this
little
piggy
bea
davenport

Legend Press Ltd, The Old Fire Station,
140 Tabernacle Street, London, EC2A 4SD
info@legend-paperbooks.co.uk | www.legendtimesgroup.com

Print ISBN 978-1-9098786-1-7
Ebook ISBN 978-1-9098786-2-4
Set in Times. Printed in the United Kingdom by Clays Ltd.
Cover design by Simon Levy www.simonlevyassociates.co.uk

Legend Press

Bea Davenport is the writing name of former BBC and newspaper journalist Barbara Henderson. She drew on her experiences as a journalist for *This Little Piggy* and also for her debut novel, *In Too Deep*, which was shortlisted for the 2009 Luke Bitmead Bursary and published by Legend Press in 2013.

Bea has a PhD in Creative Writing from Newcastle University. The children's novel written as part of the PhD, *The Serpent House*, was shortlisted for the 2010 Times/Chicken House Award and published by Curious Fox in June 2014. She lives in the Northumberland border town of Berwick-upon-Tweed with her partner and children.

Visit Bea at beadavenport.com
Follow her @BeaDavenport1

one

Come on, baby, little baby, wake up. Just wake up. Give us a smile. It's only me. Wake up and we'll do a game, like we always do. Peep-oh. Who's there?

12th July, 1984

Screams were not uncommon on the Sweetmeadows estate. But the sound that tore through the stifled silence on that hot July afternoon was something more than that. It was a visceral howl, a primal, animalistic wail. It was the sound of a mother whose baby was gone.

The women on the estate ran out first, barefoot, hopping on the sticky tarmac, blinking in the grey-white glare of the sun bouncing off the concrete buildings. One or two men followed, half-dressed and slow, all dazed by the stagnant heat. On the third-floor balcony of the flats, a young mother leaned over, clutching at her hair, howling, her words too incoherent to make out. But the women knew, as they ran towards her, joining in with the cries. "The bairn. It must be the bairn."

*

Clare Jackson pulled out her dog-eared list of phone numbers. One last round of calls for the day: police, fire, ambulance, coastguard. Then off for an early evening pub crawl along all the seafront bars. She'd kept the thought at the back of her

5

mind all through the deadly-dull Thursday: get to the end and there would be a bucket-sized glass of white wine, so cold the condensation dribbles down the sides, a bowl of olives and all the gossip from head office. All the stuff she'd been missing, stuck out in the newspaper's cell-like district office, where nothing ever happened. The journalist's equivalent of house arrest. Still, anything was better than heading home.

As usual, the calls brought nothing from the cops. It was as if they'd taken a vow of silence when it came to the press. And as for the others: waste of a phone call. Must be the easiest job in the world, being part of any emergency services out here, Clare thought. Nothing ever happens, or that's what they always say when the *Post* calls. They must spend all their time with their feet up. In her head, Clare rehearsed this into a gag for later on in the pub.

She was hoisting her bag over her shoulder and jangling the bunch of office keys, ready to leave and lock up, when the phone rang again. It was Joe Ainsley, from their sister paper. "Clare, am I glad I caught you. Thought you might've buggered off for the day. Heard about the murder?"

"Yeah, yeah. Very funny. Are you going for a drink?"

"I'm not kidding. Clare, there's been a murder. It's a baby."

Clare sat back down on the desk and dropped the keys with a crunch like a broken bell. "You're taking the piss, right?"

"Wish I was. I was halfway into town. There was a pint with my name on it waiting at the bar. But we can both forget it for now, kiddo."

Clare closed her eyes for a second and rubbed her temples. "Where are you?"

"Heading to the police station now. Come with me and we'll see if we can squeeze anything out of them."

Four minutes later, outside, Joe's car horn hooted.

Clare grabbed her bag and clattered down the office stairs. She jumped into Joe's passenger seat and yelped. "For

Christ's sake, Joe. It's like an oven. These plastic seats are taking a layer of my skin away."

"Tell me about it. I swear these company cars breach some kind of health and safety laws. I've been driving round in a mobile furnace all day."

On the way, Joe filled Clare in on everything he knew – not much, but bad enough. A baby's body had been found on the Sweetmeadows estate. Word was the kid had actually been thrown over a balcony. From about the third floor up.

"Seriously?" Clare leaned her head out of the car window, trying to catch some cool air, wiping her hair out of her eyes. "That's a new low even for Sweetmeadows."

"It's what I was told. I only heard because I stopped in the corner shop for a cold drink. Everyone's talking about it. Rumour is it was the mother."

"Not a bloody word from the police," Clare grumbled. "I was halfway to the pub when you called. If I'd left thirty seconds earlier, I'd have been safely at the bar."

"Don't mention it." Joe steered into the police station car park and pulled on his handbrake with a crunch that made Clare wince.

They made their way to the front desk and asked for Chief Inspector Bob Seaton. After a few moments they were shown through the maze of airless, narrow corridors to his office.

"Not much to tell, at this stage," said Seaton, leaning back in his office chair. He gave Clare a wink and clicked his tongue in the side of his ruddy-toned cheek. Clare gave a quick smile and held her pen, ready to write.

"Whatever you've got, mate," said Joe. "Anything you can tell us. Baby's name?"

"Jamie Donnelly. Aged nine months." Seaton read from the papers on his desk. "Mother called the police to her home at Jasmine Walk, Sweetmeadows, in a distressed state, reporting that the baby was missing from his pram. A short search by the neighbours in the meantime found the body of a child in the rubbish bin area of the flats. It would appear he somehow fell from the balcony and died from his injuries. That's about as much as we've got for you right now."

"And you've charged the mother?"

"Not charged. Not yet. We're talking to the mother. She says she left the pram out on the balcony because it was a warm afternoon. Came back outside to find the baby gone." Seaton paused. "She says."

Clare chewed her pen. "Those balconies at the Sweetmeadows flats. Anyone can walk around them, right?"

"That's right," said Seaton. "But I wouldn't run with any rubbish about a killer on the loose. I think we'll charge the mother before the evening's out."

Clare glanced at Joe and gave a slight curl of her lip. If they charged the mother, the paper could only print the barest details. If no one was charged, they could speculate as much as they liked. "You couldn't wait until this time tomorrow before you officially charge anyone?"

Seaton gave a short laugh and shook his head. "Not even for you, bonny lass."

"Is the dad around?" Joe asked.

"Yes. One of Sweetmeadows' rare two-parent families, the Donnellys. He was picking the other kids up from their grandma's house when it happened. Lots of people saw them. Looks like Dad's in the clear."

Clare and Joe scribbled down the names of the rest of the family. Mum, Deborah, 26. Dad, Robert, also 26, worked at the Sweetmeadows Colliery, which gave the estate its name. Two other kids: Becca, five, and Bobbie, three. Joe tried to draw the conversation out, but Seaton wasn't giving anything else away.

They got up to go. "Just a question," Clare said. "Probably a stupid thing to ask. But is their flat just above the bins?"

Seaton smiled at her as if she was his prize pupil. "I haven't been out there myself. Why would you ask that?"

"It's just... it seems like a funny place for the kid to land. That's all."

Seaton's smile widened. "Well spotted. You're quite right. The baby couldn't have fallen from the walkway directly on to the spot where his body was found. Someone moved the little lad after he'd fallen and dumped him there among the bins."

Clare raised her eyebrows. Seaton held up his hand. "Forget it, Miss Jackson. There's no psycho out there. It looks like a very poor attempt at hiding the body. Probably made by someone in a disturbed state of mind. Such as an over-stressed mother who'd lost all idea of what she was doing."

"Probably," said Clare, putting her notebook in her pocket.

"I mean it," said Seaton. "We'll be charging. Imminently. That means reporting restrictions are about to kick in. Don't you two go out to Sweetmeadows whipping up panic, you hear?"

"As if we would," said Joe, as they closed the office door behind them.

Outside, they opened the car doors and stood for a few moments, trying and failing to waft in some air.

"He doesn't half fancy you, that Seaton," Joe said.

Clare shook her head. "He's a middle-aged bloke. It's his default response to any female in the room, whatever they look like."

Joe sighed. "If I made that tongue-clicking noise at you, you'd smack me in the face."

"I know. Life's unfair, isn't it?" Clare slid onto the car seat, wincing again at the feel of the hot faux-leather. "So." She looked at Joe. "It's off to Sweetmeadows, to whip up some panic, yes?"

The Sweetmeadows estate was one of those places where Clare felt glad to have Joe alongside her. It was a joyless collection of Sixties-built, flat-roofed, box-shaped flats, up to four storeys high. The local council had paper plans for knocking down the whole estate and rebuilding, but they'd been gathering dust in someone's office drawer for the last five years. There was no money. And while all the half-decent council houses in the borough were being bought up fast and cheap by the tenants, no one wanted the damp, mould-ridden properties at Sweetmeadows. Dozens of the flats were empty and boarded up. Most of the tenants that were left were among the most desperate on the council's list.

"If I had a proper car, I'd never leave it here," said Joe, pulling up and peering out of the window to read the street names on the concrete walkways. "But this thing's not even worth nicking. I live in hope."

Clare jumped out of the car. "Why is it that the more rural-sounding the name, the nastier the estate actually is?"

"Bucolic," said Joe. "Sweetmeadows sounds bucolic. But it ain't."

"Good word," said Clare. "You could've been a writer." She squinted in the late afternoon sun. "Look. That's Jasmine Walk, over there."

The area underneath and around Jasmine Walk was taped off and a team of police officers was scouring the ground, watched by a small crowd of people. It wasn't difficult to get the residents' reactions, although some weren't waiting for the formal police procedures. Amongst themselves, they had already charged and convicted Debs Donnelly of throwing her baby over the balcony, then panicking and trying to hide the body in the bin sheds.

What was Debs like? Did she have problems? Was Jamie a difficult baby? No one really knew. It wasn't the kind of estate where people knocked on each other's doors and popped in for morning coffee.

What about the balconies? That was an easy call. Word a question in the right way and you always get the answer you want. Of course everyone told Clare they wanted the balconies made more secure. In her head, she wrote her 'Safety plea on baby death balconies' copy in a few short minutes. It might pad the story out, especially if Debs Donnelly was charged, ruining the chance of a front page lead.

10

"Hey, missus, are you a reporter?" A child's voice called over and Clare turned. There was a little group of four or five kids, hanging around next to Joe's car.

"Here we go," said Joe, under his breath. "Wait for it: *Are we gonna be in the paper?*"

"Are we gonna be in the paper?" one of the kids asked straight away. Clare answered all their questions and told them to buy the *Post* the next day.

"We need to get all this news sent over now," she told them. "Don't suppose there's a working phone box anywhere near here?"

The kids all shook their heads.

"You can use our phone if you like, missus," said a stringy little girl of around nine or ten, dressed in a tiny vest and shorts. Joe and Clare looked at each other. It would certainly save a car trip back to the office. They followed the girl up the concrete steps, Clare wrinkling her nose at the smells of mould and urine.

On the fourth floor, the little girl pushed open the door. There was a loud bark and a huge dog – a sort of cross-breed, but with definite German Shepherd in there somewhere – lolloped over towards them.

Clare breathed deeply and braced herself to pat the thing. She wasn't much of a dog person, but pretending to like people's pets was part of a journalist's skill. The inside of the place didn't smell too good either, but none of these flats ever did. "Where's your mum then? Or dad?"

"Me mam's out," said the kid, holding the huge dog back by hanging onto the fur at the back of its neck. "But you can use the phone anyway, she'll not mind. It's just there." The phone sat on the bare floor just next to the door, its wires trailing back into the living room.

"If you're sure." Joe dialled first and told the late duty photographer to come out and get some pictures of the estate.

Clare called her own newsdesk and got the late reporter to type in her copy. She put a pound on the little table next to the phone. "Tell your mam thank you."

The girl watched all this carefully. "Will you put me in the paper then?" she asked.

"Er, what for?" Joe fondled the huge dog behind the ears. Clare winced and tried to smile at it.

"Letting you use me phone. Me name's Amy."

"It doesn't work like that," Clare said. The girl pouted. She was a strange-looking little thing, with shiny eyes the colour of tea and hair that was thick and fuzzy on top, but trailed into rats-tails down the back of her head.

"Tell you what, though," Clare went on. "We'll be back tomorrow, doing some more stuff about this poor little baby. Does your mum know the Donnelly family? I see you live just about above their flat."

"Yeah, me mam knows Debs. So do I. And I knew the baby." Amy cocked her head in the direction of the floor below.

"Righto," Clare said. "Tell your mum we'll give her a knock tomorrow because we'll want to talk to people who knew the baby's family."

"You can talk to me. I knew Jamie," said Amy. "He was dead cute. Like a Cabbage Patch doll. I love babies, me. I used to play with Jamie, and Becca and Bobbie."

"How old are you, Amy?" Clare asked.

"Nine. Nearly ten."

"Well, we can't do a proper interview with you, not without your mum being around. We're not allowed. So you ask if we can come and see her tomorrow. Then we can talk to you and put you in the paper. Maybe with a picture."

"Yeah?" Amy's pale face split into a grin. "You promise?"

"I promise." Clare propped her business card onto the dial of Amy's phone.

Outside, the chimes of an ice cream van plinked out a warped version of *Greensleeves*. "Here," Joe said, pulling cash out of his pocket. "Get an ice cream."

"Ta." Amy's eyes gleamed as she shoved the pound coin

into the pocket of her shorts.

Clare and Joe clattered down the steps. "Jesus. That place stank," Joe said. "The kid wasn't much better."

Clare stopped on the next level down. "We could just give the Donnellys a knock? I guess they'll tell us to bugger off, but at least we've tried."

A female uniformed police officer stood guard on the balcony. "Reporters?" she asked them. Then she moved her feet wider apart to block their way a little more. "I'm not letting you past. Sorry. The family doesn't want to talk."

Clare tried not to show her irritation. "Can we just ask them ourselves? We're only the local papers, not the red-tops. Sometimes people like to... "

The officer's expression didn't change. "No chance," she said. "And I'm here all night, or at least one of us will be. So don't bother coming back. I've been told to tell you there's a press conference in the morning. You'll get everything you need then."

Clare and Joe turned to leave. And just as Clare was shoving her notebook into her bag, a voice called out. "She didn't do it! Print that, will you? She didn't hurt him!"

Clare turned to see a man with a toddler in his arms, standing behind the policewoman. His face was red and blotched with crying.

"Mr Donnelly?" Clare asked, getting out the notebook again.

The young PC interrupted. "Mr Donnelly, I'd advise you to go back inside. The reporters are leaving now."

Clare deliberately moved her head to the side to look past the officer. "It's okay, Mr Donnelly, you're entitled to talk to us if you want. I'm Clare Jackson from the *Post*. You're saying your wife has been wrongly accused?"

Rob Donnelly clutched his little boy tighter. "That's right. The police are saying she threw our laddie out of the pram. She wouldn't do that. She just wouldn't."

"What do you think happened, Mr Donnelly?" Joe asked,

and when the policewoman tried to speak again he held up his hand. "You have the right to ask us into your flat, Mr Donnelly, if you want."

"Aye, come in, then."

The officer's face reddened slightly as she stood aside, and Clare heard her get straight onto her radio to contact someone higher up. They'd have to be quick.

They stepped into a suffocatingly warm living room where the TV was blaring and toys were strewn all over the floor. The toddler in Rob Donnelly's arms began to squirm and he placed him gently on one of the few clear patches of carpet. He picked up a wind-up musical toy in the shape of a TV set and shook it until it spat out a few bare notes. *This little piggy went to market...*

Rob didn't ask them to sit down. Clare glanced at the TV. In spite of the mess, this place was cleaner than Amy's flat, though there was a distinct smell of nappies.

"I'm waiting to see if there's anything on the local news." The voice from the sofa was that of an older woman, who they hadn't noticed before. This must be Grandma: Debs' mum, perhaps, or Rob's. Hard to tell.

"Did you see anyone come round with a camera?" Joe asked.

The woman shrugged. "No one came in here."

"I don't think they'd say much anyway," Clare said carefully, "if they think Mrs Donnelly's going to be charged."

"She won't be charged," said the woman. "My Deborah's innocent, I know that."

Rob screwed up his eyes and balled his fists. It was like he was trying not to explode, Clare thought. "You say Debbie couldn't have done it?"

"She wouldn't," Rob said, taking in a gulp of a breath and wiping his eyes. "Debs was mad about Jamie. She would never have hurt him. I'm sick of telling people that."

"What do you think happened?" Clare asked again, trying to smile at the toddler as she drove a toy car over her toes.

"I don't... " Rob ran out of words. He shook his head and held up his hands.

"It's obvious why someone's done it," said the woman, who Clare established was Rob's mother-in-law, Annie Martin. "The bastards. This is how low they'll go."

"Why's it obvious?" Joe asked.

Rob swore and stamped out into the kitchen. Annie reached for her handbag and pulled out a pack of cigarettes. She held it out to Joe and Clare. Clare shook her head but Joe reached across and took one. He didn't smoke anymore but it was one of his tactics, taking a fag from someone he was interviewing. It created a little bond with the other person, he said. Stops you looking superior. He even kept a lighter, just for work, and he used it now.

Annie took a long drag. And a longer outward breath. She nudged her head slightly in the direction of the kitchen. "He went back."

"Oh." Clare and Joe glanced at each other. There was no need to ask what Annie meant. For all the men round here who were working, and there weren't so many of them, there were only two choices, both of them impossible. You either stayed out. Or you went back. They were four months into a national miners' strike, hitting all the pits across the country. And Rob was a scab.

"You've had other trouble, then?" Joe asked.

Annie nodded, pressing her lips together and blinking. "Trouble. Aye. You could say that. But you never think they'd target the bairns... " She gave a low sob and Clare squeezed beside her on the sofa, and put a hand on her arm.

"He only went back last week. I never agreed with it. I knew it wasn't right. But Deborah said he did it to pay the bills, you know? That's all. Not for greed and extra money and all of that. Just to feed the little 'uns. And they were trying to get out of this hell-hole, into a bigger house. With a garden."

She shook her head and rummaged around for a tissue.

Clare always had a pack in her bag, and she handed it to Annie. "So what happened? Since Rob went back?"

"Nothing we couldn't put up with. A window out, the first night. Calling in the street. Spitting. Stuff through the letterbox. But this... "

Joe was doing the scribbling. He'd give Clare the quotes later. "You're saying someone's killed Jamie because Rob broke the strike?" He couldn't keep a questioning note out of his voice. Clare glared at him.

"That's right, that's what I'm saying. Otherwise, who else would do it? Who would pick a little bairn out of a pram and...? " Annie started to sob again, mingled with a deep, choking smoker's cough.

"You're talking rubbish, woman." Rob was standing in the doorway to the kitchen. "They're me mates. This strike's nearly over, it has to be, and then it'll all get forgotten. None of them would hurt my little lad."

"Some mates." Annie's tarry voice was full of scorn.

Rob punched the wall, so hard it made flakes of plaster and paint flutter to the floor. The little boy jumped and looked at him, blinking. The music box had stopped.

Clare glanced at Joe. "So what do you think happened, Mr Donnelly?"

Rob didn't answer. He knelt down on the floor and picked up a toy telephone. He held it out to the toddler, who was busy smearing a stream of clear snot across his face. He held out his sticky hands for the toy.

"Jamie's," he said. Rob put his face in his hands and Clare watched as his shoulders shook, without making a sound. She waited in the mounting silence for him to howl out loud.

Joe asked Annie a few bland questions about the family, wrote all the details down. "I hate to ask this, but have you got a photo of Jamie we could borrow? We could copy it and I promise we'd get it back to you tomorrow."

"There's one in my purse." Annie delved in her bag again, pulling out keys and fag packets and matches.

There was a loud rap at the door. Clare looked at Joe. "That'll be the cops coming to throw us out."

Two uniformed officers walked in. "All right you two, out you go. There's a press conference tomorrow at nine. Leave this family in peace now, please."

"Come on, lads. Mr Donnelly okayed it," Joe said. "He asked us in."

Uniform took a step towards him. "They're in shock. They let you in, they'll have to let the rest of the pack in too. Don't make me phone your editor."

Clare got up. "We're about finished anyway. Thanks, Annie. Take care, Rob." She left her business card on the mantelpiece and followed Joe out of the door.

They didn't speak until Joe had driven away from the estate. He parked outside the office and read through his notes, Clare scribbling the quotes and details down in her scrawling shorthand.

"Shame the cops arrived just before we got the photo of the baby," Joe said, flicking back through the pages of his notebook to check he hadn't left anything out. Clare smiled and slid a colour snap out of her notebook. Joe grinned. "You're a good 'un."

"Reckon we'll be able to use any of that stuff Rob and Annie said?"

Joe rubbed his nose. "Not if they charge Debbie Donnelly tonight. But we can save it for the backgrounder when she comes to trial."

"I suppose." Clare opened the car door. "Coming for a quick pint then?"

"Sure?" Joe asked. "I'm up for it, but didn't you have an early start this morning? I'd have thought you'd want to get home."

Clare gave a quick downturn of her lips and shook her head.

"Okay," said Joe. "Suits me."

It was too late to drive into the city centre to find the

others from head office who would, by now, have left the pub and gone on to somewhere to eat. It meant another night at the Bombay Palace, known as The Bomb, which was so close to the office it almost felt like part of it, but Clare didn't mind. Anything would do if it staved off the moment when she would have to go home.

Joe didn't even glance at the laminated menu. "I know this thing off by heart. If they ever put anything new on it, someone would have to notify me in person, because I think the last time I actually read this menu we had a Labour government."

Clare did read it every time, but always ended up choosing from the same couple of dishes. Lately, the food held little appeal. It was the wine she was really looking forward to. She held up her glass across the table to Joe. "To a front page lead tomorrow."

Joe raised his beer and nodded. They both took large, silent gulps.

two

Friday 13th July

Clare woke up hot and dry-mouthed. The baby was the first thing that made sense in her just-woken thoughts. All the way through her shower, through trying to pick out make-up and earrings from the dusty clutter on her bathroom shelves, through forcing down two bites of toast, half a mug of tea and the daily dose of paracetamol, she thought about Rob Donnelly, his crumpled face and Annie's bitter certainties about what had happened. The strange, stray idea that kept coming back to her was: what a waste. What a waste of a little baby. To be thrown away like that, like washing-up water.

She splashed cold water on her eyes, which were red around the lids. She often cried in her sleep, these nights. Then she scraped her hair into a ponytail. It was too hot to have it loose. Thank goodness the perm, a huge mistake, was beginning to loosen up and the ash-blonde curls weren't quite so tight any more. She sponged make-up lightly over her face. Anything to look a bit healthier. If one more person said she looked tired out, she'd hit them.

Clare opened her front door, squinting at the morning sunshine, digging in her bag for her car key. Damn. She'd left the car at the office so she could have a drink last night. She glanced at her watch. She'd have to pay for a taxi to the police HQ, something she could really do without the week before her wages were due, and blag a lift back with Joe.

She called the newsdesk from home first. "Just checking in," she said. "I thought I'd go straight to the presser."

"No need, Clare." It was the deputy news editor, Sharon Catt, who'd picked up the phone. Clare closed her eyes. Sharon was known among younger reporters as Poison Pen because of her notorious sour temper. In her eighteen months at the paper, Clare had never seen Catt smile. "When you didn't pick up the office phone I thought you might be off sick again. So I've sent the chief reporter."

Clare swallowed. The phrase 'chief reporter' was unnecessarily cruel of Sharon. She could have just said 'Chris Barber', but Catt mentioned his title to remind Clare, as if she was likely to forget, that this was a post that she'd applied for herself. On the day of the interview, Clare had been unable to get to work, although she was damned if she was going to explain to her bosses exactly what stopped her.

And she was equally damned if she was going to let this story be swiped away. She took a deep breath. "Okay, Sharon. Let Barber do the easy bit. I'll go to Sweetmeadows and speak to some of the people from last night. There are some things I want to follow up."

"I think Chris might want to do that," Catt started, but Clare spoke over her, a little too loudly.

"I got some great stuff. It was well worth working so late. It's all on Dave Bell's desk, ready to go. Two versions: one for if the mum gets charged and one for if she doesn't. I need to know as soon as things change."

Catt was silent for a beat.

"No need to thank me. It's the joy of running my own patch, just like you promised," Clare added and hung up.

She sat on the bottom of the stairs and gazed at the pile of shoes, bags and unopened letters in her hallway. Dust motes floated like a swarm of tiny insects in the slit of sunlight coming through the glass. One day, soon, she was going to have to sort all this out, but for the moment, the important thing to do was get into work every day, out-splash everyone else and make them sorry they'd appointed the wrong chief reporter.

There was no urgency anymore, so Clare took a bus into the town centre and found her car parked outside a newsagent's. The paper's district office was above the shop. It was a tiny room with nothing more than a desk, phone, kettle, typewriter and a teetering pile of back copies of the *Post*.

"Morning, Miss Beautiful." Jai greeted her the same way every day and Clare couldn't help raising a small smile. "I came in to sort out the papers this morning and I saw the car. I thought, oh, that naughty Clare. She's been out drinking wine again."

"It would be naughtier to get in the car and drive home, though," Clare said, picking up a carton of milk to take upstairs for her coffee.

"That's true, very true." Jai handed her change and leaned across the counter. "Sad news this morning about the little baby, eh? Every one of my customers is saying something about it."

"I bet they are." Clare turned to go upstairs, stopping for a second to grasp the rail and take a steadying breath.

"But, you know, Clare, this is a funny job. Sometimes people say things without thinking about them first. They pick up their newspaper, they look at it and they come out with these words. I feel sure they don't mean what they say. Because they say some shocking things."

Clare put the milk carton on the stair and turned back to Jai. "Some people are just mean and stupid, Jai. We're not all racist idiots."

"It wasn't that today. It was a terrible comment, though, about the little baby."

"About the baby? What did they say?"

"Just one person." Jai shook his head. "Just one person said something nasty. I don't even want to repeat it, it was so bad."

Clare folded her arms. "You can't say that, Jai, and then not tell me what was said. Come on."

Jai shook his head again. "One man. He said, 'what goes around comes around.' And I said, that's a strange expression to me, you'll have to explain what you mean. And he said… " Jai stopped and looked down at the counter. "He said to me, 'people don't deserve to have children if they don't look after their brothers and sisters.'"

"This man, did you know him?"

"I've seen him before. I think he lives on the estate. You know what I said? I said to him, Mister, no one deserves to have their child taken from them like that. So cruel. No one deserves that."

"Good for you." Clare picked up a packet of chewing gum and dug in her purse for more money. "This man. Do you think he was talking about the miners? Do you think he meant that Rob Donnelly was a strike-breaker?"

"I don't know what he meant. But you know, sometimes people come in here and they spit out these words. And then I get left with them. These angry words just stay here with me, all for the rest of the day."

Clare squeezed Jai's hand.

After a quick coffee, she headed out to Sweetmeadows again. The searing July sunshine did nothing to improve her headache or the look of the estate. It made the concrete look dustier, it shone floodlights on the litter and dog dirt. A couple of sorry bouquets were already wilting in the heat, next to the dustbins where baby Jamie's body was found. But the whole place was quiet. No kids, Clare noticed. It was a school day, of course. And it was only nine-thirty in the morning, so the tenants without kids may not be up and about yet. At the windows that weren't boarded up, most of the curtains were drawn.

Clare decided to start with Amy's flat on the top floor of the block. She was in luck. A woman who had to be the girl's mother was sitting on a canvas chair on the balcony outside her front door. She was wearing a bikini top, with a black pencil skirt. Her feet and legs were bare. She was skinny overall, like her daughter, but a small roll of pale flesh folded over the waistband of her skirt. She was young. Clare reckoned she couldn't have been more than mid-twenties.

"Are you Amy's mum?"

"Who's asking?" The woman folded her arms across her stomach. "I've sent her to school, if that's what you want to know."

Clare shook her head. She explained who she was. "My colleague Joe and I, we chatted to Amy last night. She kindly let us use your phone. I left some money for the call and a business card?"

Amy's mother raised her eyes. "I never saw any money. Little bugger."

"She said you knew the baby who died? And the family?"

"Oh, aye, we did." The woman leaned back in her chair. "Mind you, you have to watch whatever that one tells you. She's always making things up."

"Amy?" Clare laughed. "She's quite a little character." She pulled out her pen. "Can I ask a bit about the Donnellys?"

Amy's mother, whose name was Tina, was a great talker. She told how she'd sometimes baby-sat for all the Donnellys' kids. What a devoted family they all were, especially Debs and Grandma Annie, who was rarely away from the flat.

"So was Debs depressed? Was Jamie a difficult baby?"

"Jamie? He was no bother. I wouldn't say Debs was depressed. Worried about money, like everyone else, of course. She'd been used to Rob earning a canny wage, you know, right up until the strike started."

"Why are they living here?" Clare chewed the end of her pen. "I don't mean to be rude. But if I had a good wage coming in, I'd move."

If Tina was offended she didn't show it. "Right enough. But they were saving up. They were going to buy Tina's mam's council house. Four beds and a garden. One of the bairns has a bad chest. Becca, I think. These flats are all full of damp, you know."

Clare nodded. "So the strike really hit them hard. What did you think about Rob going back to work?"

Tina shrugged. "That was up to him. None of my business. Debs wanted him to go back, I know that. Maybe if it was my man, I'd be telling him the same, but it comes at a hell of a price. Not many round here will even look Rob in the eye."

"When you heard what had happened to Jamie, what did you think?"

"Shock, just total shock. My Amy was in pieces. She loved him. Scary for all the kids, isn't it, to think of that happening. She was up in the night, crying her little eyes out." Tina opened a pack of cigarettes and pulled one out. "Because I'll tell you something. Debs didn't do it. No way would she hurt any of her bairns. No way."

"Some people round here think she would," Clare said.

"Yeah, the ones who didn't know her. Or the ones who think that the Donnellys are like the bloody devil, because Rob scabbed on the strike."

"So if Debs didn't do it," Clare began.

"Aye, that means there's a killer still walking around. Amy didn't even want to go to school this morning, not that she's ever very keen, to be honest. She was sweet on that baby. She's soft with all the little 'uns. But I said to her that's where you'll be safest, at the school. It's terrifying, when you think about it. Any kid could be next."

"Annie Martin thinks it was revenge because Rob broke the strike. What do you think, Tina?"

"I can't see that. They're angry, the strikers. But they wouldn't go that far." She thought for a moment, toying with her cigarette. "Mind you. I'm not a miner and I'm not married to one. So I can't really say."

A ringing sound came from inside Tina's flat. "Sorry," she said, getting up and going indoors to answer the phone. A minute later, she reappeared wearing a T-shirt and plastic

24

sandals. She threw the end of her cigarette onto the ground, stubbing it out with her sole.

"Amy's been sick," she said. "I have to go and pick her up from school." She glanced at Clare. "Just missed the bus, too."

Clare took the hint and offered Tina a lift. They were on the way out of the estate, Tina leaning out of the car window and smoking again, when Clare noticed Joe's clapped-out car coming in the opposite direction. He flashed his lights at her and she slowed up.

Joe rolled down his window. "They've let Debs Donnelly out."

"Told you so," said Tina. "She'd never do that to any of her kiddies."

"So what are the police saying now?" Clare asked Joe.

"They haven't got the first clue," said Joe. "Or that's how it looked at the press conference. How come they sent that knob Chris Barber instead of you?"

Clare shook her head. "Don't ask. I'll be back in twenty minutes and I'll catch up with you at the office." She nodded towards Tina. "This is little Amy's mum, by the way. You know, the one who let us use the phone last night. We're just going to get her from school."

Joe nodded back. "Nice kid."

Tina made an eye-rolling face. "Aye, sometimes. She's a nice nuisance today."

Amy gave a huge grin when she climbed into the back seat of Clare's Mini. She was wearing the school summer dress, a blue and white checked nylon pinafore, greying white socks and what the kids called Jesus sandals.

"I love your car," she told Clare. "I want a Mini. I want a red one like this. Hey, we had to say prayers for baby Jamie in assembly today."

"You did?" Clare asked a few more questions about what the teachers said. Amy filled in the details.

"Loads of us were crying," she added.

"You don't seem very ill to me," Tina said, narrowing her eyes at Amy's reflection in the passenger seat mirror. "Did your teacher actually see you being sick?"

"Well, no, because she doesn't come into the toilets with me, does she?"

Tina looked sideways at Clare and shook her head. "She'll do anything to get out of school."

Amy picked up Clare's notebooks and pens from the back seat and started looking through them. "Your writing's funny," she said. "It just looks like squiggles. Is it in foreign or something?"

Clare grinned. "It's shorthand."

Amy didn't know what that meant so Clare explained. "It's a kind of writing that people do when they need to write things down very fast."

"Is it like a secret code though? So other people can't read it?" Amy was tracing a finger along some of the outlines.

"It's not supposed to be. Though sometimes I have trouble reading it back myself." Clare winked at Amy in the mirror. "It's really good if you're doing a report from court, because people speak quickly there and you can't ask them to say it again."

"You go to court? To see the prisoners? Do you go into prisons?"

Tina gave a sigh. "Police, prisons, detectives. She loves all that. I reckon she's going to be a copper one day."

"No, I'm going to be a reporter," Amy said. "I've just decided. I'm going to drive a Mini and write the news and learn the code for writing fast."

Clare pulled up the car and smiled at Amy. "It's called Teeline. It's quite easy, actually. I'll show you some quick words sometime, if you like."

"*Yessss.*" Amy looked as if Clare had offered to take her to Disney World.

Tina opened the car door. "Come on, you. Leave the poor

26

reporter alone." She glanced at Clare. "Can't get her to do her homework, you know, but she'll sit and learn bloody shorthand with you."

"One thing," Clare said, quickly. "Can we send a photographer to take a pic of you? And Amy," she added. "It'll be in an hour or so?"

"If you like." Tina held the car door open.

Amy didn't move. "What're you doing now, Clare?"

Clare swivelled round in the seat. "I have to get back to my office and type up my story. And you'd better go and lie down, right?"

Amy frowned.

"You've been poorly, remember?" Clare reminded her.

"Oh, yeah." Slowly, Amy heaved herself out of the car. She stood waving at Clare until she'd driven the car round the corner and out of sight.

Joe was lingering outside Clare's office, drinking a can of Coke, his sleeves rolled up. "You took your time."

"I've been talking to that Amy again. She makes me laugh. Says she wants to be a reporter. I've got some stuff about the school assembly and how scared the local kids are. I just need to send a photographer round to get some shots."

Inside, Clare picked up the office phone and propped it under her chin, wriggling out of her jacket as she talked. "Anyone take some copy?"

Joe scribbled down some of Clare's quotes as she dictated her story over to head office. He waited as she chatted to her news editor, Dave Bell, and watched as she put the phone down and grinned at him. "He loves it. He said it was all really good stuff. Says I can knock off early today if I want, for working late last night."

"Jeez. My editor never says that to me. Swotty suck-up."

"Yeah, yeah. Tell me about the press conference."

"Not much to tell, except they're not charging Jamie's mum. The dad was there, Rob, and they meant him to make some sort of appeal for information, but he just broke down in tears and no one got a word out of him."

"Except us. First and exclusive," said Clare. "What a team we are. So Chris Barber didn't get much from trying to pinch my story."

"He's a waste of space anyway. All he can manage is following up other people's exclusives and pretending they're his own. Chief reporter my backside."

"Yes, okay. There's loyalty, Joe, and there's layering it on with a trowel. I'm over it, I promise."

"You should've got the job though."

Clare reached out and took a drink from Joe's can. "Yes, I should. But if I don't get the front page today, there's no justice." She grimaced. "That's warm."

"You will get the lead. There's bugger all else going on. Even the picket line was quiet today."

"Speaking of which." Clare told Joe about the man in the newsagent's shop and his comments to Jai.

"I still can't see it," said Joe. "Yeah, the strikers are angry about the men who've gone back. They'll probably never have a pint with them again. But they wouldn't do anything so violent. Surely. And especially not to a baby."

Clare shrugged. "That's what Amy's mum said. Then she didn't seem so sure. The thing is, otherwise, there's absolutely no motive, is there? If it's not the mother run ragged at the baby crying and it's not revenge on Rob, then what is it? It's a completely senseless death."

Joe nodded. "I know what you're saying. But it just seems like a stage too far. The miners are single-minded, but they're not psychotic." He drained the can, crumpled it and threw it into Clare's bin. "Want to go for fish and chips then? Celebrate your splash?"

Clare wouldn't budge from the office until the delivery van arrived with the first editions. She took two stairs at a time on the way down and fidgeted while Jai cut the string around the pile of papers.

"Here you are, Miss Beautiful," he said, handing her the

top copy.

Clare held it in front of her and stared at it. She looked up and blinked as Joe came down the office stairs. "It says Chris Barber on the story," she said. "They haven't given me a by-line."

Joe swore and took the paper out of Clare's hands. "But this is all your stuff. There's just one line about the press conference. This is all your work, from being out on the estate."

Clare nodded. She didn't want to speak aloud, in case Joe realised how choked she felt.

"Bunch of bloody bastards." Joe rolled up the paper. He reached out to put an arm on Clare's shoulder, then drew it back again. "Come on, let's go out. I'll buy you a glass of wine and you can leave the car here again."

Clare shook her head, lips tightly pressed together. "Sorry, Joe. Not in the mood anymore."

"What will you do? Just head home?"

Clare's shoulders slumped. "Don't feel like doing that, either. Shit."

"Come on, slugger. What happened to the stroppy mare that used to be Clare Jackson? I know they're behaving like gits. You should've got the chief reporter's job and you should've got a by-line today and you don't get paid anything like enough. But we all feel like that from time to time. You've been down in the dumps for weeks now."

Clare didn't look up. "Yeah, I know."

"What is it?" Joe sat on a stair and folded his arms. "Something else?"

Clare shook her head. "Nothing. Just the usual bitterness. Ignore me."

"You're my mate. Anything I can do?"

Clare shook her head again. Upstairs, the phone rang. Clare ran up to the office and answered to find Sharon Catt on the end of the line. "Clare? Dave says he's sending you home early because you worked late last night."

"That's right." Clare made a face, for Joe's benefit, at the phone. "Is there a problem?"

"I just wanted to warn you that it's your turn for picket duty next week. Seven-thirty Monday morning, outside the Sweetmeadows Colliery as usual." She paused to let this sink in. "Enjoy your long weekend."

Clare dropped the receiver into the cradle and swore. "I don't call finishing an hour early on a Friday and starting at seven-thirty on a Monday morning a particularly long weekend, do you? She's done that on purpose."

Joe groaned. "Not the picket line on Monday?"

Clare nodded. "Everyone's favourite job."

Joe got up and gave Clare a gentle punch on the shoulder. "Watch yourself out there, won't you? And try to have a good weekend."

Clare raised a hand. "You too."

The thought of picket duty would loom over the next two days, Clare knew. Ever since the miners' strike started, the paper sent a reporter and photographer to wait outside the pits early every weekday morning, in case there was any drama. The editor's regular hard-line editorial columns, denouncing the strike, meant that the miners would turn on the paper's car, kicking it and spitting on it, and reporters that got out of the car risked getting the same treatment. Clare hated it. She wore 'Coal Not Dole' stickers on her jackets and always put money into the NUM collection tins, but it didn't stop her from the queasy feeling that she was part of the other side. Or certainly that was how the pickets saw all the press, tabloids and local papers alike.

Clare put a key in her front door and pushed it open with an effort. More mail and today's free-sheet paper were blocking the movement of the door. She picked all the papers up and, without glancing at them, shoved them on top of the growing pile of envelopes, flyers and magazines on the little hall table. She clicked down the deadlock and flung her bag down on her living room floor. Then she lay down on the sofa and stared at the grey-white ceiling. Shoals of dust flecks floated around this room too, highlighted in the bright afternoon sun. Everywhere needed a good clean. She wasn't even sure if the flat smelled too fresh. There was probably some vegetable, long-forgotten in the back of the fridge, which had converted itself to a noxious gas, a faint but detectable odour. She should definitely scrub the kitchen, properly, not merely running the odd glass or cup under the tap to make it just about fit to use again. Maybe clean sheets on the bed would help her to sleep through the night.

She could even emulsion the living room walls, put some posters up… Then again, she ought to wait until her wage cheque went into the bank. So next weekend, not now. With a vague sense of relief, Clare closed her eyes.

It was almost seven in the evening when she woke up, her neck painfully twisted, and her brain too fuzzy to recognise the ringing of the phone for a few moments. She let it ring. She ought to get one of those answerphones, she thought, so it could lie for her and pretend she was out. Another thing to do after pay day.

three

Monday 16th July

Clare had had enough of the day already, and it was only ten o'clock in the morning. She sat at her typewriter, staring at the wedge of blank copy and carbon paper waiting on the table and held in place by the little metal fingers. It was no good writing about what had happened to her on the picket line, because she'd always been trained to believe the reporter was never part of the story. So the miners could shout and spit and gesture at her all they liked and it would all go unreported. Anyway, Clare thought, she knew why they were angry. She wanted them to be angry. Her newspaper, along with almost all the others, was doing the miners over. And she felt like swearing at the strike-breakers herself.

A few weeks ago, she'd mentioned to her news editor that the picket lines were tricky places for women reporters.

"It's not just that they're furious with our paper because of these editorials Blackmore keeps writing," Clare said to Dave Bell. "All the reporters get the backlash for that. But when they see a female reporter it's worse, because they shout 'get your tits out' and all that stuff, all the bloody time. It's a pain, Dave."

Her news editor shrugged. "Yeah, sorry, but think of it this way. At least as a woman you're less likely to get thumped."

Sharon Catt had been listening. "Anyway," she'd cut in.

"If Dave didn't send the female reporters out to the picket lines you'd probably call it sex discrimination, wouldn't you, Clare?"

Clare glared at the ceiling for a moment. "No, Sharon, I don't think I would."

She caught Dave Bell's eye. His mouth was twitching. Clare shook her head at him and walked away. There was no need for male chauvinist pigs in her newspaper office, when Sharon did such a good job of demeaning all the other females at every opportunity. Why was it some women were so horrible to each other? A philosophical question for the girls in the pub later, Clare decided. Catt never bothered coming out for a drink with them. Just as well.

The mood on the picket lines outside Sweetmeadows Colliery was both angry and resigned today, writes Clare Jackson. *As the bitter strike drags into its nineteenth week, the miners are more determined than ever not to give up. Shouts and insults were hurled at the heavily protected van that rushed the handful of strike-breakers past the pit gates this morning. But the continued police presence, with lines of officers armed with riot shields keeping the picketers at a distance, meant the miners were prevented from physically attempting to stop it going through.*

The number of men who've broken ranks with the union is so tiny that no production can be taking place inside the pit. But the very principle of their action means...

Clare's phone rang. At the other end of the line, there was a silence, breathing and a muffled giggle. For a second or two, Clare thought it was some kind of prank caller. Newspaper offices were prone to them. Then something told her who it was.

"Amy? Is that you?"

"Hiya, Clare. How'd you know?"

"Hi. Just a guess. You okay?"

"Yeah. I just thought... I just wondered... are you coming to teach me the fast writing today?"

"Today?" Clare ran a hand through her hair. "I don't think so, Amy, sorry. Not today. I'm quite busy."

Clare could hear Amy's breathing but the child didn't say anything. Clare could almost hear her disappointment, coming in waves down the telephone. "Sorry," she said again. "Another day?"

"I stayed off school today, 'specially."

"You did?" Clare bit her lip. "You shouldn't have done that. I didn't promise."

"I know you didn't. I just thought." Amy's voice sounded livelier, suddenly. "Are you doing a story about baby Jamie today?"

"No. It's about the miners' strike."

"You should do something else about the baby," Amy said. She paused for a moment. "I've got a big story for you."

"Yeah?" Clare was cradling the phone receiver between her head and shoulder, while continuing to type her picket line story. "What's it about?"

"Baby Jamie, of course." Amy gave a little sigh. "Stupid."

Clare laughed. "Sorry. Has something happened?"

"Come over and I'll tell you. It's really important."

Clare glanced at the clock. 11.15am. "Okay, listen, Amy. I have to finish writing this story but it won't take me long. Then I'll pop over for a few minutes. About twelve? How's that?"

"*Yessss*. Could you bring some chips?"

Clare hesitated. "Chips? As in fish and chips?"

"Yeah, but no fish, thanks, just gravy?"

"What for?"

"For me dinner, you stupid."

"Yes, I realise that, but where's your mum? Is she not giving you some lunch?"

"She's out. She said it was okay for you to bring me some chips in."

"She did, did she?" Clare shook her head at the phone. "I'll see what I can do."

Clare typed out her miners' copy and three shorter local stories, then left them in an envelope with Jai. The paper sent a runner out to pick up Clare's copy at around mid-day, if there was nothing urgently needed before that. The miners' stuff would get in the later edition and the rest would be held over until tomorrow. She told her newsdesk she was going to have another scout around Sweetmeadows to see if there were any new lines on the baby's death. And before she left the newsagent's shop, she bought a shiny red Silvine notebook and a cheap black pen.

Pressing down the niggling feeling that she shouldn't get involved, she bought two bags of chips and a carton of gravy at the shop next door. When she pulled up in the car, she could see Amy hanging over the fourth-floor balcony, waiting for her.

"You shouldn't lean over like that," Clare told her, as she reached the top of the stairs and Amy grabbed the bag of chips out of her hands. "You could fall. I felt sick just watching you."

"Yeah, I know. Me mam's signed a... a... thingy about it."

Amy had two little plastic chairs and a table waiting out on the balcony. "It's kind of like a picnic, isn't it?"

Clare looked at the brutalist blocks of flats, with the pit head in the near distance, and waved away a couple of wasps. "I'm not sure it's a very scenic view. But yes, let's sit here and have a chat. It's too sunny to be inside. Although," she went on, giving Amy a mock-glare. "You really shouldn't have bunked off school."

Amy swallowed a mouthful of gravy-smeared chips. "It's the last week before the summer holidays. We're just messing about, watching telly and drawing pictures. I can do that here."

"Hmm. Do you like school, usually?"

Amy wrinkled her nose and shook her head. She stuffed in another handful of chips.

Clare decided not to press on that subject. "What did your

mam sign about the balconies?"

"It was like a long piece of paper with people's names on it? There's a word for it."

"Petition?"

"That's it. You're right clever. Do you have to be clever to be a reporter?"

Clare laughed. "Not if some of the idiots in my office are anything to go by. Anyway, you're clever too. I can tell. Thanks for telling me about the petition. I'll do a story about it for tomorrow's paper."

Amy licked gravy off her fingers. "That wasn't my real story. That wasn't the one I'm going to tell you about. Mine is more important."

Clare raised her eyebrows. "Let's hear it, then."

Amy wiped a hand across her mouth and shook her head. "You have to teach me the writing first. Don't you want those chips? I'll finish them for you."

Clare grinned. Amy was pretty good at getting what she wanted out of people. "Okay. Just for ten minutes, though. I have to get back to work." She pulled out the brown paper bag. "For you. A reporter's notebook, for practising your Teeline."

"*Thanks.*" Amy sat with the notebook and pen poised, just like Clare.

Clare started off writing down the alphabet in Teeline. She explained that one of the ways that made it faster than other writing was that it missed the vowels out of most of the words. She showed her a few: 'mum', 'flats', 'dinner'. Then she showed her how to write 'Amy', marking two little dashes under it to show it was a proper name.

Amy chewed her lip while she was writing and the end of the pen when she wasn't. "It's dead hard," she grumbled.

"It's not. At least, maybe it is at first. But you get used to it really quickly. So over the next few days, practise writing out the alphabet and then put some letters together to make some words. We can do some more another day."

36

Clare pushed her own pen and notebook back in her bag. "Okay, I need to find the woman who started that petition. Where's her flat?"

"Number 440. But don't you want to hear the other story? My story?"

Clare glanced at her watch. "Come on then."

Amy looked around and lowered her voice a little. "I saw them do it. I saw them drop baby Jamie over the balcony." Then she fixed her gaze on Clare, who saw the child's eyes go a little watery.

For a moment, Clare didn't know what to say. "You're telling me you saw it happen?"

Amy nodded. Clare leaned forward. "Listen, Amy. It's really important that anything you say about this is true, right? You mustn't make anything up about baby Jamie. Because the police are trying really hard to find out who did it. If someone sets them off down the wrong path, then a real killer could get away. Or even do it again. You understand?"

Amy's grubby face flushed a little and she blinked back tears. "I'm not making this up. Why does everyone say that?"

"Amy, I'm not actually saying you've made anything up. I'm just... I don't know. I'm a bit shocked, that's all. Tell me what you saw."

"I was looking down over the balcony. I saw everything. This man came and he picked Jamie out of his pram. He held him up and there was another man down on the ground and he threw the baby down to him. I think maybe he was supposed to catch the baby but he missed."

Clare squinted at Amy in the bright sunlight, trying to make out the expression on her face. "Then what happened?"

"The man on the ground, he picked Jamie up and ran off. The other one ran down after him. There was a bit of blood on the ground. I saw it. The police saw it too, when they came."

"Did you see where the two men went?"

"I saw one of them go over there," Amy pointed towards the concrete stalls where the bins were kept. "I never saw where the other one went though."

"Did you go and tell anyone? Straight away?"

Amy shook her head.

"Didn't you think you should? The police? Or Jamie's mum?"

"I was scared."

"Yes, I'm sure you were, but… " Clare noticed that Amy's chin had dimpled as she started to cry, silently.

"Hey." Clare reached over and put a hand on Amy's clammy arm. "Have you told anyone else, Amy?"

Amy sniffed and nodded. "Yes, I told the policemen. When they came knocking round all the doors and taking everyone's fingerprints. But they never believed me. And my mum said I make up stories all the time, so she told them I'd probably made this one up too. But I never. Not this time."

"What did these men look like, Amy?"

"The one on the balcony had a baseball cap on. Dark blue, I think. And it was pulled down low, so I couldn't see his face."

"And what else did you notice? About their clothes or anything?"

Amy stared down at her feet. "Just that they were wearing jeans and stuff. That's all. I know I should've written it down or something but I never." She looked up at Clare. "You would've writ it all down, wouldn't you?"

"Did you see the other guy's face? The one who picked up Jamie from the ground?"

"Yes, a bit, but," Amy shrugged. "I don't know how to tell about it. It wasn't, you know, special. Like, I didn't see a scar or a big nose or anything."

"After the men ran away, what did you do?"

"Nothing. I just sat and watched. I knew Debs was going to come out and go mad when she saw the baby was gone."

"You didn't think you should go and tell her what you'd seen?"

"Thought I'd get into trouble." Amy started to cry again.

"Amy." Clare squeezed the little girl's sticky hand. "Would you know either of them if you saw them again?"

"Maybe. Yeah, the one on the ground. I thought it was someone from round here, but I'm not sure."

"Last question: did either of the men see you?"

Amy shook her head. "Don't think so."

"That's good," Clare said.

"But what if they did? Would they come back for me?" Amy's eyes went huge and round. She suddenly looked much younger than nine years old.

"That's not going to happen." Clare put her notebook away.

"No one else believes me." Amy folded her arms and looked at Clare. "But you do, don't you?"

Clare paused for just a moment. "I've got no reason not to believe you, Amy." A tactical answer, one that would get past most adults, never mind a nine-year-old, but Clare couldn't help feeling a guilty little twinge inside when Amy's face broke into a gap-toothed smile.

Even after leaving the estate, it was hard for Clare to push Amy's face out of her head. If she was mine, Clare found herself thinking, what would I do with her? Get her to write her stories down, for a start. Let that crazy imagination run wild. Clean her up, she couldn't help thinking too. For Tina, who seemed too bored and impatient to be a really good parent, Amy was just a nuisance. Whereas Clare could have... she shook the thought away and reached in her bag for some headache pills.

Later, Clare called at the police station and asked to speak to the chief inspector. Seaton was always pleased to see her, especially on her own, when he could flirt more outrageously. He sent a secretary to make Clare some tea, which arrived dark and strong in the regulation thick white cup and saucer. She tried not to wince when she took a sip.

"Any developments on Jamie Donnelly?" Clare started.

Seaton blew air noisily out of his wide nostrils. "One or two lines of enquiry."

"Anything the paper could help with? An appeal, or... "

Seaton gave a snort of a laugh. "Nice try. But there's nothing I'm about to go public on, not just yet."

"Nothing from the scene? You know, fingerprints or... there was blood, wasn't there, on the ground?"

"There was. Young Jamie's blood. No one else's, though. As for the fingerprints... " Seaton shook his head, looking exasperated. "The baby's body was found beside the bins. The tenants put their rubbish there, the bin men come and collect it every week, the kids play round there and the local druggies meet there at night. You can imagine how many people's fingerprints are left behind. And not just that, they're all mixed up with each other. All we've got is a load of partials."

"So what can you do with them?"

"Not much, to be honest. We've had officers doing the whole house-to-house, eliminating as many local people's prints as we can. Fat lot of use it's been."

"This is going to sound daft." Clare crossed her legs and looked down at her notebook. Seaton leaned back in his chair and made it obvious he was enjoying the view. "There's a kid up on Sweetmeadows who says she saw a man throw the baby over the balcony. She says there was a second man on the ground who picked the kid up and that they ran off towards the bins, where Jamie's body was found."

Seaton gave another sharp laugh. "You've been talking to young Amy Hedley."

"That's right."

Seaton took a slow sip of tea. "I wouldn't pay her too much attention, Miss Jackson. She's a fantasist. The mother's been known to us for a while. Nothing serious, just the odd bit of shoplifting. Class B drugs. Drunk and disorderly."

"Tina?" Clare couldn't keep the surprised tone out of her voice. "She seemed quite responsible."

"She is, if you're comparing her with most of the tenants on that estate. Though I wouldn't set too much store by anything she says."

"But little Amy? She seems really bright. And I got the sense that she was quite scared by the whole thing."

Seaton shook his head. "She has, how shall I say it... a very vivid imagination. Does it sound likely to you? It doesn't to me."

"You checked it out, though?"

Seaton raised his wiry brows. "We did. We check out every line of inquiry, no matter how far-fetched it seems."

"Sorry. I'm not suggesting you ignored her. It's just that it seems to be a massive thing to make up, even for a kid with a vivid imagination."

"I'd have thought journalists would be used to people making things up. That you would come up against that every day."

Clare gave Seaton a small smile. "We do. But children, they tend to tell it how it is, in my experience."

Seaton shrugged. "Welcome to my world, Miss Jackson. Sometimes the kids are worse than the adults. Even Amy's mother swears the lass made it up, just to get some attention. Anyway, we asked her some questions. Her story kept changing around, from one version to another. It just doesn't get us anywhere, I'm afraid."

Clare chewed the end of her pen. "So are you checking out this idea that it was some kind of payback for Rob Donnelly breaking the strike?"

Seaton gave a low sigh. "We have to look into it, because that's what the family are saying. Some of the family, anyway. Not Rob Donnelly, I notice. He thinks it's all rubbish."

Clare sat forward a little. "But what do you think? Is there anything in it?"

"We're asking questions, of course we are. But you know, I've known these men all my life. My dad was a miner, my granddad was a miner. I was the first lad in our family not to leave school and head straight down the mine. Things aren't good between the miners and the police at the moment, but that'll all blow over soon enough."

He shook his head again. "Most of these men are the absolute salt of the earth, if you ask my opinion. Decent men with wives and kids, pushed into a hopeless strike, all wanting nothing more than to get back to work and bring some money in. You're not telling me that any one of the strikers from round here would harm a kiddie. I don't believe it."

Clare slotted her pen into the spirals at the top of her notebook. She thought about Amy again. "Funny, isn't it? How differently everyone thinks about the strike. The miners don't think it's pointless, they think they're fighting for their jobs.

"And I've been out on those picket lines, just like you have. There's so much anger against those who don't support it, whether it's the press, the scabs, the police. You can see it. It's hard to predict what that kind of anger will drive people to do."

"I'm disappointed, Clare," Seaton said. "You're trying to drum up a problem about the strikers. We've only had little incidents up here. No big trouble like they have down in Yorkshire or Nottingham. Let's keep it that way, eh?"

"Okay." Clare cast around for a way of keeping the peace. "Did your dad work round here?"

"He worked at a few of the local pits. Sweetmeadows was the last place he worked before he retired. I went to school with more than half of the men on that picket line today. The last thing I want is any aggro."

"What does your dad think about the strike, then?"

Seaton paused. "He's not around to say. He died about a year after he retired. Lungs."

"I'm sorry."

At the end of the day Clare lingered in the office, putting off the point when she would have to go back to her own flat, her fingers clacking listlessly at the typewriter keys. She tried to write up Amy's story in a way that seemed credible.

Police are running out of leads into the horrific murder of little Jamie Donnelly. But they dismissed rumours that the baby was killed out of revenge after dad Rob broke the bitter miners' strike and went back to work at Sweetmeadows Colliery.

One witness, who the Post *has decided not to name, claims to have seen a man lift baby Jamie out of his cot and throw him over the balcony at Jasmine Walk. Another man picked the baby up and ran away towards the bins where Jamie's body was later found, the witness claims.*

The young witness was too afraid to speak out immediately but later told the police what they saw. Chief Inspector Bob Seaton said the claims had been looked into but that they were not pursuing them any further.

Meanwhile, police also dismissed as 'unlikely' the fears by the Donnelly family that the tragedy was carried out by supporters of the four-month-old miners' strike. Rob Donnelly's mother-in-law, Annie Martin, told how the family had been subjected to name-calling and spitting in the street, as well as two broken windows at their home. Chief Inspector Seaton said that although the police were pursuing all possible lines of enquiry, he did not believe that supporters of the dispute would resort to such a violent act.

Clare yawned and rubbed her eyes. It was late but still light and breathlessly warm. She should go back to the flat, of course. She should tidy up, she should open some post. But she knew it would be all she could manage to pick her way through the mess and fall into bed. She kept promising herself that any day now, she'd wake up and feel different, that she would somehow find the energy to sort everything out. But over six weeks on, she still wasn't feeling any better.

Tuesday 17th July

The miners' union office was in a prefabricated hut across

the road from the colliery and attached to the workers' social club. Clare could hear the loud, gruff voices coming from inside and she took a deep breath before turning the door handle. It was always an intimidatingly male environment, off-putting even before the strike got under way and the miners' feelings towards the local reporters changed for the worse. Clare was hoping that George Armstrong, the long-time union official, would still be civil to her, in spite of the *Post*'s editorial stance on the strike, which had been openly hostile from Day One.

But when Clare pushed open the door to the smoke-fugged room, she wasn't prepared for the way the voices stopped dead, the way everyone looked at her like she was an apparition of Margaret Thatcher herself. She swallowed, tasting the smoke and male sweat in the air.

"Er, hi, I'm from the *Post*." She was well aware that most of them knew that already. "I just wanted a quick word with Mr Armstrong?"

One of the men swore. George Armstrong held up a hand, but another man stood up and leaned towards him.

"You couldn't wait, could you?" He stabbed a finger towards Armstrong's face. "You told the papers before you even told your comrades. That says it all."

Clare looked at the little group of men, baffled, as Armstrong shook his head and said, "Nah, nah, it never came from me."

He looked grey-faced, Clare thought. "Should I come back in a few minutes, if you're in the middle of something?" Anything that avoided getting their backs up any further.

"Why, no, have a seat, I think you might as well hear what we all think about our wonderful leader." A stocky little man stood up and offered Clare his chair. For a moment, Clare wasn't sure whether to take it or not. She couldn't work out the atmosphere and what exactly was going on. She looked at the only one she knew by name. "George?"

George wiped his hands across his face. "I'm resigning

from the union."

Clare blinked. "Because of the strike?" A few weeks earlier, George had given her a long interview in which he'd told her the miners had no choice if they wanted to protect their jobs and the strike was a moral responsibility for all the men. "What's changed your mind?"

"I'm trying to tell them. We need to have a proper ballot before we carry on. And I'm sure we're walking into a bloody great trap that the government's made for us."

"The ballot would be a waste of time."

Clare looked over at the new speaker, a tall, broad-shouldered man in his late twenties. "The fact that we're all out there on the picket line is enough to show the men support the action. And what's the choice? Roll over and let Mad Ian McGregor close all the pits down?" There were murmurs of agreement.

"No, just to do some more talking, that's all. To make a strike official, through the proper channels, if that's what it comes to."

George Armstrong had been in the union for twenty-five years and he'd been the branch leader for fifteen of them. Clare had enough biographical details to turn the story into a front page lead, with just a few more quotes.

"So, George, if you're leaving the union, does this mean you'll be crossing a picket line?"

Armstrong screwed up his face as if the very thought was causing him physical pain. All the men were staring at him.

"George. Don't do it, man. Change your mind right now and we'll all forget about it." It was the tall young man from the back again. Clare couldn't remember seeing him before today.

She followed Armstrong as he walked out of the office and into the bright daylight, squinting and blinking hard. Clare pretended not to notice he was struggling not to cry. They chatted a little longer. Armstrong refused to let Clare send a photographer out, but it didn't matter. The paper had a folder full of library pictures they could use.

"George, I'm really sorry to ask this right now, but the reason I came out to see you was because of this baby's death at the flats."

George looked at her as if she was talking another language. "What's that got to do with me?"

"Nothing, I hope. But some of the Donnelly family are saying the baby's murder might've been linked to the strike. Because Rob went back to work. I just wanted to know what you thought about those rumours."

George gazed across the road at the colliery gates. Clare waited for him to say the idea was outrageous and an insult. Instead, he shook his head. "I don't think it's very likely. If anything bad happens these days, someone tries to blame a striking miner. But it's no good asking me, love." He jerked his head back towards the union hut. "Go in and ask someone from the new regime."

"Who's taking over from you?" Clare asked.

George twisted his mouth. "I'd put my money on Finn McKenna."

"Which one's McKenna?"

"You saw him in there. The gobby one at the back."

"Have I met him before?"

"It's unlikely. His family's from round here but he was working down Nottingham way. He wasn't even a miner. Says he was in security or some such at the pit. And the strike made him join the union and come out on the picket lines. Or that's his story, anyway."

"You don't get on with him?"

"He's already taking over in the union. He's the one to watch."

An hour later, Clare phoned her copy over direct to Dave Bell, who promised she'd get the front page lead in the late night final edition. "You're turning in some brilliant stuff, Clare. I was telling Blackmore that your baby death copy's been spot-on."

"Is that why you gave Chris Barber the by-line on Friday?"

The phone line crackled as Bell sighed hard. "That was a mistake, Clare. Don't get paranoid. Not when you've just given me this cracking good story and made my day."

Just after she'd ended the call, Joe rang. "Fancy going back out to Sweetmeadows? I want another go at the Donnellys. Five days on and the police are no further forward with finding Jamie's killer."

"I'll wait outside the office." On the way, Clare bought some bubblegum and a Double Decker bar, pushing them into her bag in case she met Amy on the estate. She followed Joe's car for most of the short drive.

"Heard about your union story," Joe said, as they each got out of the cars and slammed the doors shut. "That's a belter. Armstrong's not answering his door or his phone anymore, so you've got the exclusive."

Clare shrugged. "It was a total fluke. I went to ask him about baby Jamie and I walked in on the guys having a big row." She thought for a moment. "Heard of a union man called Finn McKenna?"

Joe gave her a sideways look. "Funny you should say that. I'd never heard the name until today. But I had a message to call him. Is he in charge now?"

"That's who George Armstrong thought would step into the breach. And he was there, this morning. I'd never seen him before either. Face of the future, apparently."

As Clare and Joe climbed the stairs towards the third floor of Jasmine Walk, the sounds of raised voices grew louder. Clare and Joe quickened their steps. One of the voices was Annie Martin, the other was a man's deeper tone. They stopped before turning the corner onto the walkway, to listen in.

"You can take your card," Annie was saying. "And you know where you can stick it. One thing we don't need is any sympathy from the likes of you."

Clare poked her head around the corner for a second, and

47

turned to whisper to Joe. "It's him again. That McKenna bloke."

Joe raised his eyebrows. He nodded towards the walkway and together they walked round the corner.

Annie turned to look at them, then turned back to Finn McKenna. "Bugger off. And take your crappy card with you."

McKenna was holding an envelope. "A lot of Rob's workmates have signed it, that's all. He might want to see it, even if you don't. You need to understand, Annie, that all the lads are sickened by what happened. It doesn't matter what Rob's done. Something like this... "

"Rob hasn't done anything, except try to take care of his kids. So don't you come here acting like you're doing us a favour."

McKenna held up his hands. "Fair enough. This is a bad time. I just wanted to make it clear that these rumours going around are all lies. None of the union lads would've harmed the baby. And we're all sorry for what's happened."

"You said that. Now sod off, like I told you."

Joe and Clare looked at each other. Joe followed McKenna down the steps while Clare went up to the Donnellys' door. "You okay, Annie?"

"That's some nerve. Coming here with a sympathy card signed by all the bloody bastards who've been posting dog shit through the door." The expression on Annie's face was hard but her eyes were wet.

Clare followed Annie indoors, without waiting to be asked. "You still think it was all related to the strike, then?"

"There's no question in my mind." Annie walked through to the tiny kitchen and filled a kettle.

"How's Deborah?" Clare perched on a little bar stool.

Annie jerked her head in the general direction of a closed bedroom door. "Still on pills. What do you expect?"

Clare nodded. "And you? Looks like you're the one keeping everything going."

"I don't know about that. But Rob's in pieces, Deborah's

out for the count, and there's still two little 'uns needing their dinner cooked and their socks washed."

"They're lucky to have you."

A pile of sympathy cards, several inches high, lay face down on the kitchen table. Clare picked one up and put it down again. "Lots of cards."

"Aye. Little Becca asked me if it was someone's birthday." Annie blinked hard again. "I have to say this. We've had cards and flowers and knocks on the door, every one offering to help. Half of them may be just being nosey, I suppose. But they slag off this estate and they call the people who live here worse than thieves, when at the end of the day, the folks all rally round to help. You should print that in your paper."

"I will," said Clare. *Tragic Baby Gran says thanks.* She glanced at a few more of the messages of sympathy and then asked, "When's the funeral, Annie?"

"We're talking about it. The priest from St Lawrence's is coming round tomorrow, if Deborah's up to it. Only thing is, we don't know if the police will release... " Annie bit her lip and swallowed. "If they'll release his body." She cast around for a hankie and grabbed a tea towel to wipe her eyes.

Outside on ground level, Amy was there, showing Joe how well she could do cartwheels and headstands, and Joe was trying to look impressed. He looked relieved to see Clare. Amy took a few steps towards her on her hands. "Did you do my story?" she demanded, her stringy hair trailing on the ground and her face slowly going pink.

Clare bent down and angled her head. "I did the petition one. It went on the front page. I'm talking to the police about the other one."

Amy jumped back to a standing position and smacked her hands together to get rid of the grit. "Them. They're bloody useless, the police. They don't know anything. And they don't listen."

"I'm working on it, Amy. Anyway, how come you're not at school again? I thought you didn't break up until Friday."

49

Amy filled her cheeks with air and blew it out again. "I got sent home."

"What for?"

"Nothing." She pronounced it, *Noffink*.

"It wasn't nothing, you little mare." Tina emerged from the stairwell. "Tell the lady why you got sent home. Go on."

Everyone looked at Amy, who looked down at her own sandalled feet and started making circle-shapes with her toes.

"She got asked to tell the class something good that happened this week," Tina began.

"Stop it," said Amy. "Don't tell."

Tina poked Amy on the shoulder. "And she stood up in front of everyone and said the best thing that happened was that the baby died."

"That wasn't... "

"The best thing that happened was the baby died, because it made the reporters come round and Amy got in the paper." Tina folded her arms and glared at the girl. "So she got sent to the head teacher. And I got dragged in to pick her up again. I could've killed her, honestly."

"Sorry," Clare said, not sure where to look. "That wasn't a very sensitive thing to say, Amy."

"It wasn't like that!" Amy's cheeks were now a deep red. "You *bloody stupids*!" She turned and ran off.

Clare made a cringing face at Tina. "I am so sorry."

"It's not you, it's her," Tina said. "She's a bleeding pain in the backside. The council is always on my back to send her to school and when I do it, I get a phone call saying I have to come and take her home again." She rummaged in her bag for her purse. "I have to go out, anyway."

Joe and Clare watched her hurry towards the bus stop. Joe spread his hands. "Tell me she doesn't think we're about to babysit her daughter?"

"I don't think she really cares. I think Amy does quite a bit of fending for herself."

Joe checked his watch. "I should get a move on. Give me

50

Annie Martin's quotes and I'll tell you about the mystery man Finn McKenna."

"Sounds like a good swap." Clare traded the story about Annie's thanks to her neighbours and how the family was hoping to sort out a funeral soon. "Might be worth calling in on the priest at that church over there, maybe tomorrow. What's it called again?"

"St Lawrence's. One of the patron saints of miners."

"Huh?"

"Just one of the many things a lapsed Catholic knows." Joe folded his arms. "Now then, Clare Jackson. You have an admirer, I think. Or I should probably say another admirer, to add to your legions of adoring men."

"Oh, for god's sake. What're you on about?"

"Finn McKenna is the new branch official for the miners at Sweetmeadows. And you certainly caught his eye this morning."

"Never mind that. What did he say about George Armstrong? And what about this card he tried to give the Donnelly family?"

"He seriously wants to quash this rumour that strikers were in any way involved in Jamie's death. I believe him, about that, anyway. He's given me some quotes but he really wants to talk to you, he says. And he asked me far too many questions about your personal life."

"Oh, honestly. Men." Clare had her pen at the ready. "Give me the quotes. And I'll call him, later."

Joe read his notes back. "If he suggests meeting you somewhere, I'm happy to come along and ride shotgun."

Clare laughed. "Why would I ask you to do that? I'd be a pretty crappy reporter if I needed a chaperone every time I went out."

"There was something about him, that was all." Joe shrugged. "I don't know. Something I didn't like."

"You don't like many people, let's face it." Clare punched Joe lightly on the arm. "It comes from being a journalist. You

51

think everyone has feet of clay."

Joe gave a little grunt. "That's because they usually do."

"Haven't you got some copy to write?"

"Yep, I'd better get going." Joe turned to his car. "Coming?"

Clare hesitated. "I might just go and see that Amy's all right. I feel a bit responsible for what happened at school."

"That little girl again? Clare, don't get too involved."

"I'm not." Clare put her fingers inside her bag to make sure the chocolate was not too badly melted. "I'm just going to make sure she's not still upset. Then I'm gone, I promise."

Joe shook his head, opened the car door and swung inside. He gave Clare a quick salute as he drove away. She held up her hand in response then turned to stare around the empty square, surrounded by its grim buildings. No one seemed to be around and the only sounds were traffic from the nearby main road, a dog barking somewhere and a piece of torn plastic skittering along the pavement in the faint breeze. The heat seemed to be keeping everyone indoors. That, and the fact that there was still a killer on the loose.

Which way did Amy run? Clare wandered in the general direction and noticed that the dark open stalls where Jamie's body was found were still taped off, although presumably any police forensics team would have taken everything they needed days ago. The tenants' bins had been moved outside, where flies buzzed around their rancid-smelling lids.

Clare was about to turn away when she heard a tiny shuffling sound. She peered into the stalls, suspecting a rat. But she spotted Amy's pink day-glo T-shirt, which the girl had stretched over her skinny knees. Amy was sitting huddled on the stone floor, watching her.

"Hey." Clare gave her little thumbs-up sign. "You're here. I was looking for you."

Amy stuck out her lower lip. "Are you going to give me wrong?"

"Not my job." Clare wrinkled her nose at the stench from the bins. "This isn't a great place to hang out, though. I've got

52

you some sweets but the chocolate's melting fast."

Amy stood up and brushed dirt off the backs of her legs. "Okay." She emerged from the little stall, her face still grubbily tear-streaked. Clare handed over the Double Decker bar and the bubblegum.

"Ta," Amy said, tearing at the wrapper. "I always used to come here when I wanted to be on my own. It was like my den. Only now it's been spoiled, because of baby Jamie."

"How do you mean?" Clare waved away Amy's offer of a bite of the sticky chocolate.

"This is where they found him. After he was dead."

"Yes, I know. That's very upsetting."

"He's still here." Amy's eyes went wide. "I hear him crying at nights. I guess it's his ghost."

Clare half-smiled. "There's no such thing as ghosts, Amy. What you hear must be something else. A different baby in one of the flats, or even maybe a cat. I get stray cats outside my flat. They sometimes sound like babies crying."

Amy shook her head, very firmly. "No, I know Jamie's cry, it's special to him. I used to live upstairs from him, remember? Babies' cries are all different. This is definitely Jamie."

Clare looked down. "Yes, but, Jamie's dead, remember? Maybe you dream it. That would be understandable."

"Not if I'm actually awake, you stupid." Amy unwrapped the bubblegum and stuffed it into her mouth, where it mingled with the chocolate. "Anyway, I know how to make him stop. I sing him a song, like how I used to do. He loves that. It always makes him smile."

"You used to sing songs to Jamie?"

Amy nodded, chewing hard. "Yes, I sing him stuff from the charts and I sing him nursery rhymes and stuff that babies like. Then he stops crying." She blew a huge bubble in Pepto-Bismol pink and let it burst with a dull, rubbery pop.

"What did you actually say to the teacher today, Amy?"

"Not what the stupid head teacher told me mam. She

made that up to get me in trouble. I just told them about you and about helping you with your stories. I never said it was good that Jamie died. I wouldn't say something like that. I miss Jamie. I miss cuddling him."

"I'm sure you wouldn't say anything so daft. I suppose people are feeling so bad about Jamie that they hear things wrong. That can happen when people are upset."

"Huh." Amy looked as if that was no excuse.

Clare hoisted her bag onto her shoulder. "I can't stay, Amy, because I've got work to do. But I think your mum went out. Will you be okay on your own?"

"'Course I will." Amy had already turned away and was wandering slowly back towards the flats. She cut a tiny, waifish figure, in her over-sized T-shirt, her thin legs bare and unhealthily pale. It was with a sharp inner twinge that Clare watched her walk away. If she didn't have all this copy to write up she would ring the desk and find an excuse to spend time with Amy, until her mother came back.

Clare tried to concentrate on typing up all her copy and out-doing every other reporter, especially Chris Barber, in terms of story count. But Amy wouldn't leave her head. You didn't have to spend long with the child to realise that she was prone to making things up, Clare thought, but mostly the lies were so preposterous that they were pretty harmless. And she clearly had loved the murdered baby, in her childish way.

But then there was this story about the two men who may have killed the baby, that everyone lumped in with all of the little girl's imaginings about ghosts and such like. The police, and even Amy's mum, filed them all under 'Fibs'. But Clare thought there was a subtle difference. Clare was sure Amy didn't really expect anyone to believe her stories about ghost-babies crying in the night: she was old enough to know the difference between what was possible and what had to be fantasy. But the girl seemed genuinely hurt that no one would listen to her version of how Jamie died. And simply by telling it and admitting that she had watched the tragic events unfold, too scared to act, Amy had laid herself open to trouble, though Clare was not sure whether the child had thought that through. She really wanted to believe Amy on this one, if nothing else.

As soon as she'd finished for the afternoon, Clare drove back to Sweetmeadows. The plan was just to make sure that Amy was okay. As she drove into the estate, she could hear music and spotted a gaggle of kids doing some kind of a dance routine. Amy seemed to be leading the troupe, all of whom were much younger than her. Clare parked and watched for a moment. The music was coming from a radio on a low wall: Grandmaster Melle Mel's *White Lines*, so loud it was distorted. Amy was the one making up the dance, a combination of something she must have seen on *Top of the Pops* and her own, manic inventions. She was singing along too, tunelessly, and every time she yelled, 'Freeze!' the other kids obeyed.

Rang-dang-diggedy-dang-de-dang. Amy was furiously crossing and uncrossing her feet, like some grubby little ballet dancer in a film on fast-forward. Clare noticed how the younger kids watched her every move and tried to copy it. Smaller children seemed to like Amy, perhaps because they weren't old enough to notice the things that were different, the things they could use to bully or isolate her. Clare decided she'd better drive away before Amy spotted her. Smiling, she steered her car into a full turn. The track pulsed in her head for the rest of the night.

four

Wednesday 18th July

Clare parked outside the office and was fishing for her keys when she heard another car door slam. She looked up to see Finn McKenna walking towards her. Clare glanced at her watch. It was only eight-thirty; too early for anyone to be sitting waiting to meet her.

"Clare Jackson from the *Post*?" McKenna held out a hand.

Clare took it, lightly, and let it go again immediately. She deliberately looked at her watch again. "You're an early bird."

McKenna gave half a smile. "You're hard to catch."

"How can I help you?"

"Let's chat," McKenna said, nodding his head towards Clare's office.

Feeling a little cornered, Clare led him up the office stairs. Jai called up after her. "No milk for your coffee this morning, Miss Beautiful?"

With her back to McKenna, Clare made an irritated face. She'd intended to say that she couldn't offer him coffee precisely because she was out of milk.

"I drink it black," McKenna said, without being asked. He picked up her kettle, shook it to check the water level and clicked it on to boil.

Clare sat at her desk and swivelled her chair to face him. "Make yourself at home."

He peered into the mugs. Clare remembered with a small flush of embarrassment that they weren't particularly clean, but she was damned if she was going to apologise for them. He didn't seem concerned as he spooned in the instant coffee.

Clare waited, determined not to make any more small talk. She didn't thank McKenna when he placed the coffee in front of her.

"I wanted to catch you before you were right up against your deadlines," McKenna began. "Joe Ainsley said yours are late morning and early afternoon, right?"

"That's right. Like most evening papers."

"You've done some good reporting for the union, George Armstrong said."

Clare shook her head. "Nope. I don't do my reporting for the union, I do it for the *Post*."

McKenna held up his hands. "That's not what I meant. George Armstrong said you were fair. Not anti-union. That's a good start as far as I'm concerned."

Clare turned over her notebook to hide the bright red-and-yellow 'Coal Not Dole' sticker. She didn't want McKenna to think she was some sort of a pushover.

"These are bad days," McKenna went on. "The men are flagging and the press are out to get us. No, they really are. Three-quarters of the stuff in the national press is not true. If we lose the war of words we'll lose the strike. As far as I'm concerned, a reporter without a built-in anti-strike agenda is like gold."

Clare shifted in her seat and said nothing. Finn was around the same age as Clare and stockily handsome. His eyes were a very pale shade of blue, his eyebrows and lashes blonde. It gave him an almost innocent appearance.

"Losing George was a hell of a knock to the lads. That's why I stepped in. They needed someone to take over, and quickly, before they lost their resolve. And then there's this rumour about the baby. That's a lie too. You must know that. You do, don't you?"

57

Clare stared into her coffee. She didn't like it black. "I just report what I hear. I don't decide what's true and what isn't. But it's only fair that people should know what's being said, isn't it? Then they can make their own minds up."

"I'm telling you," McKenna sat forward. "Yeah, we're angry at the strike-breakers, but most of our men have got families of their own. Not one of them would hurt a kid. I'd swear to it. On my own life."

"To be fair, Rob Donnelly doesn't think so either," Clare replied. "But his mother-in-law does. And given the sort of stuff the family's had to put up with since he broke the strike, it's probably understandable."

McKenna took a long drink of the coffee.

"Spitting at the family in the street? Putting their window out? You don't think that might have upset Rob's kids?" Clare raised her eyebrows at him.

"The union doesn't condone any of those things," McKenna said. "Although you have to understand that the men felt badly let down when one of their mates turned into a scab. But even you can see that there's a big difference between that and committing a murder."

Clare gave a small shrug. "The good news for you is that the police don't believe it either. So no one's pursuing that line of inquiry."

"Except for you."

"I'm not pursuing anything. I just report what people tell me, like I said."

"Sure. We both have a job to do. I thought maybe we could help each other out."

"How do you mean?" Clare folded her arms.

"I'll make you my first port of call for any union stories I get. And there are plenty, these days."

Clare narrowed her eyes. "And what do I have to do?"

"All I'm asking is for fair reporting. Fair. Not one-sided towards the union or the strike. Just not skewed the other way, by default." McKenna paused and rubbed his nose.

58

"And maybe… "

Clare sat up. "Maybe what?"

"What if you report on the odd positive thing? Like the fundraising we're doing, like the food kitchens, that sort of thing."

"I've always wanted to cover those things. But you don't tend to ask the press along."

"I want to change that. You can understand how people feel about reporters these days. The strikers and their families are sick of getting stitched up. But my view is, we have to work with you, not shut ourselves off."

"I'd agree with that. Obviously." Clare hesitated. "And I think I'm pretty fair already."

"So do I. That's what I'm trying to say, it's why I've come to talk to you. You've got a dirty job, that's all."

Clare allowed her mouth to drop open a little. "That's rich, coming from a miner."

McKenna laughed. "Okay. But technically I'm not a miner. I was in security, but I quit when the strike started. And now I'm just a full-time union man."

Clare hesitated. "Look, here's a thought. Can I do a profile piece on you?"

She expected him to protest, but he didn't. He just nodded. "Fine. As long as it's not a hatchet job."

Clare held up her hands. Then she glanced at her watch. "I've got stuff to do. I should've done my calls by now and I need to ring the newsdesk. Can we meet later?"

McKenna scribbled down his numbers. "Office and home. A pint after work?"

Clare gave a non-committal nod. "I'll call you. Might not be tonight."

She stood at the window watching McKenna head for the car, ducking backwards when he turned to look back up at her.

When Clare called her newsdesk, they told her to go straight to the police station for a news conference.

"Not sending the chief reporter?" Clare couldn't resist asking.

"He's on the picket lines today." Dave Bell didn't respond to Clare's sarcasm.

"I'd have thought that was beneath him," Clare said. "I thought that was for the likes of us lower life forms."

Bell sighed. "It is beneath him, at least in his opinion, but Tony was due to go and he's off sick today."

Clare allowed herself a small smirk at the telephone. She hoped the miners' aim would be good when they started spitting.

In the police meeting room, Joe looked pleased to see her. "It's you. That's a relief, I thought it might be Barber. Every time I see him I want to thump him."

Clare sat down beside him and pulled out her notebook. "That's very loyal of you."

"Not really," Joe said. "I've always wanted to thump him, even before he pinched your job. He's just got that kind of face."

"Any idea what this is about?" Clare asked, glancing at the police officers who were taking their seats along a table in front of the small press contingent.

Joe shrugged. "All Seaton would say on the phone was that it's not an arrest. They still haven't got the killer."

It turned out the police had discovered that when baby Jamie's body was found he was missing an item of clothing: a blue-checked sunhat. His mother insisted that he'd been wearing it when he was out in his pram, but no one could find it. The police were also releasing a new photo of Jamie, taken when he was wearing the little hat.

"It may be that the hat can provide us with the crucial evidence we need to find baby Jamie's killer," Seaton announced.

Clare shot up her hand. "Have the police always known the hat was missing?"

Seaton took a slow breath. "Mrs Donnelly told us the hat

60

was missing, the day after Jamie's death. But before we put out any public appeal to find it, we wanted to make sure that in her distress she had not made a mistake."

"You didn't believe her?" Clare pressed.

"We wanted to be certain about any information we made public, with regards to this highly sensitive case. I'm sure you can understand that, Miss Jackson." Seaton gave a heavy sigh. "It is possible that the sunhat fell off during the fall and was lost, but to date close examinations in and around the site of Jamie's death have failed to retrieve the item.

"So another possibility is that Jamie's killer has kept the hat as a kind of memento or trophy of the murder. It's therefore essential that the public keep their eyes open and if they discover such a garment then they must report their find to the police without delay."

Joe looked at his copy of the new photo. "He was a cute kid," he said to Clare, as they got up to go.

"Yeah." Clare pushed the picture into her bag without looking at it. "All babies are cute, though, aren't they?"

Joe frowned at the back of her head. It wasn't like Clare to play the hard-nosed reporter. Sometimes, these days, he got the feeling that he was getting on her nerves, and he had no real idea why.

Clare drove into head office with the photo and found a desk where she could sit to type. She still didn't let herself look at the picture. Dave Bell came over and perched on the edge of the desk. "How're you doing, Clare? You still okay out there in the sticks?"

Clare stuck out her lower lip and shrugged.

"You've done some great stories," Bell went on. "The baby stuff's been brilliant. Some of the strike stuff's been pretty good too."

"Thanks." Clare gave a small sniff.

"I know you're sore about the chief reporter's job. Between you and me, I reckon all you had to do to get that job was turn up on the day of the interview. But we never got to the bottom of what happened, did we?"

"I told you." Clare kept her eyes fixed on the beaten-up old Olivetti that sat on the desk. "I wasn't well. Some sort of a bug."

"You said that. But you're never ill. And I know you, you'd have done the interview anyway, even if you were at death's door. And ever since you seem to have... I don't know. Lost some of your spark."

"That's probably because you gave that idiot Barber the job and then you sent me out to the news equivalent of the salt mines. Anyone would lose their spark after that."

"You're taking it way too hard."

The office door burst open and Chris Barber strode in, red-faced and panting, making his way straight towards Dave Bell. "That's it. I'm never going to a picket line again. Have you got any idea what they're like, those bloody strikers?"

Dave Bell glanced at Clare. She noticed a small glint in his eyes. "Clare knows. She's done picket duty a few times, haven't you?"

Clare nodded. "Weren't they nice to you, Chris?"

"They spat at me. Animals. And you should see the state of my car. It's been kicked so hard there are dents in it and the paintwork's ruined. I'm billing the paper for the repairs, Dave."

"You took your own car?" Clare asked. "What, that red sporty thing? What were you thinking?"

"I can't drive the company car," Chris said, wiping sweat from his face. "It's too small. I'd get a back injury. And I was sitting in my car when a whole mob of them came up and started rocking it back and forward. It was bloody terrifying."

Clare laughed. "They do that almost every time, Chris. They've never actually turned one over. Yet."

Bell got up and walked away, with Chris Barber following him. "I think I should write about the way the miners behave towards the press. It was a disgrace."

"I don't think so," Bell replied. "No one cares about

reporters. They just want us to do our job and report the news. Doesn't matter if we get beaten up a bit along the way. And it definitely doesn't matter if a journalist's flashy sports car gets a scratch or two."

Clare decided she wouldn't stay to hear any more of the row. "I'm going to talk baby clothes with the lovely people at Sweetmeadows," she told Bell.

"I should come with you," said Barber.

"Because?"

"To get my face known round there. This story's getting bigger. It was one thing when it looked like a stressed-out mother battering her baby. It's more important now that there's a killer on the loose."

Clare looked at Dave Bell for support.

"It's something the chief reporter should be covering, and you know it," Barber added, looking at Bell.

"A chief reporter," said Clare, swallowing down her anger, "should be bringing in their own exclusive stories. Not piggy-backing onto stories that other reporters have been covering, perfectly well."

Dave Bell rubbed his eyes. "Maybe it would be a good idea if the two of you went out there together anyway. Safer." He gave Clare an apologetic look. "I'd feel happier."

"Joe's usually with me," Clare argued. "I haven't had any bother at all, anyway."

"Not yet. And technically, Joe's part of a different paper. Even though you two go round in a pair like Cagney and bloody Lacey."

Clare chewed the inside of her lip, trying to come up with a way to get out of this. "Tomorrow, maybe. But don't you need to get your car fixed, Chris?"

Barber glanced at his watch. "I suppose I'd better sort that out. We'll go there tomorrow, right? You can introduce me to some of your contacts."

"Yeah," Clare said, turning to go. "Like hell," she added, under her breath, as she strode out of the office.

She was pleased to spot Joe's car parked at the edge of the Sweetmeadows estate. He was talking to some young mums who were having a sort of picnic with their toddlers, on blankets spread out on a balding patch of grass. The heat was making the little ones grizzly and the women slow and disinterested. Joe smiled when he saw Clare and wandered towards her, wiping a hand across his brow.

"I swear there's more than orange juice in those beakers," he said, out of earshot of the group. "And I don't just mean the mums' drinks either."

"Don't," said Clare.

"What's up?" Joe was rather too good at spotting Clare's moods before they'd even passed a word between them. It was because they went back a few years: they'd gone to the same journalism school, suffered the same hangovers, passed their proficiency tests at the same time and followed each other through the same group of newspapers.

"Two words." Clare screwed up her eyes and put a hand up to shield them from the sun.

"Ah. Chris and Barber, by any chance?" Joe elbowed Clare lightly. "I heard he got his nice car messed up this morning. What sort of a prat takes a red sports car out to a miners' picket line? He deserves everything he gets. What's the latest?"

Clare told Joe about Barber's plan to muscle in on the murder story. Joe made a whistling noise through his teeth. "Does he have some sort of death wish?"

"What's even worse is that Dave Bell is so utterly spineless. He lets Barber flounce around the office like he owns the place. And he won't stand up for anyone else. So I'm expected to escort that idiot round my patch tomorrow and hand him my contacts book for good measure."

Joe looked over Clare's shoulder. "Uh-oh. Here comes your Amy-shaped shadow."

Clare turned to see Amy skipping towards them, wearing her stained blue school dress. "You've finished school early,"

Clare commented.

"Got sent home again," Amy said, cheerfully. "Felt sick."

"You look the picture of health to me," said Joe. "Underneath the muck."

"Yeah." Amy wasn't concerned. "It was probably the school dinner. It was a pile of puke." She pulled out the little notebook from her pocket. "What's the story today then?"

Clare's lips twitched. "The police are looking for some of baby Jamie's clothes."

"Right." Amy nodded. "Would it have, like, fingerprints on and stuff?"

"I expect so."

"So if they find it, would they know who killed Jamie?"

"They might. It would definitely help them."

"How would it?" Amy put a finger in her mouth and chewed at the skin. "Like, what would they know from it?"

"There might be forensic evidence on it," Joe began. "That's when… "

"I know what it is, I've seen it on the telly," said Amy.

"Pardon me," said Joe.

Clare smirked. "Yes, don't be so patronising. I think they'd look for traces that would link the killer to Jamie. But it gets harder, the more time has passed. The police should've started asking about the hat ages ago."

"Stupid police." Amy wiped at her eyes.

"Hey, you okay?" Clare put a hand on Amy's skinny shoulder. "I'm sorry. I know thinking about Jamie upsets you."

Amy shrugged. "Hey, look." She pushed the notebook up at Clare. "I've been practising my Teeline."

"Wow, look at that. Well done." Clare avoided meeting Joe's eyes, but she could sense him giving her a look. "Amy's going to be a reporter, Joe."

"Good for you, kid. But it's not as glamorous as it's made out to be. You might find yourself reporting on horrible stories like this one."

"I wouldn't mind." Amy was gazing at Clare, waiting for her verdict. "It's still not very fast though," she added, pointing to the pages of shorthand.

"No. That takes practice," said Clare. "It took me three goes to pass my shorthand exam. But I got there in the end." She flicked through the little book. "You've done really well, Amy."

Amy gave a big grin as she stuffed the book back into her pocket.

Joe nudged his head to one side to indicate that he and Clare should go. "I've got enough quotes from people here," he said. "You can share them for the price of a pint later on."

"See you, Amy," Clare said, turning towards her car. "Keep your ear out for any stories for me."

"I will. And I'll let you know if anyone finds Jamie's hat." Amy wandered off.

Clare stared at her back view for a moment, then turned to look at Joe, bracing herself for what she knew would be a lecture.

"Clare. Don't you think you're a bit too involved with that kid? You know you shouldn't make friends with anyone you're doing a story about."

"I know, I know." Clare got into Joe's passenger seat and winced again at the heat. "Don't have a go. She's just a bit lonely, that's all."

"Which is exactly why you should keep your distance. How's she going to feel when the police arrest someone, the story's dead and you don't come back here again? It's bad enough getting too close to adults, never mind kids."

"Okay. Get off my back, Joe. I know what I'm doing."

"Yeah? Only you've been weird lately. I've never seen you like this before. You sure there isn't something going on with you?"

"No more than usual. Look, will you give me your quotes? And I'll buy you that pint tonight."

Joe flicked open his book and read back from his

impeccably neat notes.

"Thanks." Clare pushed down the car door handle. "I'll catch you later. The drink's on me but if you lecture me, I'm leaving."

She left Joe shaking his head at her and went to sit back in her own car. But she didn't drive away. Mentally, she went over and over the last exchange with Amy. Then she got back out and walked across the estate. She went up to the fourth storey and tapped on Amy's door. The dog started its deep bass barking and Clare peered in at the window. Then she called through the letterbox. "Amy? It's Clare. Are you in there?"

The door opened a little and Amy slid out, pushing the dog back inside. "Hiya! I thought you'd gone away."

"I'm about to. I just wanted to ask you something."

"Yeah?"

"You know I said the police were looking for some of Jamie's clothes?"

"Uh-huh. I haven't got them."

"I didn't think you had. It's just that I said 'clothes'. But you said you'd look out for Jamie's hat. I was wondering, how'd you know it was a hat?"

Amy's face went a dull pink. "You said hat."

"No, I don't think I did. Amy?"

Amy dug her hands in the little side pockets of her school dress and looked at the ground. "Joe did, then."

"I'm sure he didn't. It's important. Please."

Amy hid her face, like a toddler might.

"Everything all right, pet?" Tina suddenly appeared.

Clare turned round. "Hi, Tina." She explained about the baby's sunhat.

"Oh, aye?" Tina gave Amy a prod on the shoulder. "Tell the lady what you know."

Amy released her hands from her face, which was now streaked with tears. "I knew it would be the hat, 'cause when the men dropped baby Jamie, his hat fell off. I saw it. And then one of them picked it up and put it in his pocket."

Tina sighed. "Not this rubbish again." She put a finger to her head and tapped it. "I sometimes think this kid's not right."

"But shouldn't Amy tell this to the police?"

"I told them already," Amy said, wiping her nose with her hand.

"She makes things up, I've told you," Tina said. "This stuff about the men is one of her stories. She never saw anything."

"Are you sure?" Clare wished Tina wouldn't talk about her daughter as if she wasn't there.

Amy made a growling noise in the back of her throat, pushed open the door of the flat and went inside. She slammed the door behind her. Clare jumped as the huge dog started barking again.

"See? She's nuts. I don't know where I went wrong." Tina gave a sigh. "Don't let her waste your time."

As Clare turned away, she stopped for a moment to blink away one of the many short spells of dizziness that punctuated her day. Maybe she hadn't taken in what Amy said, or maybe she had said the police were looking for Jamie's hat. It wasn't fair to pick on a nine-year-old child when the mistake was likely to be her own.

In the pub, Clare found it hard to lift her mood. Watching the news hadn't helped: the shooting of twenty-one people at a McDonald's restaurant in California and speculation that Margaret Thatcher was about to declare a state of emergency because of the miners' and dockers' strikes. Clare wasn't sure what that would mean but it sounded desperate. Joe was rambling about governments abusing people's civil rights. Clare couldn't pay attention.

"Bloody hell, that one didn't touch the sides," Joe said, as Clare tipped her glass to drain the last mouthful of wine.

"I'm not sure if I can stand another minute in the company of Chris Barber," Clare said, holding out her glass for Joe to get a refill.

"Understandable. But it's not just that, is it?"

Clare sighed. "Joe, that little girl... "

"... is not your responsibility," finished Joe. "What is up with you? Is your biological clock ticking or something?"

"Do you mind?" Clare rapped Joe's fingers with her pen and laughed when he yelped. "It's not that. She's just such a funny little thing. So bright. And that mother of hers doesn't seem to be remotely interested in her."

"I really don't care," Joe said. "I mean, I am sorry for the kid. Who wouldn't be? But the mother's not half as bad as some of them on that estate. And you can't step in. It's absolutely not your problem to sort out."

Clare gave a small groan. "That's easy to say. But if I see her left on her own for hours on end, sometimes without any food, and I don't do anything about it, then I'm neglecting her too, aren't I?"

"If you think it's that bad, you could call social services. And then she'd probably get whisked off into care, where at least she'd get three square meals a day. And they might make her have the occasional bath. Don't look at me like that. It's how things are, that's all."

Clare raked her fingers through her hair. "Okay. Let's change the subject."

"Hey." Joe's eyes lit up. "This strike business. It's starting to look like the miners have a chance of winning, don't you think? It might even see off Thatcher. That'd be interesting, wouldn't it?"

Clare nodded, closing her eyes and allowing her thoughts to drift off. Amy somehow knew it was the baby's hat that was missing, even though Clare was now sure she hadn't mentioned it. Surely that meant she really had seen something happen? It made it more likely the girl was telling the truth, Clare thought. Why was she the only one paying Amy's story any attention?

Thursday 19th July

Clare spent a dull morning at the local magistrates' court, eking out the sort of stories that were known as 'fillers': petty thefts, benefit frauds and burglaries. She'd gone there to get out of escorting Chris Barber round the Sweetmeadows estate, telling Dave Bell that she'd had a tip-off about an interesting case. The way courts worked, it was easy to spend a morning there and then claim that the hot case just hadn't gone ahead. As long as she came back with a sheaf of smaller stories, the desk wouldn't complain.

And there was another reason why Clare sought out the local courts that morning. There was always a duty social worker there, in case something came up in one of the cases and they were asked to step in. Thursdays were Geoff Powburn's days, and he was a friendly sort of guy who always had ten minutes to hang around in the canteen and chat. Around 11.30, when Clare had a handful of copy to take away with her, she found Geoff in the corridor and offered to buy him a coffee. She knew he never said no.

"Well, Miss Jackson, I hope this isn't an attempt to bribe a council employee into giving away confidential information," Geoff winked at her and dunked his Bourbon biscuit into his cup.

"Nothing like that," said Clare, pushing her own biscuit towards him. "But I was wondering if you could give me a bit of advice."

Geoff wiped sugar from his mouth. "You know I can't talk about individual cases?"

Clare nodded. "I don't need you to. I just want to talk about a... a 'for-instance' sort of scenario."

"Go on."

Clare hesitated over how to word her question. "Suppose a child wasn't being cared for properly, what would you lot do about it?"

"That depends."

"On what?"

70

"On the level of neglect, really. If we thought a child was in imminent danger we might have to take them away and into care. But that's a last resort. We'd rather kids stayed in their own home and with their parents. We might be able to work with the family to improve things."

"That's a lot of 'might's."

"Every case is different." Geoff gave her a sharp look. "If you have cause for concern about a child I have to officially urge you to tell someone. Me, if you like. In confidence."

Clare sighed. "That's the problem. I don't know if there is anything to be concerned about. I might be getting worried about nothing."

"Can you give me a name? We might already be aware of the case."

Clare shook her head. "I don't think so. I don't want to name names in case I'm way off the mark."

"There's our problem, these days. No one wants to get involved in case they're wrong. That's how everyone feels, right up until the point when a kiddie's found dead."

Clare inspected her nails. "I'll think about it, I promise. I just don't want to cause a lot of trouble. I'd be mortified if I was wrong."

"I'll say it again though. That's what everyone thinks, Clare. If this is a real child you have in mind, possibly being neglected or abused, you ought to tell us what's going on."

"Hey," said Clare, deciding to change the subject, at least a little. "You must do a lot of work up on the Sweetmeadows estate. What did you think about the baby murder?"

"Don't seem to be any issues with the Donnelly family. We'd never been made aware of them before."

"Right. But the police don't seem to have much of a clue, do they?"

"On that estate? I can't blame them. It could've been almost anyone. Except for the Donnellys themselves, I'd say. Although no one has any time for Rob, of course. Not since he broke the strike."

71

"I know, I pick that up when I'm chatting to people. Even now, they say how sorry they are for Annie and Debs and the kids. It's like Rob isn't part of it. Or that he doesn't deserve their sympathy."

Clare was about to leave the court when a friendly usher lifted his hand and beckoned her over. "I'd stick around for about another half-hour, if I were you."

Clare scanned the list of cases and pursed her lips. "What would I be waiting for?"

"It's not listed. But you'll be interested. Court One."

"A clue?" Clare gave the usher a hopeful smile.

"This morning's picket line. That's all I can say."

"Thank you!" Clare noticed there was a flurry of activity among the duty solicitors. She wondered what had happened. As it turned out, she didn't have to wait long before the magistrates' clerk came back in. He looked over to the press bench. "News travels fast this morning, eh, Miss Jackson?"

"That's right," Clare smiled back, trying to look better informed than she was. And then a police officer came in with a troupe of striking miners. And Finn McKenna. They were all pointed towards the dock. She couldn't help her mouth opening just a little. Whatever you've done, Mr McKenna, it's a story now, she thought. Even if you've just dodged your TV licence.

McKenna looked over towards her and gave a brief nod. Everyone got to their feet as the magistrates came back into the court.

"The court session has been resumed in order to deal quickly with a number of related cases that occurred earlier today," said the magistrates' clerk. The Crown Prosecution Service solicitor stood up. He told the court that all the men were involved in trying to stop a coach taking miners across the picket line into the Sweetmeadows Colliery. Stones had been thrown at the coach and the picketing men had got into a brawl with the police as they tried to hold them back.

"The police, however, are happy for all of these men to be

bound over to keep the peace. All, that is, with the exception of Mr Finn McKenna, against whom the charges are more serious."

The five other miners in the dock all agreed to be bound over to keep the peace, which meant that they walked away from the court without a fine or a prison sentence. As they filed out, they all clapped McKenna on the back. McKenna nodded at them and stood facing the magistrates' bench.

Clare scribbled fast as the court heard that McKenna was to be charged with assaulting a police officer, leaving him with a broken nose. When asked how he pleaded, McKenna replied: "Not guilty".

After a few moments, the court agreed to set a date for a trial and that McKenna should be granted bail on the condition that he didnt go to the picket lines. McKenna spoke into the ear of the duty lawyer, who asked the court if that condition could be waived, given McKenna's position with the miners' union. His request was turned down.

Once the magistrates had left, McKenna made his way across to Clare. "I suppose all of that has to go into the paper," he said.

"It does," Clare replied. They looked at each other. "It doesn't stop me from doing that profile piece on you, if you're still up for that. Any chance we could do it in the next day or so?"

"Now's as good a time as any." He had a purpling bruise across his upper cheek and, Clare noticed, cuts across his knuckles. There was no denying he'd been in some sort of a scrap. Finn noticed Clare looking at him and grinned. "The pig came off much worse. But you can't quote me on that."

He suggested the pub across the road from the court and they were making their way across the car park when Clare spotted Chris Barber, jumping out of his red car and half-running towards the court. He spotted her and groaned. "Don't say I've missed the miners."

"'Fraid so." Clare worked at keeping the glee out of her

voice. "Don't worry, I've got all the details."

"I don't suppose... "

Clare raised her eyebrows at Barber and he stopped. "Okay, forget it." He turned to McKenna instead. "Can I ask you for a comment on what happened on the picket line this morning?"

Clare made an eye-rolling face. "He's being charged with assault, Chris. That means he's not in a position to say anything about this morning." She resisted the urge to add, 'You should know that.'

"What are you up to then?" Barber demanded.

"I'm doing a profile," Clare told him. "And I need to get on, Chris. Sorry. We'll have to meet another day."

Barber handed McKenna one of his business cards as they walked away.

"He seems full of himself," McKenna said, dropping the card in the nearest litter bin. "That flashy car of his didn't make him any friends on the picket line."

Clare just smiled.

McKenna insisted on paying for drinks and a quick lunch, in spite of Clare's arguments. "I'd never live it down if the lads heard I'd let you pay for your own drinks," he said.

"What century are they living in?"

McKenna laughed and shook his head.

It turned out that Finn McKenna was exactly the same age as Clare and they shared a passion for seventies punk music.

"You don't look like a punk," Clare said.

"Not now," McKenna said, with a grin. "I had a few piercings though. Anyway, you can talk about not looking like a punk. You could pass for a model."

"I'd need to be a few inches taller." Clare's face felt warm. "Anyway, I've still got my ripped-up leather jacket. The last vestige of my teenage rebellion."

"I'd love to see that sometime."

Clare found McKenna easier to talk to than she'd expected.

The Miners' Leader Banned from the Picket Line was going to be a very easy write-up. And it had driven Chris Barber mad to see her walking off with a prized interviewee. The day was turning out to be not quite as bleak as she'd expected.

Back at the office, she dictated her string of court stories, then put in a call to Joe.

"I've been hearing your name from the other side of the office," he told her. "You'll enjoy this. Chris Barber was shouting at your newsdesk and accusing them of giving you all the good stories. The ones they're supposed to be giving to him, of course."

"Cheeky sod. What did Dave Bell say?"

"Something about you getting your own stories, all by yourself. I was doing my best to listen in, but I couldn't catch it all."

Clare grinned widely. "This day keeps getting better. Barber wouldn't know how to find his own stories. He thinks being chief reporter means you get given the best story of the day, by some sort of divine right."

"So what're you up to now?"

"I've got this profile to type up."

"I'm pleased to hear you're not going off and mothering that little stray from Sweetmeadows."

"No need for that sort of comment."

But Joe had touched a nerve: Clare was indeed wondering whether she ought to drive past the estate just to check on Amy. Or maybe that was entirely the wrong thing to do. She tried to push the little girl out of her mind and concentrate on typing up her profile of Finn McKenna, who was also taking up more space in her brain than she wanted him to.

five

Clare stood outside the door to her spare room, with her fingers around the handle. She hadn't been in the room for more than six weeks. She found her heart was thudding and her hand felt slippery. When she swallowed, her throat felt thick and dry. She pressed down the handle, pushed open the door and stepped inside. The first thing she saw was the dark brown mark on the floor. Dried blood on a cream-coloured carpet. She should've dealt with it straight away. She wasn't likely to get it out now. It would mean telling the landlord... what? Telling him something. And offering to replace the carpet.

Clare wrapped her arms around herself. The room was cool but the air was stale and dusty. She found herself staring into the stain and noticing that there were flecks of blood around the room and a dirty-looking smear along the door. That would have come from her own hand as she struggled to make it to the hallway. Clare didn't want to look at the rest of the room but she forced herself to turn her head.

A sudden hammering at her front door gave Clare such a shock that tears came to her eyes. She shut the bedroom door hard and stood behind the front door, not opening it. "Who is it?"

"It's *uuusssss!*" The voices were the women from the paper's head office. "Open up, we've brought wine! And food!"

Clare didn't know what to say. She slipped the chain on the door and opened it a tiny crack. "I didn't know you were coming."

"Yeah, surprise!" There stood Nicki, Jools and Di, her drinking partners when she was based at the city office. They were waving bottles and supermarket carrier bags. "Come on, open up. This wine's getting warm out here."

Clare didn't move the door chain. "I'm sorry, girls, it's not a good time for me."

Nicki squinted back at her through the narrow gap. "Clare, what's up? We haven't seen you for ages. Joe told us you seemed a bit down. We reckoned you must be fed up, all on your lonesome in that horrible, cramped old office. So we thought we'd come and cheer you up, that's all."

Clare glanced back at her dusty hallway with its piles of newspapers and unopened post. "That's sweet of you, honestly. But I'm all at sixes and sevens in here. I've... I've had a little flood. It came from the upstairs flat. The place is all dust and plaster. I need to sort it out."

"We'll help," Nicki said, and the others all chimed in. "Don't worry about that." "We'll clean it up quicker if there's a few of us."

"No." Clare's tone was sharper than she meant it to be. "No, sorry. I just need to sort it all out myself. Look, I'll come to the pub tomorrow and buy you all a drink."

Nicki looked quickly round at the others. "Tell you what, Clare, we'll drive down to the seafront and if you get sorted out you can catch us there. We'll be somewhere near the car park, okay?"

"Okay." Clare shut the door fast and breathed out. She went into the bathroom, doused her face in cold water and looked at herself in the mirror. "Pull yourself together," she told her reflection. "They must think you've lost the plot."

She dug out some clean clothes, freshened up her make-up and spritzed on some perfume. Then she called a taxi to take her down to the seafront.

"Someone's been very organised," Clare commented as Nicki handed her a plastic glass full of still-cool wine.

"That'd be Jools," said Nicki. "She thought of everything. Wine coolers, ice box, cheeses, bread, strawberries. The girl's a genius."

Jools did a mock flutter of her eyelashes. "Never mind me, though. What's going on with you, Clare?"

Clare pulled a face. "Been better. It was one thing being sent to the district office wasteland, but then as soon as the decent stories started happening, that git Chris Barber tried to muscle in on them. It's driving me mad."

Di put an arm around Clare's shoulders and gave them a squeeze. "You mustn't let him get to you. We all thought you should've got the job. He knows it, that's why he's too insecure to watch you get any by-lines at the moment."

"You never told us what went wrong," Nicki said. "You know, not turning up for the interview and sort of disappearing for a few days afterwards. Sharon Catt would still have you sacked for that, if she had her way."

"Sharon's such a bitch." Jools offered Clare the punnet of strawberries. "I don't get what her problem is."

Clare shrugged.

"Never mind that," Nicki said. "We want to know that you're coping, Clare."

"Yeah, sort of. I suppose I'm going to have to look for another job though, or else working with Sharon and Barber is going to do my head in. And I like it here, otherwise."

"Joe's worried about you." Di raised her eyebrows at Clare.

"Right." Clare nibbled at a strawberry. "There's no need for anyone to worry. And he's got no business to go round talking about me like that. I'm just a bit down about the chief reporter's job. And this baby story… "

"What about the story? It's a belter," Nicki said. "Your stuff with the grandma was great."

"It's depressing." Clare licked pink juice from the end of

her fingers.

"Right." Jools folded her arms. "I suppose it is, if you think about it too much. It's not like you to get so involved with a story, though."

"What's Joe been saying, exactly?"

Jools widened her eyes. "Nothing, really. Just that. That he thought it had got to you, a bit too much."

Clare shook her head. "No, it hasn't. But murdered babies don't make me happy, Jools, not even if they come with a big by-line."

Clare was aware of the looks passing between the other women. She closed her eyes and rubbed her forehead, as the grass beneath her spun a little.

"Clare?"

Clare screwed her eyes tight to rid herself of the flashing lights behind her eyelids. This had happened a few times, since… but she couldn't let it get to her. She just couldn't.

Jools put a hand on her shoulder. "You've lost a stack of weight, too. What happened to our curry queen?"

Clare shook Jools' hand away. "I'm fine, for god's sake. Will everyone stop acting like my mother?"

Her voice came out louder than she'd meant. There was a second or two of silence. Then Nicki said, "Any more of that wine?"

Back in the flat, Clare poured herself a huge glass of water to put by her bed, spilling it in globs on the kitchen bench when she tried to add some chunks of ice. It was going to be another sleepless, airless night and past form meant that she would go over and over the evening's conversation, wishing she hadn't been quite so brusque with the friends who were trying to do her a favour.

She couldn't decide whether she was furious with Joe for telling people that she wasn't coping, or touched at his concern. Her feelings for Joe switched from impatience to something like fondness, at least a few times every day. There certainly had been days recently when she didn't even want to look at him, and she also knew that wasn't fair. She wasn't going to let him know any of this, though: she'd be sure to tell him to keep his nose out of her personal life in future.

In the end it was Finn who made his way, unasked, into Clare's dreams. When she woke up after an hour or so, she felt warm inside, for just a few moments. Until she remembered, and the chill inside came back.

Friday 20th July

At seven-thirty the next morning, Clare found herself sitting in the newspaper's most beaten-up car with Stewie, one of the staff photographers. She hadn't been scheduled for picket duty but once again Tony Warton, a new-ish young reporter, had called in sick when it was his turn for the job. Sharon Catt, who'd phoned Clare at home at around six in the morning, was unapologetic. "Get yourself turned round and down to the picket line. The Sick Man of Europe's having another day in bed, apparently."

"Tony?" Clare happened to be wide awake, after a predicted night of very little sleep, and she was proud of her ability to sound alert at that time in the morning. "Sounds like there's something seriously wrong with him. He's had a lot of time off. Has anyone spoken to him about it?"

"I'll tell you what I think is seriously wrong with him," said Sharon. Clare could hear her leafing through the morning papers on her desk. "He's an idle tosser who doesn't fancy doing the difficult jobs. He's always ill on the days when he's down to go to the picket lines. I told Dave Bell that if it happened one more time we should give him an official warning, and that's what we're going to do."

"Maybe he's got some personal reason… " Clare started to say.

"Reporters don't have personal anything," Sharon snapped. "You want to be a decent reporter, forget about your own lives. Otherwise you won't get anywhere."

Not with you in charge, at any rate, Clare thought. Poor Tony, with his startled expression and his Marks and Spencer shirts and co-ordinating ties, so obviously chosen by his mother. Maybe he was genuinely ill, but news editors have a habit of automatically assuming that anyone who rings in sick is faking it. Clare knew this at her own cost. More likely, the thought of covering the volatile picket lines left the poor lad terrified. Either way, Catt would make him suffer.

So Clare sat doodling on her notebook while Stewie played around with his camera.

"Nice to have you for company, anyway," Stewie remarked. "You're easier on the eye than Tony."

"He's heading for trouble," said Clare. "Catt's got him down as swinging the lead."

Stewie shook his head. "It's not that. Some of his family are strikers. They gave him a hard time the last shift he did. I think he's trying not to fall out with them."

Clare sighed. "Trouble is, he can't keep avoiding it forever. If he claims to be ill one more time, Catt's out for his bollocks."

"I think he was hoping it would all be over quickly. I mean, none of us thought we'd still be here four months on, did we?" Stewie looked out of the car window at the row of men standing at the colliery gates with their placards: *No Pit Closures. Victory to the Miners. Coal Not Dole.*

"I guess not. You have to admire them, though. Can't be easy, living off nothing for all this time. Yet we're more worn down than they are."

"Here we go." Stewie jumped out of the car as the mini-bus carrying the handful of strike-breakers headed towards the gates. The line of police officers pushed back the picketers as they took up their shouts of "Scabs!" and tried to get at the bus. Clare watched as the bus went in, someone behind the window giving the picketers the V-sign, and Stewie's camera making its constant clicking, whirring sounds.

Once the bus had gone through the gates and the shouts

quietened down, Clare went up to the picketers as they stood, swearing, shaking their head in the direction of the pit. "Smell that bacon," one commented, glaring at the line of police officers. "Bunch of pigs."

"How's it going?"

They looked at her, their faces hostile. "You're the bird that was in the union office the other day," one of the men said.

"That's right. I just wondered what the mood of the men is, at the moment."

"We're fine," said the same man. He nodded in the direction of the pit. "See that bus? There were about five or six scabs on it. Know how many men work here, on a normal day? Two hundred. Just remember that, pet. There are hundreds of us still out on strike and we'll keep it up until we win. That lot... " he jabbed a finger towards the colliery. "... they're pathetic. They'll be begging us to come back, in a week or two. You just watch."

When Clare went into the newsagent's, Jai had an envelope for her.

"From your mining friend," he said, as she headed up the stairs to the office. The room felt claustrophobic and already too warm, even though it wasn't yet eight-thirty. It would only get more stifling as the day went on. Clare had a go at opening the little window, brushing away the cobwebs and dead flies that had accumulated along the sill and behind the plastic blinds. It wouldn't budge.

She tore open the envelope. It was a ticket to a benefit that evening at the miners' welfare club, to raise money for trips out over the school holidays. Clare fingered the ticket. It just said: *Benefit Night for the Miners' Families. £3 Waged, £2 Unwaged.* There was no note with it, but she knew this was Finn giving her an 'in'. She'd mentioned to him the other day that she particularly wanted to do something about the miners' wives and families. This would be a great start. Good job she'd stayed out of trouble on the picket line. She pushed slips of typing and carbon paper into her typewriter and began: *Striking miners remained upbeat on the picket lines today as the bitter dispute continued well into its fifth month. Defiant men told the* Post *that they were in no mood to give up in spite of the handful of strike-breakers who were bussed into the pit...*

Clare followed it up with a feature-length piece marking eight days since baby Jamie's death, detailing how the police were no further forward and families on Sweetmeadows were still living in fear of a psychotic killer. At the end of the working day, though, Clare had around half an hour spare before heading along to the miners' benefit. She'd planned it that way. She had a carrier bag full of sweets, pens and comics for Amy, seeing as it was the start of the school summer holidays. She made sure to scurry away before Joe or anyone else from the office called to persuade her out to the pub: she didn't want questions asked, either about the miners' benefit or why she'd felt compelled to put together a bag of treats for a kid she barely knew.

As Clare approached the door to Amy's flat, she could hear music. Amy was singing along, loud and unabashed, to Cyndi Lauper's *Time After Time*. Clare grinned as she rapped on the knocker and the singing stopped abruptly. The dog began his automatic barking. Amy didn't come to the door. Clare lingered for a moment or two, then knocked again. She could hear the dog snuffling just on the other side of the door. She leaned towards the letterbox and spoke into it. "Amy, it's Clare. Are you okay?"

The door opened immediately and Amy squeezed herself out of it, pushing the dog back inside.

Clare thought Amy looked even more scruffy than usual. Her hair was even more dishevelled and she'd obviously been picking at some scabs on her arms.

"Course I am, why?" Amy's gaze travelled to the carrier bag, with a kid's sixth sense that there was something in it for her. "You doing a story tonight?"

"Not here, but I thought I'd bring you this."

Clare held out the bag and Amy grabbed it and pushed her face inside. "Wow. Thanks!" She pulled out a handful of sweets and the copy of *Smash Hits*. "No way!"

"I didn't know if you like any of those bands. It's got George Michael in it and…"

"I like everyone, just about," said Amy, riffling through the rest of the bag. "The charts is my favourite thing. This is so brilliant. What's it for?"

"It was your last day at school today, right?"

Amy paused. "Oh. Yeah, that's right."

"You didn't go to school today, did you?" Clare asked.

Amy smiled and shrugged. "Not really."

"Not at all?"

Amy shook her head. "Thanks for this though. Can we go get chips or something?"

Clare glanced at the door. "Is your mum not around?" She resisted the word 'again'.

The girl unwrapped a tube of sticky, melting Rolos. "Can you keep a secret?"

"That depends what it is, Amy."

"You have to promise or I can't tell you."

Clare promised, knowing she shouldn't.

"She didn't come home last night."

"Your mum?" Clare's stomach clenched. "She was away all night? Is that why you didn't go to school?"

"I never woke up in time."

"Right." Clare felt out of her depth. "So have you had, I don't know, breakfast and lunch and stuff?"

"I had Sugar Puffs. We never had any milk though."

"Dry cereal, that's all?" Clare sighed. "Okay, let's go get something right now. And Amy, your mum. Do you know where she is?"

Amy followed Clare down the stone steps and across the bare courtyard that fronted the blocks of flats. "No. But she'll turn up tonight, probably. She always comes back in the end."

"Always?" Clare repeated.

There were groups of kids hanging about. Even the idea of a killer roaming around wouldn't stop them from playing outside on the first evening of the school holidays. And there had to be safety in numbers, although Clare noticed that a couple of mums were sitting on a wall, smoking and chatting but keeping a casual eye on the children. Parents' faces kept appearing at the windows and glancing out, in a way that wouldn't have happened before Jamie died. Amy linked arms with Clare as they walked past the others, showing her off.

Clare got into the driver's side of the Mini and pushed open the passenger door for Amy. "Are you saying she does this quite often? Goes away and leaves you on your own?"

Amy put a grimy finger to her lips. "You promised not to tell anyone, remember?"

"I did." And I'm regretting it, Clare thought. "But you know she shouldn't be doing that, don't you? You're too young to be on your own all night."

"I'm fine. And I've got Max."

"Who's Max?"

"My dog, who'd you think? He'd take care of any burglars."

"Hmm. By slobbering them to death, I suppose. But where does your mum go?"

"I don't know, do I? Out with her boyfriends and stuff. I told you, I'm okay. Only usually she leaves me some money and this time she forgot."

Clare watched, finding herself unable to eat, as Amy tucked away her sausages, chips and gravy, all slathered in salt, vinegar and ketchup. "Look, I have to go somewhere for work. I can come by later on to make sure you're all right."

Amy shook her head, quickly. "Don't do that. If me mam's back she'll kill me for telling on her."

"But what if she isn't back?"

"She will be, honest."

Reluctantly, Clare left Amy back at the flats and drove

to the miners' social club. She felt slightly sick. She'd just played a part in leaving a little girl alone in her home, with only a half-feral-looking dog for company, on one of the worst estates in the district, where only a week ago a baby had been brutally killed. And where, if she was to be believed, the same little girl was the only one to have seen the killer or killers in action. Clare pulled on the handbrake, checked her reflection in the car mirror and decided to give the benefit event no more than an hour. If anything happened to Amy, she'd never forgive herself.

The woman on the door of the social club looked Clare up and down, as if she was trying to find a reason not to let her in. Clare waited, shifting from foot to foot.

"Finn McKenna gave me the ticket," she said, after a minute or two. "I'm here to write something about the benefit, for the *Post*."

"Write what sort of thing?" The woman didn't look impressed. "The *Post*'s no friend of the miners, that much we know."

"I can't help what the editor writes," Clare said, trying to look past her into the function room, to see if McKenna was around. "But personally I'm on your side. I want to write something positive. That's why Finn gave me the ticket."

The woman said nothing, but turned to the couple standing behind Clare. She took that as an agreement that she could go in. The room was dark, thick with cigarette smoke and the smell of beer. Someone was operating a small portable disco, with a few coloured lights flashing half-heartedly on and off, but no one was dancing. Kids were running around, chasing each other in and out of the tables and sliding across the polished floor. Clare couldn't see Finn McKenna anywhere. She walked up to a long table where two women were pulling cling film away from paper plates, heavy with sausage rolls, pork pies cut into sections, chunks of cheese speared with cocktail onions and homemade cakes. She introduced herself and noticed how people's faces seemed to close down.

"I want to write about how people like you are trying to keep things together," Clare said. One of the women grunted and kept unwrapping food, but the other nodded. "Everything's a help. Tonight is to raise money to take the kids on some days out over the summer."

Clare started making notes. She found her way around the organisers and chatted to some mums and kids. She listened to the start of the set by a local band, singing local folk songs and the old songs that had been reworked for the strike: *Which Side Are You On? We Are Women, We Are Strong.* When no one was watching, she slipped some money into the collection buckets.

The hour passed quickly. Clare was heading for the door with a sheaf of good quotes, when she spotted Finn in the lobby. She waved at him.

"You came. Thanks. Let me get you a drink," he said, putting a hand on her arm to steer her back towards the bar. He smelled of a fresh, lemony aftershave and his hand, with its strong fingers, felt cool on her slightly clammy arm.

"I'm just going. Sorry." Clare held up her notebook. "But it's been great. Everyone's been really helpful. I should be able to get a good piece out of it."

"Come on, one drink." McKenna's hand didn't move. "It's Friday night." He had a camera on a strap round his neck and he nodded down at it. "Promised I'd take some snaps."

Clare moved to the side a little and made an apologetic smile. "I really have to go."

"Hey, Finn." The woman taking the tickets stood up. "There was a lass in here a few minutes ago, looking for you."

"That was me," said Clare.

"No," the woman said. "Another one. Someone called Jackie?"

Finn's expression was hard to read but Clare sensed he wasn't pleased. "Jackie? You sure?"

"Aye. I sent her to your mother's house."

"Damnit." Finn turned to Clare. "I need to go and sort

87

something out, but I'll be back. Wait for me."

Clare smiled and sidled past him towards the door. "I'm sorry. I have to be somewhere." She pushed open the door and breathed in the warm evening air and the faint, beery smells that drifted out of the building. She turned back for a moment. "Hope you sort things out. I'll let you know when the piece is going in the paper. Thanks for the ticket."

In the car, Clare wondered, briefly, why she hadn't quizzed Finn further on his personal life. It could have made a decent line, particularly if his girlfriend had an interesting job or was supporting him through the strike. Instead, she'd only asked if he was married and when he'd said no, she hadn't pressed him further. With a warm rush of embarrassment, she remembered that at that point the conversation had got a little flirty in tone. Truth was, he was very attractive. She didn't want to feel anything for him, but there it was. She worked hard at pushing Finn McKenna out of her thoughts as she drove, as fast as she could get away with, towards the Sweetmeadows estate.

Clare hadn't really worked out exactly what was going to happen when she went back to check up on Amy. She'd just have to play it by ear. Clutching a couple of the sugary cakes from the social club, wrapped in a paper napkin, Clare ran up the steps and tapped on the door of Amy's flat. It was Tina who answered the door. She stared at Clare.

"What is it?"

Clare opened and closed her mouth. Then she said, "I'm so sorry to bother you at this time of night, Tina. I was chatting to Amy earlier on and I think I might've left my notebook here?"

"You came in here?"

"No, I was just talking to Amy at the door." Clare didn't want to drop the girl in trouble with her mother. "I thought she might've picked it up."

Tina looked back over her shoulder for a second, then shook her head. "Don't think so."

"Oh, okay. Maybe I've dropped it somewhere. Sorry to have disturbed." Clare walked backwards along the balcony, then turned and almost ran back down the steps. She threw herself into her car and sat back in the driver's seat, placing the backs of her hands on her hot face to try to cool it down. Tina must have thought she was a complete flake.

As Clare headed home, her embarrassment gave way to something else. In part, relief: Amy's mother was back home and the child was no longer in the flat on her own. But there was something else that she was trying to ignore. Vaguely, and without really articulating in her head how it would happen, Clare had pictured herself rescuing Amy. Clare didn't need to root around inside her brain to find what was compelling her to meddle in Amy's life; she knew exactly what she was trying to replace in her own. But it turned out she wasn't needed. And that was a good thing, for everyone. Though, as she put the key into the door at home, kicking aside the papers on the mat, she couldn't shake the feeling of flat, overwhelming disappointment.

Saturday 21st July
These days, Clare didn't like weekends and was keen to try to fill them up with things that would keep her out of the flat. She always woke too early, for a start, around five-thirty in the morning, sometimes even earlier. So she showered and dressed as if she was going to work, then drove into the office. The newsagent's shop had just opened and Jai was putting the last of his morning papers out.

"It's Saturday, Miss Beautiful," he said, grinning at her. "You should still be in bed."

"I know, I know. But I've got something to write up." Clare was glad to have the excuse of last night's miners' benefit to take her into work, but in fact she had been coming into the office every weekend for the last five weeks or so. It was just about the only advantage of having an office to herself, that she could see. No one, except Jai, was there to ask questions if you were there late into the night, early in the morning or on days when you should have been having a life.

So she sat down and started typing: *Young miner's wife Margie Jeffries wasn't looking forward to the school summer holidays. With husband Micky out on strike, she wondered how to help her two boisterous boys – Christopher, six and Andy, eight – fill the long six weeks. Thanks to a fundraising benefit held at the Sweetmeadows Social Club, however, she and some of the other miners' families can look forward to some trips out...*

When midday arrived, Clare had written the benefit night feature and six other dateless stories that would see her through any quiet days next week. What's more, if anyone were to tot up her story count, they couldn't fault her: she was outstripping every other reporter by a long way. Particularly Chris Barber, which was partly the point of the frenzied work. The other point was filling that aching hole in the rest of her life. Other people's stories were a great way of doing that. Sometimes, Clare thought, being a journalist turned you into a big blank page, waiting for other people to come and write on it. Your own life was what ended up on the spike.

She'd banked on the phone ringing at least once, with some lead for another story. It hadn't. So with a long afternoon and evening ahead of her, Clare faced the prospect of going home. She'd just been paid, though, so maybe some of the girls could be persuaded to get together and do something, if they'd forgiven her for being such lousy company the other night.

On the other hand... Clare flicked through her contacts book for Finn McKenna's number. She held her fingers over the dial for a few moments, then called him. "Hi, it's Clare Jackson. I just wanted to say thanks for the invitation last night. People were kind to me. I think it'll make a great piece."

"You're working today?"

Clare hesitated. "Sort of. No, not really. I just had a few

things to do in the office."

"You finished?" Finn paused on the end of the phone and then said, "So what're you doing now? Come for a drink?"

"Umm, yeah, I could do that, for a few minutes, maybe."

They arranged to meet at a seaside pub, a few miles out of town – Finn's suggestion. It didn't escape Clare's notice that he could have picked somewhere much nearer, but where they would both be much more likely to be spotted. Not that there was any reason to hide. After all, it was perfectly reasonable for a reporter to be having a drink with a local union leader in the middle of a controversial national strike.

Finn was wearing a pressed white shirt and his aftershave smelled freshly-applied. The shirt looked expensive. It must have been a pre-strike purchase, Clare told herself. She toyed with the notion of asking who did Finn's ironing as she couldn't quite picture him doing it himself, at least not quite so painstakingly. But she didn't.

"I'm glad you went along. Those women deserve a bit of recognition for their work," Finn said, handing her a glass of orange juice clinking with ice.

"I want to do more on the women. The wives and mothers," Clare said. "They're the ones trying to hold things together, right? I want to do something about how it is to try to live on – what is it? Twenty-six quid a week supplementary benefit? Like maybe a diary-style piece for a week, from one or two of the women. What they're eating and what they're going without and which bills are not being paid."

"You're right, that would work. Take my mam," Finn said. "My dad is on strike, so's my uncle and so am I. She's had a good wage coming in for the last few years and now she's got none. No family to help out. Two big men still to feed, though."

"Would she talk to me?"

"I think so. And," Finn wrote a name and number down in Clare's notebook, "this is someone who wants to form a Women Against Pit Closures group, like they're doing down in Yorkshire. Maybe if you talk to her and put something in the paper, she'll get a few more women joining in."

"Brilliant." They sat outside, looking over towards the cliffs. The breeze from the sea brought the temperature down, making the heat more bearable, but Clare wished she'd brought her sunglasses, to stop herself blinking and wiping her eyes in the bright sunshine. She hoped she wouldn't get one of her dizzy spells. The last thing she wanted was someone chivvying her along to see a doctor.

"Tell me something, how do you feel about the men who're breaking the strike?"

Finn kept gazing out towards the sea. "Is this on the record?"

"Everything's on the record with me, Finn."

"I'll be honest. Bloody angry. I'd like to shake them. And you can guess which ones are going to crack first. Rob Donnelly – everyone said he was never quite one of the lads. But at the same time, I know what's going on in their heads. They're always wondering where the next meal's coming from and how they're going to get through the next couple of days, never mind the next few weeks. So I know the pressure they're under. That doesn't stop me thinking that what they're doing is wrong."

"But aren't they just putting the needs of their families first? You know, the ones like Rob Donnelly, with a troupe of young kids?" Just two young kids, now, Clare thought. Not so much of a troupe.

"We've all got families. I haven't got young kids of my own, but I've got a mother and a sheaf of red bills. We're all going through it. Some of us are just a bit stronger than others. More determined, if you like." Finn took a long drink of his pint. "The thing is, this can only work if we stick it out. If they chip away at us, bit by bit, with more and more men going back to work, we can't keep going. So tough as it is, we have to hang in there."

"Do you think you can win? Be honest."

"If I didn't think that, I couldn't get up in the morning. Yes, we will win. Only a tiny minority have cracked and gone through the picket lines."

Clare frowned. "I just can't see Falklands Maggie and her crew backing down. Can you? Really?"

Finn smiled. "It'll take a union as strong as the miners to beat her, that's for sure. But we'll stick it out. They're trying to starve us back, but it's not going to work. We need more reporters on side, though. The lads pick up *The Sun* and they get disheartened. It might not be outright lies they print, but it's distortion. There's only one point of view, which is anti-union. It wears you down."

Clare nodded. She was conscious of Finn giving her the odd appraising look, his gaze lingering on her bare legs. She shifted in her seat.

"I'm sorry," Finn said, suddenly. "I shouldn't be staring at you like that. I'm embarrassing you."

"You're not." Clare wondered how obvious her body language had been. Truth was, she liked being the object of Finn's attention.

"You're very attractive, that's all."

Clare looked at her drink. "Thanks."

"I'm making it worse now."

Clare shook her head. But she decided it was time to go. "Look, thanks for the drink, and there's really no problem, but I need to be somewhere shortly. Sorry." She remembered telling Finn earlier that she was free for the afternoon, but he didn't argue. She didn't want him to know how much she really liked him.

Just as she was getting up and hoisting her bag over her shoulder, she noticed Finn look past her and saw his face change. She turned to see two men in plain clothes, who were almost certainly police officers, walking up to them.

"Finn McKenna?" one of the men asked.

Finn gave an almost imperceptible nod.

"We'd like to ask you some questions in connection with

the death of Jamie Donnelly on 12th July."

Clare sat back down next to Finn and looked at him. He gestured to the officers to sit down, but they stayed where they were.

"At the station, if you don't mind, Mr McKenna."

Clare expected Finn to protest, but he just shrugged and stood up. She stared at him, at the two men, and back again. Then she grasped at his hand. "What's going on?"

Finn looked down and gave her a half-smile. He folded his fingers around hers. "I don't know. But I know I have nothing to worry about, so neither have you."

"But… "

Finn squeezed her hand and then, in a quick movement that was over in a second, he leaned down and kissed her knuckles. Then he let her go. "I'll call you when they've finished wasting everyone's time. Let's get this over with, then." He followed the officers out of the bar. Clare stayed where she was, with everyone else in the bar staring at her, then she hurried out to the car.

She wondered where she could find to go. Anywhere but back to her flat, as usual. She set off almost without thinking about it towards Sweetmeadows, forming ideas in her head as to what she could do when she got there. Have a word with Annie Martin, perhaps, and see if there were any definite plans yet for Jamie's funeral. That would be the next big story, she thought.

The Donnellys' flat was Clare's first call. She was relieved that Rob Donnelly was out, but Annie was there. "He's taken the kids to the beach," Annie said, on the doorstep. "I'm minding Deborah."

Clare made a sympathetic face. "Still no better? Not that it's surprising."

"Come in." Annie walked into the flat and Clare followed, stepping over the plastic building blocks and trying to avoid pressing broken crayons into the carpet as she walked. Things looked no worse than the day of Jamie's death, though. That would be Annie, cooking, keeping on top of the cleaning and washing as best she could, while Deborah – the sunken-faced husk of a woman hunched on the sofa, swamped in a faded track suit – remained on heavy medication.

"This is the woman from the *Post*," Annie said, loud and slow, as if to a little child.

Debs just blinked.

Annie shook her head. "Drugged up to the eyeballs. But otherwise I think the pain would be too much."

Clare nodded. "How's Rob coping?"

"He's just getting on. You know, the way men do. By working and not talking about anything and going around like nothing's happened." Annie reached for a cigarette. "I don't know which is worst."

Drugs or denial. Clare wasn't sure either.

"I wondered if there was any news on the funeral?"

Annie shook her head. "Deborah can't think about that right now. What's bothering us is that the police still haven't caught the bastard." She sucked hard on the cigarette. "Worse than bloody useless, the lot of them."

"They still don't seem to have any real leads," Clare agreed.

"We've decided." Annie stubbed out a half-smoked cigarette in a red tin ashtray that had come from a pub. "If there's no news by tomorrow, we're going to go and protest outside that police station."

"Who is?" Clare wrote *Sunday - protest* in her notebook.

"Me and some of the other women from the estate. We're going to go outside that police station with pictures of Jamie and we're going to take candles and torches and we're going to stand there all night. We want to shame the police, for doing bugger all for more than a week."

"We'll be there," Clare promised. "We'll get you some coverage for that."

She toyed with the idea of telling Annie that Finn McKenna had been arrested, but decided against it. She was sure – she found herself hoping – that he would be released without charges after an hour or two. No point in getting Annie worked up about something that would almost certainly come to nothing.

"There are women round here who haven't let their kids play outside since it happened. They're having to keep them indoors in this stinking heat because they don't want to let them out of their sight. Not when some madman's roaming around throwing bairns out of their prams."

On the sofa, Debs made a snuffling sound. Clare and Annie looked at her, but Debs just stared down at her own fingers and said nothing. She looked as if she was fading into her own sofa, as if she barely existed. She looked like someone who'd had her insides wrenched out. Clare's own guts twisted painfully.

"See, if it was because of Rob breaking the strike, that would be one thing," Annie went on. "No one else from this estate has been stupid enough to do that, so it follows that everyone else would be safe, right? But the police say they don't think it's anything to do with that. So we're no further forward, and every mother thinks her kid might be next."

Outside, Clare could see Amy leaning casually on the car. She waved when she saw Clare walking towards her. "Hey, Clare, what've you been reporting on today?"

"Some of the mothers are holding a demonstration outside the police station tomorrow night."

"Yeah, that. Me mam's going. I'll go too, if you're going to be there."

"I will." Clare noticed Amy was wearing the same shorts and neon T-shirt as the other day, and they didn't look or smell as if they'd been through a wash in the meantime. "How've you been?"

"Great. I love not being at school." Amy did a little hopping dance. "I did some more shorthand. I did it watching telly the other night. I'm getting faster."

"That's brilliant. Only try to write it in your notebook, not on your arms, eh? Why don't you like school, anyway?"

Stupid question, really, Clare thought, after the words had tripped out. All kids hate school. She'd disliked it herself. More than disliked.

Amy scratched her head. "Everyone gives me wrong all the time."

"Like, for what?"

"For things I say. I never mean to say the wrong thing but I always do. Me mam says, 'Amy, I wish you'd learn to keep your daft gob shut.'"

"What about lessons?"

Amy shrugged. "They're okay. Some of them. I like writing stories and all that."

I bet you do, thought Clare. "What about your friends?" She hoped it was okay to ask that.

Amy gave a long, outward sigh. "Not 'specially."

"You don't have a best friend or anything?"

Amy shook her head. "Sometimes they let me play. Sometimes they don't. They say I'm dirty and that I smell."

"That's horrible. Take no notice, Amy. You don't smell." Clare hoped her lie sounded believable.

"I sometimes play with the littlies instead. They're not so mean." The girl shrugged.

Clare nodded. She knew what it was like to be the weird kid who didn't quite fit in. She knew how much those tiny daily humiliations – not to be allowed to join a group, not to have the right clothes, shoes or hair – could hurt.

"What else are you doing today?"

"Mmm, something about the miners' strike."

"Oh, yeah." Amy didn't look interested. "I'm dead sick of all that."

"Amy. You haven't been left on your own today, have you?"

"No, me mam's up in bed."

Clare glanced at her watch. It was getting on for four in the afternoon. "Is she poorly?"

"Nah." Amy laughed. "She's with a fella."

"Oh." Clare wondered how often the little girl found herself wandering the balconies and streets while Tina entertained a boyfriend. Amy's tone of voice didn't suggest today was out of the ordinary. "Do you like your mum's boyfriend then? What's he called?"

"Don't ask me, I don't know anything about this new one. 'Cept he snores."

Clare smiled. She pulled a sheet of paper from her notebook and wrote on it, while every professional part of her brain screamed at her not to do it. "Look, Amy. This is my home number. If you're ever on your own at night again, or… or you're ever feeling scared and your mum's not around, I want you to give me a call. Promise?"

Amy nodded and stuffed the paper into her pocket. "Promise."

"Okay. Good. Listen, I need to go, but I'll see you tomorrow at this demo." Clare opened the car door and turned back to Amy. "Sure you're okay?"

"Yeah, see you."

Clare watched Amy cartwheel her way across the deserted courtyard. It was eerie, the way she was the only kid playing outside here on such a warm summer's Saturday afternoon. But whoever did commit the murder, whoever found it in themselves to pick up a sleeping child and throw them over a balcony to smash their little skull on the concrete below, was still out there, somewhere.

Clare drove into town and battled the Saturday shoppers in her local DIY store. Almost without thinking, she found herself at the counter with a trolley-load of disinfectant and carpet cleaner, tins of emulsion paint and a set of rollers. She winced at the total bill. But it was time, although she could not find a rational reason as to why, to tackle that spare room.

Her resolve felt less solid when she arrived back at the flat. So she made herself a mug of tea and sat in the hallway, looking at the closed door to the little box room. Somehow, she was going to have to find the courage to go in there and look at the place again, otherwise the paint tins and cleaners were just going to add to the clutter that had built up in every other part of the flat for the last month and a half. It took almost an hour, some of it spent sitting on the floor with her head between her knees and taking deep breaths, before Clare found the energy to change out of her work clothes and into an old T-shirt and jeans. Then she put her hand onto the spare room door handle and, ignoring the sweat on her palms and the tremor in her fingers, she pushed the handle down and leaned against the door with her shoulder. It opened and Clare stepped inside.

In the airless room, that stain on the carpet was still there. A matt, dark, accusing colour, it looked even more difficult to shift than it had before. Clare crouched down and touched it, lightly. It was stiff and crusted. Clare filled a plastic bucket with the cleaner and added a large splash of the disinfectant, in the faint hope that it would help bleach the mark away. She put on the gloves, gagging at the mixture of smells: rubber and whatever chemicals made up the disinfectant. It was so strong it made her eyes smart and as she knelt down and tried to mop at the stain, tears ran fast down her face. She didn't bother trying to stop them. Clare dabbed at the mark gently at first, but it made almost no impact on the crusted fibres of the carpet. She started rubbing harder, blinking and sniffing continually, feeling almost as though she was dissolving into a heap of tears and snot. The stain wouldn't budge. Clare scrubbed more and more vigorously, making involuntary groaning and panting noises that eventually turned into sobs. There was no way that cleaning fluid was going to shift the stain. It needed something industrial strength. Or, more likely, a new carpet altogether.

And then there was the rest of the room. Without focusing on it, Clare turned and went back to her living room, ripped off the rubber gloves and dropped them on the table with a slap. She picked up the Yellow Pages and looked for the numbers of local charities. She picked on the first one she recognised and called the number. There was no one there, but there was an answer machine.

"Hi," she said, awkwardly. She hated speaking into recording machines. "I've got some stuff to donate, but I can't transport it. Could you pick it up? It's... " she stopped, swallowed. "It's a baby's cot. Brand new, not used. And there's baby bedding and clothes. And a Moses basket. And some other bits and pieces. It's all really nice, still in its wrapping." She left her number and address. "I'd like it collected as soon as possible, if you can do it. Thanks."

There. That was a start, at least. She could get rid of all that stuff, give the spare room walls a couple of coats of paint and turn that little room into somewhere that... what? What was she doing it for? Clare didn't want to acknowledge the half-formed idea that was playing in a corner of her mind, the notion that another child could occupy the space meant for a half-wanted, half-unwanted baby.

She had a long hot shower, although even her strongest scented soap didn't seem to entirely lift the smell of the rubber gloves around her fingers and arms.

In all that time, though, Finn still hadn't called. Clare tried ringing the station and asking for Seaton, but he wasn't on shift and she didn't know who else she could persuade to leak any information.

She sat for a few more minutes, staring at the phone, willing it to ring. This could go on all night, she thought. I'll send myself mad. So she dialled Nicki's number. "Hey. It's Clare. I wanted to say sorry for being a pain in the neck the other night. Any chance I could buy you all a drink later on?"

She was relieved to hear that Nicki and the others were happy to spend an evening propping up the bars with large glasses of white wine, soda and ice. Afterwards, maybe a club and its most lethal selection of cocktails. Which would mean not getting back home until the small hours of the morning, having drunk enough to make sure she would collapse into bed and sleep for at least a few hours.

Sunday 22nd July

On weekday nights, if she hadn't been out drinking, she would almost always wake in the grey early hours, and she was used to the fact that she would not, after that, get properly back to sleep. Once or twice, she'd fallen heavily asleep just before the alarm went off, but most of the time, Clare resigned herself to lying awake, her limbs aching with the unmet need to get comfortable and stay still, her eyes sore from staring into the half-dark. This morning, after the drinking and clubbing, Clare fell into her bed at around three-thirty, and managed around four hours of hot, fuggy-headed sleep before the sound of traffic and birdsong penetrated enough to wake her up properly. She tried gulping the tepid water from the glass beside her bed and lying back down with the pillow over her head, but after a few minutes she gave up and rolled out onto the floor.

The smell of yesterday's disinfectant was the first thing that hit her as she opened her bedroom door and she ran into the bathroom and leaned over the basin, retching dryly. It was going to be a long day. She switched on Radio 1 and Amy's uninhibited singing and dancing came to mind. If she had just a fraction of that child's energy, Clare thought, she could sort out this flat in no time. Maybe she could just tackle that pile of newspapers and stuff lying in the hallway. That would be a start. Clare dressed in old clothes again and bent a little over the pile of papers that came up to her thighs. She picked the first one up and looked at it. Free-sheet. That could go. She started a pile of things to be thrown out and after a short time, staggered to the bins outside with the old papers and managed to stuff them in, although it meant she couldn't put the bin lid back down.

Back inside, though, the newly-created pile of unopened post was harder to face. On the very top was a brown envelope with a red-bordered bill inside it. Clare decided she'd had enough cleaning for the day and took a shower and a walk. She bought the Sunday papers, aware that this would just start the pile all over again. She also bought some bread. Alone in the house, these days, she rarely bothered eating. It was something she often only remembered to do when she was out with other people. So today, the two slices of toast she managed at around four o'clock in the afternoon were real progress.

Clare liked putting on her work clothes: smart skirts and white shirts. They were part of a costume, making her appear so very normal, as if she was functioning properly. No one would be able to look at her and guess there was anything wrong, although they would if they set foot inside the flat. She was becoming something of an expert at keeping people out. It occurred to her, as she listened to the start of the Top 40 countdown on the radio, that Amy and Tina usually kept people on their doorstep too. She pictured Amy listening to the same programme and wondered which were her favourite songs.

At six, she was outside the police station, where a large group of women from the Sweetmeadows estate were already gathering. Most had their children with them. Some carried homemade placards with pictures of Jamie, or hand-written messages: *Who Killed Baby Jamie?* And *Get Off the Picket Lines and Find Jamie's Killer.* And *When Can Our Kids Sleep Safe?* Some of the women held candles to light when it got darker. Clare knew that was a bigger deal than it looked: some of the strikers' families were lighting their home with candles, the electricity having been cut off. They would be using up their supplies.

Clare waved at the duty photographer, Stewie, who she'd called yesterday. He followed her, the squeak-and-whirr sound of his camera behind her at every point. Clare started by having a quick word with Annie Martin. She reckoned there were around fifty mothers and kids there.

"This is a good turn-out," Clare said. "Are you pleased?"

"I knew it would be." Annie looked around at the crowd. "When it comes to something like this, the people on Sweetmeadows support each other. In spite of what everyone says about us."

Clare wrote down some quotes from a few other mums: "I daren't let the bairn out of my sight." "Everyone's terrified. The place will never be the same again, not till that bastard's found and locked up." And most often: "The police are doing nowt. Too busy clocking up their overtime on the picket lines to do their proper jobs."

The crowd had been there around half an hour when Chief Inspector Seaton came out and spoke to them. He looked hot and even redder in the face than usual. "I understand your concern. Of course I do. But let me promise you, we are doing everything we can to find the killer of little Jamie. Demonstrations like this won't help. I have to ask you now to leave and go back to your homes. Let the police do their job."

"Are you any further forward?" Annie Martin shouted out. "We've been told nothing for days. My family is in shreds." A couple of women stepped towards her and put their arms around her shoulders and back, pulling her close to them.

"This investigation is proving very difficult," Seaton went on. "What I would ask you all is to think very hard. Does anyone know anything they should tell the police? This baby died in broad daylight. But no one claims to have seen anything. If you did, or if you know someone who's been acting strangely since the murder, it's your duty to come forward and tell the police."

Clare cringed: bad call, Seaton, she thought. Sure enough, his comment was followed by a low muttering from the little crowd. "So it's our fault. He's saying we're hiding the killer."

"Do your bloody job and stop blaming everyone else," shouted one woman and there was a hail of shouts in agreement.

Seaton held up a hand and raised his voice. "You've made your point, now take the children home, please. This is no scene for them to see."

Annie stepped forward. "And it's no place for them at home when the police are doing nothing to find our Jamie's murderer."

The women started marching forward, raising their voices, brandishing their placards. And it seemed that from nowhere, a whole posse of uniformed officers ran out of the station doors and towards the crowd, blocking the women from getting too close to the chief inspector. Clare stepped back, her mouth slightly open, as some of the women started grappling with the police. Kids were kicking the officers in the shins and women were pulling at the police officers' faces, swatting them with their placards. There was a low roar and – again, as if from nowhere – a group of men from the estate hurled themselves around a corner and into what was becoming an affray. More police buzzed out of the station, the noise and shouting got louder, along with the sounds of children screaming, women yelling and Stewie's camera clicking incessantly in her ear.

Some of the men and women ended up being dragged inside the police station. Clare saw others moving away, carrying crying toddlers in their arms, or nursing cuts and bruises. Annie Martin climbed up on to a low wall, and yelled at everyone. "Stop it! It wasn't meant to be like this! Stop it, everyone! Go home! Go on, home!"

That had an effect. The men and women who weren't being arrested started walking away, tugging bewildered kids along with them.

Clare turned to stare at Stewie. "What the hell just happened there?"

"Are you okay, kid?" Stewie started putting his camera back in his canvas bag. "Good job you tipped me off. That just went mad, didn't it? I've got some bloody brilliant shots."

"Great. Well done, Stewie. Another lead tomorrow, you and me." Clare felt light-headed. She put a hand on Stewie's arm for a second, steadying herself.

Someone tapped her on the arm and she swung around to see Amy. "Hiya, Clare."

"Amy. Did you just get here?"

"Yes, and I've got another story for you."

Tina appeared alongside her daughter, cigarette in hand. "It all kicked off here, then. I knew it would. I wasn't going to come, but this little pest made me."

Amy tapped her mother's arm. "Yes, but tell Clare why we're late."

Clare looked from Amy to Tina. "What?"

"The ambulance came," Amy said. "They took Jamie's mam away."

six

Clare stared at Amy, the words not quite sinking in. "Seriously? What happened? Is she all right, do you know?"

Tina gave Clare a meaningful look and shook her head. Clare noticed a small crowd of women were leading Annie Martin away. She couldn't see Annie's face.

"She had her head covered up when they put her in the ambulance. That means she's dead, doesn't it, Clare?" Amy looked up with interested eyes.

"I'm not sure," said Clare, carefully. Further along the street, she heard Annie Martin give a loud, heart-breaking howl. She felt tears spring to her eyes and tried to blink them back.

"That's what me mam said too," Amy went on, looking over at the women leading Annie away. "That she didn't know. But on the telly, when someone's in an ambulance with their face covered up, it definitely means they're dead."

"Shut up, you little ghoul," said Tina, cuffing Amy lightly on the back of the head. "She gets it all off these bloody detective shows. They show all these horrible things, don't they?"

Don't let her watch them, then, Clare thought, but didn't say.

Tina gave Clare a quick nod. "That's right, though. She was covered up, on the stretcher."

"Christ." Clare looked at Stewie. "Come with me, back to Sweetmeadows?"

"I wouldn't let you go there on your own, not tonight. What do you want to get?"

"Reaction to this demo. And to whatever's happened to Debs Donnelly."

But they found the estate was quiet, people closing their doors and drawing their curtains. "Out of respect," one woman told Clare. "For Annie and Debs. And those poor little bairns."

Not for Rob, Clare noticed. People never quite knew what to say about Rob. Rob the strike-breaker, the one who cracked and gave in, the one who let the other lads down and who somehow seemed, although no one said it, to have brought all this horror on himself. Clare wondered what it was like to be Rob Donnelly right now, to know that every journey to work needed police protection and involved being shouted and spat at. That was his choice, though. He could have guessed at that. The terrible death of his child was something else, and yet no one could quite find it in themselves to put their hand on his shoulder or look him in the eyes to offer their sympathies. In the dark of the night, when his other children were asleep, Rob Donnelly must surely be asking himself what he'd done.

"In," Tina told Amy, sharply, pushing her in the back.

"Awww, no!" Amy stamped her foot. But Tina gave her a hard-eyed look and the girl's shoulders slumped. She turned to Clare. "You coming back tomorrow?"

"Probably." Clare gave Amy a wink. Amy grinned and turned to go home, Tina walking behind her, shaking her head. Later, a call to the ambulance service confirmed that a neighbour had called them out to Deborah Donnelly's house but that the young mother was dead when the crews arrived on the scene.

It was after 11 o'clock and Clare was trying to talk herself into going to bed, when Finn rang. Clare picked up the phone on the second ring. "Finn, where the hell have you been? I've been worried sick."

"You know where I've been." Finn's voice sounded calm. "Thanks for worrying, though."

"So what happened? Why did the police want to talk to you?"

"They've been back out doing door-to-door on the Sweetmeadows estate. Someone told them they remembered getting some flyers about the strike on the day that the baby died. They thought I'd probably delivered them."

"And did you?"

"Yes, me and a mate. So we were around the estate that afternoon. The cops wanted to know if I'd seen anything, that was all."

"So?"

"No, as I told the police, I didn't see a thing."

"But you must've put a leaflet through the Donnellys' door?"

"Jesus, Clare, I've just come to the end of one interrogation, so don't start. Yes, we would have put something through Rob's door, but to be honest, I can't even remember whether the pram was there or not. I suppose it was, but I didn't notice it. We leafleted a couple of hundred houses that afternoon and then we were so hot and knackered that we went to the pub."

Clare sighed. "It's a shame. I bet the police thought you might've seen the killer."

Finn gave a short laugh. "You mean, they had a great excuse to bring me down to the station and leave me locked up for a few hours, for nothing. They're playing with me, that's all. I reckon I can expect a lot more of this, the longer the strike goes on."

"I'm sorry. I thought it was awful, the way they turned up at the pub like that. It did seem like they were out to humiliate you."

"They'll have to work harder than that, then." Finn paused. "Thanks for being on my side, though. It means a lot."

"Take care. See you soon, yeah?"

"I'll call you," Finn promised.

Clare was surprised at how relieved she was to hear from him and know that he was in the clear. Suddenly, she felt that she could go to sleep.

Monday 23rd July

Clare and Joe were outside Chief Inspector Seaton's office before nine on Monday morning. "You were actually there last night," Joe said. "Everyone in the office is singing your praises this morning. This might be a good time to ask for a little bonus or a week off, or whatever else that journalist's apology for a heart desires."

"Chris Barber's bollocks on a dish? To feed to the birds, obviously."

They were sniggering together when Seaton stamped along the corridor and waved them into his room. "I haven't had the greatest start to my week already. Seeing you two is no improvement."

Clare gave him her most practised smile.

"Let's have it, then." Seaton sat down heavily and glared at them.

Joe nodded to Clare. "Ladies first. Or eye witnesses, anyway."

Clare took a breath. "Bob. Last night. What the hell happened?"

Seaton gave a grunt of a laugh. "Don't beat about the bush, Miss Jackson, say what you mean." He breathed out a long sigh. "We were happy for the residents of Sweetmeadows to register their concerns. But when it started to get out of hand, for the safety of all concerned, we decided to break the demonstration up."

Clare raised her eyebrows. "Why do you think it got out of hand? I mean, at what stage, exactly, do you think the mood turned?"

Seaton knew what she was implying. "Off the record, and

I mean that, we expected trouble from the start. The folks from Sweetmeadows don't do peaceful protest."

"But it was all women and children."

"With a gang of men round the corner, waiting for the slightest reason to get involved. Doesn't matter what the police do at the moment, they're in the wrong. Everything gets mis-reported and misrepresented."

"Funny," said Joe. "That's how the miners feel too."

"That's true. And what's the common factor? You lot. The press. Stirring up trouble in every quarter, under the guise of reporting the facts."

"That's not like you, Bob," said Clare, sitting back suddenly. "We usually have a good working relationship, don't we?"

"Like I said, Miss Jackson, I am not having a good day. There's an internal inquiry going on into last night's events. My role and that of all of the officers involved will be very carefully scrutinised, I can tell you."

Clare paused for a moment. "Do you have any sympathy with the mothers from Sweetmeadows, though? It's more than a week since Jamie Donnelly died. It does feel as if you're no further forward. Can you appreciate their anxiety?"

"I can, Miss Jackson, yes. I too am anxious to find Jamie's killer, I promise. It would certainly help, though, if the people on the estate weren't quite so reluctant to talk to the police."

"You see," Clare put down her pen. "I think that's what changed the mood of the protest last night. When you suggested that people were knowingly hiding the killer, just because they don't like the police. I think that's what sparked... "

"Perhaps you'd like to give evidence to our inquiry," Seaton cut in, dryly. "Anyway, it's a fair point, isn't it? They all seem more than happy to chat to you, at length, and read it all back in the evening paper. But if a copper asks them a question they're struck dumb." He sighed. "Perhaps we should take you with us when we go round trying to eke information out of the people round there."

"To be fair, that little girl tried to tell you that she'd seen it happen, and you wouldn't take her seriously."

"Amy Hedley? I've warned you about her. She's not a credible witness to anything. Anyway, we double-checked her story. There were some union men around the estate, dropping leaflets through doors. We think she may have seen them and assumed they were responsible for the baby's death."

"But you arrested Finn McKenna at the weekend and kept him in overnight," Clare said.

Seaton raised his eyebrows and Joe turned to look at Clare. She avoided his eyes.

"You're very well informed," Seaton said. "We talked to Mr McKenna, yes, because he certainly was in the area, around the time that Jamie died."

"And?" Clare persisted.

"He's out on police bail. That's all I can say."

Clare blinked. "So you might talk to him again?"

"I am not going to get drawn into a discussion about Finn McKenna, Miss Jackson. We can draw that subject to a close."

Clare frowned down at her notes. Seaton made it sound as if the police were still questioning Finn's story. That wasn't the way Finn put it across the night before. She was relieved when Joe moved the conversation on.

"Are you saying, then, that someone may know more than they're telling the police about what happened?" Joe said. "I mean, are you actually saying someone on Sweetmeadows is deliberately hiding the killer?"

"I'm afraid I am saying that, yes, Mr Ainsley. And that's on the record."

Clare and Joe darted a quick look at each other. It was their 'He-just-Said-a-Headline' look. *Who is hiding Jamie's killer? Police chief slams Sweetmeadows silence.* They asked a few more questions and learned that an inquest into Debs Donnelly's death would be opened the next day.

"Does it look as if she killed herself?"

Seaton hesitated. "That's one line of inquiry. She had some very strong prescription tranquillisers from her GP. But we can't rule out a link with whoever killed her son. We're still in the early stages here. That's also not for publication yet. But you can say that the police send their condolences to the family."

"Right." Clare moistened her lips, which were getting dry in the airless office. "Do you think Debs might've coped better if Jamie's killer had been found by now?"

Seaton looked as if Clare had just slapped his hand. "That's not something I can speculate on, Miss Jackson. Now I'm sure you understand that I have better things to do than chat to you all day." He stood up and held an arm out towards the door.

Back at the office, Clare added Seaton's comments to the two pieces: one about last night's affray and a sidebar about Debs Donnelly. It didn't take long and she told Dave Bell she'd drive to head office with the copy. "You'll have the updated version for the late edition," she promised.

"Bloody good work last night, Clare. And today."

"Thanks, Dave. Joe said I should ask you for a bonus."

Dave Bell laughed. "Clare, if I had control of the budget, I'd send you on a Caribbean cruise. Well, once this baby story's done and dusted, anyway."

As soon as she put the phone down, it rang again. This time it was Amy. "Are you coming over today, Clare?"

"Not today, Amy, sorry."

"I thought you would?"

"I can never promise. It depends on what else is happening and whether there are any more stories."

"You have to come today, Clare. Promise you will."

"Why today?"

There was a short silence on the line. "It's my birthday."

"It is? Wow. You should've told me before. Double figures?"

"Ten."

"Then I'll make sure I get over at some point, I promise. You having a party or anything?"

"Nah."

"So, have you had any good presents?"

"Not yet. Me mam's out. I really, really want a Sony Walkman. But she says they're too expensive, so I won't be getting one of those."

In the newsroom, Clare dumped a sheaf of copy paper onto Dave Bell's desk. "So this is the Sweetmeadows latest?" Bell handed it to Sharon Catt. "Take this straight to subs, would you?"

Clare waited as he leafed through the other stories, including some of the ones she'd written at the weekend. "Jesus, Clare. You're not a reporter, you're a machine. How do you get all this done in half a day?"

"You know me, Dave. Superwoman."

"And modest with it," Catt snapped. "We're going to have to rename the paper the *Clare Jackson Post*, at this rate." Her tone of voice wasn't complimentary.

"I'll tell you something else," Dave Bell went on. "I had a few phone calls actually praising your piece about the miners' benefit. I can't remember the last time someone called to say something nice about the paper. You're a star, Clare."

Clare shrugged, but stole a look at Chris Barber, whose face was hidden by the early edition of the paper. Inside, she smiled.

"Look, you've done more than enough stories for today. I seem to be making a habit of it, but go on, go home. You've earned a half-day off."

"Again?" said Catt. "Don't start to expect it every day, just for doing your job."

"Thanks." Clare treated Catt to a wide smile, just to irritate her. "Oh. Anyone know how much a Sony Walkman is?"

"About thirty quid," said Dave. "Treating yourself?"

"Not myself, no. I'm thinking of buying one as a present."

"Must be a special someone?"

Clare slid out of the newsroom door before anyone could ask any more questions. And then she headed for the shops. In her head, she'd already worked out the possible scenarios. If Tina had been bluffing, the way parents sometimes did, about not getting Amy a Walkman for her birthday, then she would keep the receipt and take the thing back. Amy would get Present B, which was the double cassette of *Now That's What I Call Music II* and a white slogan vest top, although it was the copycat version from the bargain clothes shop, not the designer version. And if Tina hadn't been able to afford the Walkman after all, Amy would get what she wanted for her birthday.

Clare arrived at Amy's house at around four and once again she found herself having to call through the letterbox before Amy would answer the door.

"Happy Birthday!" she said, holding out a card. "Is your mum still not around, then?"

Amy shook her head. "Out."

"Right." Clare looked past Amy, trying to see into the flat, but the girl wasn't opening the door any wider. "Never mind. Are you having a good day? What did you get in the end?"

Amy blinked a little. "Noffink. I think she must've forgot."

"No! Maybe that's where she is, out shopping for you. Mums don't forget their kids' birthdays."

Amy sniffed. "It wouldn't be the first time. I never got anything last year either. She just forgets, that's all." She wiped her hand across her nose. "Doesn't matter."

"Oh, Amy. It does matter. Here," Clare held out the wrapped-up Walkman box. "And this." She handed her the second present too.

When she opened the first present, Amy's eyes went wide. "I can't believe it. You're not giving this to me? Is it a real one?"

114

"I'm not going to give you a toy one, am I? Look, if your mum asks, it's only because someone gave it to me and I didn't need it."

"She won't be bothered." Amy tore at the paper and pulled out the cassette. "This is ace. I can't believe it."

"You said that already." Clare laughed at the child's face, which was pink and open-mouthed. "Give it a go, then. I put batteries in."

With a grin stretched across her little face, Amy clicked the tape into the Walkman and popped the tiny headphones into her ears. "I love all these songs so much. I'm going to dance to them all night. I'm not even going to bed." She was smiling so hard that Clare wanted, for a sharp moment, to cry.

"Hey." Clare waved to get Amy's attention back. "Have you eaten?"

Amy shook her head.

"Come on then. I've finished work for the day. I'll get you something. Leave a note for your mum to say where you are."

Amy ran inside, shutting the door behind her, and came out wearing the new T-shirt, its whiteness highlighting the grubbiness of her shorts.

"That was quick. You left a note, like I said?"

"She won't care."

"But you left a note?"

"*Yep*. I'm starving. Can we go to the Wimpy?"

"We'll go wherever you like. It's your birthday."

For a tiny scrap of a girl, Amy could put away some food. After her burger and chips, she started eyeing the menu again. "I can't decide whether to have a Banana Boat or a Brown Derby or a Knickerbocker Glory. What'll I get?"

"Whatever you want. They all look disgusting to me, I'm afraid."

Amy looked shocked. "No, these are gorgeous. They're my favourite foods ever. Are you on a diet then? My mam's always going on about dieting. You don't need to do it, though. I think you look beautiful. As beautiful as Lady Di.

Beautiful-er."

"Okay, just for that, you can have two desserts if you like. Don't be sick, though, or your mum'll kill me." After ordering the desserts, Clare tried to eke a little more information out of Amy. "So, your mum. Does she have a job?"

Amy shook her head, her mouth full of ice cream.

"Where does she go, then?"

"I've told you. Out with a fella." She grinned, her mouth smeared in a dark red sauce. "It's better than when she stays in with a fella, anyways. I hate that."

"How come?"

"Just, you know. What they do. It's yuck. And I don't like all her boyfriends."

Clare nodded, finding Amy's lifestyle hard to picture. She was shocked at the thought of Amy being left on her own for hours on end, and just as horrified that the child would have to put up with a string of strange men in her home. Clare's mum had been no prize-winning parent, but she'd barely let Clare out of her sight as she was growing up. Clare had no idea what passed for normal, when it came to bringing up kids. Talking to Amy made her feel lost. And utterly helpless.

Later, sitting at home and staring at the TV screen without taking anything in, Clare couldn't push Amy out of her thoughts. There was something about her. Clare could listen to her prattling for hours, about pop music and TV and school. She made Clare laugh, and it took a lot to do that these days. Just for the day, she'd decided to stay off the subject of baby Jamie and Amy's story about the men who, she claimed, had thrown him over the balcony. After all, if Amy had forgotten about it, temporarily, then she didn't want to scare her by bringing it up again. Let the kid enjoy what was left of her birthday. Such as it was, with what seemed to be only one card and a couple of presents, from someone the girl barely knew, and a mother who'd gone out with a boyfriend and forgotten all about her.

She'd dropped the girl back outside the flats, knowing that

the little thing was probably going back to an empty home and the threat of a child murderer still on the loose. But what was she supposed to do, exactly? Tell the authorities, with all the consequences that would set in motion? Take her back here, to her own neglected flat, and get accused of acting unprofessionally, and getting too involved? She was already crossing that line, she well knew. Clare clutched her stomach, wishing she hadn't had any food, because her insides were aching.

A little after the nine o'clock news, Clare's phone rang. It was Joe. "Hi, kidder. I need to talk to you. Can I call round?"

"Here? No," Clare said, a little too quickly. "Is it urgent?"

"I'd just rather talk to you when you're not typing a story with one hand and only half-listening. Why can't I come round?"

"Can we just... I'll meet you. Name your pub."

Clare found Joe propping up a smoky bar near the docks. "So who are you hiding at your flat? Some new bloke? Given that your love life is such a complete mystery these days."

Clare laughed. "No one. And my love life isn't a mystery, it just doesn't exist. I wanted to come out and have a drink, that's all. And you always take me to the best places." Joe didn't smile. "Okay, so what's this about?"

"Couple of things. There's something you need to know. Look, I was in the office most of today and I think I should tell you that Chris Barber spent most of the day whingeing. About you."

"What've I done? I'm the one who should be whingeing about him, surely."

"True. But he's telling anyone who will listen that, as the chief reporter, he should be covering the murder story, not you. And that you're being given special treatment as a sop for not getting his job."

"Bloody cheek. I don't suppose anyone is listening, though?"

"Most people think he's an arsehole, you're right. But I

happened to be next to your newsdesk when he was saying all this to Sharon Catt. And he got quite a sympathetic hearing. Sharon doesn't have many allies in that office."

"How do you mean?"

"I heard her telling him that she would have a word. That it might be time to send him into your patch, while it's so newsy, to get his name established. That, er, you might spend a bit of time on the features team."

Clare slammed her glass down and swore. "I don't believe it. Features! The bloody nursery. No way."

"I just thought I should warn you. Knowledge is power and all that. I thought you could prepare your argument so that if they ask you to move over for him, you're ready to talk your way out of it."

"Thanks. I appreciate it. Jesus Christ, that man. He got the job that everyone tipped me to get. They sent me out to the sticks and said I needed experience of running my own patch. I didn't want to go but I made the best of it. And now he wants to take that from me as well. I can't win."

Joe nodded sympathetically. "That's your argument, then. They told you they wanted you to run your own patch. Surely they can't take it off you just to hand Barber the best stories of the day?"

"They can do whatever they want, that's the problem." Clare took a long gulp of her gin and tonic. "But thanks for the tip-off. Forewarned and all that. Did you say there was something else?"

It was Joe's turn to take a slow drink of his beer. He stared into what was left of the drink. "This is a bit awkward, to be honest."

Clare swallowed. "What? Out with it."

"Okay. Promise not to get angry with me."

"I'm not promising anything."

"Look, it's just this. I was walking past the Wimpy Bar at tea time. And I swear I saw you sitting in the window with that weird kid from Sweetmeadows."

118

Clare gave a deep sigh. "And?"

"Does it even need an 'and'? What the hell were you playing at?"

"I don't know what you mean."

"You're not in the habit of eating there, so don't make out that you just bumped into her. What's she called again?"

"Amy."

"Right. Amy. You took it upon yourself to take this Amy out for something to eat? Why?"

"I'll tell you why, but you have to promise to keep it to yourself. Because it was her birthday and she was all on her own and her selfish bitch of a mother hadn't even remembered to buy her a card."

"I'm sorry to hear that. Now shall I list all the reasons why it's not your problem?"

"Don't bother." Clare swirled her drink around in her glass. "I already know them."

"So how come I spot you sitting having a banana split with the scruffiest of all the scruffy little beggars on that estate?"

"I don't know. Except I just felt really sorry for her. And I just couldn't walk away and leave her. She's only ten, Joe. Ten years old. And she looks after herself almost all the time, from what I can see. Only this was her birthday."

Joe shook his head. "I never had you down as such a soft touch. Remember what Seaton said about her? She makes things up. And anyway, that's not the point. The point is, you're only spending time with her because she lives on Sweetmeadows and you happen to be doing a running story there. When it's all finished, she's going to expect you to keep calling round. You absolutely shouldn't be getting so mixed up with her. It's not fair on the kid – on Amy."

Clare drained her glass. "Now tell me something I don't know."

"So what's going on with you?"

"Nothing's going on, as you put it. I know you're right, so you can spare the lecture. I shouldn't have taken her for

119

tea. I should have left her alone and hungry, on her birthday, right? Because I'm not a human being, I'm some sort of news robot."

Joe groaned. "Are those violins I can hear?"

Clare slammed her glass down on the table. "Stop it. Just for one minute, can't you drop the Harry Hardnose act? Don't you ever get sick of pretending that you're not quite part of humanity, you're just someone who stands on the sidelines and takes notes?"

Joe looked startled for a moment. Then he laughed. "Is this a competition to see how many clichés we can stuff into a single sentence? Bet I can beat you at that."

"Funny." Clare fixed her gaze on her glass.

"Oh, please not the silent treatment. Come on, we might not agree about everything, but at least let's talk to each other."

Clare breathed in and out, hard. "What's the point? You won't get it."

Joe touched Clare's hand. "I'll try."

Clare slid her fingers away. "Look, when I was Amy's age, I was a bit like her. Not for the same reasons, not because my mother didn't care about me. My mother – she wasn't well. She had, you know, problems. So sometimes I didn't have clean school clothes and sometimes I couldn't afford the same things as everyone else, or go on the school trips.

"So I got picked on, just like Amy does. Kids can be meaner than you can ever imagine, unless you've been through it. So now when I see Amy, I want to help. More than that. I need to help."

Joe sighed. "But Amy isn't you. You can't rescue her, Clare."

"I know. But she looks up to me, you know? I can't just be another person who lets her down, who just doesn't care. Especially not when I know how it feels." For a fraction of a second, Clare wondered if she should tell Joe the other reason why Amy seemed to be filling a painful gap. But she pushed the idea away.

"Look," said Joe. "If you think the kid's being neglected, then tell the social services, like I said. That's the right thing to do. It's sensible and it's legal. Then your conscience is clear. But you can't take her on by yourself." He paused while Clare nibbled the edge of the lemon slice from her drink. "Tell me you see that?"

"I do, sort of. But I can see another side to it too. Okay, I'll be careful. But don't tell anyone, Joe. The social services might take her away or something. I don't want to be responsible for that."

"Not even if that's what she needs? Maybe she should be in care, if she's being left alone like you say. You can't go wading in, trying to sort it out yourself."

"You promised not to tell anyone."

"No, I didn't, actually. But I won't, for now. Just back off, though. For your own good and for the kid's sake too."

"I promise. Another?"

"Going to give me a hint on tomorrow's Barber-blasting exclusive then?"

"Not a chance."

Clare bought another round, but things felt cool between them, in spite of Joe's attempts at cracking jokes and changing the mood. Clare wondered if Joe guessed he wasn't being given the whole story. Then he looked over at the door. "Uh-oh," he commented. "Look who's just come in."

Finn McKenna was making his way to the bar, where Clare noticed that the men slapped him on the back, shook his hand and offered to buy him a pint. They may have been loyal to George Armstrong but McKenna was the new man of the moment. He spotted them and came over, the foam from his pint trickling slowly down the side of his glass.

"Oh, look, it's the enemy within," Clare said, and McKenna grinned at her.

"I'm thinking of getting that on a T-shirt. Thatcher hasn't done herself any favours with that remark. It's put people more on our side, if anything." He and Joe gave each other a brief and not entirely friendly nod. Then he pulled up a stool. "I'm glad I ran into you, Clare. I called you earlier, but you were out. Something you might be interested in."

"Go on." Clare was conscious of Joe watching them closely.

"A concert to raise money for the strike. Thursday night at the City Hall. Two bands and a couple of comedians. I've got you a ticket, thought we could both go along."

"Thursday night? Yep. Sounds great."

"Brilliant. Seven-thirty. Shall I just see you outside?"

"I'll be there. Thanks."

Finn stood up and looked towards the bar. "Better get back to the lads." He winked at Clare.

Clare cast around for something to say. "This used to be George Armstrong's pub. He stays away now, I've noticed."

Joe gave a grunt.

Clare fished the lemon slice out of her drink again and started chewing the edge of it, waiting for Joe to say something. There were a few moments of strained silence. Then he said: "Are you seeing Finn McKenna? As in, are you going out with him?"

Clare raised her eyebrows at Joe. "No. Well, not exactly, not entirely."

"What does that mean?"

"It means I've had lunch with him, once, and he's just asked me to go to a gig with him, but I don't know whether that's a date. He might just want to get some good press coverage."

"Sounded like a date to me." Joe glared down at his pint. "And you knew about him being arrested, at the weekend. You never even gave me a hint about that."

"What if it is a date?"

"I don't trust him. There's something not right about him. He's being questioned by the police. And... "

"What are you, my dad, all of a sudden? What's it to you

who I go out with?"

"Well... " Joe raised his eyebrows and for a moment, Clare wondered exactly what he was going to say. Then he seemed to think better of it. "It's just... okay. Maybe it's the same thing as I was saying about that little kid.

"You're getting way too close to your stories, you're getting personally involved with the people that you should be keeping at arm's length. It'll stop you being detached when you write. If you start seeing Finn McKenna out of work, you won't want to write anything critical about the strike. And then if the whole romance crap goes wrong, you won't even want to talk to him for a quote when you need to. It's got disaster written all over it."

"Okay, you've made your point. Now can you let me make my own decisions?"

Back at the flat, fired up by a couple of gins, Clare made herself go into the little box room again. She'd got as far as putting some of her unwanted purchases into black bin bags, waiting for the charity to come and collect them. She pushed the heavy bin bags into the middle of the floor so that she didn't have to look at the stain on the carpet.

Something made her take the next step. She used the back of a spoon to prise open the first tin of emulsion paint. The clean smell took her by surprise. It'd been a long time since she'd smelled anything so fresh, or that said 'new start' quite so clearly. The thick paint made a satisfying glooping sound as she poured it into the tray, its texture reminding her of Amy's melting ice-cream. She'd also forgotten how satisfying the process of painting something as simple as a wall could be. Most of it was covered in minutes, a shade of white with a hint of pink, the latest decorating fad. The freshly painted wall made her think of a new page in her notebook, of 1st January. And of a newborn baby. But she pushed that image away. Compared to the faded colours of the rest of the room, the wall's brightness made her blink. And smile.

Tuesday 24th July

The day didn't get off to a good start for Clare when she called in to find that Dave Bell was on leave and it was Sharon Catt waiting to take her news list.

"Okay, well, to start with, there's the opening of the inquest into Debs Donnelly, down at the coroner's court this morning. I'm expecting that… "

"We've got Chris Barber down to do the inquest."

"How come?"

"Because we have. It's the biggest story of the day and he's our chief reporter."

"I'm not likely to forget that, Sharon. But this is supposed to be my patch. And actually, I don't think… "

"Clare, I don't have time to argue with some prima donna reporter who thinks she should get the splash every single day. What else have you got?"

Clare decided not to tell Catt that it was quite likely the inquest would be opened but go no further, meaning there wouldn't be a lot to say. Her diary also read: *Police protestors up in court?* She decided not to mention that. The coroner's court and the magistrates' courts were in the same building and she didn't want Barber to get that story too. "Umm, otherwise it's looking a bit quiet. Tell you what, Sharon, I'll have a dig around and come back to you in an hour or so." Then she headed for the car and drove to court.

Around ten men and women were standing in a small huddle outside in the car park, smoking. Clare recognised some of them from the protest. The usher directed her into Court One, where Geoff Powburn was sitting, just in front of the press bench. He swivelled round to chat. "How's your social worker training going?"

"Eh?" Clare gave him a baffled smile.

"The last time we spoke you were worried about some child that was being neglected?"

"Oh. That. No, everything's fine now. You expecting much here?"

Geoff nodded. "I am, as a matter of fact. Word is the magistrates are going to come down hard on these protestors. Make an example of them and stave off any more trouble from Sweetmeadows. And if they do, there'll be problems, because some of them are strikers and no way have they got money for a big fine."

As the magistrates came in, Clare recognised two local councillors on the bench, who were well-known for taking a tough stance when they sat in court. She sat with her pen at the ready. These two were unlikely to be sympathetic to anyone accused of causing an affray. Nor were they disposed to be in favour of the miners' strike.

Sure enough, the magistrates refused to agree to the group being bound over to keep the peace. Instead, they heard charges of violent disorder and suggested the maximum possible fine, to be paid back at a high weekly rate. There were little gasps from the defendants and their friends and family in the public seats, and one of the magistrates told everyone to be quiet.

The hapless duty lawyer stood up. "Your worships, all of the defendants are currently not working and are struggling financially. The defendants Wilson, Cook and George are miners and you will be aware of their present situation, in that they are on strike and not currently earning a wage… "

"Perhaps they might consider going back to work," a magistrate commented, to an audible intake of breath from members of the public.

The duty lawyer didn't comment on this. He continued, "Mrs Johnson is a single mother of two children and owing to a dispute with the Department of Health and Social Security, she has received no benefits for two weeks… "

"If the defendants are saying they are unable to meet a fine then the other option available to the bench is a short prison sentence," said one of the magistrates, as the clerk, sitting in front of the bench, visibly cringed and stared down at his law books.

The people in the public seats started to whisper amongst themselves. The magistrate smacked the desk. "If there is any more disorder in the court I will ask that you all be charged with contempt."

In the end, three of the eight were given two-month jail sentences and were taken down into the police cells with bewildered expressions on their faces. The others agreed to heavy fines and Clare guessed it would only be a week or two before they were back in the dock for non-payment. Everyone stood up as the magistrates filed out of court. Geoff Powburn swivelled round to look at Clare and gave a little whistle. "What did I tell you?"

Clare shook her head. "Unbelievable. I don't see the sense in that, to be honest."

It was at that point that Joe appeared at the court room door. "You're here. Thank god for that. I've just wasted an hour sitting in an inquest and it's going to make the grand total of two pars of copy. And I've missed the protestors."

"You certainly have." Clare looked past him. "Chris Barber isn't on your tail, is he?"

"He didn't know about this so I damn well wasn't going to tell him. If it makes you feel any better, the whole thing took ages because the coroner dealt with a whole load of admin first. And then it was only opened and adjourned because they haven't got a full pathologist's report. So he'll hardly get anything out of it at all. Certainly not a big enough piece for a by-line."

Clare grinned. "Excellent. Come and listen while I phone the story in, and you can take it all down. Then we'll go get some reaction down at Sweetmeadows."

On the estate, Clare felt she could almost taste the worsening mood. Clusters of people were standing around talking, with grim expressions on their faces. She overheard a small group of young teenagers complaining about 'fascist pigs'.

A woman came up and jabbed a finger at Clare and Joe.

"You want to write something about the way this estate's been written off. No one's listening to us. There are kids round here who can't sleep at night because some psycho's on the loose. The coppers say we all know who killed the bairn but that we're not saying. It's a lie. They just think we're scum."

"That's right." Another woman joined her. "My brother-in-law's just been sent down, all because we went to tell the police what we thought of them. My sister's in bits. And in the meantime someone who's killed a kiddie is still wandering the streets. Our streets."

"That's the trouble with living here," the first woman went on. "You get branded. If it was some posh couple's baby, the police wouldn't drive the mother to her grave by making out it was her that did it. And if anyone else complains about the police they have to sit up and take notice. But when it's Sweetmeadows, it's just, oh, it's that lot again. They call us swine and treat us like rubbish. Bastards."

Clare and Joe were soon surrounded by people, shouting about how badly they'd been treated, how the investigation was a joke, how the fines and prison sentences were unfair. They could barely take notes fast enough. Afterwards, with pages of hurried shorthand to compare, they headed for Joe's car. Clare sat back and took a deep breath. "Wow. That was quite some reaction. *Fury on the 'Forgotten' Estate.*"

"Let's get it written up. I'll buy you a drink. I promise not to tell you how to live your life this time."

"I'm glad to hear it."

"I'm sorry." Joe gave an embarrassed smile. "It's just that you haven't seemed yourself, for ages now. You always look a bit, I don't know, strained."

"Thanks a lot."

"Sorry. Did I say strained? I meant gorgeous."

Clare smacked Joe on the thigh. "Stop that right now."

"But still strained," he went on. "You've been working too hard, I reckon, and I totally understand it. It's because you want to prove they made a mistake in not giving you that job.

127

But I think you're over-tired and not always making the best decisions. That's all."

Clare put her hand on the car door. "What happened to 'I won't tell you how to live your life'? It took you about thirty seconds to break that promise."

Joe screwed up his face. "Damn. Sorry again. I will shut up now, honest."

"Okay. I mean it. You're a good mate, but if you tell me once more that I look like hell or that I'm losing my mind, I will find someone else to go drinking with."

"Like Finn McKenna?"

Clare swore. "You can't leave it alone, can you?" She pushed the car door open. "I've had it, Joe. Come and see me when you've remembered that I'm all grown up and I don't need a minder."

"Sorry!" Joe leaned out of the car and tried to persuade her to get back in. But she strode off towards the office.

"Another front page," Jai commented as she walked into the shop. "I don't think you ever stop working."

"Yeah?" Clare picked up the evening paper and smiled as she read her by-line. The report continued onto Page Three, where a small sidebar mentioned that an inquest had been opened into the death of Deborah Donnelly, the mother of murdered baby Jamie. "Two whole sentences on the inquest. Great morning's work for a chief reporter."

She took great pleasure in ringing Sharon Catt. "I've got some brilliant reaction to the court sentences. The people on the estate are really angry."

"Get it sent over, then." Catt didn't sound as pleased as a duty news editor should sound, when they've just been offered a lead story.

"I'm about to. I just wanted to give you a heads-up." Clare paused for a moment. "Not much came out of the inquest, then. Bit of a waste of Chris's time."

There was a second's silence on the end of the phone. Clare pictured Catt gritting her teeth.

128

"Don't gloat, Clare. I wish you'd start acting more professionally."

"Professionally? Sharon, you sent me out to a district office and you knew I didn't want to go. But ever since, I've worked really hard. I come in every day and sometimes at nights and weekends and I never complain about it. How is that unprofessional?"

"You're still resentful about not getting the chief reporter's job, that's obvious. Even though you didn't turn up on the day of the interview and didn't even bother to give us a call. For days, remember? We had to send Dave Bell round to bang on your door to make sure you weren't dead. And then we got some pathetic story about having a virus. Talk about 'the dog ate my homework'. You might be able to bat your lashes at Dave and the other men in the office, but you've got some way to go before I think of you as professional. And you've only got yourself to blame, so stop trying to make Chris Barber into Public Enemy Number One."

Clare blinked hard, surprised at how much Catt's words stung. She held the phone away from her face so that she could try to gulp back her urge to cry, without Catt hearing her. She swallowed and hoped her voice wouldn't come out too thick. "Okay. Point taken." She put the receiver back in its cradle and reached for a tissue. She held it, scrunched up, against her wet eyes for a few minutes. She could easily rescue her reputation, just by being honest about what had happened on the day of the job interview. But she couldn't bear the thought of everyone knowing about it.

seven

The phone rang again. Clare took a deep breath before picking up the handset.

"Hi, Clare, it's Amy. I might have a scoop for you."

Clare couldn't help smiling when Amy used words like that. She hadn't the heart to say that real reporters would never say 'scoop' these days. "Go on, then."

"You have to come and see it."

It turned out to be quite a good story, about one of Amy's neighbours who'd found a cockroach crawling in her baby's cot. When she'd seen the state of the flat, with its patches of black fungus growing on the walls and its insect infestations, Clare knew she could write a weighty feature about the conditions in the last occupied flats on the estate. A quick quote from the council would finish it off. Another double-page spread, Clare reckoned.

On their way out, Amy linked her arm into Clare's. "Have you noticed anything?"

"Like what?"

Amy stopped and sniffed the warm air. "I'm not sure. But it's like... it's like something's about to happen."

Clare looked at her and frowned. "What sort of thing?"

"I don't know, do I? I'm not Russell Grant or someone, am I? I can't, like... " she wiggled her fingers in the air, "...see into the future. But it just feels different round here."

"In what way, different?"

Amy screwed up her face. "It's hard to say. But the air is all buzzy. It felt like that before Jamie died too. I could sort of smell it. Like something's about to change."

"I wish I knew what you meant."

Amy traced a circle round and round with her toe. "I wish I knew what I meant, too."

"You're a funny girl, Amy."

Amy gave a little sigh. "That's what everyone says."

Clare nudged her gently. "Doesn't mean I don't like you."

"Good. 'Cos that's what most people mean."

The strangely mournful-sounding ice-cream van cruised slowly around the corner. "Want a lolly?" Clare asked, glad to change the subject.

"Yessss. Can I have a Funny Feet?"

They sat on a low brick wall and Clare handed Amy the lolly. It started melting its Germolene-pink drips almost straight away, but Amy was deft at catching them with her tongue.

"Baby Jamie loved ice-cream," she said. "If I had one I would put a bit on my finger and he would lick it off. He loved it."

"You still missing him?"

Amy nodded and for a few moments she stopped eating and let the lolly drip onto the floor. "I've got no one to sing to any more. Or do games with. He used to like doing Round-and-round-the-garden, and having his toes tickled."

"Try not to think about it," Clare said. "I know that's hard, but you should try not to dwell on it like this."

Amy turned her attention back to the ice lolly.

"So you think there's a strange atmosphere on the estate?" Clare tried again.

Amy frowned. "A strange what?"

"You know, like things feel odd and different. You were saying that, remember?"

Amy nodded and made a slurping sound as she tried

to stop any drops of ice-cream from falling to the ground. "I don't know how to say it. It's like things are all shifting about. Changing. But I don't know how, really."

"What makes you feel like that?"

Amy stared around her and sighed, trying to find words that would properly explain her thoughts. Clare watched her, remembering how it sometimes felt as a child to lack the right words to tell someone how you felt. To know that something was happening but not to understand it.

"Everyone's cross or sad or worried. More than usual, I mean. And the kids hardly ever come out to play anymore. All anyone talks about is baby Jamie or the strike or not having any money. No one says anything nice or funny these days."

Clare looked at the ground. Not just on Sweetmeadows, she thought. "These are hard days, Amy, for lots of people. You're right. And when something really bad happens – you know, like Jamie being killed – people can feel it's wrong to be happy. At least for a while."

"And there are these boys that hang around at night," Amy went on. "Some girls too. And they have stuff to drink and they shout and throw things around. A woman told them off and they smashed her windows. I get scared of them. I can't sleep when they're out there."

"Has anyone told the police about them?"

Amy gave Clare a pitying look. "The police? Nah. Why would they? They wouldn't do anything to stop it, anyway."

"So how long's this been going on?"

Amy gave a little shrug. "Three or four nights. I watch them from my bedroom but I keep the light out. I don't want them to see me watching."

"Do you know who they are?"

"A couple of them. One of them's the brother of a boy in my class. He stopped coming to school a while ago, though."

"I'm sorry you're scared. But they're not interested in you, Amy, they're just letting off steam. They'll soon get sick of hanging around here with nothing to do. Especially when the weather gets colder or it starts to rain."

"I wish it would rain."

"You do?" Clare smiled. "How come?"

"Maybe then it won't feel so... crackly. Maybe some of the bad stuff here will get all washed away."

Clare nodded. "The funny thing is, you're right. People do fewer crimes in bad weather. Look, I need to pop back to my office to finish some work. But I'll come back tomorrow. I might get a story out of the way these yobs are terrorising people on the estate. Ask your mum if I can talk to her about it, will you?"

Amy pouted. "You'll be lucky getting any sense out of me mam these days. She's got this new bloke and she spends all her time running after him. I hate him."

"Why do you hate him?"

Amy made a face. "Just because."

Clare glanced at her watch. "Ask your mum anyway. And if there are any other mums I could chat to, you could point me towards them, yeah?"

"Yeah, okay."

Clare waved Amy goodbye, and headed for the nearest phone box to call the picture desk. "Hey, Stewie? I'm glad it's you. I need you to come to your favourite place. Yes, Sweetmeadows. I need you to take a pic of a cockroach in a jar."

Wednesday 25th July

It didn't take long for Clare to find people on Sweetmeadows to complain about the way small gangs of teenagers were disturbing the estate at nights, although she preferred the word 'terrorising'. *Yobs terror on murder estate.*

As she knew she would get stuck there for a while, Amy's mum was her last door-knock of the day. She was half-surprised to find that Tina was around, pale and sleepy-looking, and she was even more surprised to be let into the flat. Usually, even Amy kept her standing outside the door.

133

The place smelled heavily of cigarettes, unwashed clothes and dog. Like most of the living rooms Clare had seen in the last couple of weeks, the place was sparsely furnished: a sofa, a rug so coated in dog hairs that it was difficult to guess at its original colour, a TV, a plug-in electric fire. There were no pictures on the wall.

"Aye, I've heard them, the little sods," Tina said, when Clare asked her about the teenagers. "Drinking and shouting and throwing things about. It keeps her awake," she went on, jerking her head in Amy's direction. Amy nodded vigorously, her arms firmly round the dog, to stop it from jumping at Clare. Clare kept half an eye on it as it wagged its tail vigorously, ready to pounce.

"What would you like to see done about it?" This was a question for which it was frustratingly hard to glean any answers. The tenants were reluctant to speak to the police about the problem and, however angry they were about the noise and disruption, most wouldn't commit themselves to a solution. They shrugged their shoulders and said they just didn't know.

Tina sighed and sucked on a cigarette. "The trouble is, there's nothing else for them to do. I remember being that age and doing the same thing, hanging around, hoping for trouble."

"So should the police speak to them? Move them on?"

"I suppose so."

That'll do, thought Clare. I can turn that into a call for the police to take action.

"Does it scare you? You know, when they smash things and stuff?"

Tina pouted. "Not really. I'm scared for them, though."

"How do you mean?"

Tina raked a hand through her hair, an unwashed frizzy perm in unnatural gold. "You know what kids are like, drinking and smoking whatever they can get their hands on. Riding round on those daft scooters. There'll be a horrible accident. That'll be another reason for everyone to call the people on Sweetmeadows worse than scum."

A death waiting to happen. Good line, Clare thought.

"Have you seen them?" Tina asked suddenly.

"Not actually seen them, myself," Clare admitted. "Just heard the stories."

"You should come round here tonight," Tina suggested. Clare was taken aback. It wasn't like Tina to show that much interest. "Come here about nine o'clock and sit and wait. They'll be round. Then you can see what happens."

"You wouldn't mind? I wouldn't be interrupting your evening?"

Tina shook her head. "Don't be daft. Come and sit and chat to Amy. She'd be chuffed, wouldn't you, kid? And then you can write about whatever you want. That'd be better than talking to me."

Clare blinked. "Okay, I will, thanks very much."

"*Yesss.*" Amy's face glowed.

Clare managed to fill her day's story quota and decided not to tell the newsdesk her plan to stake out the Sweetmeadows estate. For one thing, Catt was still in charge and there was every chance she would hand the story to Chris Barber. For another, they might decide to send someone else with her – a photographer, for example – and for reasons that she couldn't quite put her finger on, she wanted to do this on her own. After all, nothing might happen. Sod's law said the more resources the paper put into it, the less likely a story was to work out. She was just checking it out, after all.

She arrived at Amy's flat at around eight-thirty with a carrier bag full of sweets, crisps and fizzy pop. When Tina opened the door, she'd changed and put on some make-up. She still looked unnaturally pale, but much more human than she had earlier in the day. A man who Clare hadn't seen before was sprawled across the sofa, watching the TV.

"Hey, Mickey. This is the reporter woman." Tina raised her voice at the man as if she was used to having to repeat herself. "What's your name again? Right. Clare. This is Mickey, my boyfriend."

"Aye." The man heaved himself up and nodded at Clare. He looked younger than Tina and as he stood up a strong waft of cheap aftershave made Clare catch her breath.

"See you then," Tina said, picking up a handbag from the floor. "Hope you get what you want. And you," she nodded at Amy, "behave yourself. None of your fairy stories."

Amy stuck out her tongue as her mother turned round.

"You're going out?" Clare tried to keep the surprise out of her voice.

"We might be late," Tina added. "So don't worry. We'll probably go to a club. Amy'll be fine, whenever you need to get off you just tell her to go to bed. Not that she will."

Clare said nothing as the couple slammed the door behind them. I walked into that one, she thought. She noticed Mickey had barely looked at Amy and hadn't bothered to say goodbye. No wonder Amy hated him.

Amy gave her a little shrug and a huge grin. "Yay! What'll we do? Shall I put my tape on?"

"You might as well," Clare said. "We've got a bit of waiting around to do."

"Hang on." Amy fiddled with the cassette in a player plugged in next to the TV. It clicked and whirred. She pressed play, then stop, then wound back a little more. "This is my favourite song, ever. I never get fed up of it."

The opening words of Wham's *Wake Me Up Before You Go Go* boomed out. Amy jumped in the air, waving her hands, then did a wild stepping dance across the floor. *Jitterbug.* "Dance, Clare!"

Clare laughed.

"Dance properly!" Amy held out her hands and Clare took them, letting Amy do most of the jigging about, until the girl was red in the face and out of breath. "I love that one. Don't you love that one, Clare?"

"Sure. That Walkman playing okay?"

"I love it. I love it so much. I take it everywhere I go. Me mam says I'm asking to get it pinched but I don't want to leave it at home. Anyway, it's meant for carrying around, isn't it?"

"I suppose it is." She couldn't bring herself to ask Amy if her mum had remembered her birthday, but she noticed there were no cards around the room.

They watched some of the news. Seventy arrests on the picket line at Babbington Colliery in Nottingham. Amy was restless. "I'm so sick of hearing about this," she said to Clare. "Strike, strike, strike, that's all anyone talks about."

"I know, but it's quite important to lots of people. That's what news is, Amy, something that matters to real people. You have to get used to that if you want to be a reporter."

"Do you ever get to meet pop stars?"

Clare half-smiled. "Not on a local paper, at least, hardly ever. But if you go and work in London you'll meet them all the time."

"That's what I'm going to do, then. Why don't you go to London?"

"I might, one day. My friend Joe keeps talking about it."

"Is Joe your boyfriend?"

"No. But anyway, you need to start on a local paper and get lots of by-lines, then you might get a job on a national paper. They're all in London. That's when you might get to meet all the stars."

"You get millions of by-lines," Amy commented.

"I wouldn't say that."

"You do. Wait there." Amy slid off the sofa and ran into her room. She came back with a scrapbook and put it across Clare's knee. "There, look. I've been keeping them."

Clare flicked through the heavy card pages. Amy had cut out and kept every story with Clare's name on it since the day after the baby's death and had gummed them into the scrapbook.

"Wow. This is what I should be doing, only I never get

round to it. I should pay you to be my secretary, Amy."

Amy giggled. "See, though? Loads of by-lines."

Clare was turning another heavily-glued page when the sound of smashing glass outside made both of them jump. They went to the window and peered out. In the square, a small group of teenagers was sitting on a low wall.

"It's them again," Amy said, keeping well back behind the shabby curtain. Clare counted five, two girls and three boys, none of them any older than seventeen at the most. They were all drinking from bottles of cheap booze. A couple of small motorcycles were parked up next to them. Clare watched as one lad drained his bottle and threw it against the wall of the flats, where it smashed, spattering shards of glass across the ground. Clare thought of how often she'd seen Amy wandering around in bare feet.

Even from four floors up, Clare could feel the group's boredom. She began to get a sense of what Amy meant when she said it was as if something was about to happen. It was coming from the desperation of the teenagers, which was so thick she felt she could reach out and squeeze it. It gave off a feeling that even something bad, something very bad, would be better than nothing.

They got back on their scooters, sped around the square, out of the estate and back again, none of them wearing a helmet. The girls perched behind the boy drivers, squealing and shrieking as they revved up the bikes. Someone came out of a doorway and shouted at them to 'shut the fuck up', but they just laughed and pumped the engines harder.

Clare turned away from the window to see Amy crouched on the sofa, her head buried in her knees. "You okay?"

Amy gave a loud sniff and looked up, red-eyed. "I hate them. They scare me."

Clare sat back down on the sofa next to her. "I can't believe someone as tough as you could be scared by those idiots down there." They sat listening to the roar of the bikes until it faded again.

"Did you see the one with the cap on?" Amy wasn't looking at Clare, but still staring at her own grubby knees. Clare nodded, waiting.

Amy wiped at her eyes. "I think I've seen him before."

"You mean… "

Amy nodded, misery on her face. "It's the same cap. And I think the same trainers, with red laces."

"You never mentioned trainers with red laces before."

"I know. I forgot. I only remembered when I saw him again."

"You said he was a man."

Amy looked up. "He is a man."

"Right." Clare frowned. "I'd have called him, I don't know, a lad. Or a boy. Or something that said he was younger." But she supposed that to a ten-year-old, perhaps the teenagers did seem much older – grown-up, even.

Amy shrugged and said nothing.

"So were they both young men? Like those ones down there?"

Amy pouted. "I can't really remember. I didn't get that good a look. It all happened really quick."

Clare chewed her lip for a moment. "Is that why you're so scared? Because you think it's the same guys who threw baby Jamie over the balcony?"

Amy nodded and her eyes filled up with tears again. Clare didn't know whether she should put an arm around the child or not. Probably not. "So when you saw it happen – when you saw someone take Jamie out of his pram and drop him over the ledge – did you think you'd seen those men before?"

Amy pouted. "I wasn't sure. It was only when I saw them again, just now, that I realised." She paused, thinking. "Those girls might've been there too."

Clare bit back the irritation she felt over Finn's arrest, which had in part been down to Amy's original story, and sighed. "But you never mentioned any girls."

"That's 'cause I'm not sure. I don't like thinking about

that day any more."

"I know, Amy. It must be awful. But you need to try to remember everything you can. Every little detail's important. Even the shoelaces. And you mustn't say things unless you're sure about them. If you keep adding bits on, or changing your mind, people think you're making it up."

"They think that anyway, don't they? Anyway, I can't remember everything at once. I can't help that."

"Okay. I know. I'm sorry. It must be hard." Clare remembered reading that people can blot out traumatic incidents from their minds, and that the memories can come back in tiny pieces, like fragments of broken china, sometimes never quite fitting back together. She took a furtive look at her watch. It was getting on for eleven o'clock and she had a bad feeling that Tina and Mickey weren't in any hurry to come home. But she couldn't leave Amy on her own, not when the kid was so scared by the gang down in the square.

Amy crouched on the sofa, her eyes fixed on Clare, waiting for her to somehow sort things out. Clare sighed and looked out of the window again. Her car was parked near the entrance to the estate and she wasn't too happy with the way the bikes kept flying past it at high speeds. "Amy, I'm going to have to go home and get to bed, I've got work tomorrow. But I don't want to leave you here all on your own."

For once, Amy didn't say anything. She wiped her eyes and gave a tiny shrug, to indicate that it was okay. Clare knew she liked to pretend she was hard-edged, but tonight it wasn't working.

"Look. You can stay here if you like, if you promise you won't go out or let anyone else in the flat. But if you want, if you're really scared, you can come back to mine and stay in my spare room. Just for tonight, okay? We'll leave your mum a note and my phone number, so she doesn't get worried."

Amy's watery eyes lit up. "I can go to your flat? For the night? Honest?"

Clare nodded. "Only if you want to. I don't want to get

you in trouble with your mum."

Amy jumped up. "Let's just go, then."

Clare suspected the last thing Amy wanted was for her mum to come home, right at that point, and spoil the little adventure. "Get a nightie and your toothbrush. And something to wear tomorrow."

Amy ran into her room and came out with a bundle of not particularly clean clothes. Clare looked around for a carrier bag and shoved them inside. "Okay, we're going to my car. When we get outside, we just walk past those kids, we don't look at them in the face or say anything to them, got it?"

Amy nodded. "Got it."

Amy did as she was told, keeping her gaze directed at the ground until they got inside Clare's car. As soon as the engine started, though, her face brightened and she chatted all the way back to Clare's flat, her mood apparently fixed in an instant. They had tea and toast, and then Clare insisted that Amy get some sleep. "You might not feel tired, but I'm worn out, and I've got a day's work to do tomorrow." She opened the door to the spare room.

Amy looked around. The paint still smelled fresh, just faintly. "Whose room is this?"

"No one's, really, it's just a spare room. It's a two bedroomed flat, that's all."

"So it's like, just a room that anyone can stay in?"

"That's right."

"It's really nice. I love the Garfield posters."

"I thought you might. Only, seriously, I need to get to bed. Go on, off you go."

Clare closed the door behind her and fell into her own bed. Part of her hoped that Tina would call to check on Amy, but part of her knew that she wouldn't.

Thursday 26th July
Clare got out of bed at six-thirty to find Amy already up and watching TV. "Your milk's gone sour," she said.

141

"I know. I was going to nip to the shop to get some more before you got up, but you beat me. Sorry."

"It's fine, I don't mind."

"Did you sleep?"

"Yes." Amy gave her a strange look. "What else would I have done?"

Clare laughed. "Nothing, I just meant… it doesn't matter. Let me get dressed and we'll go and find some breakfast."

Somehow, Amy persuaded Clare to take her to a cafe usually used by lorry drivers. Clare, who almost never ate breakfast, found herself with an unfamiliar rumble in her stomach as she ordered Amy a bacon sandwich. She watched, the heat and steam making her eyes water, as Amy opened the greasy slices of bread and used the tube of ketchup to squirt out a heart-shape on top of the glistening bacon slice, then picked up the brown sauce and added an arrow going through it.

"Who's the love heart for, then?"

Amy's cheeks flushed. "George Michael."

"No one at school? No boyfriends?"

Amy made a gagging face. "I don't like *real* boys."

"Very sensible. I don't think I do either, very much."

"Aren't you in *luuurrve* with Joe, then?"

"No. Don't be silly."

Amy polished off the sandwich and followed it with a doughnut. She licked her fingers and used them to pick up every last remaining grain of sugar from her plate.

"I really don't know where you put it all," Clare said. It was strange how much she enjoyed watching Amy eat. "Anyway, when you've finished hoovering up all that sugar, I'd better get you home."

Amy pouted but then said, "Yeah, I suppose, because if me mam didn't come home last night, I'll have to feed Max."

It was obvious to Clare that Amy was more than used to her mum staying out all night. It was a routine.

After dropping Amy back at the estate, Clare put in a few calls. Then she drove round to see Chief Inspector Seaton.

"Why do I always think there's trouble on the way whenever I see you these days, Miss Jackson?"

Clare smiled. "I really couldn't say." Were those extra lines on his face? The stress of the baby murder was definitely getting to him.

"Come on, then. What have you stirred up from Sweetmeadows this time? I take it that's what this is about."

"You're not going to like it. But just hear me out, please. That little girl… "

Seaton groaned. "Hasn't she wasted enough of our time already? That tale about the men came to nothing."

"Wait. I'm doing a story today about a gang of kids that's causing a load of trouble on the estate. Four or five teenage lads and girls, buzzing around on scooters, making a racket, drinking, vandalising the place."

Seaton arranged his pens and pencils into neat lines on his desk. "Vandalising Sweetmeadows? Can anyone tell?"

"Yes, because they're smashing things up and they're an accident waiting to happen."

"Has anyone reported it to us?"

"No."

"Because?"

Clare paused, so Seaton answered his own question. "Because it's Sweetmeadows and no one there talks to the police."

"Because they don't think anything will get done."

"It bloody well won't get done if no one reports it. The police are many things but we're not telepathic."

Clare looked at him, with her pen hovering above her page.

"My apologies. I shouldn't have raised my voice and I shouldn't have sworn in front of a lady."

"I'm no lady, I'm a reporter."

Seaton gave a little snort.

"Just thought I'd get that one in before you did." Clare clicked her pen in and out. "Anyway, I wanted to check that the police weren't aware of it. And if there is anything you can give me by way of a response."

"You can tell the good folks of Sweetmeadows that we'll be looking into it."

"Right. Thanks. Now the thing is, remember when that little girl said she thought she saw two men carry out baby Jamie's murder?"

"Ah, we're back to Amy Hedley. A complete stranger to the truth."

"You said that. But the thing is, I was with her last night when we were watching these kids running around the estate and she got very upset. She thought she recognised one of them."

"How do you mean, recognised?"

"Amy told me she saw two men around the estate on the afternoon that Jamie died, remember? She saw one of them pick the baby out of his pram and the other one was down on the ground, waiting. She told me a while ago that one of them was wearing a baseball cap."

"You do realise it would be quicker for me to bring in everyone round there who doesn't wear a baseball cap? It hardly narrows the field."

"So last night she thought it was the same guy. And she said he had the same trainers on, with red laces."

Seaton sat up a little. "She didn't mention that before. She told us something about Support the Strike stickers, but we looked into that and got nowhere."

"No. And what Amy calls a man, I'd call a young lad. But she says she only remembered the trainers with red laces when she saw them again, last night."

"Red laces?" Seaton thought for a moment. "Okay. That might lead us somewhere quicker than a baseball cap. Unless it turns out that all the low-lifes are wearing them right now. I'm no expert on street fashion. But I'll send an officer round

144

to speak to Amy Hedley and we'll follow that up. Thank you."

Clare clicked her pen in and out again, then stopped when she caught Seaton looking at it with obvious irritation. "You will… I mean, your officers will be nice to her, won't they? She's just a kid. Kids don't think straight, the way we want them to, do they? And she was really scared last night."

"We will be nice, as you put it, yes."

"You know where she lives?"

"As I've said before, her mother is well known to the boys in the station. We'll have no trouble finding her, thank you." He picked up some papers on his desk and shook them, unnecessarily, into a neater pile. Clare took the hint and got up to leave.

Back at the office, Joe called. "Not doing your daily visit to Sweetmeadows then?"

"I've already got something else to write up."

"Something else? Do you remember when you used to have slow news days? Before you became editor of the Sweetmeadows Chronicle, that is."

"Yes, I suppose, it's been a stream of stories, hasn't it? I'm not complaining."

"I know someone who is."

"Tell me it's Chris Barber again?"

"It is. I'm warning you – he's still seriously trying to push you out of here."

"Yeah, yeah. Surely they can't budge me when I'm turning stories round as fast as this?"

"Since when were newspapers a meritocracy? It's about who shouts the loudest and whose face fits, you know that. Just keep watching your back, Clare."

At seven-thirty, Clare arrived outside the City Hall, where she spotted Finn already waiting, wearing one of his very freshly-washed and pressed shirts. He leaned down to give her a quick kiss on the cheek. "I wasn't sure if you'd remember.

I thought about giving you a call to remind you and then I thought that would make me look like a total prat."

Clare laughed. "Of course I remembered. Have we time for a drink?"

Finn steered her towards a crowded bar, where he somehow managed to get served straight away just by nodding his head at the woman behind the counter.

"Good that there's such a crowd," Clare said, taking a sip of her wine.

"We've still got a lot of support. In spite of what you might read in the *Daily Mail* and *The Sun*."

"Any progress, though?"

"The lads in Yorkshire are having a lot of trouble with the police. It's much worse than it is up here. We've only had a few scrapes, nothing really bad. But it could get worse. I've noticed a few unmarked cars hanging around near the pit. I reckon they're spotters, looking out for flying pickets. And if they try to turn anyone back, there'll be bother."

When Finn talked about the union's work, Clare felt a mixture of admiration and an uneasy sense that her own work was trivial in comparison. Finn insisted that fair publicity was a help, but to Clare it paled next to walking the streets with collection buckets, wrangling with lawyers and winning concessions on benefit payments.

"Did the police ever get back to you? About that baby business?"

Finn shook his head. "They're keeping me on their books because they're still none the wiser." He took Clare's hands and she felt a pleasurable jolt of heat through her limbs. "You don't think I had anything to do with that, do you?"

Clare shook her head. "Of course not."

She noticed Finn's gaze wandering around the crowd as they chatted. "Are you looking for someone?"

Finn snapped his attention back to Clare. "No. Sorry. By the way, you wanted to do something on the women involved in the strike? Can you get to my mother's house tomorrow morning, elevenish? There'll be a few there, having a coffee and talking about setting up a group. They'll talk to you, I've primed them."

"That's brilliant. I'll be there."

At the end of the concert, Clare's head was ringing with protest songs and she'd put more money than she could afford into the collection bucket. It felt like all she could do and it also felt hopelessly inadequate. Finn put an arm lightly around her shoulder as they made their way through the crowd leaving the City Hall. She had no idea how to respond, but didn't try to shake it off.

"Come for a last drink?"

Clare made an apologetic face. "Work tomorrow. I'd better not, sorry."

"Can I see you home?"

Clare laughed. "I'm not sixteen. I can jump in a cab all by myself."

"That's not the point, I'd like to… " Finn stopped and gave a little shrug. "Okay, okay. But I've had a great night."

"Me too. Thanks for the ticket. I'll write something up. They're always short on the reviews page."

Finn gave Clare a note with his mother's address and phone number. He leaned down and Clare stood on her tiptoes to kiss Finn's cheek, as he put his arms around her waist to hold her there for a minute.

"I should go."

Finn stepped back. Clare smiled as she waved at him and turned towards the taxi rank. She held the feeling of the kiss and Finn's faint scent – of washed cotton and aftershave – in her head as she rode home, enjoying the sensation of a quickened heartbeat that took most of the journey to return to its normal pace.

Friday 27th July
It was unusual for Clare to wake up feeling optimistic about the day ahead. For several weeks, after light, fitful sleep

at best, she'd woken up clutching her stomach, and with a sickening feeling of emptiness inside. Getting up, washing, dressing and all the other morning routines were things that she forced herself to do, with a sensation of dragging herself along. This morning, though, she found herself almost looking forward to the next few hours, rather than steeling herself simply to get through them. It wasn't a feeling she could rationally explain.

Dave Bell was back on the newsdesk, to Clare's relief. When she offered a news feature story on the women affected by the miners' strike, he liked the idea. "You've got some good sources, I can tell," he told her. "I've been having a look through the last few days' papers and you're still turning out some great stuff. Well done."

"How are you for stories today? Can I take a bit of time over this miners' thing?"

"I could do with something short for the early edition. Find me an overnight story for Saturday as well and I'll be happy."

"That shouldn't be a problem."

Clare sent a few paragraphs about the Sweetmeadows protestors and the union's plan to appeal against their court sentences. She already had a small pile of holdable stories, ready for weekend editions, and the entertainment editor was happy to take a review of the benefit concert from last night. It meant Clare was free to spend the rest of the morning with Finn's mother.

Mary McKenna's neat council house was only a few streets away from Clare's office. As Clare tapped on the door, with the highly polished knocker, she suddenly felt jittery inside. Winning Mary's approval would be important. Not just for the sake of the story.

Mary was a tiny woman in her late fifties, with hair in a short grey bob, and her house was intimidatingly clean. As Clare passed a series of framed photos on the wall, she couldn't help wondering quite how this little elfin-shaped woman had managed to produce what looked like a small sports team of tall, muscle-bound lads.

Two small coffee tables were set out with cups, saucers and plates of biscuits. The mantelpiece over the fireplace was lined with ornaments – crystal and china figurines of animals and ladies in period dress. And down on either side of the hearth, polished but battered, were two old miners' lamps.

"One's my dad's," Mary said, as she noticed Clare looking at them. "The other belonged to my father-in-law." She picked up one of the lamps and handed it to Clare, who ran her fingers along the bumps and dents in the brass.

"The mining goes back generations in our family," Mary went on. "And almost any family round here will tell you the same. But they expect us to sit back and do nothing when they're taking a whole way of life away from us."

Clare nodded. "I do get that," she said. "But I suppose they claim the unions are scaremongering. That there's no big plan to close all the pits down."

"I don't trust anything that comes out of the mouth of a Tory government. I've got a long memory. We've been here before, back in the seventies, and the miners won. The Tories never got over it. This is payback time, I'm telling you."

The doorbell pinged and Mary scurried off to open it. Four women arrived together and all piled into Mary's little living room, fussing around the tea pot and biscuits, squeezing onto the sofa as Clare tried to breathe in and take up as little space as possible.

"These are fancy biscuits," one of the women remarked.

"Don't worry, they're still in date. Just."

"First off, I've got two of us on the van going down to London on Saturday," one of the women announced. "Collecting for the food banks and the fighting fund. See if anyone down there's got more money than we have."

"Good, we're running low. And with the school holidays, everyone's finding it harder. We could do with some local firms helping out, with treats and maybe some days out, that sort of thing."

"You could sort that out, couldn't you?" The woman next to Clare gave her a nudge. "If you put something in the paper, some business people might come forward."

"I could try." Clare wasn't sure if the editor would let her effectively advertise for people willing to support the strike, but she was prepared to give it a go, disguised as a story about the new women's group. "So, summer activities for the kids and helping raise funds towards the strike. What else is the women's group going to do?" As if that wasn't enough, she thought, realising how the question might sound.

"We've got big plans." Mary had a way of talking that meant Clare didn't doubt her. "We need to make sure the women and kids are okay, because they're what will keep this strike solid."

"But you must be under so much strain already," Clare said. "Trying to manage on – what?"

"Supplementary benefit," one of the others chipped in. "Though what it's meant to supplement, I've no idea. Bare bones benefit, that's what it is."

"How can you take all this on?" Clare asked. "With nothing?"

Mary smiled. "Because doing something useful is what gets us through the bad times. And the worse they make it for us, the harder we'll fight. You just watch."

Clare smiled back. "Good luck, then. I'll do what I can."

Mary nodded. "Our Finn said you would help."

Clare found her face growing a little warm. She knew Mary was watching her closely. "I'll do my best."

"Finn's taken quite a liking to you," Mary added. Clare was conscious of all the other women turning to stare and size her up.

"Is he not with Jackie anymore?" asked the woman next to Clare, staring at her as if she had just landed. "You're joking. I thought they were just about to name the day."

"So did I. So did poor Jackie, I reckon." Mary gave a little

150

shake of her head. "But you know our Finn. I've never been able to fathom him and I'm his mother."

Clare squirmed awkwardly in her seat, although it wasn't easy with the woman's large hips keeping her firmly pressed against the side of the sofa. Everyone was looking at her.

"How long had they been seeing each other? Since they were at school, wasn't it?"

Mary nodded. "I know, I know. We're all sorry about it. But if it's not right it's best that he says so now, before they're down the aisle or in the maternity ward."

"Aye. I suppose." The woman next to Clare didn't sound convinced. She looked Clare up and down. "Your Finn's always been a dark horse, though."

Mary sighed. "Tell me about it. And I don't know what went on between him and Jackie, but there's more to it than either of them are letting on. It's something to do with him working for the union, I think. But I'm proud of him for it. It's great to have him back at home."

"Is it? I'd have thought it was one more mouth to feed."

"Yes, but he's such a help. He gets things done, he chips in with money." Mary's powdery cheeks went slightly pink. "I don't always ask where he gets it from."

"Aye, well." The woman on the sofa shifted again and Clare tried to compress herself into an even smaller space. "These days, you take what you can. I'm glad he's here for you, pet."

"I think I'd better get going, anyway," Clare said, squeezing painfully out of the sofa and standing up. "You've been so helpful. Thanks for letting me come along today. Is it okay if I get a photographer to call you, to come and take a picture to go with the piece?"

"I suppose so," said Mary, though the others shrieked with laughter and said they wished they had the cash to get their hair done first.

Outside, the sky was cloud-grey but the air was still hot and heavy. Clare fanned herself, uselessly, with her notebook, wondering why those last few minutes had been quite so embarrassing. What exactly had Finn told his mother? Did he think they were some sort of an item, just because they'd been for a drink and out to a gig together? Were they? She found herself hoping so. Although whatever had happened with his long-term girlfriend, Clare hoped she wasn't unwittingly responsible.

The office phone was jangling as Clare ran up the stairs, and she somehow sensed it had been ringing for some time. Amy sounded impatient on the other end of the line. "I've been calling you for ages and ages."

"I was out doing a job. That's what I do most days, Amy."

"You need one of them phones you can carry around. I saw them on the telly. Why don't you get one of those?"

"Because they cost a fortune and they weigh a ton. Only posers have them. Anyway, what can I do for you? Are you okay?"

"The police want to talk to me. They were banging on the door."

"What did they say?"

Amy gave a dry little laugh. "I never let them in, you stupid. You don't let police in unless you have to, that's what me mam says. But they were knocking and knocking for a long time. I just hid in my bedroom till I was sure they'd gone."

"So how do you know they want to talk to you?"

"They pushed a note through the door. They want me mam to bring me to the station."

"That's good, isn't it? You can tell them about that man in the trainers and the cap. Then they can check him out. It might make you feel better."

"Yeah, but me mam won't take me. She thinks I'm making it all up. And she hates the police anyway. She won't go to the station unless they drag her kicking and screaming, she says."

Clare raked a hand through her hair, thinking. "Would it help if I came and talked to your mum?"

"Maybe."

"Is she around?"

"She said she'd be back at tea time."

Clare sighed. "Okay, tell your mum I'm going to pop in around five-ish just for a chat. Only, listen, Amy, tell her I can't stay long, so I'm not babysitting again, okay?"

By six, Tina still hadn't turned up. Clare sat, drumming her fingers on the edge of the sofa, whipping them away when she felt Max's slippery tongue. Amy spent the time showing Clare her clumsy attempts at Teeline, dancing to her favourite pop tracks, and asking a barrage of questions about working as a journalist.

"I've got an idea," said Clare. "How about I pick you up tomorrow and take you for a look in the newspaper office? You can see the papers coming off the presses. It's really good to watch."

Amy caught her breath. "I'd love that."

"Okay, if your mum says you can."

"She won't care."

"I'm sure she does care. I'm not just waltzing you off without permission."

"But what if she doesn't come back tonight?"

Clare felt a slight sinking feeling inside. "Do you think she might not?"

Amy looked down at her feet, which were bare and filthy, with chipped polish on the toenails. "Maybe."

Clare took a deep breath. "Amy, how often does your mum leave you on your own for a whole night? Be honest with me."

Amy didn't look up.

"I won't tell, I promise. But I want to know. Does it happen a lot?"

Amy shrugged, stretched out her leg and made invisible patterns on the floor with her toe.

"Please, Amy. You can trust me, can't you?"

153

"Sometimes. It happens sometimes."

"Once a week? More than that?"

"It just depends. Sometimes the boyfriends come here. But she doesn't like that, not after... " Amy's voice tailed off.

"After what?"

Amy shook her head and went silent.

Clare waited a moment. "So if she goes out with a boyfriend, what happens? You stay here on your own? She doesn't usually get a babysitter?"

"I'm too old for a babysitter, stupid."

"Not legally. Anyway, how often does she stay out all night?"

"She goes out a lot with this one. Mickey likes going out better than staying in with me. But I'm safe, because Max guards me."

"That's really not the point." Clare felt as if she had been handed a very heavy weight, one that she could never quite give back again. "So how do you feel about being on your own?"

"I'm not scared."

"That's not true, is it? You were scared of that gang."

"Yeah, but... " Amy kept her eyes fixed on her feet. "That was 'cause it was them. I'm not normally scared of being on my own. I'm not a baby."

Clare was about to argue that there was a killer roaming around somewhere, unsuspected, and it was hardly childish to be worried about that. But she stopped herself from making Amy feel worse. That was an argument to put to Tina, when she eventually bothered to come back home. In the meantime, Clare wasn't sure what to do.

"I know you're not a baby, of course I do. I'm just worried that you're still a kid, although you're a very smart one. That means you shouldn't be here all alone, even with a great big dog. That's all."

"But you won't tell? You promised."

"Who would I tell?"

154

"Me mam says if I tell anyone they'll take me away. I'd have to live in care and she says that's the same as being in prison."

Clare frowned. "I'm not sure that's right. But stop worrying about that. You're not going to be taken away." She glanced at her watch. Almost seven.

"I could come to yours again," Amy said, looking up. "I'd be no bother, honest."

"I don't know, Amy."

"Go on."

Clare gave half a laugh, half a mock-sigh. "Oh, go on then. Let's leave a note with my number on it and if your mum wants you back tonight, I'll bring you straight home."

"*Yessss.*" Amy ran into her bedroom and came out with a carrier bag. "Here's my stuff."

Clare narrowed her eyes. "Was that already packed?"

Amy just grinned.

Clare was pleased she'd got some food in, just in case. Bread, milk, breakfast cereals, biscuits. A new pop magazine lay on the bed in the spare room. The truth was, Clare knew, that she and Amy had wordlessly conspired with each other, without even realising it.

"You've already tidied up," Amy said, as soon as she walked in. "It smells nicer."

"I've done a bit of cleaning," Clare admitted. "It needed it."

"I sometimes clean up at home. I quite like cleaning," Amy said. "I like the way things look when you're done. But I haven't got any stuff to clean with, right now."

The phone rang. It was Finn. "How did you get on with my mother and her mates?"

"Really well, I think. They were helpful. Plenty to write about. Tell your mum thanks."

"Are you doing anything tonight? We could go for a drink."

"I'm sorry, Finn. I've got someone staying with me tonight."

155

"Oh. A man?"

Clare paused. "Just a friend."

"Tomorrow, then."

"Was that your boyfriend then?" Amy wanted to know, when Clare put the phone down.

"No, it wasn't, nosy. What do you want to do? Watch some telly?"

Amy shrugged. "If you like. That's what I usually do. I like *Starsky and Hutch*."

Clare cast around. "I don't have any games or anything but I've got a pack of cards."

Amy looked blank. "I don't know how to play cards."

"You don't? I'm no expert, but I can teach you a couple of games."

They started with Beggar My Neighbour and moved on to Pontoon. Amy was a fast learner and soon trounced Clare again and again.

"I love doing games," Amy said, as Clare went into the kitchen to get some drinks. "But there's never anyone to play with at home."

"You'll have to teach your mum."

Amy made a spluttering noise. "As if she has time. I got Monopoly at Christmas and I set it all up and everything but she never played it."

"Well, Christmas is busy. Sometimes mums don't get the chance to play."

"No, I mean she never played it *ever*. It stayed set up on the floor till it got all dusty and then I put it away. You can't do Monopoly on your own."

"Oh." Clare wasn't sure what to say for a moment. "It's years since I've played Monopoly. Next time, I mean, *if* you have to come and stay again, you could bring it with you."

As the time ticked on to almost ten, Clare thought she ought to tell Amy to go to bed.

"But I don't usually go this early." Amy sounded genuine and Clare believed her. Clearly Tina often wasn't around to tell her daughter to go to bed at a decent time.

"But you should. You must be tired when you go to school in the mornings."

"Sometimes I don't go to sleep all night anyway."

Clare frowned. "Are you still having dreams about the baby?"

Amy folded her arms. "I told you, they're not dreams. I still hear him crying though. Sometimes he stops when I sing, like I used to. But I can't make him laugh any more. I can't tickle his toes or do finger games, and they were his favourite thing." She sighed. "Sometimes I wish I could just be with him."

"Perhaps you should talk to someone about the way you feel and these dreams you're getting. I mean, maybe you could talk to your mum?"

"No way. She'd say I was mental. She says that anyway, lots of the time."

Clare sighed. "Maybe you'll sleep better here, tonight. You shouldn't hear any crying here."

"Ohh-kayyy." Amy heaved herself up from the chair. "That room seems sad though."

Clare blinked at Amy. "What do you mean?"

Amy screwed up her face, thinking. "I'm not sure. But you know when you go somewhere and you get a feeling about it? Well, that room feels like it's sad, that's all." She looked at Clare, whose mouth was slightly open. "But it's still a nice room, honest. I'm not, you know, complaining about it or anything, 'cos I really, really like it. It's not scary-sad, it's just, I dunno… sad-sad."

Clare shivered. "I'm pretty tired myself, Amy, so let's go to bed, eh? Off you go. I'll see you in the morning."

Amy didn't move. "Do you know why the room is sad? Does it have a ghost?"

Clare stood up. "It definitely doesn't have a ghost, because there's no such thing, okay? Go on. You can go to the bathroom first."

Amy chewed her lip. "Are you cross with me?"

"No. No, of course I'm not. But I think we both need to get some sleep."

Amy skipped off into the bathroom. Clare went into her own room, sat on the bed and stared out of the window into the greying night.

eight

Saturday 28th July

Amy was up before Clare again, at around six-thirty.

"I've made toast," she said, brightly, handing Clare a plate.

The toast was already cold, so Clare wondered how long Amy had been up. Or if she had been asleep at all.

"Your mum didn't call, then."

"I never thought she would."

"You think she stayed out all night again?"

"I don't know, do I? Probably."

Clare dialled Amy's home number, but there was no answer.

"She might be worried about that note from the police," Amy said. "She won't want to take me to speak to them."

"That's daft, though. They just want to talk to you, because you might be able to help them. You haven't done anything wrong, remember. Nor has your mum."

"She won't get me to the police station, though, like the letter says." Amy chewed the skin on her finger, her nails already bitten down to the nub. "So they'll be looking for me. I'll be Wanted."

"Are you worrying about this?"

Amy nodded.

Clare sighed. She tried calling Amy's flat once again, but there was still no reply.

"I suppose I could go in with you this morning. We could just make sure that you tell the police what you know and what you've seen. And then it would be over with and your mum won't have to go and talk to the police. How would that be?"

Amy's face brightened. "That'd be brilliant." Then her expression fell again. "Will it be hard? Will they give me wrong?"

"No. I'll be there and I won't let them scare you. I promise."

After Clare chewed her way through the cold toast, they drove to the police station. Clare asked for Chief Inspector Seaton and was shown to his office by the desk sergeant, who knew her.

Seaton raised his eyebrows when he saw Amy. "These reporters are getting younger all the time," he said. Amy went into peals of laughter, which seemed to please Seaton. Clare watched her carefully, guessing that the forced laughter was a way of covering her nerves.

"Look, I've brought her along to talk to your officers, because her mum's not keen on coming along. Is that okay? Can I be with her?"

"I suppose you qualify as a responsible adult. Just about."

Seaton took them along to a tiny beige interview room and sat them at a table. "I'll find an officer to take a statement. I'll describe you as a friend of the family, for want of a better way of putting it."

"But she is my friend," Amy said, pushing her chair a little closer to Clare's.

After a few minutes, a female officer came in with a sheaf of headed paper, followed by another officer with tea for Clare and some watery orange juice for Amy.

"Amy, I'm Margaret. Now, there's nothing to be worried about." The officer wrote down Amy's name and address. "When's your birthday, Amy?"

Amy didn't answer. She stared down at the desk.

"It's the 23rd of July," Clare said. "She's just turned ten. Amy, please don't look so anxious."

Margaret gave a thin smile. "Right. What did you get for your birthday, Amy?"

Amy beamed. "A Walkman."

"Very posh. Lucky you."

That was the small talk bit, Clare thought.

Margaret went on: "I understand that you think you saw something on the day of baby Jamie's death. I just need you to tell me again everything that you saw that day, as truthfully as you can. As much as you can remember."

Amy started to recount her version of what happened. It was a painfully slow process, because the officer was writing everything down by hand and kept asking each question two or three times.

"You need to learn shorthand," Amy told her. "I can do Teeline shorthand. Clare showed me. It helps you write things faster."

"I'll bear that in mind," Margaret said. Clare made an apologetic face in her direction, but she couldn't help feeling a tiny spasm of pride at Amy's enthusiasm.

"The thing is," Margaret went on. "I'm trying to imagine you watching these men. Especially the one you say went up to the balcony and picked the baby out of his pram. I'm trying to work out how exactly you could see him, if you were on the balcony above. I can't work out how you were at the right angle."

"I wasn't on the balcony above."

"But you said… "

"Well, I wasn't on the balcony all the time. I was on the stairs for a bit."

"You didn't say that before. Why were you on the stairs?"

"I thought I heard Jamie crying."

"So?"

"So I went down to see him. But I saw this man go along

the balcony."

"I see. And then what?"

"I told you. He lifted baby Jamie out of his pram."

"And what did you do then?"

"I went back up the stairs. To my balcony."

"Why?"

"I dunno. I just felt a bit scared, that's all. I wanted to get out of the way of the man."

"Why were you scared, at that point?"

Amy nibbled at her fingers. "He was acting funny. Like… like he was on drugs or something."

Margaret gave Amy a hard look. Clare shifted in her seat. Sometimes Amy did sound as if she was making things up as she went along. But that might be because she was only ten. And because she was afraid.

"How would someone on drugs act, then?" The officer tapped her pen lightly on the table.

"Like… jumpy. And his eyes were kind of like *this*." Amy's eyeballs swivelled around.

Clare frowned. All this was new to Amy's story.

Margaret's expression was hard to read. "I thought you couldn't see his face. I thought he was wearing a cap."

"That was the man on the ground."

"I thought you said it was the other one."

Amy shook her head. Clare was having trouble keeping up with the details. So, it seemed, was the police officer, who read and re-read her notes and scribbled something Clare couldn't read. "So you went up to the balcony and you saw what exactly?"

"I saw baby Jamie fall all the way down. There was blood on the ground."

Margaret's tapping got a little faster. "So you didn't actually see this man throw the baby?"

Amy thought for a moment. "Yes. I mean, no, not exactly. But he must've done."

Margaret wrote something else on the sheaf of papers.

Clare couldn't read it upside down and when Margaret saw her tilting her head, she placed a hand over it.

"And then? What about this man on the ground?"

"He sweared."

"Did he shout?"

Amy shook her head.

"So how did you hear him, if he was four levels below you?"

"Mmmm," Amy thought about this, her head on one side. "He must've shouted, then."

"So why do you think no one else heard? Jamie's mum, for instance?"

Amy's face was a little pink. "It was quite a quiet shout."

Clare chewed the inside of her lip.

Margaret sighed. "You can't shout quietly, though, can you? If it was quiet, how did you hear it, all that way up?"

"Maybe it was the man on the balcony who sweared, then. But I heard it. Then he picked Jamie up and ran off with him."

"Right." Margaret's voice didn't disguise the fact that she no longer believed Amy's story. "Could you see where he went?"

Amy shook her head. "Just that he went towards the bins."

Margaret paused as she skimmed back over her notes. "I still don't understand why you didn't do something. Why didn't you tell Jamie's mum? Or phone the police?"

"She was scared," Clare interrupted.

The officer glared. "Let Amy tell her story in her own words, please."

"But that's right." Amy gave Clare a grateful smile. "I was scared. I thought I might get into trouble."

"Why would you get into trouble?"

"Because I never saved Jamie."

"That doesn't make sense, does it?"

Amy blinked.

"Actually, it does make sense, if you're ten," Clare interrupted again. "Can't you remember what it's like to be a kid? You do think things are your fault, when actually you're not at all to blame. And sometimes you do get into trouble for things that you couldn't help. You don't think rationally, like an adult would."

"The thing is," Margaret said, ignoring Clare and directing her stare at Amy. "First you say one thing and then you say another. You told the police a while ago that the men who threw baby Jamie were miners and that it was all because Mr Donnelly was a… because he went back to work. Now you say it was these teenagers who're bothering you at nights. It's hard to believe a story that keeps changing."

"If you're upset by something," Clare interrupted, "you don't always remember it properly. I don't think turning this into an interrogation is helping. It's not like Amy killed the poor baby. She's trying to help you, so stop treating her like she's the one in the dock." Clare put a hand on Amy's arm. The girl was trembling.

Margaret said nothing for a moment. Then she made Amy tell her more about the gang of young people who were hanging around the estate. Amy said she thought she knew who some of the young lads might be. The whole thing took almost an hour and, at the end of it, Clare's head was aching. Amy slipped her hand into hers as they stood up to leave. It was hot and clammy. Clare could still feel the little girl shaking as they headed out to the car. "Well done," she whispered to her. "Brave girl."

"The police woman never believed me," Amy pointed out.

"She didn't say that," said Clare, although she knew it was true.

"She looked like she didn't believe me," Amy sniffed.

"You did your best. Sometimes the police forget that you're just a kid, or that you might not remember every bit in perfect detail. But it's over now, okay?"

At the newspaper office, only the duty weekend staff was in. Most of the desks in the long newsroom were empty. Nicki was one of the duty reporters. "Can you not stay away, Clare? Oh, hello, who's this?"

"Nicki, this is my friend Amy. She's come to watch the newspaper being printed."

"Oh, you'll love it. The first time I saw that I was really excited. I nearly wet myself when I saw my name in print."

Amy sniggered. Clare gave Nicki a mock-glare. "Come on, let's leave this very rude person behind and go down to the printing presses."

As Clare had expected, Amy went wide-eyed when she saw the huge reels of paper being loaded in. She stuck her fingers in her ears, laughing, when the machines started to whirr into action and watched with bright eyes and an open mouth as the newspaper pages rolled across the high rails and clattered off the presses, packaged up by the machines. The familiar smell of oil and ink made Clare smile. Nicki was right – you never got tired of watching the papers print.

One of the printers brought out a pile of early editions to take up to the newsroom. "Want the first one, then?" He handed a paper to Amy, who looked at it as if someone had handed her some newly-minted bank notes.

"Wow. I just saw that get made. That was amazing. Are you in here today, Clare?"

"Let's see." Clare leafed through the pages. "Yes, look. There's my name on this piece about the women raising funds to support the miners' strike." She was pleased with the show, which went across two pages towards the middle of the paper.

"I would love it. My name in the paper like that. It must feel amazing."

Clare was about to say the novelty had worn off. But she looked at Amy's eager face and said, "Yes, it is pretty amazing. Maybe that'll be you one day, eh?"

Amy nodded, with a child's confidence that nothing would stop her doing whatever she wanted when she was older. Clare hoped it wouldn't be knocked out of her too quickly.

She remembered the teachers at her own school telling her to give up her dreams of being a journalist. 'Surely,' the careers teacher had said, looking down her nose, as if Clare had said she wanted to be a stripper. 'Surely you can think of a loftier ambition than that? You want to spend your days sticking your foot in someone's door?'

It was the wrong thing to say to Clare, who quite liked the idea of sticking her foot in someone's door. Imagine being paid to get up people's noses. It sounded like it might be fun. And it was, for a long while. She couldn't tell Amy that she'd reached a point where it felt like something of a grind. That nothing was really new, in news, any more; that in local papers, the same sorts of stories came around again and again like fairground horses. And meanwhile many of the national papers seemed to be writing about worlds that she didn't even recognise, with a ruthlessness and an agenda she hadn't been trained to expect.

Back in the newsroom, Nicki told Clare a long version of how Catt had made her cry. "She was just shouting at me. I couldn't get a word in. I was trying to stop the paper printing a mistake and she wouldn't listen, she just shouted me down."

"She's a bully," Clare said.

Amy nodded wisely. "You should smash her face in."

"I should." Nicki let Amy sit at her desk and clack out some words on her typewriter. Clare grinned at Nicki as Amy's grubby index finger pressed down hard on the keys.

"Why are the letters all mixed up, I mean why isn't A at the start of the line? What happens if you make a mistake? How d'you rub it out? What do you do when you get to the end of your piece of paper?"

She liked the bicycle-bell pinging sound when the carriage lever was pressed and eventually, after taking several painfully long minutes to type 'By Amy Hedley', she lost patience and clattered her fingers all over the keys at random and laughed as she pulled the paper out.

"Ah well. Makes about as much sense as some of the

166

stories that get written in here," Nicki said. "It just takes practice, Amy."

"Like Teeline. So you get faster and faster?"

"That's right. Although some of us still only use two fingers."

"I would love a typewriter. Then people would stop saying my writing was messy. It would be brilliant. I'd practise and practise till I got super-fast."

Clare took Amy to a bakery for her lunch, where she tucked away an impressive amount of pastries, then drove her back to the estate. She resisted Amy's pleas to be allowed to stay with Clare for another night.

"Your mum will think you've left home," Clare said, as she stopped the car.

"She won't care."

"Don't be silly. Of course she will. She might've been ringing my home number while we've been out. Go on, off you go. I'll see you soon."

"When, though?"

"I don't know. Next week sometime, I promise."

Slowly, Amy got out of the car and turned to give Clare a mournful look.

"I said, I'll see you soon." Clare gave Amy a wave. "Remember to tell your mum about the police station."

Back at her flat, Clare put her head around the door of the little spare room. On the bed was a piece of paper with a drawing in felt tip pen. It looked a bit like a newspaper's front page, done in Amy's scrawl, and the mock-headline read: *Clare Is The Best!!! From Amy!!!*

Clare picked it up and took it through to her kitchen, where she pinned it onto her cork notice board. She was just wondering how to spend her evening when the phone rang. It was Finn.

"You're not going to knock me back two nights in a row," he said.

Clare smiled, surprised at how her insides felt full of

bubbles when she heard his voice. "You're right. I'm not. What do you want to do?"

They met in one of the quieter pubs just outside the town centre.

"You look great," Finn said, giving Clare a quick kiss on the cheek. "Tell you what, I was seriously grilled by my mother after you'd gone. You'd think I'd proposed to you, the way she carried on."

Clare folded her arms. "Really? When I was there I got the distinct impression they thought I was leading you astray. There was some reference to a girlfriend of yours?"

Finn nodded. "Jackie. We'd been going out for a long time. But it wasn't going anywhere."

"How come?" Clare kept her arms crossed.

"We'd known each other since we were at school. We'd drifted a bit, that's all."

"Why, though?"

"Honestly? I think she thought she was seeing someone with prospects. She's a lot less impressed with a striking trade union leader who hasn't had any money coming in for four months."

"That's a shame. Especially if you've known her so long."

"It was for the best. She'll see that, in the end."

Clare liked listening to him getting passionate about the strike, and the way he was more angry and raw about the subject than Joe, who looked at everything with a journalist's detachment. She noticed that sometimes Finn avoided answering the odd question about simple things such as his last job, but decided not to press him. I have to stop talking to everyone like I'm grilling them, she thought. This isn't an interview. I have to stop being so paranoid.

At the end of the evening, Clare found herself outside her flat with Finn enveloping her in a tight hug. "I should go," Clare said, freeing one hand to rummage inside her bag for her keys.

"Make me a coffee?"

Clare shook her head. "I'm done in. I've had a long day."

"It's Sunday tomorrow, no reason to get up early."

"There is for me. I've got some stuff to write up," Clare lied. "Honestly, Finn. Not tonight. Sorry."

Finn stepped back and shrugged. For a moment, he looked like he might be about to punch the wall. Then he shook his head and smiled.

Clare opened the front door as narrowly as she could and slid into it, closing it quickly behind her. That must have looked really weird, she thought. But having a kid in the flat is one thing: they don't really care about piles of rubbish and mess. Finn, on the other hand, would think she was some sort of mad hoarder who couldn't look after herself. Maybe that was true, to an extent. She stumbled into a pile of carrier bags lying in the hallway. She liked Finn. Part of her wanted to take the next step and ask him inside. The strange combination of her attraction to Finn and her urge to help Amy was having an unexpected effect, on her body and her head. For two months now, she'd felt like rock: cold, numb, unable to move. Now she could felt herself shifting, softening, giving way. It was good and it was terrifying, at once.

She ran the tap in the kitchen for a long time, waiting for the water to cool. Then she took a series of long gulps. She'd hardly had anything to drink over the course of the evening and she felt bone-tired. It had to be the heat.

The jangling, persistent phone ringing was the last sound Clare wanted to hear. She sat up slowly, clutching her head, and looked at the bedside clock. It was one in the morning. She swore as she threw herself out of bed and shuffled to the living room.

It was Amy. "Clare, Clare, you have to come over," she gabbled on the other end of the line. She sounded breathless and tearful.

Inwardly, Clare groaned. "What is it, Amy? Do you know what time it is?"

169

"No. Midnight or something. But you have to get here quick. Horrible things are happening. Please."

"What sort of things? What do you mean?"

"There are fires. And people are running round and smashing things up. I'm scared. Clare, please hurry up."

"Are you on your own again?"

"Max is here. But he's scared too. He keeps crying."

"Where's your mum?"

"How should I know? Clare, please?"

Somewhere behind Amy's voice, Clare could hear the sound of sirens.

"Okay then. Hang in there. I'll be as quick as I can."

She flung on some clothes and trainers. Then she picked up the phone and called the duty police desk. "Hi, it's Clare Jackson from the *Post*. Can you tell me what's happening on the Sweetmeadows estate? I've heard there's some trouble."

"Working late, aren't you?"

Clare swallowed back the urge to shout at the officer. "Yes, I am. Can you just give me an idea about what's going on?"

"Hold on." The phone went quiet for a few moments. Then the officer came back. "We're not making any media comments on Sweetmeadows at the moment."

"What do you mean, you're not making any comments? That's ridiculous."

"It's what I've been told to say to you. It's an ongoing situation."

"Fair enough. I'll go and find out for myself. Thanks a lot."

Clare dropped the phone with a growl. She was about to run out to the car, when a thought struck her. She didn't usually do this, as a matter of principle, but she decided to let someone know where she was going. She dialled Joe's number.

It took him what felt like many minutes to answer.

"I'm sorry to wake you up."

"This better be bloody good, Clare."

170

"It's going to sound daft but I'm about to drive out to Sweetmeadows, and… "

"Tell me you are kidding. Do you realise it's… Jesus, it's quarter-past one in the morning. Have you finally lost the plot?"

"No, the thing is, I've heard there's some trouble going on. It sounds bad."

"Stay out of it, then. Pick it up on your calls in the morning."

"I have to… I think I should go and see for myself."

"You're not expecting me to come with you?"

"Of course not. I just wanted someone to know where I was and I picked on you. Sorry. Wish I hadn't troubled you."

There was silence on the end of the phone, apart from Joe's breathing.

"Okay, so you can go back to bed now."

"I will." There was a curt click on the end of the line. Clare swore at the phone and ran out of the door towards her car.

As she drove into the road leading into the estate, Clare noticed a faint orange glow to the sky overhead. A row of police cones indicated the road was closed off, so she parked up and started heading into the estate on foot. A fire engine sat on the corner, its engine thrumming, and as she passed it she looked up to see if she recognised any of the crew.

One of them leaned out of the window. "Hey. You're not going in there on your own, are you?"

Clare looked up. "I have to. There's someone I need to see."

"I'd advise you to wait, love. It's not safe. We're not going in there ourselves at the moment and that's on the advice of the police."

"How do you mean, not safe?" Clare looked at the sky again. She could smell sulphurous smoke. "Something's burning. Surely you need to… "

"We've been in already. We were pelted with bricks and all sorts. We had to get out or one of our lads would have

171

been hurt. I'm telling you, don't go in there on your own."

"Who's doing it?"

"Group of kids, protesting about some mate of theirs who's been arrested, I gather."

"Are the police there?"

"Same problems. They're on the edges of the estate, waiting until things calm down."

"But... " No wonder Amy sounded so terrified and even that brute of a dog was scared. "You can't just leave the people who live there to sit and watch the place burn down around them, can you?"

"We're told the building that's alight is a derelict one, some sort of storage unit. As far as we know, there's no one in immediate danger. We can't go rolling in there and put ourselves at risk for that. We need to wait until things settle down a bit. That's on the word of the police too. We can't operate if we're being pelted with missiles, I'm sure you can understand that."

Clare looked across at the estate. "I still have to go and find my friend."

"I'm advising you not to go in there."

"Yes, but advising me isn't the same as stopping me, so thanks, but I still need to get in."

As she turned the corner, Clare could see two fires going on: one was a car that was burning itself out, and another was some sort of outbuilding, as the fireman said. The smell of petrol and smoke caught at Clare's throat and made her eyes smart. Little groups of people were standing around watching: older people standing back with their arms folded and younger kids running around in some sort of strange excitement, as if it was a late-night party. Across a wall, a sheet had been draped, and on it was painted the misspelled slogan *Craigy is Inocent*. Around a dozen teenagers were sitting along the wall, drinking from cans.

Walking across the square, Clare felt small and very exposed. She could sense that she cut a conspicuous figure, like walking into some sort of no-man's-land. A young lad strode towards her. "You live here?"

Clare shook her head. "No. But I need to go and find someone. What's going on?"

The lad pointed to the painted banner. "See that? Craigy's our mate. He got taken away today, for nothing. We want everyone to know that he's innocent."

"What happened to him?"

"Someone grassed him up for taking a bike or something. They put him in a van and he hasn't come back."

"So you're protesting?" Clare decided to take a gamble. "I work for the paper. I could write about this and get you some publicity." A small group of teenagers were circling her.

"Tell the paper this. Craigy is innocent."

"How old's Craigy? What's his full name?"

"Jason Craig. He's seventeen."

"Does he live here?"

"Aye, over there." A girl pointed up towards one of the flats. "He's not done anything."

"We want to know who dobbed him in it," someone else added.

Clare thought about Amy and hoped there was no way they'd be able to find out that she'd been talking to the police.

"Do you think," Clare asked, carefully, "that what you're doing might make things worse? Or that maybe you might be making people frightened?"

"Whose side are you on?" a girl asked, stepping nearer.

"No one's side. I just report things. Is anyone prepared to give me their name?"

Everyone shook their heads and the girl turned her back.

Clare looked up towards Amy's flat. She was sure she could see a small shape bobbing about behind the window. She ought to get up there.

As she turned to walk away, one of the teenagers tapped her hard on the shoulder. "Hey. What'll you be putting in the paper?"

173

"What you've told me. And I'll ask the police about Jas - er, Craigy."

"You can't say we started the fires. They'll get us too."

Clare held her hands up. "I didn't see who started anything. And I don't even know your names, remember? But why not let the fire crews in to put them out? Before someone gets hurt?"

She didn't wait for an answer but walked towards the flats, hoping she sounded more self-assured than she felt inside.

Amy practically leaped on her when she arrived at the door of the flat. "You've been ages."

"Amy, are you telling me your mum didn't come home at all, not since Friday? You've been on your own all this time?"

"You won't tell?"

"I keep promising that. I need to know, though."

Amy put her skinny arms around Max's thick neck. "I haven't seen her for a couple of days. She's probably staying at her boyfriend's, but I don't know where he lives."

"I don't suppose you have his phone number either?"

Amy shook her head. "So can I come to yours again?"

"I think you'll have to, for the rest of tonight anyway."

"What about Max? I think he knows something's going on. He keeps making whiney noises."

"I'm not allowed pets, Amy, I only rent the flat."

Amy hugged the dog a little tighter. "I can't leave him here tonight. He'll be scared. And I've run out of his food too. He's really hungry."

Clare sighed. "Have you got a lead for him? And a collar?"

"He doesn't like it."

"Tough. He's lucky I'm taking him at all. Get a lead on him and we'll get going."

Max had to be dragged down the steps. The shouting and the smell of burning were terrifying the animal. His loud whining was upsetting, even for Clare, who had no patience with dogs. On the ground, Amy squeezed herself up against Clare as they walked across the square, watched by all the teenagers. They had to stop again and again because Max kept sitting down and would only move with the combined pushing and pulling efforts of Clare and Amy.

As they rounded the corner, Clare saw that Joe was there, talking to the firemen. "There you are," he said. "You are a bloody liability. These guys told you not to go in there, didn't they?" He looked at Amy. "It's you. I might've known. What's going on?"

Clare paused. She couldn't say that Amy was on her own, not in front of anyone official. The firemen might talk to the police… "What are you doing here, anyway?" she fired back at Joe. "I thought you were getting your beauty sleep."

"Yeah, well." Joe shifted from foot to foot. "Once you woke me up, I couldn't drop off again."

Clare made a snorting noise. "Had to come and see what was happening, more like. I don't suppose you called a photographer out?"

"I did, as a matter of fact." Joe scratched his unshaven chin and looked down at Amy, who was half-hiding behind Clare. "So where are you two going?"

"I'm just giving Amy a lift," said Clare, carefully.

"Where to? Where's her mum?"

Clare was conscious of Amy tensing. "At an auntie's. Amy's mum went out and missed her last bus, so I'm just dropping her round there." Clare nodded back towards the estate. "Obviously Amy can't stay there tonight."

"Right." Joe didn't sound convinced. "When you've done that, do you want to swap some notes?"

Clare hesitated. "It'll have to wait until the morning. I'm worn out."

They tugged Max around the corner to Clare's car and pushed him into the back seat. He made a low whining sound as they drove away.

"He's really hungry." Amy said. "I gave him some Frosties but I don't think he liked that very much. It was all there was in the house."

175

"I don't suppose he did." Clare thought for a moment. "Okay, I've had an idea."

Clare parked outside Jai's newsagents and, as Amy waited in the car, used her office key to get inside. She picked up some cans of dog food and left the money on the counter. She'd come up with some sort of explanation to Jai the next day.

Then they drove back to Clare's flat and dragged Max inside. When Clare mashed the dog food into a bowl, the animal gobbled at it until the plate was clean.

"I've never seen a dog eat so fast," Clare said. "I think he'd better have another tin. He's a big beast, after all."

"Can he come into my room? Otherwise he might feel strange, in a new place all night," Amy said.

"I suppose so. Amy, we are not making a habit of this, okay? And you look pale. Go on, get into bed and take that brute in the room with you. Don't let him chew anything."

"Thanks, Clare."

Clare shook her head at Amy's back view as she headed for the spare room. This couldn't go on, she knew. If Amy was regularly being abandoned – for days on end, it seemed – then Clare was going to have to do something about it, or at the very least tell someone who could step in. She just wasn't sure what would happen to Amy after that.

Sunday 29th July

Clare managed to grab a couple of hours' sleep, but thoughts of all the writing up she would have to do prodded her awake at around six in the morning and wouldn't let her rest any longer.

She made breakfast for Amy while the little girl took the dog outside for a quick walk and then fed him again. Clare was glad she'd picked up several cans of dog food.

"Now then. I have to go into work to write up what happened at Sweetmeadows last night. We'll call your home, but I'm guessing your mum won't be back yet. So how about you wait here for a couple of hours, until I get back?"

"Yeah, great."

"You'll be sensible? Promise you won't go wandering off or anything?"

"Promise."

"Right. I'll go into head office." Clare scribbled the number on a piece of notepaper. "You can call here if you need me. I should be back around lunchtime. I'll bring something to eat."

And when I get back, Clare thought, we need to decide what we're going to do about you. I'm supposed to be the grown-up around here but somehow I've ended up helping keep your secret.

Joe pounced as soon as she walked into the office, shortly after eight. "Right. What the heck went on last night with you and that weird kid?"

"I told you. She phoned me and told me there was all this trouble going on. I went to do the story and then I thought I ought to take her to…"

"Her auntie? Yes, you said that. So where does this aunt live?"

Clare grabbed a sheaf of copy paper and slipped two sheets of carbon paper in between the leaves. "Not far from me, as it happens. That's why I thought it would be okay to give her a lift. I could hardly leave her there, could I?"

"How many times? That kid is not yours to sort out. You're going to end up in trouble yourself at this rate."

Clare fed the paper into the typewriter. "Want to share my notes? Or do you just want to go on and on like a poor man's policeman or something?"

Joe pulled a chair up next to her desk. "I'll share your notes."

"Good."

"For now."

Clare filled Joe in with the details of the teenagers and their friend's arrest.

"You get writing and I'll find you a police comment," he told her. "I'll even get you a coffee."

Clare gave him a quick smile as she started typing. She'd written around half of the story when Sharon Catt came in, followed by Chris Barber. Catt stopped dead and stared at Clare. "What are you doing in here? It's not your weekend on rota, is it?"

Clare shook her head, her fingers continuing to tap rapidly at the typewriter keys. "I was out at Sweetmeadows last night. I'm writing it up for tomorrow's first edition."

Chris Barber swore.

Catt shot a look at him, then turned back to stand over Clare, reading over her shoulder. Clare stopped typing and looked up. "Something wrong?"

"Yes, Clare, there is. I picked up the stuff about the Sweetmeadows disorder on my calls this morning and I dragged Chris in on his day off to cover it. I really think you could have let someone know what you were doing."

Joe walked up to the desk, a plastic cup of vending machine coffee in each hand. "The picture desks knew we'd covered it," he interrupted. "And we were out until the small hours of the morning, as it was all going on. You can't blame Clare."

"Don't tell me how to manage my news team, Joe."

"I'm only saying that… "

"Haven't you got your own stories to write?" Catt swept towards her desk and threw herself into her chair. She started to flick fast through the Sunday papers. Clare made a face at Joe, who turned and started to stroll, deliberately slowly, to the other end of the office.

"Looks like I'm a spare part," Chris said. "Again."

Clare stuck out her lower lip and mimed crying. She stopped before Catt looked up again. "You must have better things to do, then. When does the Olympic coverage start?"

"Not until late," Chris said.

"Yes, off you go," Catt interrupted. "There's no point in

paying for extra reporters on a Sunday. And Clare's jumped in yet again, without being asked. I haven't agreed this with you, Clare, so don't expect any overtime."

Clare bit back a reply and carried on writing. Joe came back when Catt left her desk and handed Clare a piece of paper with a typed police comment about the disorder.

The police say Jason Craig is still helping them with their enquiries into a range of offences. They urge young people on the estate to calm down and warn that anyone involved in any further disorder will be arrested and charged.

Joe had written *PTO* on the slip of paper. Clare flicked it over to read: *Seaton says he has something interesting to tell us. Come and see me when you've finished writing up.*

Clare raised her eyebrows, finished her final sentence and typed 'Ends'. She handed the copy to Catt and asked: "Okay if I go now?"

"I'm sure we'll manage without you. Hard as that is to believe."

Clare signalled to Joe and he followed her out to the car park at the back of the newspaper office. "Seaton wouldn't say what it was about over the phone. Just that we'd be interested."

At the police station, Seaton called for tea and it arrived with biscuits.

"This is the VIP treatment," Clare said. "What's going on?"

"I'm sorry, officer, she's a terrible cynic," Joe added.

"She is." Seaton dunked a digestive into his cup. "And here's me giving you a tip-off."

They waited as Seaton sucked at the soggy remains of his biscuit. "Inquest re-opening tomorrow morning on Deborah Donnelly."

"Only re-opening? I'd have thought you would be able to give a full report by now." Clare sat forward. "I'd assumed she'd taken too many sleeping pills."

"That's what everyone thought had happened. Who'd have blamed a mother who'd lost a baby for overdosing, accidentally or on purpose? Turns out there were pills in her mouth, not swallowed. There's been a bit of a delay with the lab reports. But we talked to Annie Martin again and there are a few odd things about how Debs was found."

"What do you mean, odd?"

"The front door was left open, for a start. Annie Martin says they don't leave their door open, especially since the family was targeted for breaking the strike. And there are signs that she struggled with someone. We're getting the pathologist to look at the case again. There's just a possibility she might have been suffocated."

nine

Clare and Joe looked at each other. "You're saying Debs Donnelly was murdered?"

"It's bloody difficult to suffocate yourself, I'd imagine."

Clare gave a quick smile. "Okay, but have you made any arrests?"

"Not so far."

"Any leads?" Joe was scribbling fast in his notebook. "Debs died on the evening of the protest outside your station, didn't she?"

"Annie Martin was there. Debs' mum. At the protest, I mean," Clare chipped in.

"And Rob Donnelly was at some meeting about work," Seaton carried on. "Nine or ten men can vouch for the fact that he was there till late. Until the police called to tell him about Deborah, in fact. His kiddies were with a relative who takes care of them sometimes when Rob's at work."

"So have the police got any thoughts?"

"We're talking again to the person who called the ambulance, just to see if we can piece together what might have happened. It was a friend of yours, in fact, Miss Jackson."

"Who?"

"The ambulance was called by young Amy Hedley's mother. It was the kiddie who raised the alarm. Apparently she looked in their window and noticed that Deborah Donnelly was lying on the floor. But then I thought you would know all that, seeing as how you and young Amy are thick as thieves."

Clare shifted in her seat, aware that Joe was looking at her. "I didn't know she'd been the one who actually found Debs Donnelly, no."

She thought back to the conversation on the night of the protest. All Amy and Tina had said was that Debs had been taken away in the ambulance. Poor Amy. That was probably something else she had nightmares about.

"So the police are nowhere near making any arrests?" Joe was saying. "I'm guessing you think there's a connection with what happened to Jamie, though?"

"We're working on those lines, obviously."

"Is it too late for any forensic evidence to be left at the scene?"

"We're looking for anything we can get."

"But most of it won't be there any more?"

Seaton coughed. "Do you watch a lot of detective shows on the TV?"

"All of them," Joe said, cheerfully. "So I'm guessing you'll be asking why no one took evidence straight away? Will there be another internal inquiry?"

"Our officers will have done what they thought was correct procedure at the time. We didn't seriously anticipate there being any other persons involved in Mrs Donnelly's death. I wish you lot would just do one story at a time."

Clare almost felt sorry for Seaton. He was doing a good impression of a man who was doing his best but being thwarted at every turn.

"And she definitely didn't take an overdose?"

Seaton reached for another biscuit and broke it in half. He mopped the crumbs into a small pile with his index finger. "We're still waiting for a report on what medicine was in her system."

"That's taking a long time, isn't it?"

"Cutbacks, Miss Jackson."

Clare frowned. "All the same... "

Seaton interrupted. "Not for publication, the original report got lost. Do not ask me to make a comment on that because it wouldn't be printable."

Joe gave a short laugh and tried, badly, to turn it into a cough. "You're really not having much luck with this whole thing, are you?"

Clare winced. "So will some of this, about the possible murder inquiry, will that come out tomorrow?"

Seaton nodded. "We've informed the family that we're working on a new line of inquiry. You can imagine their distress, given what they have already been through after the loss of young Jamie. So I don't have to tell you to respect their feelings when you go knocking on their door, which I am sure you're about to do."

"Just out of interest," Joe said, as they stood up to leave. "Any reason for the tip-off?"

Seaton gave an exaggerated shrug. "You know I like to keep my friends in the press happy. It would be nice if they paid me back with some friendlier pieces about the police, for a change."

Clare waited until they got back out to the car before saying anything. "I can't promise that," she said. "Seems to me the police are making an almighty cock-up of everything to do with Sweetmeadows at the moment."

"I'd say that's a fair comment," said Joe. "Shit. So another death-knock at the Donnellys. There must be better ways to spend a Sunday afternoon."

"Joe."

Joe turned to her, his hand on the car door. "What? Let me guess. The name 'Amy' is heading my way, isn't it?"

"She stayed at my flat last night."

Joe's mouth opened and closed. "Tell me you are kidding."

Clare shook her head. "She had nowhere to go. It was late and she was scared. I couldn't just leave her alone in the middle of all that stuff, could I?"

"I knew you weren't telling the truth last night. You're a pathetic liar. Don't give me those big eyes." Joe breathed out hard and swore. "Okay, listen to me. We'll go back and get her and take her home, on the way to door-stepping the Donnellys. And then listen to me, just for a change, and back off."

"But what if there's no one home again? I can't just leave her all on her own."

"If there's still no one home, that's neglect. We'll call the council."

"But I promised I wouldn't do that, Joe. She's terrified about being taken into care."

"That's tough. You'd still be doing the right thing."

Clare found her stomach churning as they drove back to her flat. As she turned the key in the door, Max gave one of the low barks that always made her shiver. The first thing that hit her as she pushed open the door was a smell of bleach. She held her breath.

"Amy?"

Amy bounced out of the kitchen. "Hi! You were ages. Can we go and eat? I am *starving*."

"What's that smell?"

Amy spread her arms wide. "I've been cleaning!"

"You have, haven't you?" Clare looked around. The place looked quite frighteningly tidy. "What's happened to - er - all my stuff?"

"I've cut all the by-lines out of the newspapers and thrown the rest of the papers away. I put your letters in a pile, over there. I took some stuff out of carrier bags and put it in your wardrobe. I never took the labels off though, in case you want to take anything back. My mam does that with clothes all the time. And then I dusted and I cleaned the bathroom and the kitchen. It was a right old mess, you know."

Clare stared around. "I don't know what to say."

Still standing on the doorstep, Joe gave a loud and

184

meaningful cough.

"Sorry. Come in, Joe. You remember Joe, who works on the morning paper?"

Amy looked at him and widened her mouth into a smile, but Clare could tell she'd rather he wasn't there. She suddenly felt the same.

"I've got an idea. Joe, why don't you head off to Sweetmeadows and see how far you get with the Donnellys? It might be better if there's just one of us. I think I owe Amy some lunch after she's done all this. And then I'll catch up with you, okay?"

Joe paused. "Fine. I'll wait for you in the square."

In other words, he was going to make sure that Clare took Amy home and came back without her. But at least she would have a chance to chat to Amy and, with any luck, to Tina, without Joe watching and butting in.

Once she was sure Amy had had her fill of fried chicken, chips and ice cream, Clare drove her back to the estate. On the way, she asked the question that had nagged her since leaving the police station. "You never mentioned it was you who found Debs Donnelly? And your mum called the ambulance?"

Amy's brow wrinkled up into tiny lines. "I thought I told you."

"Nope." As she drove, Clare glanced at Amy out of the corner of her eye. "That must have been very upsetting."

"Yeah, it was." Amy breathed onto the car window and started drawing a pattern on the clouded glass.

"So what happened, exactly? How come you found her?"

"I sometimes play with Becca and Bobbie. I knocked on the door and, when no one answered, I looked in the window. Debs was lying on the sofa and she looked all funny."

"On the sofa?" Clare was sure Seaton had said she was on the floor. "How do you mean, she looked funny?"

"Like, her arm was dangling down to the floor and her head was hanging off the sofa. I thought you wouldn't be able

185

to sleep like that, so I thought she must be ill. And her face looked a weird kind of white-y yellow-y colour."

"So what did you do?"

"I banged on the window to wake her up, but she didn't move. So then I went inside and gave her a shake, but she wouldn't move."

"Do you mind me asking questions about it?"

Amy shook her head and continued steaming up the window then doodling on it.

"Okay. So the door was open?"

"Uh-huh." Amy nodded.

"Was that normal? I mean, wouldn't it usually be locked?"

"Dunno."

"Right. When you tried to wake Debs up, did she feel strange? Like, did her skin feel cold?"

"No, I don't think so."

Clare thought about this for a moment. So Amy must have found Debs very shortly after she was killed. "Did you see anyone coming out of the flat, or anyone nearby?"

Amy shook her head.

"So you told your mum?"

"Yes, and she rang 999."

"Good girl. You did the right thing."

Clare thought for a moment. "Amy, I don't want to upset you. But the police think someone might've killed Jamie's mum."

She looked sideways at the girl. Amy rubbed out her latest doodles, so fiercely it made the glass squeak, but she said nothing.

"I want you to think really hard about that day. If you remember seeing anything else, you have to tell me, okay?"

Amy nodded. After a moment, she put her head down between her knees.

Clare glanced at her. "What's up?"

"I feel a bit sick," said Amy's muffled voice.

Clare tutted. "I thought that ice cream was a step too far.

186

I'll have to apologise to your mum."

When Tina came to the door of the flat, Clare breathed out. She realised that if no one was there yet again, she really didn't have a plan.

Tina, her hair short and newly white-blonde, held open the door for Amy and Max. "Have you had fun?"

"It's been brilliant," Amy said, tugging Max inside along with her. "We ran out of dog food though. I like your hair."

"Thanks for having her." Tina looked ready to close the door.

Casually, Clare slid her foot forward so that her toe would stop the door from closing fully. "Can I have a quick word, Tina?"

Tina didn't reply but just waited, the door still hovering halfway between open and closed.

Clare wasn't certain how to start the conversation. "Do you think Amy's okay? She was telling me about finding Debs Donnelly. I think she's still upset about that, and about the baby, of course."

"I think she's fine."

"You'll know about all the trouble on the estate last night? She got quite upset." And you weren't here, Clare thought, but didn't say.

Tina gave a little shake of her head. "She's got too much imagination, that's her trouble. She sees things that aren't there and she makes things up. Don't you worry about her."

"I need to tell you that she talked to the police about some of the troublemakers. I was with her. I hope you don't mind."

"Oh, aye? It's a bit late if I do mind, isn't it?"

"Well." Clare couldn't stop herself. "You weren't here to ask. Amy didn't even have a number for you. She was effectively looking after herself for two days. Longer."

Tina glanced behind the door and reached for a packet of cigarettes. She took a minute or two to take one out and light it up. She didn't say anything. She blew a stream of smoke

187

just past Clare's face. "Did she tell the coppers that?"

"No." Clare wafted some of the smoke away with her hand. "And neither did I. Tina, look. I'm not having a go at you. I don't know what it's like to bring up a kid on my own and I'm sure it's hard. But you just can't leave Amy for that amount of time. She's a clever kid, but she's too young. She's only ten."

"Nine, actually. I thought you were a reporter, not a frigging social worker. What's any of this got to do with you?"

"It wouldn't have anything to with me, except that I've been minding Amy for the last two nights. I couldn't just leave her on her own."

Tina threw her half-smoked cigarette onto the ground at Clare's feet and stamped it out. "You need to get your own life, pet."

Clare held up her hands. "Probably. But Amy's really great. I'm... I'm fond of her. Is there no one who can look after her when you go out? To make sure she's safe?"

Clare was surprised to see the start of tears in Tina's eyes. "What am I supposed to do, eh? She's not easy, that girl. If I bring a man back there's always trouble."

"What sort of trouble?"

Tina blinked rapidly to force back the tears. "None of your business. What am I supposed to do, live like a nun? I'm half-mad looking at these walls anyway. I need to get out."

"I'm sure. I'm not judging. I know it sounds that way, but I don't mean it to."

"I don't want her to end up in care. It happened to me, you know. When I was about Amy's age. I bloody hated it. So I don't want that for her. But... " Tina's voice went quiet. She flexed her fingers as if they were missing something, then reached for another cigarette. "But I don't always think I can manage. She's hard work. You'll have found that for yourself."

Clare decided not to contradict Tina. She was also aware

of a movement in the flat behind Tina and guessed Amy was listening in. "It won't come to that, will it? But stay with her tonight. There might be more trouble and she gets scared, that's all."

Clare turned at the sound of a loud whistle. She looked over the balcony to see Joe waving at her. "I need to go. It'll be okay to come and see Amy again, won't it?"

Tina nodded.

"She might have over-eaten, a bit. Sorry," Clare added. Tina didn't reply and Clare heard the door slam as she ran down the steps to meet Joe.

"You took your time," Joe grumbled. "But at least you haven't got a little street urchin hanging off your arm."

"She's hardly a street urchin."

"She's like an extra from *Oliver Twist*, if you ask me." Joe waved his notebook. "Anyway, I talked to Annie Martin. The police only told them yesterday that the cause of Debs' death is being treated as suspicious. And that was only because the family has been pressing them to release the body. They still have two funerals to arrange and no sign of anything being sorted out. They're furious, as you can imagine."

"That's awful. Share your notes?"

In Clare's office, Joe worked at getting one of the thickly-painted windows to open as he read quotes from a notebook propped on the sill. Eventually he swore and slapped his dusty hands against his trousers. "It's stuck fast, sorry. We'll have to swelter. Annie Martin calls the police a waste of space. At least, that's the printable bit of what she really said."

Clare nodded. "You can't blame her. Did they have any thoughts about who would want Debs dead?"

"I have to say Annie was rambling a bit. She's still blaming herself. If she hadn't gone out to that protest, she'd have been in the flat when whoever killed Debs turned up. But no, they have no idea who might've done it. Problem is, neither have the police."

"Was Rob there?"

"No. His sister and parents are looking after the kids between them at the moment. Rob's staying with them. Annie says he can hardly face coming back to the estate these days."

Clare loaded her typewriter. "Let's get this written up then."

By eight o'clock that evening, Clare was on her sofa, half-watching a film on TV and eating Chinese takeaway out of its box. Occasionally she stared round at her newly-tidied flat and enjoyed the thought of Catt's face when Joe handed her another sheaf of copy written by her least favourite reporter. Aggravating Catt could become a new mission in life.

There was a knock at the door and Clare opened it to find Finn, holding up a bottle of wine and some beer. "I heard you've been working hard, again," he said. "Thought you might want to unwind a bit."

Clare held the door open for him. "You can save me from Sunday night telly."

"Not a sports fan then? Not even for the Olympics? I thought all you women were quite happy to watch Daley Thompson."

Clare made an eye-rolling face and flicked the TV off. She poured the drinks into glasses. "You've heard about all this trouble at Sweetmeadows then?"

Finn stretched himself across Clare's sofa. "Can't say I'm surprised. You should take care going out there though, especially on your own. I'm surprised the paper lets you do that."

"I usually don't tell the newsdesk what I'm doing until after I've done it," Clare grinned. "That way they can't stop me." She sipped at the wine. "Anyway, how do you know I was out there on my own?"

"I have my spies. Well, actually, I was having a chat to a fireman who was out there last night. He spotted you."

Clare nodded. "They tried to talk me out of going onto the

estate. It feels like being back in Victorian times, the way you blokes go on."

"To be fair," Finn said, "they were talking everyone out of going there. Not just women. I heard the place was like the wild west."

"I was fine."

"You mean, you were lucky."

Clare shrugged. To change the subject, she went over to the record player and held up a couple of albums for Finn to choose from. They settled back on the sofa and Finn picked at the remaining carton of takeaway food.

"We had a great day collecting money for the strike fund," Finn told her. "We should have had the miners' gala today but it's been called off because of the strike. So we went out with buckets instead. You'd be amazed what people were giving us."

"You wouldn't think anyone had any money at the moment," Clare said. "Never mind the strikers. Highest ever unemployment rate since the Depression, wasn't it, just the other month?"

"That's right. In fact people were queuing up to give us money – actual fivers. And some of the lads are down in London today. They've got pots of cash down there. It's fantastic. We're bound to win, you know, with support like this."

"And women like your mum. I don't think even Thatcher would last five minutes in a room with her."

Finn laughed. "She's a force to be reckoned with, I'll give you that." He smiled. "She likes you, though."

"That's a relief."

"Yes. Because so do I." Finn leaned forward and in the fraction of a second that Clare had to wonder how to respond, the phone rang, the sound making both of them jump.

"Leave it," Finn suggested, as Clare wriggled off the sofa and went to answer it. She picked up the receiver and listened. There was noise on the other end of the line but no

191

one was speaking.

"Hello?" Clare said, twice. But the faint background noise went on. "Sounds a bit like someone's dialled and then left the phone off the hook. There's no one there but I can hear something in the background. A bit like a TV or something."

She put the phone down. Finn held open his arms. "Come back here."

Clare gave an apologetic smile. "Hang on," she said and went to lift the needle off the album, which had come to the end of one side and was making repetitive soft bumping and clicking sounds.

"I'll just… " she nodded her head towards the bathroom and scuttled towards it. Once inside, she examined her face in the mirror. It looked flushed. That would be the wine, she thought. She ran the cold tap and mopped her face with a cloth. It was time to make a decision.

She sat down on the sofa again, then leaned in closer to Finn. He placed a hand under her chin, tilted her face towards him and kissed her. The gentleness of it took her by surprise. She put her own hand up to pull his face closer, make the kisses deeper. A rush of heat went through her body and it felt like the first stirrings of real life, as if she was just coming out of some sort of cold, heavy paralysis. Finn stood up and pulled her lightly to her feet, and she led him by the hand into her bedroom.

Later in the night, as Finn lay asleep, the unfamiliar sound of a man's heavy breathing kept Clare wide awake. She slid out of bed and crept to the kitchen, where she poured herself a glass of water and added some ice. Something made her look at the telephone, and pick up the receiver again. She listened. The line still hadn't cleared and she could still hear the TV or radio noise rumbling in the background. She could also hear something else. It was the sound of a child, crying. More than crying, it was deep sobbing. Clare felt as if the receiver was glued to her ear. She couldn't move, even though the sound was almost too distressing to bear. "Hello? Are you there?

Can you speak to me? Are you all right?"

But no one came to the phone to speak.

Monday 30th July

Two Tribes on the radio alarm woke Clare up, earlier than she'd have liked. She smacked the snooze button just to stop the noise for a moment and sat up, her head feeling heavy and sore. She'd sat on the carpet, cradling the phone, until the early hours, until her limbs were numb, wracking her brains for anything she could do to help. But she couldn't think of anything. And when, eventually, the crying seemed to stop, Clare clicked the phone back into place and stumbled into bed for a disturbed night, hearing a child crying in her dreams.

Finn sat up, leaned over and kissed her tangled hair. "You didn't sleep so well."

"There was an alien in my bed."

Finn tried to pull her back under the sheets, but she twisted away, groaning, wishing she could sink back onto his body and lay her head on his chest, just above his heartbeat. She'd forgotten how good it felt to be so close to someone else. "I'd stay if I could. I have to go to work. I'm not idling around on strike like some people here."

Finn sat up with a sigh. "When can I see you again?"

Clare resisted the urge to say, just stay here, don't get dressed, wait for me to come back. "We'll see," she said, instead, enjoying his look of mock-anguish.

As she got ready for work, Clare knew she had to find time to call on Amy today. She had no way of knowing for certain it was Amy who dialled her number last night and whether that was Amy she could hear, or just some completely coincidental mis-dial. But she needed to put her mind at rest.

She called the newsdesk from the court. "I'm going to the inquest for Deborah Donnelly, which is going to say that the police are now saying it might be a suspicious death. It may not all go ahead, though."

193

"Okay. You cover the inquest and I'll send Chris out to talk to the family," said Catt.

"No need. I did that yesterday."

"Of course you did. Silly me, for imagining you might let anyone else get a look in."

"No need to thank me. Joe's dropping the copy off round about now."

Catt sniffed. "And here he is right at my shoulder. Did you synchronise your watches?"

Clare gave a false laugh. "I'll call you when the hearing's finished."

Inside the court, Clare gave a brief nod to a drawn-looking Annie Martin, who looked as if she was being held up in a standing position by the women who flanked her on either side. In only a couple of weeks, she'd lost a grandson and a daughter. Clare, who recognised that what she'd been through was nothing in comparison, felt like she was only just learning to function properly again. She couldn't understand how Annie even got out of bed in the mornings.

Joe ran up to the press bench and threw himself on a seat next to Clare, who grinned at him. "You gave Catt my copy then."

"I did," Joe said, quietly. "I'd like to say she said thank you. But she was too busy doodling a bloodied knife on her notepad."

"Can't think who she'd like to use that on, can you?"

"You're full of the joys this morning, aren't you?" Joe narrowed his eyes. "What's happened?"

"Nothing." Clare smiled again before the coroner walked into the room and they both stood up.

When the coroner heard the inquest was to be delayed again, he told Rob Donnelly and Annie Martin that his sympathies went out to them and that he hoped the police were doing all they could to bring matters to a swift conclusion.

"That's as good as telling them to pull their fingers out," Joe said, afterwards. "It's about as close as that old duffer will ever get to criticising the police."

"They're just bumbling around and getting nowhere fast. No wonder Seaton's got even more grey hairs than he had three weeks ago."

Clare dictated her copy from the payphone in the court canteen. When she'd finished, the copytaker asked her to wait on the line. Then she heard Dave Bell's voice. "Good work again, Clare. Are you about to head off on another story?"

"Not immediately. Have you got something for me to do?" Clare paused. "I thought this was one of your days off rota, anyway?"

"Obviously not. Unlike you, this is not where I choose to spend my days off. Anyway, can you just pop into head office? I need to have a word."

"Sure. Right now?"

"Now, yes."

"Should I be worried?"

"No, of course not. Just get your arse over here when you're told."

Clare laughed. She was delighted to have Dave back on the desk. Although it was odd that when she arrived, he put on his jacket and beckoned her out of the newsroom.

"Let's get out of here for a bit. We can chat without anyone listening in and I could do with some air."

Clare found her stomach twisting with nerves as she followed him to the nearest cafe. Any little chats, whether they were for praise or a complete bawling out, always happened in the full glare of the newsroom. Something was up. The few minutes of small talk about Dave's recent holiday were almost unbearable as Clare waited to hear what this was all about.

"Anyway, glad you had a good time. Expect you're pleased to see the back of those kids now, eh? And I'll be glad to speak to you instead of Poison, er, Sharon in the mornings. So... what's this in aid of?"

Dave stared into his coffee for a long moment. "Clare.

195

You've been doing some amazing stuff. I've been looking through and you've virtually filled the paper single-handed. We thought that you might like a little... a little bonus."

"Wow. Money?"

"Yes, I've talked to Blackmore and I've negotiated quite a generous chunk of... let's call it merit money."

"Amazing. That's got to be a first for the *Post*. I'm stunned. Thanks, Dave."

"Only there's a condition."

"How do you mean?"

"We want you to spend it on something specific."

Clare was baffled. The conversation felt surreal. "Such as?"

"A holiday."

Clare started to laugh. Then she stopped. "I don't understand. Is this some weird joke?"

"No joke." Dave couldn't seem to look Clare in the eye. "We all think you look exhausted. You've lost weight. Everyone's mentioned it. And you never seem to stop working. It's not good for you. You don't have anything to prove, Clare, not to me."

"I don't remember the *Post* ever being so paternal."

"I know. But I'd feel very bad if you... I don't know... had a car accident or something, through sheer exhaustion."

Clare tried to filter the information. That now-familiar wave of dizziness was washing over her. She couldn't understand why Dave was looking so uncomfortable. After all, he was giving her good news. Wasn't he? She rubbed her eyes and blinked to get rid of the shapes floating in front of them. "Umm, okay, thanks. I'll book something for a couple of weeks' time when things have quietened down a bit."

"No, Clare, now. You need to go now."

"Pardon?"

"The point of this is that you need to have a break right now. Starting this minute."

Clare felt her head start to throb. "I can't, Dave. There's

too much going on. There's a murderer, probably a double-murderer, on the loose in my patch. I don't want to take a holiday now, I'll do it when it's all a bit quieter."

"Clare, I'm your boss, remember? And I am telling you to take this money and go on holiday, and do it now. Understood?"

"No, I bloody well don't understand. Sorry," she added, aware that people in the cafe had turned to look. "I didn't mean to shout. But what's this really about?"

Dave sighed hard. "It's not just that everyone's worried about your health. Catt thinks your attitude's a problem. And she says no one's getting a chance to do any big stories because you keep jumping on them."

"You mean, I hear about them before our supposed chief reporter, because they're in the patch that she wanted me to cover? So I go and do stories from my own patch, and that's somehow a problem?" Clare took a long breath in and out. Her head reeled and she hoped she wouldn't disgrace herself by fainting.

"She's trying to give Chris a chance to find his feet. Usually, with something big like a murder, the chief reporter would cover it."

"Then he should start building up contacts, like I have. And then he'd get some exclusives. Like I do."

"It's not just the murders. Apparently last week Chris tried to do some feature relating to the miners' strike and the men told him they'd only talk to you. On the instructions of their union rep, apparently."

Clare pressed her lips together to stop herself smiling. Good old Finn. "I didn't know about that. But again, that's because I spent time building up trust. Chris will have to be patient."

"Can't you try to be a bit nicer to Sharon? Maybe not nicer, but a bit more respectful? That would be a start."

"It'd have to be mutual, Dave."

"You're one difficult woman. If you weren't such a good

197

reporter you wouldn't last five minutes. But listen, there is still the health thing."

"That's real? Not just an excuse to get rid of me for a couple of weeks to give Chris Barber a piece of the action?"

"No, it's real. We all agree that you look wrung out. I admit, Sharon wouldn't be so keen to give you time off if she wasn't championing Chris right now, but there it is. Jesus Christ, Clare. I bet you're the only person in the whole company who would find reasons to object to a paid holiday."

They caught each other's eyes and laughed.

"I'm not going, Dave. Not right now. Sorry."

"Don't make me insist, Clare. I don't want us to fall out."

Clare blinked again. She didn't want to be seen to cry. "You can't make me." She knew it sounded childish, even to her own ears.

"I think I can. But I would rather you agreed. At least go home for the afternoon and think about it. We'll speak again in the morning, eh?"

Clare didn't trust herself to reply, in case Dave picked up a catch in her voice. So she just nodded.

Back in her office, she called Finn. "I hear you've made me the designated strike reporter. Just wanted to say thanks."

"Like I said. It helps if we have someone we can trust." Finn paused. "Are you okay? You sound kind of flat."

Clare told him what had happened.

"I don't think he can force you to take a holiday when you don't want to. I'd challenge it, if that's how you feel. You in a union?"

"Yes. But the rep isn't exactly Arthur Scargill. Or you. I'm not sure how much support I'd get."

"Go and see him anyway and get your concerns written down. If they start victimising you, it's best to have a record from the start. Shall I come round tonight?"

"I'll be rotten company."

"I'll be the judge of that. See you later."

By the time Finn turned up, at around eight o'clock, Clare was even more on edge. She'd called round to see Amy, but there'd been no answer at the flat. She'd spoken to her union rep, who glumly said that it sounded as if she was being offered a very good deal and that he would be happy to swap places with her. And then she'd had a row with Joe, who'd also said he thought she should take a break.

"But by the time I get back, the killer could've been caught and there'll be no story. The miners' strike could be sorted out. I could be reporting school day trips and teddy bears' picnics for the rest of the summer."

"It doesn't matter. Stories come and go. You should take a step back, it'll be good for you," Joe said.

"I can't believe you're saying this. I thought you were on my side."

"I am. That's why I'm saying it."

Clare put the phone down without another word.

So when she answered the door to Finn, her first words were: "I hope that's a bottle of wine."

"No, I'm just pleased to see you."

Clare forced a smile. "I've had a horrible day."

She put her arms around his waist and leaned her head on him, breathing in his smell and the solidity of his body. Then Finn filled her glass and listened as Clare recounted the last few hours.

"Not joining me?"

"I have to drive back tonight, I've got an early start in the morning. But I'm happy to watch you drink it."

"Cheers, then." Clare took a deep swallow of wine and screwed up her face as the taste hit the back of her throat. "That's really nice. It tastes expensive. You shouldn't be spending your money on me."

"I want to."

"So what've you been up to?"

"Manning the new soup kitchen."

"Oh." Heat washed through Clare's whole body. "Shit. I'm

199

sorry. All my stuff is nothing compared to what's happening with the strike."

Finn shrugged. "It's important, if it matters to you."

"Yes, but… a soup kitchen. That's so… " She took another drink. "Hey, can I come and do a piece on it?"

"From a beach somewhere?"

"Hah. I'm not going anywhere. I've decided."

"Is that official?"

"It's official. They'll have to change the office locks and frogmarch me to the airport."

Clare's phone rang. When she picked up, Joe was on the line.

"Don't hang up, listen. The rumour is that the police have made an arrest and they're looking to charge someone tomorrow for the murder of baby Jamie."

"You're kidding me."

"Seaton won't confirm it yet. But more important, he won't deny it either. So it must be right. As of tomorrow, there'll be bugger all left to say about Sweetmeadows, until the trial. I think you can safely pack your swimsuit and get going."

"I don't know, Joe… "

"Think about it. You take them up on their very generous offer and head for the Med. And just as you do, the story dries up, so Chris Barber won't get a sniff at it. He'll be furious. You'll win, Clare."

In the kitchen, Finn made a point of clattering the glasses.

Clare gave him a wave. "I have to go. Thanks for the tip."

"But what're you going to do?"

"I'll decide in the morning. See you, Joe." Clare hung up the phone.

"He's quite fond of you, that Joe Ainsley," Finn commented.

"You know what? Every man I speak to alleges someone else is interested in me. I don't know what it is with men. Do you just see all women as some kind of Helen of Troy?"

"Just protective, I guess. You do have that sort of face.

Makes people want to look after you."

"It's pathetic." Clare fidgeted for a moment with the end of her watch strap and then checked the time. "Actually I might just make a quick call. And check out what Joe's been saying."

Finn closed his eyes. "Can't you just leave it?"

Clare gave an apologetic shrug and picked up the phone.

The desk sergeant was someone Clare knew. "Jack, hi. I know it's late. Is your chief inspector still around?"

"He is. But he's very tied up."

"That's fine. Can you just confirm for me – off the record, if you like – whether someone's been arrested for the Jamie Donnelly murder?"

"Off the record?"

"Promise."

"It's more complicated than that. We did make two arrests. But something went a bit wrong. I can't say what, not right now. But there's trouble on Sweetmeadows estate again, as a result. We're about to go in to try to calm the situation down."

"Something went wrong? What, exactly?"

"That's all I can say. I shouldn't even be saying that. You'll find out soon enough without me risking my job."

"So what's happening out on the estate?" Clare thought of Amy and hoped she wasn't alone.

"It's a repeat of the other night. Cars are being torched, the fire bobbies are being lobbed with bricks when they try to get near. Kids roaming around, out of their heads and looking for trouble."

"And this is because of the arrests?"

"That's the excuse. But you know that place. It's a tinderbox. It's a riot waiting to happen."

"Thanks, Jack."

"Don't quote me. And I wouldn't go out there tonight. It'll be bad. Let things simmer down."

Not likely, Clare thought.

Finn was drumming his fingers on the edge of the sofa.

"Sorted out?"

"Sorry, Finn. There's more trouble on Sweetmeadows. I think I'm going to have to go out there."

"Now?"

"Sorry."

"You've had a drink."

Clare swore. "I'll have to get a taxi then. Unless... " She gave Finn a hopeful look.

"Jesus. Yes, I can drive you. And keep an eye on you at the same time."

Clare gave Finn a quick hug. "You're a star."

Finn took a back route to the estate. The night sky looked as if it was on fire itself, the rust-coloured glow was so vivid. The hellish smell of burning made them both cough before they'd even opened the car door. There were sounds of bikes buzzing around. And shouting.

"There are no lights on in any of the flats," Clare said. "Why's that, do you think?"

A man was running towards them. "Finn, man," he said, holding out a hand for Finn to shake. "How did you know?"

"Know what, mate?"

"George Armstrong's having an asthma attack. We can't get an ambulance to him."

"How come?"

"The bastards have taken out the sub-station. No one's got any leccy. Can you run us to the hospital, Finn, mate?"

"Jesus Christ." Finn looked at Clare.

"Take him," she said. "Go. I'll be fine."

Finn's friend seemed to notice Clare for the first time. "Don't stay here on your own, pet. It's bad, bad stuff." He pointed to the concrete balconies behind them. The words *PIGS MURDERERS* were sprayed across them in red.

"What's that about?"

"Some young lad got arrested. And now he's dead. Managed to top himself in the police cell. At least that's what they're saying, the pigs." The man's words came out so fast

Clare could only just make them out.

"Jason Craig?" Clare asked.

"Aye, Craigy, they call him. They're saying the police wanted to lay the baby murder on him. But he's no more than a bairn himself. Sixteen, seventeen, something like that."

"So that's what this is all about?" Clare looked around. The doors to the little mini mart on the outside edge of the estate were wide open, all its windows were smashed and, although it was in darkness, she could see the shelves had been stripped. A couple of young lads were kicking around inside, trying to see if anything was left. Where the hell are the police? Clare thought. It's complete anarchy.

"Finn, mate, we need to go." The man was panting and sweat was running down his face.

Finn turned to Clare. "I'll get George to the hospital and I'll be straight back. Don't do anything stupid."

"Off you go." Clare waved Finn away and watched as he ran towards a ground-floor flat, along with his friend.

Clare stared around. The fires, the stripped-out shop and the way all the flats were blacked out made the place look like a scene from some far-off war zone. The dark air was thick with the smell of smoke and chemicals. The lightless windows all around made it look as if the whole estate was closing its eyes to what was happening. She walked towards a small group of teenagers hanging around the edge of the square.

"It's you again," a girl said. "You following us?"

Clare shook her head. "I just heard there was trouble. Can you tell me what's happening?"

Some of the lads turned away. One pulled a cap low over his eyes. "Craig's dead. The police killed Craigy."

"I heard he killed himself in the police cell. What did you hear?"

The girl stood close to Clare, right in front of her face. She was a little taller than Clare, with fierce, furious eyes. Clare smelled alcoholic sweetness on her breath. "They wanted to

203

fit him up for the baby murder. So they've done him in, that's what's happened. Or they've sent him mental. So now he can't talk back."

"You're saying the police killed Craigy? But why did they think he'd killed the baby?"

"They don't, not really. They can't. They just wanted someone to blame."

Another girl tapped the teenager hard on the back. She had what Clare always called the 'hard-girl's-hairdo' – a tight ponytail stretched high on top of her head – and she was clutching a can. "Don't talk to her, you stupid mare."

The first girl gave a direct glare into Clare's eyes and they turned and moved away. Clare knew better than to argue. As she walked away, she pulled her notebook out of her pocket and started scribbling down a few notes about the scene. *Graffiti: 'Pigs Murderers'. Torched cars still alight. Shop looted and stripped. Power cut after fire at elec sub-station. Friends claim Craigy is innocent. Stench of burning.*

Glancing behind, she was aware of the little gang of teenagers following her at a short distance. She stuffed the notebook back inside her pocket and kept walking. She could knock on Amy's door, just to make sure she was okay, and then she could make a phone call to Stewie to see if he was up for driving out and taking some pictures. Trying to look confident, she quickened her stride towards the stairs that led to Amy's floor.

She didn't quite make it to the stairwell. Someone ran up behind her, pulled at her shoulder to stop her walking, then kicked at the back of her knee, making her buckle and fall down to the ground. She felt a foot on the small of her back, pushing her flat down onto the concrete. Her skin grazed on the ground and she tasted grit in her mouth. She held her breath as the foot pressed down harder.

"What were you writing in that book?" It was the voice of the second girl, the one who'd warned the other not to talk to Clare.

"Nothing about you," Clare muttered, wincing at the pain in her leg and hands.

The girl kicked her hard in between the shoulder blades. "Give us the book."

"No way." Clare rolled over a fraction so that she was pressing down on the pocket with the notebook. The girl crouched down, put her knee on Clare's back and tried tugging on Clare's arm, but she stiffened and refused to budge. In the next moment, her head was wrenched backwards as someone pulled hard on her hair. Instinctively she put both hands up to her head and then doubled up as she was repeatedly kicked in the back, thighs and stomach. Spasms of pain were shooting through every muscle and limb. She tried calling out, but the sharp ache in her stomach made it difficult to catch enough breath to make a noise. Someone grabbed her fingers and forced them backwards and as she tried desperately to move her hands back with them, to stop her fingers breaking, she felt someone pull the notebook out of her pocket. At the same time, the weight came off her back and her hands were released. Slowly, her eyes streaming, Clare tried to push herself up, her numbed arms and fingers barely taking her weight. She watched, shaking but unable to act, as the girl pulled pages out of the book, without looking at them, and tore them into little pieces. She scattered the papers across the ground.

Another young girl turned back to Clare and gave her a hard thump that landed on the side of her face and made her fall back down to the ground again, clutching her head. She lay there, pain pounding through her whole body, no longer trying to fight tears. The agony in her head washed over her, wave after blackening wave.

ten

Slowly, Clare became aware of someone calling her name. "Clare. Clare!"

She blinked repeatedly, unable to focus properly, and raised her head, groaning. Amy was standing over her with tears running down her little face. In her hands, she was clutching as many pieces of torn paper as she'd been able to find. "I've got some of them back for you," she said. "The fucking bastards."

Clare gathered her thoughts together enough to say, "Amy!"

"I'm sorry, Clare," Amy said, in a tone that suggested she was the one doing the telling-off. "But that's what they are."

Clare pushed herself to her feet and brushed herself down, screwing up her face and moaning involuntarily. Everything throbbed.

"Look," Amy said. "Here's your friend."

Finn was running towards her. He came to a stop and Clare thought she saw him visibly blanch. "There's an ambulance on the edge of the estate, but the crews have been told not to come in. Let's get you there. Can you walk?"

"Of course I can." That wasn't quite true. Her legs felt reluctant to move and there was a searing pain across the side of her head. "And I don't need an ambulance, I just want to get home."

Finn took her arm. "What the hell happened?"

Clare took a step forward and wobbled. She clutched at Finn. "Hang on. I just feel a bit sick."

"Have you... does your back feel okay?"

Clare closed her eyes and tried to breathe slowly. "Nothing feels okay. How's George Armstrong?"

"In good hands. Never mind him. I think we should get the paramedics to check you over. "

"Don't be silly. I've got a few bruises, that's all." Clare shivered, although the night air was warm. She tried to suppress the urge to vomit. "And I feel like a prat."

"This isn't your fault." Finn put his arm around Clare, and she gave him a small smile.

"Though you probably shouldn't've got your book out when you did," Amy chipped in. "You should've waited till they couldn't see you."

Finn stared down at her. "What's your part in all this?"

Amy shrugged. "I was watching, that's all. If you want to get the bastards I know where they went."

Finn followed the direction of Amy's eyes.

"Hey," Clare said. "I'd just like to go home, if that's okay. I don't want anyone getting anyone else, you hear me?"

Amy made a disgusted *puhh* sound. "Want these?" She held out the crumpled, torn shreds of paper.

"Go on then. Thanks for picking them up." Clare stuffed them into her pockets. "I take it your mum's out again?"

Amy thought for a moment. "No, it's okay. She's in the house."

"So how come she's letting you wander around at... " Clare looked at her watch and squinted, her eyes taking a while to focus. "Around half-one in the morning?"

"She's asleep."

"She's asleep? Through the power going down and the fires and all this racket out here?"

Amy nodded. "Yep."

Finn coughed. "I think we should get out of here, Clare.

Think about yourself right now."

Clare squinted at Amy. "Promise me? Promise you're not on your own in that flat?"

Amy shook her head. "Uh-uhh. I'm fine."

Clare didn't entirely believe Amy, but she was too wracked with pain to argue. "Go to bed then. I'll come and see you tomorrow, I promise."

Clare looked around. The place was still in darkness but there were fewer people around. The trouble seemed to be damping itself down.

They started to move slowly forward again, Clare hobbling and gritting her teeth.

"Hang on," said Finn, stopping. He scooped his arms under Clare's legs and round her shoulders and lifted her up. Clare made wincing noises. "You don't have to do this, I can walk."

Finn strode forward. "It's like carrying a little bird," he said. "Tell me if I hurt you."

Clare tucked her head under his chin and closed her eyes, grimacing at the way every movement caused fresh agony. "What I want to know is where the police were? Not a sign of them anywhere."

"They're around, but they're on the edge of the estate," said Finn, pausing for a moment to hoist Clare a little closer to him. "The main roads into Sweetmeadows have been blocked off. I spoke to one of the lads and he said it was orders from on high, not to actually go into the estate. For their own safety."

"Never mind anyone else's safety," Clare grumbled.

"To be fair, you were warned not to go in and you took no notice. Not that I'm taking the pigs' side," Finn said, quickly, as Clare gave him a sharp look. "Plus, they're short of manpower. It's their own fault, because they've shipped a load of officers off to earn the big money on picket duty down in Yorkshire. So they were caught on the hop when this all kicked off. It took them an hour or so to get some extra officers together."

208

Clare tried to breathe slowly, to calm the pains shooting across her head and body. It had no effect. "Meanwhile the place is going up in flames and there are old men having asthma attacks who can't get an ambulance. And families with kids and no electricity in their flats. That shop is the only one that's actually on the estate, and it's been torn apart. If the police aren't supposed to move in when all that's going on, I don't know what they're there for."

Finn stopped walking. Clare spotted two paramedics walking towards her.

"Hey. How are you doing?" one of them said.

"I'm fine. A bit sore, that's all." Finn lowered her gently to the ground and, as she placed her feet on the pavement, she clutched at him for balance. Her head swam.

The young woman paramedic took her arm. "Can you walk over here to our ambulance? We'd just like to give you a quick once-over. I'm Jill, by the way."

"Hi, Jill. I really don't need a once-over," Clare argued, but she let herself be lifted into the back of the ambulance. Jill examined her bruises and gently felt the side of her jaw. Clare cringed as more spasms bolted through her head. She touched the tender skin on her face and checked her fingers to see if she was bleeding. Jill shone a small light into Clare's eyes, which started to water.

"I'd be happier if you spent the night in hospital. You're badly bruised and you've hit your head, so I'd feel more comfortable if someone was observing you for the next few hours."

"I'd feel more comfortable if I could just go home and have a shower and get into my own bed."

Jill ignored this. "Are you coming with her?" she asked Finn, easing Clare down onto a stretcher and propping her head and shoulders up. Finn nodded.

"I get no say in this, obviously." Clare watched as the ambulance doors were closed. She felt too weak, sore and exhausted to put up a real fight.

Tuesday 31st July

The sound of a trolley clattering with tea cups woke Clare with a painful jolt. When she'd worked out where she was, rather slowly, she closed her eyes again with a moan. Everything still ached, or at least that was how it felt, on every part of her body. A nurse leaned over her and asked, in a whisper, whether she wanted a cup of tea. Clare nodded, wondering why the nurse had bothered to lower her voice when the trolley made enough noise to wake everyone along the whole corridor.

Clare asked the time and was told it was just after eight in the morning. "Damn. I'd better get to work," she said, slowly pulling back her sheet. She had a vague memory of being helped into the hospital nightgown and hoped that by that point Finn had gone home.

"I don't think so," said the nurse, holding up a hand. "The doctor needs to see you before you go."

"I can't wait very long then," Clare said, sitting back with her tea, hoping her head would stop spinning if she lay still for a moment. "I'll be in trouble if I'm late for work."

The nurse gave Clare a long look. "I've seen you before," she said. "Recently. Am I right?"

Guilt made Clare's skin prickle. She hadn't recognised the nurse, but it was possible that she'd been on duty two months ago, when Clare had to be admitted as an emergency.

"I don't think so," she said.

The nurse frowned and looked at Clare closely. "I'm sure I am," she said. "I don't get faces wrong. I'm sure you came in…"

"It wasn't me," Clare said quickly. "I just have one of those faces, everyone thinks they've seen me before from somewhere. Common, I think they call it."

The nurse laughed. "Well, you should know whether or not you've been in hospital recently. But you shouldn't be fretting about work. I can call someone for you and tell them you're here."

Clare shook her head. "No need. I'm fine to go to work, really."

"You don't look fine to me." It was Joe's voice.

"What the hell are you doing here? How did you even know I was here?"

"Bob Seaton told me. You went out to Sweetmeadows last night, in spite of people telling you not to do it, and you got beaten up by a bunch of toe-rags who thought you were about to dob them in to the police. Well done, Clare. That's a prime piece of fuckwittedness, even for you."

"That's a warped version of what actually happened. Nurse, is he even allowed in at this time of the morning?"

Noisily, Joe scraped a plastic chair to the side of the bed. "Yes, I am, because I called the ward sister and asked if I could drop in before work. I'm quite ready to believe that I don't know the whole story. Does the name Amy Hedley feature in it, by any chance?"

"Not in the way you think. I went out to do a news story on the mini-riot that was going on. Amy had nothing to do with that. She only turned up at the end. She tried to rescue the pages from my notebook, bless her."

"I'm told you're lucky that you didn't get a broken jaw. Or even a brain injury."

"Really." Clare folded her bruised arms and glared at Joe. "You know, I could do without this kind of bedside manner."

"And I gather the boyfriend was with you. Fat lot of use he was, the big tough miner. Letting you get beaten up by a bunch of kids."

"Actually, Finn was taking George Armstrong to hospital. He had a serious asthma attack and Finn probably saved his life. Get your facts right before you write the headlines."

"You're not expected at work, by the way. I spoke to Catt this morning, as soon as I found out."

"Throwing a party, is she?"

"Don't be like that. If nothing else, this is going to make you have some time off. Every cloud and all that."

"That's not the way I see it."

Joe put a morning paper on the bedside table. "I thought you'd rather have this than flowers."

Clare gave him a weak smile. "I would. Thanks. Hey, what did Seaton say about this young lad dying in the police cells?"

"They're saying he managed to hang himself with something. They're not telling us what he used. But he was only seventeen. Seaton says the team interviewed him about Jamie Donnelly and he got very distressed, so they put him in the cell to calm down. When they next went to check on him, he was dead. Of course, he shouldn't have been left with anything that meant he could do himself harm. There's another inquiry hanging over Seaton's head. He looks like a man with the world on his shoulders."

"And do they really think this Craig lad killed baby Jamie? Why would he do that?"

"Seaton says he could have been off his head on some sort of drugs. But he's going to have trouble making that stick."

"It fits with Amy's story, that's for sure. But it just doesn't seem like enough of a reason. What did he say about all the trouble on the estate?"

"It was a policy. Contain the trouble, don't confront it. So they decided to let it burn itself out, literally. Risky, I think. Questions are being asked."

"Yes, by me, apart from anyone else."

Joe stood up. "I have to go, but I'll call later to see how you are. Try to stop thinking about work. If they do let you out, I can come and give you a lift home."

"That won't be necessary, thanks."

As soon as she was sure Joe had gone, Clare slipped out of bed and hobbled slowly along the corridor to the payphone. She called the paper and sweet-talked the receptionist into accepting the charges, then asked to be put straight through to a copytaker. She dictated the story of the night before, with Seaton's comments added on, courtesy of Joe.

212

"If you wouldn't mind just dashing all that along to the sub-editor, so they can get it in the first edition, that'd be great," Clare said, crossing her fingers. The copytaker said she would and Clare hoped that, with luck, the sub would just lay the piece out for that day's paper, without it having to be okayed first by Dave Bell or Sharon Catt.

Later the doctor told Clare that they wanted to X-ray her jaw to be absolutely certain that there were no fractures. "We can't do that until mid-afternoon, I'm afraid. So if I were you I should settle down with a magazine and try to rest. Don't worry, it really looks like you've got away with it. But we just want to be sure we're not missing anything."

Clare dozed for a while, but only minutes after she woke up she felt she would go mad with boredom. Just after two, Finn arrived, with some roses wrapped in paper.

"You shouldn't have bought flowers," Clare said. "They're a waste of money."

"They're from my mother's garden," Finn said, sheepishly. "She said you'd like them anyway."

"I like them better, then."

Finn gave Clare a light kiss on the top of her head. "How're you doing?"

"I just want to get out. Hey, you could drive me back?"

"Not until we're happy," said the nurse's voice behind her. "You know, I was sure that you were here before and the reason I remember it is because you discharged yourself. Against advice. Are you sure... "

"Really, that wasn't me. It must've been my evil twin."

The nurse laughed. "If you insist." She turned to Finn. "Don't take her anywhere until the doctor says she can go."

Behind the nurse's back, Clare made a stabbing motion with her hands.

"I feel responsible for last night," Finn said. "I shouldn't have left you on Sweetmeadows on your own, not when things were so tense. It could have been so much worse."

"Stop beating yourself up, it was my decision." Clare

213

squeezed his hand.

"My mother's the one doing the beating-up now. She actually cuffed me across the head when I told her what happened. Called me an idiot for not looking after you."

"I like your mum, so much."

Finn grinned. "Call me when you can escape. Promise?"

Clare nodded.

Finn turned to go, then fished in his pocket. "Oh," he said, as an afterthought. "You dropped these." He put Clare's keys on the bedside table.

After the X-ray, Clare decided not to wait for the results. She was heading down the corridor away from the ward when she spotted Dave Bell walking towards her. She swore under her breath and tried to duck into a side ward, but it was too late. He'd seen her. He waved a rolled-up copy of the *Post* at her.

"I should hit you with this," he said. "What do you think you're playing at?"

Clare widened her eyes. "What?"

"I had no idea you'd written this story about last night's riots, or whatever you want to call them. And nor had anyone else, until we opened the first edition."

"I sent something over to the copytakers. Didn't they show it to you?"

"No, because you told them to take it straight for subbing. You're a sneaky cow."

"What's wrong with it?"

"There's nothing wrong with the copy. It's great, as always. You write better with concussion than most of the reporters do when they're fully *compos mentis*. That's not the point, as well you know."

"I haven't got concussion. Look at me, I'm fine. I'm being set free."

"Remember the conversation we had yesterday? And that was before you hit your head. I haven't changed my mind. I want you to take a break."

"But…"

Dave brandished the rolled-up newspaper again. "Go home, Clare. Don't come back for at least a week. That's an order."

Clare went out into the hospital car park and for a few moments wondered why she couldn't remember where she'd left her car. Then, cursing, she recalled being brought here by ambulance and that she hadn't asked anyone to give her a lift home. She hailed a taxi.

Inside her front door was an official-looking letter, a folded-up piece of notepaper and a small, crumpled paper bag. Inside the bag were some grubby-looking sweets: a slightly squashed Anglo Bubbly gum and a candy banana with a distinct thumbprint on it. The folded paper was a makeshift card from Amy. It had a drawing of what was clearly meant to be Clare lying on the ground next to an ambulance and it said *Get Well Soon! Come Back! Love Amy!!!* in multi-coloured felt-tip pen across the front. Inside there was a message written in Amy's attempt at Teeline. It read: 'Git well son. There is a fat man going round pretending do be a reporter. I've told no one to tack to him. Amy.'

Clare couldn't help giggling. She enjoyed imagining Chris Barber trying to persuade people on Sweetmeadows to talk to him, his sports car parked up somewhere out of sight of the local kids, wondering why he was getting what Joe liked to call the bum's rush. She sniffed at the bubble gum, its synthetic, chemo-sugary smell coming through the wrapper on to her fingers. She remembered how, to a child of Amy's age, sweets were such important currency. Giving someone one of your sweets, with nothing like-for-like in return, was a big deal.

Minutes later, she wondered how Amy had got to her flat to drop the things through the letterbox. Without a car, Amy would have had to walk a few miles or else get two buses. Clare gently touched the top of her head and gave out a small moan. Her brain felt fogged: this should have been her first thought, not something that occurred to her quite so slowly. She really needed to know that the little girl was okay.

Idly, Clare tore open the brown envelope. Usually, she would have thrown it on top of her growing pile of unopened mail, but she couldn't, for the moment, see where that was. The place seemed half-empty. It was from her electricity company, saying that her supply would be cut off within twenty-four hours, due to non-payment of her bills. She read it a couple of times, rubbing her temples, wishing that she could trust her brain to work properly. Then she sighed and picked up the phone.

When she got through to the right department, Clare started a rambling story about forgetting to pay because of problems at work.

"There's nothing to worry about, Miss Jackson," said the voice on the other end of the line. "The bill's been paid in full. You don't owe us a penny."

"No, I really haven't paid it," said Clare. "I'm behind with all sorts of things. I haven't got round to paying any bills lately. You must be looking at the wrong account."

The voice read out Clare's address and account number. "That bill was paid in cash, at one of our branches this morning." The voice paused and Clare sensed the operator was smiling. "I wouldn't argue about it, if I were you."

"Right. No, I guess not."

As soon as Clare put the handset down, the phone rang again. Clare shuddered at the noise. She had more of a headache than she wanted to admit. But she was delighted to hear Amy's voice on the other end of the line.

"Wow, Amy. You must be telepathic."

"Telly what?"

"I was just thinking about you. Thanks for the sweets and the card. That was thoughtful."

"I've got a story for you. I know what happened to Craigy."

"The lad who died in the police cell? Go on."

"The police sent him doo-lally. So he hung himself with

216

his shoelaces."

"What do you mean, the police sent him doo-lally? And how do you know this, anyway?"

"You know his friend, well, I know his little brother, and he told me... "

"Slow down. I've got a sore head, remember? Who's his friend?"

"His friend is Stevie Simpson. He got nicked along with Craigy. Stevie's brother Liam's in my class at school."

"Right. And Stevie's back home now?"

"Yeah, they let him out. And he told Liam... well, he told his mam, and Liam was listening, that the police did this awful thing and Craigy went ballistic."

"What exactly did the police do?"

Amy took in a deep breath. "They threw a baby down on the floor in front of him. To make him remember what he'd done."

"Amy. That doesn't sound right. The police wouldn't do something like that."

"Liam says they did. He says it was all wrapped up in a blanket and they threw it down at him from the stairs at the police station. And blood came out. He says Craigy went off like a bomb and it took three coppers to hold him down and get him back in a cell."

"It couldn't have been a baby, Amy. I think your friend Liam is making this up."

"He's not. He's not very nice but he doesn't tell fibs like that, he's too dumb to even make them up. He says Stevie keeps crying and shaking and his mam's had to have the doctor out to give him a pill."

Clare tried to imagine how something like this could happen. "Could it have been a baby doll, do you think?"

"Nuh-uh, because it had blood, remember? Stevie said there was a big puddle of blood on the floor."

"Hmm. I'm not sure I'm buying it. And Liam just told you all this? Maybe Liam was trying to scare you?"

"No, I had to pay him. Well, I had to give him a Twix. So I haven't got any sweets left, by the way."

"You shouldn't give people sweets or money for stories." Clare stored the phrase 'choc-book journalism' for her next conversation with Joe. "You see, it might make them ramp up their stories, so they feel they deserve the payment."

"Oh." Amy paused for a moment. "But is it a good story?"

Clare sighed. "Sort of. It's a good story if I can stand it up. I mean, if I can get someone to tell me, for sure, that it really happened. Someone other than Liam, obviously. But that might be a problem."

"What about Liam's mam?"

"She wasn't there. And it just sounds so... far-fetched."

"Right."

Clare could almost hear the waves of Amy's disappointment surging down the phone line. "Listen, though, you did an amazing job for getting the story. A Twix is a good price. Newspapers sometimes pay thousands of pounds for stories. And if your story is true, it's a cracker. You around tomorrow?"

"I'm not going anywhere. You have to be a miner's kid to get a day trip out round here."

"Okay. I promise to come round and bring some sweets, how about that?"

"*Yessss.*"

Wednesday 1st August

Clare woke up after a night on the sofa, every limb still pulsating with pain and every movement making her groan out loud. She couldn't even remember falling asleep, but it was sometime after fielding phone calls from Finn, Joe, Nicki and Dave Bell. She'd promised all of them in turn to go straight to bed, to call if she needed anything and definitely not to go to work the next day. In the shower, the extent of her bruises took her by surprise, as did the tenderness of her scalp as she washed her hair. She was trembling so hard as she put on her clothes, it felt as if they were all that were holding her together.

218

Over a coffee, she tried to work out how best to spend the day. It would have to be with people who weren't aware that she'd been barred from working: the police, for a start, and maybe the women of the strike group. She could get an update on how things were going.

She started by asking for a meeting with Bob Seaton. As soon as she went into the police station, she could sense an atmosphere. The desk sergeant kept his eyes lowered when she chatted to him and gave one-word answers. It wasn't how things usually were. Clare noticed that everyone she passed in the corridors, from officers to secretaries, wore grim expressions. And none were as grim as the look on Bob Seaton's face.

"You look tired," Clare commented as she sat down. "I suppose all this stuff is really taking its toll. Everyone seems to be... I don't know... tense."

Seaton rubbed his hands across his face. "It's my fifty-eighth birthday today, Miss Jackson, and I don't need to be reminded of how much I'm ageing, thank you."

Clare smiled uncertainly, not sure how much of that was intended as a joke. "Happy birthday, then. I'd have brought a card if I'd known."

Seaton sighed. "You've been in the wars yourself. Those bruises look nasty."

"I'm absolutely fine."

"Those toe-rags at Sweetmeadows didn't do too much damage then? I was furious when I heard about it. I mean, hitting a woman like that. And the size of you. You're barely worth hitting."

Clare smiled again. "Thanks, I think. No, not much damage, bumps and bruises, that's all. And they were girls too. I might have asked for it."

"Do you want to press charges?"

"Definitely not."

Seaton nodded. "Understood. Anyway, you'll have to be quick-sharp today. There's so much going on round here that

I hardly have a minute."

"Oh." Clare wasn't sure how to approach the subject in a quick or direct way. "It's about Jason Craig. The thing is, I've been hearing these wild stories about why he killed himself in custody. I just thought I'd run them past you." As Clare spoke, she noticed Seaton's face flinch, almost imperceptibly, before he resumed his usual impassive expression. Something is definitely up, she thought.

Seaton put on his formal voice. "As you know there is to be both an inquest and a full internal inquiry into Mr Craig's death and what may or may not have led up to it. So I couldn't possibly say anything about it at this stage."

Clare chewed her top lip for a second. "Yes, I realise all that, but I just wanted a bit of a steer, to make sure I'm not chasing a lot of nonsense. Off the record, obviously."

"You'll have to tell me what you've heard."

"It does sound very odd, so bear with me here. I'm just repeating what I've been told."

"Go on, then." Seaton folded his arms.

"The rumour is that when the young lads were in the police station, some of your officers dropped something in front of them. Something that looked like a baby. And that this sent Jason Craig over the edge. Mentally speaking, I mean."

Seaton stared at her for a moment. If he knows about this, Clare thought, he's a very good actor.

"Say all that again," Seaton said, slowly. "Something that looked like a baby? Such as what? A doll or a dummy of some kind?"

"No. Something that seemed to bleed when it hit the floor. I know, it sounds… "

Seaton had put his face in his hands.

"Are you okay?" Clare leaned forward a little.

He looked up. "Miss Jackson, everything I am about to say is off the record. It is as far off the record as it is possible to be. Understood?"

Clare nodded.

"I was not on duty here on the night Jason Craig and Steven Simpson were interviewed and when Mr Craig died. I was away at a meeting at another force. You'll know we're all very stretched at the moment, what with the strike and everything, so we'd drafted in a couple of officers from down south. I know there was some sort of funny business around what happened to Mr Craig, and I've been trying to get to the bottom of it. I'm meeting nothing but silence, even amongst my own men."

Clare opened her mouth and closed it again. "You mean something like that could have happened?"

Seaton rubbed his eyes. "Whatever this stunt involved, it won't have been a living thing. But if they did something – anything – along the lines you're suggesting, then it could well have sent a volatile teenager over the edge. And don't even ask me why he was allowed to keep his shoelaces when he went in the cell. I've asked that one until I'm blue in the face. Apart from anything else, they were supposed to be testing the kid's clothes. This station is falling apart, Miss Jackson, and my sanity is going the same way." Seaton sat back heavily in his chair. "Off the record."

For just a moment they both looked at each other, as if neither could quite believe the conversation they'd just had.

"I can't report any of this, then, can I?" Clare said.

Seaton half-smiled. "It's a bugger. For you, anyway. But no, you can't."

Clare's mind ticked over, more slowly than she wanted. There had to be some way to get some of this story out into the open. "If I find someone to accuse the police of mishandling Jason Craig to the point where he killed himself, would you comment?"

"I'd say I couldn't comment until the inquiry and the inquest had both reached a conclusion."

They stared at each other again, Seaton twisting his pen round and round in his fingers.

"Who's saying that, anyway?" Seaton looked as if he

might be about to snap the pen in two. "Steven Simpson?"

"Have to protect my sources," Clare said, with a shrug. She certainly wasn't going to admit that the information was second-hand and extracted from a ten-year-old boy for the price of a Twix.

"Must've been him." Seaton stared out of the window for a moment at the grey-white sky. "Or someone close to him."

"I couldn't comment."

There was a light knock at the door and a secretary put her head around it. "Joe Ainsley, also wanting to see you."

"Damn," said Clare, without meaning to.

Seaton raised his eyebrows. "Something wrong, Miss Jackson? I thought you and that Ainsley fellow came as a set."

"I don't suppose there's a way I could get out of here without actually passing Joe in the corridor?"

"There could be. I'd like to know more about what this source of yours is alleging, though."

"I'll see what I can do, if we agree that as far as Joe's concerned, I wasn't actually here today. And anything I tell you is also off the record, chief inspector. Much as I hate that phrase."

Seaton gave a dry chuckle. "Agreed."

He instructed his secretary to get Clare out to the police staff car park at the back of the building before letting Joe up to his office.

Outside, Clare sat in her car and massaged her temples. Her head still pounded and there were moments – no more than seconds here and there – when she felt so light it was as if she was floating, like the moments before falling asleep, and she had to pinch herself to bring herself back round. She hoped it was the unrelenting heat and not anything related to her injuries. The next stop was the newsagents. As Clare filled her bag with chocolate bars, gum and the sort of pastel-coloured, penny-priced sweets that went into kids' mix-up bags, Jai laughed at her. "Is it someone's birthday?"

"Not exactly. Don't ask," said Clare, scanning the shelves. "What's the most popular thing with the kids these days, Jai? I'm out of touch."

"No contest. These." Jai pointed to some packets of crisps that looked as if they were fish and chips wrapped in newspaper. "That's why I keep them on the counter. Anywhere else and they all get pinched when I'm not looking."

"Okay, give me a couple of bags of those too," Clare said.

Jai handed her change. "You might have to have to find a new office soon, I'm afraid."

"Oh, no. Why?"

"I don't want to be here anymore, Clare. My cousin's shop at Sweetmeadows was burned out. He's been left with nothing. His family are broken-hearted. And I don't think it's worth it any more. People are cancelling their papers and their magazines because they have no money. All the little things they don't need, they're cutting them out. And it's only a matter of time before someone trashes my shop too. I don't want to be here when it happens."

"So what will you do?"

"I'll put it up for sale. It may take a while. But then I will join my brother in London. Things are not so bad there, I think."

"I'm sorry. I'll miss you."

"And I you, Miss Beautiful."

Clare went out with a heavy carrier bag full of sweets and put it on the floor of the car, blasting on the fan to keep the chocolate as cool as possible. So I'm about to bribe some vulnerable kids into telling me an anonymous story about someone who was probably a criminal, she thought. And I might trade the info to a police officer who's involved in the death of a prisoner. It's about as unethical as I can possibly get. She took a deep breath and started driving.

Amy appeared immediately as the car pulled up and Clare guessed the girl had been watching out for the red Mini.

"Did you bring sweets?"

Clare laughed. "That's why you were so keen to see me. Yes, don't worry, I haven't forgotten. But listen, Amy. Is there any chance I could talk to your friend?"

Amy looked blank. "Friend?"

"Steve Simpson's brother. Did you say his name was Liam?"

"He's not my friend." Amy stuck out her tongue in disgust. "He says I stink. But you should see him. He… "

"Okay, not your friend. But he's the lad who told you about Jason Craig and what happened to him? I've brought some extra sweets if he'll agree to talk to me. On the Q-T, you understand. I don't want to get him into trouble." Even as the words came out, Clare thought she must sound like a child predator. "Could you find him and ask him?"

"I s'pose." Amy scratched her head and scanned the estate. "His mam went out before and she had Stevie with her. I think she was taking him to the doctor's, because Liam said he was going to have to get more pills to calm him down. That means Liam might be in the house on his own."

"Will you show me?"

Amy beckoned and Clare followed to a third-floor flat. It wasn't too far from the Donnellys', Clare noticed. Maybe there was bad blood between the families.

Amy banged on the door and a plump, fair-haired boy opened it. "What do you want? Me mam's not here."

"This is my friend Clare. She wants to hear your story about what happened to Stevie."

Liam folded his arms and put his head on one side. I bet that's what his mother does, Clare thought.

"Why should I? Me mam says I should keep me gob shut about it till she's talked to a s'liss-it-er."

"She's got sweets." Amy pointed to the bag.

Liam pouted but Clare could see he was thinking about it. "What you got?"

Clare pulled out the fish-and-chips crisps. Liam's face changed. "Aye, all right. Come in, but you'll have to be quick."

Liam made Clare hand over the crisps, chocolate and gum before he said a word. Amy's eyes became wider and wider, the more Clare pulled out of the bag. "Don't worry, there's some for you in the car," Clare promised.

Liam retold his brother's tale, cramming the crisps into his mouth as he talked and getting his T-shirt covered in a dusting of salty, powdery coating. It was more or less as Amy had said.

"Stevie says they made them stand in the yard at the back of the police station and then this thing came crashing down. It landed on the ground right in front of them. And all this blood came out. He says Craigy went mental, shoutin' and runnin' about and cryin'. And a couple of big coppers jumped on him and held him down. And then they took him off to the cells to calm down."

"Where did Stevie go?"

"Another cell. He says he was all cryin' and shakin' too. And he says the blood splashed on him and everything. He says when he went to the cell he was sick in a bucket."

"He got blood on his clothes? Has he still got them?"

Liam shook his head. "Nah. Because he was wearing some sort of police thing. Like a jumpsuit made out of papery stuff, he said. Because they were doing tests on his real clothes. Then he got his things back when they let him go."

"What does Stevie think it was? The thing that was thrown down?"

Liam pouted and made a 'don't know' face. "He thought it was a baby. It was wrapped up in a blanket. And he said it was about the size of a baby too."

"When did he find out what had happened to Craigy?"

"When they let him out. They just said, 'By the way, son, your big mate's topped himself'." Liam poked at the bars of chocolate, deciding what to eat next. "And he's just cryin' now, all the time. So me mam's gone to get him some more sleeping pills. And she says she's gonna sue the coppers too."

Clare nodded. "Liam, do you know why the police arrested

225

Stevie and Craigy?"

"Aye. For the baby. Some crackpot's been saying they saw them do it. But they never would, you know. Our Stevie won't even kick the dog when it pees on the floor. He's right soft, on the quiet." Liam licked chocolate from the tips of his chubby fingers. "But if he ever finds out who grassed them up to the police he'll kill 'em. I know he will. And all Craigy's mates will help."

"Thanks, Liam." Clare glanced at Amy, who was squatting on the floor trying to persuade Liam's oily little terrier dog to come over to her. She didn't react. "Hey, let's not tell anyone about this, eh? I don't want to get you into any trouble."

As her words came out, Clare's stomach squirmed. This is how easy it is to get a kid to keep a secret, something you should never ask them to do. Just make them feel as if they're in the wrong. After all, some kids grow up thinking they're in the wrong anyway, just by being around, so it's not difficult. It's precisely why Amy thought she'd be the one in trouble when she saw someone murder baby Jamie.

Liam shook his head. "Me mam'd kill me. You're not going to put me in the paper, are you?"

"No, I promise." Clare raised her eyebrows at Amy, who jumped up from the floor. She pointed at the window. "That big fat reporter's back," she said. "He's wandering round out there."

Clare made a face. "Can we go to yours for a bit, Amy? I don't want to run into him."

"Do you not like him?"

"Not very much, no."

"Why not?"

Clare thought about it. "It's a long story. But in a nutshell, he got a job I really wanted, even though he's not very good. And now he's trying to muscle in on my patch and do my stories."

Amy shook her head. "What a bastard."

Clare couldn't help but smile, and followed Amy as she

scuttled like a rat along some back fire escape stairs. The girl delved into the pocket of her shorts and pulled out a Yale key. "Here," she said. "Me mam's not in, so you can go in and wait."

"Where are you going?"

Amy grinned. "I'm going to talk to that fat reporter."

"Why?"

"I'm going to make sure he goes off somewhere else."

"No, Amy, don't... " But Amy had already started running down the steps.

Clare shook her head. She felt too tired, achey and fuzzy-headed to argue. And she knew quite well that Amy had a mind of her own.

She turned the key in Amy's door and stepped inside. It smelled even worse than usual: a combination of dog and rotting rubbish and god knows what else. Clare found herself gagging and had to hold her breath, stick her head outside again and take a deep gulp of air. Max gave a single bark and got up slowly from the corner of the room.

"Hi, Max." Clare looked at him, her hand over her nose. Usually he almost deafened her with his barking and Amy would have to hold him back from leaping up at her. She braced herself to give him a pat on his large head. He whimpered but wagged his tail.

Clare frowned. "Are you okay? You don't seem right today." She was talking to a dog. Maybe she did have mild brain damage after all.

Clare stared around the sparsely-furnished room. In the corner where Max had been lying, on layers of free-sheet newspapers, there were pools of dog mess, and when Clare put her head around the kitchen door she found several overflowing bin bags of rubbish, with flies buzzing around their open tops. Bottles of soured milk sat on the bench and ants were scurrying all over the surfaces. The plastic bowls on the floor were empty apart from old, crusted chunks of dog food that had dried up. Clare leaned over the sink and wretched.

There was a tap at the door and Amy's voice called through the letterbox. "I'm ba-ack!" She bounced inside. "I told the stupid man that there'd been a big fight this morning and that the police had arrested about twenty people. He's gone running off to the police station. He's really dumb."

Clare looked at Amy, who didn't seem at all fazed by the stench or the state of the flat. She didn't know quite where to begin. "Is your mum around today, Amy? Has she gone off with her boyfriend again?"

Amy shrugged. "Don't know."

"I don't think your dog's very well. Look at the mess he's made on the floor. And he seems all floppy, doesn't he?"

Amy's face fell. "I know he's sick. I told me mam last night but she said she hasn't got money for the vet so he'll just have to get over it. And Mickey, that's her boyfriend, he said there was nothing wrong with him. I was just hoping he'd get better."

"Okay, we'll think about that in a minute. But what about all this mess? Rubbish and dirt and... I don't know. You shouldn't be living in this, you'll get ill. When did your mum last do any cleaning around here?"

Amy pouted. "She doesn't like cleaning. I do it, usually. But we've run out of stuff to do it with. And Max getting ill made it worse."

Clare closed her eyes for a minute. "Right. Let's start by getting Max to the vet. And then we'll start cleaning up."

Together they half-dragged, half-pushed a whimpering Max down the stairs and onto a pile of newspapers on the back seat of Clare's car. Amy squeezed in beside the dog and stroked him while Clare drove.

"I don't suppose you have a vet that you know? No. We'll just go to this one here, then. I know nothing about vets either."

The session was an uncomfortable one. The vet said straight away that Max had picked up an infection, probably by scavenging through rubbish for food, and that he seemed dehydrated. "Stray, is he? Where'd you pick him up?"

"Er, yes, that's right," said Clare, giving Amy a warning look. She guessed that Tina hadn't bothered with a dog licence. "Near to Sweetmeadows."

"So you're going to take him on? Remember to do all the paperwork. He's going to take a bit of looking after, poor old invalid that he is. He's got fleas too, you should know."

Clare sighed. Of course he did. Damn thing.

When she paid the bill for a series of injections and several kinds of medication, Clare winced. She could quite understand why Tina hadn't wanted to pay out for a vet. But Amy linked her arm on the way out and hugged it to her. "Thanks Clare."

"No problem," Clare said.

Then they called into the local Co-op for bin bags, rubber gloves, bottles of Jif and Domestos and a huge box of Flash powder. "Are you ready for this? If you're going to go back home we want to make it fit for human habitation. Fit to live in, I mean," Clare added, seeing Amy's blank expression.

"We can try," said Amy, "though you can't wash that black mould off the walls. I've tried."

They managed to clean up the living room and the kitchen, although by the end of it Clare had to sit down. She put her head in her hands. "Sorry, Amy, I'm beat. I'm still in a bit of pain from the other night."

"It's okay. I can do the rest sometime. Told you, I like cleaning, when I've got all the gear."

"Your mum needs to be around more, though. It's not right. I know I keep saying this."

"But she brings her horrible boyfriend. I hate him."

"Why do you hate him so much? Is it because your mum spends so much time with him?"

Amy pursed her lips. "Worse than that."

"What, then? Tell me. Because I don't understand."

"You won't be cross with me?"

"Of course not."

229

Amy swallowed hard. "He pinched my Walkman. He took it without asking and he sold it in the pub. And then he just laughed at me and said you could buy me another one sometime." She sniffed. "That was the best present I'd ever had in my whole life. And he stole it."

"Oh, Amy. I'm sorry. That's a horrible thing to do." She echoed Amy's earlier words. "What a bastard."

"I said I was going to ring you and tell you what he'd done. So he hit me."

Clare put her face in her hands for a minute. "Hang on. Was that last Sunday?"

"I can't remember. Maybe."

"You did call me, didn't you? I could hear you crying on the end of the phone."

"Yeah. He mustn't have put it down properly." Amy brushed her eyes with the back of her hand. "You still can't tell anyone though?"

"Mmm. But I'm going to have to speak to your mum. Look, I want you to ring me up when she gets back so that I can come round and catch her. Will you do that?"

Amy nodded. "Your flat was a right old rubbish tip too. I tidied it."

"It was, yes, but it wasn't as bad as this. And I hadn't been... well. I'd had a lot on at work."

Just then the door was pushed open and Tina stumbled in. She was followed by her boyfriend. Amy made a sulky face at him. Strong fumes of lager and cigarettes came off both of them.

"Hiya, pet." Tina ruffled Amy's hair and the girl ducked out of the way. "Oh. Hello again," Tina added, in Clare's direction. "You can't keep away, can you?"

"Tina, I really need to talk to you. When I came here today, Amy had been left on her own again. There was nothing to eat and the dog had made a mess everywhere, in fact I've had to take him to the vet."

"Don't expect any money from me," Tina cut in.

"They're a rip-off, those vets," Mickey said, switching on the TV and throwing himself down onto the sofa.

"Never mind the bloody vet." Clare felt her face going red. "The point is, Amy was left alone again. You can't keep doing this, Tina. It's not safe. She's only ten."

"Nine," Tina said, "since you think you know so much about her. But I still don't see how this is any of your business."

Clare looked at Amy, who was sidling out towards her bedroom. So Tina still hadn't remembered that her own daughter had had a birthday. "I don't know what sort of a person knows that a little kid is being left on her own in a filthy house full of dog shit and then decides it isn't their business."

Mickey got out his cigarettes and threw one across at Tina. "Fucking do-gooding posh bitch. I think you should go home, sweetheart."

Clare stood up. "If you like."

"Hang on." Tina stepped in front of Clare, her fingers trembling as she lit her cigarette. "What are you going to do? You're not going to tell the social services, are you?"

"I should." Clare was well aware that Amy was probably listening at the door. "I promised Amy I wouldn't. But... " she dropped her voice and took a step closer to Tina. "If I come here one more time and find her on her own, that is exactly what I'll do."

She was surprised to see Tina's eyes fill up.

"Don't," she said, still visibly shaking. "Give her some money for the vet, Mickey."

"I don't want any money for the sodding vet. I want Amy to be safe. I don't get it, Tina. She's such a great kid."

"Yeah?" Tina blinked her tears back and Mickey gave a loud snort. "Try having her for more than a night and see how you get on. Try getting your head around her fairy stories and trying to work out what's true and what isn't. She's a bloody handful."

Clare shook her head. "One more time, Tina. I mean it. Amy's your responsibility. Do your job."

She walked quickly out of the flat and ran down the flight of steps, her heart thumping. She half expected Mickey to follow her down and threaten her.

When a woman's voice shouted, "Hey!" she jumped hard. Turning, she saw Annie Martin, carrying a shopping bag.

"It's you, isn't it? The lass from the *Post*?"

"Clare. Yes. How are you, Annie?"

"You got a minute?"

Clare nodded and followed Annie into the Donnellys' flat. It was a little tidier than before. Becca and Bobbie were sitting on the floor, watching TV. Annie beckoned Clare into the kitchen and put the kettle on. "I need a word. We could use your help."

"Go on."

Annie clattered two mugs onto the kitchen bench. "I don't know where to start."

"Let me ask you, then. How are you coping?"

"We're not good."

"No. But I wondered if maybe it helped that there'd been some arrests?"

"The arrests? Ridiculous. Disgraceful. A complete fit-up. Everyone knows it."

"How so?"

Annie pursed her mouth. "That poor lad Jason Craig. He wouldn't have done anything like that. The police are trying to say that he threw Jamie out of his pram and then did for our Deborah because she worked it out. It's all rubbish. For one thing, Jason's some cousin of Rob's. Or second cousin, maybe. He was always a naughty lad, but never a violent one. And that daft mate of his, Stevie, he's just the same."

"So why would the police arrest them in the first place?"

Annie sipped her tea. "The word is, someone tipped them off. But it was clearly malicious. Or maybe the police just wanted to close the case and this seemed like an easy answer. I don't know. But I've already been round to Stevie's mum and said I don't believe a word of it. And what the pigs must've done to young Jason to get him in that state, I don't want to think."

Clare stared into the bubbles on the surface of her tea and blew gently onto them. "So you think the killer's still out there?"

"I know it." Annie thumped her chest. "I know it right in here."

eleven

Clare swallowed. She didn't know how to answer Annie. "So how is the family coping?"

"We're not. Rob goes out to work, and that's all wrong in my opinion, and then he goes off with the other scabs and drinks all night. The kids hardly see him. And I'm looking after them now, because I'm off the school dinner duties for the summer holidays."

Clare nodded. "It must be really hard."

"The thing is, we can't… " Annie stopped and took a long breath. "They won't let us have the bodies back. I still can't bury my grandson and my daughter."

Clare shook her head. "Why's that?"

"They just won't release them. I've asked and asked. We need a funeral. I need to put my daughter and her baby to rest in peace. The family needs to move on. And they won't let us."

"What's their excuse?"

"It was 'continuing inquiries' and all that rubbish, although a fat lot of good their inquiries did. And then they claimed that Jason was the killer, so although I don't believe that, I asked them for my family back. So that I could sort out the funeral. But they're still saying no. I can't stand… " Annie's voice cracked. "I can't stand thinking of them still lying in a mortuary somewhere. All cold and on their own and with a label round their feet, or whatever it is they do. I want my daughter and her bairn put to rest."

"How can I help?"

"You work for the paper. They don't like it when they get criticised in the press. If you do a story about it, that might make them change their minds."

Clare sighed. "I can try. We don't always have the clout people think we do. But I'll give it a go."

Annie nodded. "Thank you. You've been good to us. Thank you." She looked at Clare. "What happened to your face?"

Clare smiled. "Long story. My own fault. You don't want to hear about it."

"It wasn't a fella, was it? If it was, get the hell away from him."

"Of course it wasn't. I got on the wrong side of some kids here on the estate, the night all the trouble happened. That's all."

Annie folded her arms. "I heard you were seeing that Finn McKenna."

Clare raised her eyebrows. "On and off, yes."

Annie put her head on one side.

"No, Annie, I promise you it wasn't him. I don't know why you would say that. He's very kind to me."

"Rob says there's something not right about him."

Clare sighed. "Well, Rob's got a reason not to get on with the union men, hasn't he? You're wrong, Annie, truly." She slipped off the kitchen stool and picked up her bag. "Look. If you're sure the two lads had nothing to do with Jamie's death – and Deborah's – who do you think did it?"

"I already told you. It was revenge. Because Rob was a scab."

"You still think that?"

"I'm sure of it." Annie glanced around, almost as if she thought the real killer might be nearby. "Listen. McKenna? Even some of the miners say he's a funny character. He came

235

from nowhere and he's taken over and there's something I can't put my finger on."

"But his mother lives around the corner, Annie. That's not exactly coming from nowhere, is it?"

"Aye, I know the family. That's not what I meant. This Finn lad was working away, by all accounts, before the strike happened, but none of the miners can find anyone who knows what he was actually doing. And now nothing happens without his say-so. They call him Stalin, down in the union offices, did you know that?"

Clare shook her head. "You're not saying he's the killer, Annie – surely not?"

"I don't know what I'm saying, except that I bet he knows more than he's letting on."

Back at her flat, Clare's phone rang almost non-stop, but she wouldn't pick it up. She felt assured that it was unlikely to be Amy. Tina was selfish, but Clare sensed that her latest threat of calling social services had struck home. So she let the phone ring, again and again. The doorbell also rang and Joe's voice called her name through the letterbox. Clare stayed in the bedroom with the curtains drawn. The last thing she wanted was to get into a conversation along the lines of 'Where the hell have you been?' and 'What do you think you're playing at?' And she wasn't ready to listen to any diatribes about how she should spend her supposed recovery time.

If she could be sure that Finn was on the other end of the phone, Clare would have picked it up. He was the one person she wanted to be with at the moment, the one person who made her feel safe and the one person who didn't keep telling her what to do. In the end, she called his office but was told he wasn't there and she got no answer at his home.

She flicked through the *Post* when it was delivered. Still no major pieces from Chris Barber. Clare smiled at the thought of Amy sending him off on a wild goose chase. She knew she should have told the girl not to make up stories like that, but she couldn't help hoping Chris had wasted a lot of time. Clare's trouble now was how to keep getting her own work in the paper. She'd made a promise to Annie Martin, for one thing, and the whole weird puzzle about Jason Craig and what happened in the police station was playing hard on her mind.

It was four o'clock in the afternoon. Clare tried to sleep, to rid herself of the nagging headache, but all the things she wanted to write buzzed round her head like mosquitoes. In the end, she got up, took a couple of paracetamol and called Joe.

"Hey. Are you up to much?"

"Clare! Where the hell have you been? We've already had an office debate about whether we should get the police to break your door down."

"Yeah, yeah. Can we meet for a quick chat?"

They met at the pub where Joe bought her a tall iced drink. "Should you even be driving?"

"No one told me not to."

"Like you would take any notice, even if they did."

"Look. I need help. A couple of really strong stories are knocking around and I want to get them out there. Preferably without a Chris Barber by-line."

"I'm supposed to tell you to stop thinking about work. You know that, don't you?"

"I do, but I don't care. Come on, Joe. You're the only other reporter I can really trust."

She started by telling Joe about Annie's call for the bodies to be released for the funerals.

"I know that Catholic priest. He's not a bad bloke. How about I go get a quote from him and Bob Seaton and then we can write this up together?" Joe tapped his pen on the desk. "I could persuade Bell that this is something you just have to do before you take a proper break. A promise to Annie Martin. We can get this in, without you having to do too much extra work."

"Yes. Thanks, Joe." Clare rattled the melting ice cubes around in her glass. "There's something else, though."

"Another story?"

"Mmm. A really complicated one."

Clare began to recount the story of the teenagers' arrests. Joe interrupted. "You can't report this right now, not if there's going to be an inquest and a police inquiry. And anyway, think about it. You've only got the word of some kid, who wasn't there."

"I know that. But Seaton knows some funny business went on, he just doesn't know what, exactly. Should I tell him?"

Joe wiped his forehead. "Shit. I'm not sure. Probably, since it's Seaton and he's generally okay. But it's tough. You don't want to land that kid brother in trouble, do you?"

Clare shook her head.

"Well. Hello." A voice behind them made them both turn round. It was Finn. "This is where you are."

Clare gave an apologetic smile. "Let me guess. You've been worried."

"I have." Finn looked at Joe. "But I see I shouldn't have been."

Joe took a sip of his pint. "Can I get you one?"

"I'm fine, thanks." He looked back at Clare. "So you're back at work?"

"Sort of. Unofficially. And before you say, 'Is that wise?' the answer is I don't care. I have stuff to do."

"That newspaper exploits you. You know that?"

"I'm a willing exploitee. Today, anyway." Clare shuffled further along the bench and patted the seat. "Come and join us."

Finn shook his head. "I've got work to do, too. I only came in because I thought I spotted your car in the car park. And I've been calling at the flat."

"Sorry." Clare gave a cringing smile. "I phoned you too, but I missed you. My head's a bit spaced out."

"You in this evening?"

238

"I am. Come round." Clare waved at Finn as he turned to leave.

Joe watched him go. "He wasn't too happy, I'd say. Anyway, going back to this mad story. I think you should leave it alone. It could bring a heap of trouble down, on you, on the police, on this kid and his family, and all for something that you can't be sure is true. It doesn't even sound plausible. It sounds mad. Just drop it until the inquiry's finished and see what comes out of that."

"You think? Really?"

"I do. I know that taking the long view isn't your strong point, but that's what I would do here."

By six o'clock, they'd co-written the funeral story, with quotes from the parish priest adding to Annie's call for the release of the bodies and two lines from Bob Seaton saying that everything possible was being done. Joe was as good as his word and talked Dave Bell into giving Clare a by-line. An hour later, though, Joe called Clare at home to say that they'd had to change the copy: Seaton had called back to announce the bodies of Deborah and Jamie Donnelly were to be released to the family the next day.

"Seriously? So that means the police are effectively saying they still think Jason Craig is the killer. That they're not looking for anyone else?"

"I put that to Seaton and he wouldn't make any comment. But my guess is they'll be pulling Stevie Simpson back in for more questions."

"It seems crazy. Even Annie Martin doesn't think those lads had anything to do with it."

"The coppers think differently. They must have some reason for it."

Clare bit her lip. "I think their best reason is that Amy thought she saw them around, the day Jamie died. At least she thought she saw someone with red shoelaces. They would be the shoelaces he used to hang himself, poor kid."

"Shit." Joe paused. "It's like the damn things hanged him

twice over."

"Don't. So Seaton wouldn't say whether they're going to make any more arrests or whether they're still looking for anyone else?"

"He wouldn't be drawn on that, no. But my gut tells me they're not looking for any other people, they're just trying to find a motive to pin on Stevie Simpson. And Jason Craig, who can't talk back any more."

Clare sighed. The more things developed, the more she worried that someone else would find out it was Amy who had given the story about the lads to the police. The poor kid would never survive the backlash. "I take it you've spoken to Annie Martin again?"

"Yes. I called her and she burst into tears. She says a special thank you to you."

"The power of the press, eh? I honestly didn't think it would be that quick. I suppose Seaton thinks this is one piece of bad publicity he can turn round quite easily."

"Don't worry. You'll still get your by-line. Dave Bell is writing in some line from Annie thanking the *Post* for its intervention. More herograms, Clare. Now go on fucking holiday, eh?"

Clare laughed.

When Finn came round, Clare could tell straight away that his mind was somewhere else. She put her arms around him and leaned her head on his chest. His body felt stiff.

He wouldn't sit down but paced the floor as Clare got him a drink. "Come on, Finn, you're making my head spin, as if I didn't feel bad enough. You're freaking me out. Is something wrong?"

"There is, yes. I can't talk about it, though."

Clare's stomach gave an anxious dip. "Hey, come on. You can't say there's something wrong and then refuse to tell me what it is. You're making me really nervous now."

Finn stared out of the window, arms folded, and Clare

waited, her heartbeat sounding too loud in her head. "Finn, please."

After a long moment, she asked: "Is it about Jackie? Are you still seeing her?"

Finn looked around at Clare, and gave a short laugh. "I wish it was something as stupid as that. That would be easy to sort out. No, Clare, I stopped seeing Jackie ages ago. You're the only woman I want, I promise."

With an effort, Clare stood up and walked over to Finn. She put her arms around his waist. "Talk to me. If you want me, tell me what's going on."

After a long breath, Finn leaned down and kissed Clare's head. "It's just that I'm back up in court tomorrow," he said.

"It's tomorrow? I didn't realise." Clare looked up into Finn's pale eyes. "Is that what you're worried about?"

"I could go to prison." Finn pulled her a little tighter to him. "Would you still want me then?"

Clare thought about the rush of heat that went through her, every time she so much as looked at Finn. It was so long since anyone had sparked that kind of response. She didn't want to think about losing it – it would be like going back to those two months of frozen semi-existence that she'd suffered before Finn and Amy had chipped her defences down. "Yes. Of course I will."

Finn picked Clare up from the ground, carefully, and began carrying her to the bedroom. "You weigh nothing," he whispered, as he laid her on the bed, as softly as if she was a piece of glass that might break at any moment.

Later, as Finn dressed, he dug in the pocket of his jeans. "I have something for you." He handed her a piece of paper.

"What's this?" Lying under the sheets and still trembling slightly, Clare unfolded it.

"It's a copy of a letter my mother sent to the *Post*, thanking you for your piece about the women's fundraising. They've had an offer of a coach trip for the kids from a local firm and a baker in the town will supply a picnic for them. So they're planning a big day out for the young 'uns. They're very excited. She reckons it's all down to the article you put in the paper."

Clare grinned. "Hang on while I polish my halo. Tell your mum a big thank you too."

Finn took hold of Clare's hand and stroked it. "Clare. I need to know. Is there anything between you and Joe Ainsley?"

Clare laughed. "Me and Joe? You're kidding. We're just good mates and we go a very long way back. We've fished each other out of too many gutters for anything romantic to ever happen."

"Does he know that?"

"Of course he does."

"Okay. Good. It's just… " Finn squeezed Clare's hand a little harder. "I like you, Clare. I really like you. And I don't want to waste my time."

"I like you too, Finn. Joe's not part of the picture, I promise."

Thursday 2nd August

Clare sat in the court car park, dressed in her work suit, wondering whether or not to go in. It wouldn't be to report on the case, as she was officially on a day off and she was sure the *Post* would have sent someone else. But it seemed harsh not to be there to see what happened to Finn. She watched everyone going in: lawyers she recognised, Chris Barber, some of Finn's union colleagues and Finn's mother, looking more frail than usual. This must be frightening for her, Clare thought, given the way things are between the police and the miners. She must be worrying about what could happen to her son in the privacy of a police cell.

A few minutes before ten, Joe rapped on her car window. Then he darted round to the passenger side and let himself in.

"I really need to talk to you. It's about Finn."

"What about him? I'm just wondering whether to go in or

not. I'm not really working, but I thought Finn might like me to be there as a show of support. But then it might look weird, me sitting in the public gallery instead of on the press bench. What do you think?"

"Clare. I had something of a close encounter with your boyfriend last night."

"What do you mean? He was with me."

"Until when? I'm talking about eleven o'clock last night when I walked out of the pub. He came up and threatened me."

Clare gave a little snort. "Don't be ridiculous."

"I'm not. Listen. I was taking a short cut down that alley behind The Ship. He came up behind me and gave me a shove in the back. Then he asked me if anything was going on between you and me."

"I've already told him there isn't."

"He hasn't quite grasped it, then. He told me to back off. And he said something to the effect that, if I didn't, I wouldn't have any fingers left to write with."

Clare sat back in the seat. "I don't believe you."

"Why would I make this up?"

"Because you think I shouldn't be seeing him. We've had this conversation."

"Come on, Clare. It's a bit of a leap from thinking you shouldn't be seeing him to making up stories about him, isn't it? This is me you're talking to."

"Okay." Clare thought about it. "I'm sorry. I do believe you. But look, he was upset last night. He thinks he's going to be sent to prison today. I'm sure he didn't mean to sound threatening, it just came out wrong because he's all on edge. Who wouldn't be?"

"I can't believe you're sticking up for him. The guy's a thug."

"That's just not true."

"Remind yourself why he's in court today? For assaulting a police officer. Doesn't that ring any alarm bells?"

"That was because the police got too heavy-handed on the picket line. He was just defending someone that was being beaten up. With a truncheon, actually. Come on, Joe, it's not like you to take the side of the police against the picketers."

"I'm not. I just think Finn McKenna is trouble. You don't want someone like that in your life."

"Yeah, well. That might not be an issue after today. He's expecting to get sent down."

Joe sighed. "Come in with me."

They got out of the car and slammed the doors shut. As they walked towards the court room, one of the union men came up to Clare. "We need a favour. Can you send us your piece for our union newspaper? We haven't got anyone else to take notes or write it up. Finn said you might do it?"

Clare nodded. "Yes, sure. It gives me another reason to be here."

Joe was waiting.

"Go on ahead," Clare said. "I'll just see what the union needs and I'll catch you up." Better to put a little bit of physical distance between her and Joe this morning, she thought. If Finn was already agitated about the prospect of being sent to jail, then it wouldn't help to see her looking too cosy next to Joe on the press bench.

It meant she had to sit next to Chris Barber. "What are you doing here?" he hissed at her. "You're supposed to be on sick leave, aren't you?"

"Not voluntarily," Clare whispered back. "Anyway, don't worry. I'm not here for the *Post*."

"You're not allowed to freelance for other papers," Barber pointed out. "Sackable offence."

"I'm not. I'm not doing it for money. I'm just taking notes for someone, that's all." She gave Barber a quick smile. "You can't get rid of me that way, so forget it."

They had a long wait for the court to get under way, so much so that Joe got restless and pestered the usher, who said some sort of discussions were going on between the lawyers.

Mary McKenna looked more and more anxious, occasionally dabbing at her eyes, two of the women from the support group sitting on either side of her. When Finn was brought into the dock, the first thing he did was look over in Clare's direction and smile. Clare smiled back and gave a little nod. She was aware that Mary McKenna was watching. Finn didn't look at Joe, who was keeping his own gaze studiously lowered on to his notebook.

The magistrates' chairman spoke first, making everyone sit up. "We have been made aware of some unusual circumstances relating to this case. These are circumstances which we are not able to make public, but we agree that this case will no longer proceed. Mr McKenna, you are free to go."

Everyone, except Finn and his lawyer, looked blank. Even Mary looked taken aback. Clare glanced over at the union men and saw them frowning at each other. No one had expected this.

"Er – what just happened?" Chris Barber hissed at Clare, as soon as the magistrates left the court.

"I've no idea. Honestly." Clare watched as Finn shook hands with his lawyer and walked out, his mother hurrying after him.

Joe marched over to her. "That was weird. In all my years reporting the courts, I've never seen that happen. Do you know anything about these state secrets that've got him off?"

"I don't think anyone did." Clare stood up too quickly and had to lean on the bench for a moment. She wanted to catch up with Finn.

"Still at large after all, then," Joe added.

"At large? Honestly. There's no need for that sort of expression. You'd think he was some sort of... " Clare paused. "You've got him all wrong, that's all."

Outside, Mary McKenna hurried up to Clare. "Thank you for coming today. I know it meant a lot to Finn. I heard what happened to you over at Sweetmeadows. Disgusting. How

245

are you feeling?"

"I'm fine, really. Everyone's making a bit of a fuss, to be honest. It wasn't as bad as it sounds. Are you okay, Mary? That must have been so worrying."

Mary looked across the car park to where her son was being congratulated by some of the other men. Her face was hard to read. "It was. I don't quite know what went on in there, do you?"

Clare shook her head. "Good news, though?"

Mary was still looking at Finn. "Yes, of course, good news," she said. Her expression didn't match her words. Then she seemed to suddenly remember where she was. "Will you come over for your tea? You can come tonight if you like. If you're not busy. And it'll save you having to bother cooking for yourself."

"That's very kind." Clare fished around in her mind for an excuse not to go. But turning down the invitation would look rude. "Yes, thank you. That's nice of you."

Mary smiled. "Good. It won't be anything very grand, not these days, but we all share what we have. It's a funny thing, this strike, isn't it? We're all worried sick and no one has a penny. But it's brought us all together, like never before." She patted Clare's arm. "There's a good side to everything that happens, even if you can't always see it." Clare looked across the car park to see Joe watching. He shook his head. Clare turned away.

As soon as she spotted Finn, Clare went over to him. "Hey," she said. "Well done. How're you feeling?"

Finn shrugged. "Good, yeah."

Clare waited, but Finn didn't say anything else. "So what happened, exactly? How come everything got dropped?"

Finn shrugged again. "Lawyers. They can argue black is white."

"Your mum asked me over for tea, did you know? Do you mind?"

"Why would I mind? She likes you. I like you."

Clare knew that 'tea' was the old-fashioned use of the word, meaning a full meal. She felt guilty that Mary was stretching her already low funds to accommodate her but she also knew that it wouldn't be expected that she should bring anything along; in fact, it would be seen as insulting. She was anxious about it, sensing that Finn had built up their relationship to his mother to be something a stage or two further along than it really was.

But Mary made her welcome, fussing around her at the table, which was set with a fiercely white tablecloth and the best china. It reminded Clare of her own parents when someone was coming round, when as a child she'd hardly dared sit at the formally-set table in case she spilled anything or ate something the wrong way.

Mary piled food onto Clare's plate. "I could not believe it when Finn told me what happened to you over at Sweetmeadows. I said to Finn, what? That lovely girl? Being beaten up? Where the heck were you, that's what I asked him."

Clare smiled. "He was on a different mercy mission, that's all. And I'm fine."

"Eat up. You're far too thin. Let's get your strength back before they start slave-driving you on that newspaper again."

Mary talked about the big day out they were planning for the miners' kids. "We're taking them down to the coast, and we've wangled free admission to the splash park. And then we've been promised fifty picnic lunches. They're going to have such a good time, bless them. It's all thanks to that big piece you did in the paper. We owe you a thank you."

"I don't suppose I could ask a favour then?"

"You can ask whatever you like."

"Just say if this is a problem. But I know a little girl from Sweetmeadows. She's not from a mining family but she's got nothing, Mary. And she's having a really tough time. I don't suppose you could find a seat for her on your coach trip?"

Mary frowned. "That's tricky. If we let in one kid who

247

doesn't have a link to the strike then we could get landed with dozens more."

Clare nodded. "Yes, I understand. I'm sorry, I shouldn't have asked. I didn't mean to put you in an awkward position."

"Well, now... " Mary got up and read down a list of names. "We have had a cancellation from a kid who's got tonsillitis. I suppose we could pop her in his place and say it was all last minute."

"Sure?" Clare gave Mary a grateful smile. "That's so kind. I think she'll be chuffed to bits when I tell her."

"That's a nice thing to do," Finn commented. "I take it you mean that funny-looking little thing that's always following you around."

Clare smiled at him. "Your mum's the kind one. I just asked a question. But thanks. At least you're not telling me not to get so close to my stories."

"I couldn't really do that, could I?"

Once they were on their own, Clare tackled Finn. "Tell me this isn't true. Joe says you warned him off me."

Finn laughed. "He said that? And when was I supposed to have done this?"

"Last night. At closing time, outside The Ship."

Finn shook his head. "We bumped into each other, sure. In fact, it was Ainsley who told me to back off. I did tell him to mind his own business and he didn't look too happy with me."

"That's all that happened?"

"I swear."

"Good." Clare gave Finn a hug. "And I'm glad the case got dropped. I don't think I could stand it if you'd been sent to prison."

Finn said nothing for a few moments, but pulled her closer and buried his face in her hair. Clare breathed him in. "Come home with me."

But a few minutes after they'd got to Clare's flat, the doorbell rang. Clare peered out of the window to see Amy, with Tina. "I'm sorry, I'd better answer this."

"We've been trying to find you for hours," Tina said, accusingly.

"I've been out."

"We guessed that. Can we come in?"

Clare held the door open and followed Amy and Tina into her living room. "What's this about? Is everything okay, Amy?"

"No, it isn't. There's been a bit of bother." Tina folded her arms and looked at Clare as a parent might look at a kid who was in trouble. She ignored Finn. "Some of the kids have started saying it was my Amy who grassed up the lads to the police."

"Where've they got that from?"

"You tell me, but I've had Stevie's mum banging on the door, asking if it's true. And making threats."

"Threats? Then you should... " Clare's voice tailed off.

"What? Call the police?" Tina leaned forward. Finn put a hand on Clare's shoulder. "This is your fault. I told Amy not to talk to the pigs, but you took her round there, didn't you? And now look what's happened."

Clare held up her hands. "I'm sorry. But I didn't tell anyone else. I don't know how it's leaked out."

"These things always do."

Clare looked at Amy, who was chewing on a strand of hair and staring at the floor. "You okay?"

Amy nodded. Clare wasn't convinced. "What do you want me to do, Tina?"

"She's not safe. Neither am I. I can go stay at Mickey's but I can't take her with me. She'll have to stay with you for a bit."

"What? She can't stay here, Tina."

"She's still here, by the way," Amy chipped in. "Why can't I, anyway?"

"Why can't you stay at Mickey's?"

Clare thought she saw a look pass between Tina and Amy.

249

"She just can't." Tina rifled in her handbag. "Mind if I smoke?"

"Yes, I do. Wait till you get outside."

Tina looked as if she'd like to slap Clare. "So, you'll hang onto her for a bit, yeah? Till things die down."

"But I can't... "

"She needs to be safe, right? I can't have her back at home with people banging on the door and shouting through the letterbox. And it's all your fault, when it comes down to it."

"I don't think... "

"Clare," Amy said. "Please. I won't be any trouble. Let me stay."

"But what about when I have to go back to work?"

"I'll just stay here. I'll watch telly or something. *Please.*"

Clare looked back at Tina, who seemed to be daring her to let Amy down. "How long do you think it'll take? Before things die down, as you put it?"

"Couple of weeks. Tops."

"A couple of *weeks*?"

Tina was already on her feet and pulling the cigarettes out of her bag, ready to light up as soon as she got out of Clare's door.

"Hang on. What about your dog?"

"The woman next door's going to look after the dog, don't worry about that."

That made things slightly more manageable, Clare thought. "Give me a number, where I can get hold of you. At Mickey's."

Tina scribbled a number down. She ruffled Amy on the head. "See you, kidder. Behave yourself, right? I don't want any calls to say you're in more trouble."

Then she was out of the door.

Clare turned and looked at Amy, who was clutching a carrier bag. "Clothes, I suppose?"

Amy nodded. "And my Monopoly game."

"You were expecting me to say yes, then. You mum sort of

forced me into it, didn't she?"

"Sorry. But I promise I won't be a nuisance, Clare. Even when you go to work."

"As a matter of fact, there is something you can do. I was going to come round and tell you about it. A bit of a treat." And she told Amy about the coach trip.

Amy looked as if someone had floodlit her from the inside. "I've never been to the splash park. That's so brilliant. Thanks, Clare."

"Get an early night. Go on."

Once Amy's bedroom door was shut, Clare turned to Finn. "I'm sorry."

Finn smiled. "I'm not sure how you've got yourself in this position, but I reckon it's because you're a nice person. I think that's why I… " His voice tailed off.

Clare put her head on one side. "What?"

"Nothing. It'll keep."

After Finn left, Clare sat down, wondering what to do next. If Joe found out, she'd never hear the end of it. It was a good job Finn seemed to have inherited some of his mother's soft-heartedness when it came to a kid who had nothing. Thoughts of him kept her going.

Friday 3rd August

The game of Monopoly had gone on for almost three hours, with a break to eat in between. Amy was a ruthless player and Clare would have been happy to let her win, but the dice kept her in the game. It was only interrupted at around nine, when there was a loud knocking on Clare's door.

She peered out of the window. "Damn. It's Joe. He's going to give me such a hard time if he catches you here."

Amy stood up. "I'll go in my room until he's gone. Don't panic."

"Thanks." Clare threw a cardigan over the Monopoly board and went to answer the door.

"Thought you were going to keep me standing on the

doorstep all night. With my injuries," Joe grumbled.

Clare stared at his swollen nose. "What the hell happened to you?"

"I've decided," Joe said, sounding slightly nasal, "that you and I are suffering too much for our art."

"Stop it. Just tell me."

"I got a tip-off that some of the Sweetmeadows miners were going a bit further afield today. Supporting the pickets down at Smithwood Colliery, to stop them getting the delivery lorries out. So I went out to see what was happening. And you'll have seen it all on the news, by now, I suppose."

"I haven't watched the news today."

"Really? You must be ill. There's been a huge battle between the police and the picketers." Joe looked at his watch. "You might catch a bit of it if you put the TV on now."

Clare switched on to see scenes of police, some on horseback, some with riot shields, charging at rows of picketing miners. "It looks horrendous. Were many people hurt?"

"Dozens in hospital, about twenty arrests. It just sort of blew up. I couldn't even work out what made it all kick off like that. But you need to know a couple of things. Finn McKenna was there. And he wasn't on the picket line. I've no idea what he was up to but it was definitely something dodgy."

Clare covered her face. "Not all this rubbish about Finn again."

Joe shook his head. "You have to listen. Please."

Clare sighed. "Come on then, let's hear it."

"There was a car parked not far from it all, with some men in caps and dark glasses. These guys just sat and watched everything going on and they had some sort of radios. I reckoned they were police, but not your average plod. Some sort of undercover thing, I don't know."

"And?" Clare glanced at her watch. She hoped Amy wouldn't get fed up and burst into the room demanding to continue their game.

"I kept looking at them, to try to work out who they were and what they were up to. Then one of them rolled the car window down and beckoned me over. He asked me what I was doing, and I said I was just reporting. He said, hadn't I seen enough? So I said no, I was planning to hang around a bit longer."

"Yeah?" Clare was finding it hard to stay interested. "You are a bit paranoid when it comes to authority, though."

"Listen. He grabbed hold of my shirt and pulled me towards the car window. Then he landed one on me. Right on the nose." Joe touched his nose gingerly. "I'm amazed it isn't broken. You should've seen the blood."

"What's this got to do with Finn?"

"He was in that car, Clare. He was sitting in the back. Yeah, he had a baseball cap pulled down low and dark glasses on, but it was definitely him. I reckon that's why his mate gave me the bloody nose. On his instructions."

"For god's sake. What a load of rubbish. It probably wasn't even Finn, just someone who looked a bit like him."

"I swear it was him. I know, I've never liked him and I wish you weren't seeing him, but I wouldn't make this up, I promise."

Clare stood up. "I don't know what I'm supposed to say. You think it might've been Finn in some car with some undercover policemen and you think he told someone to lamp you for nothing. You have to admit it sounds ridiculous."

"Don't I get any sympathy here?"

"Sorry. I can give you a packet of paracetamol, if you like."

"I was thinking more about a curry and a stiff drink?"

"Not tonight. I'm still a bit battered and bruised myself, remember. I was going to have an early night."

Slowly, Joe heaved himself up. "It's bad enough when we get called Cagney and Lacey. But we're more like Laurel and Hardy these days, eh? Seriously, though. I'm starting to think

McKenna is not all he says he is. Just how did those charges get dropped, eh, Clare? I bet he's never explained it. Watch out for him."

Amy bounced out of the bedroom as soon as she heard the front door close. "Come on. You have to land on my hotels sometime."

Saturday 4th August

Clare watched as Amy lined up with the other kids to get onto the coach. "Anyone you know?"

Amy looked up and down the queue. "Yeah, some of the kids."

"You'll be okay?"

Amy nodded.

They'd had to dash out as soon as the shops opened to buy Amy a swimming costume. Clare had tried to get hold of Tina, but the phone number she'd left didn't work. Clare suspected that was deliberate. "I don't suppose you know where Mickey lives?"

Amy shook her head.

"Do you know his second name?"

Amy scowled. "Gitface, I'd guess."

Clare shook her head. "Sometimes your language is worse than I hear from grown men in the pub. I've managed to get you this trip as a favour, so don't show me up by swearing in front of everyone."

Amy made a face that was meant to look innocent. "Promise I won't."

Clare went up to Mary and gave her a hug. "Is Finn with you?"

Mary gave her a tight-lipped smile. "You haven't heard from him, then? I was hoping he was with you."

Clare shook her head. "Why?"

Mary sighed. "He's done one of his disappearing acts. He does them from time to time. Just because he's a grown man doesn't mean I don't worry about him."

"Oh." Clare felt her stomach clench a little. "So you haven't seen him since…?"

"Yesterday morning."

"Right." Joe couldn't be right, though. Finn was such a passionate strike supporter. "I'll let you know if he calls, I promise."

Mary looked at the queue of kids waiting restlessly to get on the coach. "He was a nuisance of a kid. Kind at heart, but he always did his own thing. We've been proud as punch since he came back to work for the union. But the older I get, the more I think your personality is set from a very young age. I bet I could make a few predictions about this lot here and how they'll turn out."

Clare looked at Amy, who was singing Jump at the top of her voice, with the younger kids jumping up and down on cue. I daren't predict anything about you, she thought.

Clare got home to find her phone ringing and hoped that Amy hadn't managed to disgrace herself before she'd even made it back to the flat. But it was Bob Seaton.

"I've been trying your office and getting no answer. Mr Ainsley told me you were having a couple of days at home. But there are some things I think I need to pass on to you. Can you call in?"

"Yes, I'm not doing anything in particular. Now?"

Clare couldn't work out what was so important that it couldn't wait until she came back from leave. Seaton made small talk until a secretary handed them the obligatory cups of tea, and then he asked her to close the office door.

"You're rather fond of that kid you brought in the other day. Or so it seems to me."

Clare tried to keep her facial expression as blank as possible. "She's a sparky little thing. She's interested in journalism. And, as you've said, the mother isn't all that attentive." Clare waited a moment and then said: "Why?"

Seaton didn't answer directly. "That story you came in with the other day? What happened to Jason Craig and Steven

Simpson when they were in custody? I've been looking into it."

"Right." Clare fished in her bag for a pen but Seaton held up a hand.

"This is off the record again, I'm afraid. Strictly for your ears only."

Clare sighed and waited.

"There was what you might call an ill-judged attempt to get Jason Craig to confess to killing Jamie Donnelly."

"In what way?"

"Those young officers on attachment here. They stunted something up to see what reaction it would get."

"Stunted something up? What, exactly?"

"They dropped the body of a baby pig over the stairwell. When Mr Craig got highly distressed, they thought they were on to something. They tried to calm him down and lock him in a cell, overlooking almost every procedure under the sun, which is why he was allowed in there with the means to harm himself."

"Hold on, go back a second. They dropped a baby pig down the stairs?"

"Not a live one, obviously. It was wrapped in a sheet and it's entirely possible that it would look, at first glance, like a baby."

Clare sat back, with her mouth slightly open. "You're kidding me."

"I wish I was." Seaton took out a white handkerchief, the sort only used by men over a certain age, and blew his nose with a loud trumpeting noise. "Excuse me. I need a holiday, Miss Jackson."

"What's going to happen?"

"The officers involved have been suspended pending disciplinary action. Four of them, before you ask. Two of them from this station. You can imagine how I'm feeling about all this happening here. Just because I wasn't on duty that night doesn't mean it doesn't stop at my door."

Clare nodded. "And what about the families?"

"We've been in contact with a lawyer representing Steven Simpson. We're discussing some form of compensation. Coupled with a confidentiality clause, I have to warn you. Jason Craig's relatives are proving harder to find. He was in council care until a few months ago."

"Right." Clare breathed out. "Poor kid."

"It gets worse. I had a young… I'll say a young lady, although it's stretching the term, who came to see me yesterday. She claims she was with Jason Craig the afternoon young Jamie was killed. And her evidence suggests that it couldn't have been him."

Clare bit the inside of her lip. "Go on."

"She was with Jason in his flat. But she shouldn't have been. Her boyfriend was sleeping off a hangover and she was playing away with his best mate. According to her, they spent a couple of hours in bed together. And she'd just got back to her real boyfriend's house when all the shouting started, because baby Jamie had gone from his pram."

"Right. Do you believe her?"

"As a matter of fact, I do. She was scared to come and see me and only did it on the understanding that her evidence wasn't made public. Her boyfriend, by the way, is Steven Simpson."

"So neither Jason nor Steven were around when Jamie was killed?"

"It would appear not. The hangover story tallies with what Simpson told us when we arrested him, as it happens. And there's more. This young lady said almost no one was about that afternoon as she made her way home. It was a very hot day, you may remember, and the kids were still at school. But she did see one or two people."

Clare wished she hadn't let her tea go cold. Her mouth was feeling dry. "Who did she see?"

"She saw a couple of men wearing Support the Miners badges, walking off the estate. She didn't know who they were, she said, but we've already tracked them down. They were dropping leaflets off about some sort of strike meeting, that's all. We don't think they had any involvement in what happened to Jamie. But this young lady also saw someone running away from the bins area where Jamie's body was found. A child, who she did know."

Clare looked down at her fingers. "Amy?"

"We think Amy Hedley might know more than she's told us so far. And we're sure that what she said about those two lads being responsible was completely false."

"What are you going to do? I'm sure she told you what she thought she saw, even if she got it wrong."

"We'd like to talk to her again, obviously. But there's no one at the flat. What's more, the officers reported that the place was not fit to live in. There was no food in the cupboards, there was dog mess on the floor and the kid's bedroom was a health hazard. Mildewed bedding and swarms of flies. We've sent a report to social services. Amy's mother is going to have to answer to them, when she turns up. We're wondering if she's taken the kid away on holiday somewhere."

Clare nodded. She didn't volunteer that Amy was staying with her. She decided that she could chat to the child first, bringing the subject up as gently as possible. "Annie Martin always said she thought it was some sort of payback for Rob Donnelly breaking the strike."

"I remember." Seaton rubbed his chin. "That still doesn't make any sense to me, though."

"No. Me neither." Clare twisted a strand of hair around her finger. "But then there's Debs Donnelly, too. Someone had it in for the family, I think."

"There's been a development there," said Seaton. "We got the reports. It turned out she did take an overdose, after all."

Clare sighed. "She wasn't suffocated?"

Seaton shook his head. "We looked into it. That wasn't the cause of death. She died because she took too many tablets. Simple as that."

258

"Poor Debs." Clare was about to get up. "Can I ask, why are you telling me this, if so much of it is confidential?"

"Couple of reasons. One, you helped me out, trading some of your information. I got to the bottom of what happened here a lot quicker thanks to you. And two, you're quite friendly with Amy Hedley. I thought I should just put you in the picture."

"Right." Clare hoped Seaton didn't know any more about her friendship with Amy than he was letting on. "Thanks." She stood up.

"And three, when I've wrapped this up I am definitely going to retire. You can come to my send-off. Add a bit of glamour to the proceedings, eh?"

Clare gave a little laugh. "I'm not sure about that. But I'll be there to buy you a pint."

Clare constantly checked her watch for the rest of the day, longing for Finn to call and wishing it was time for Amy to come back. Poor Amy. She'd obviously been much more traumatised by baby Jamie's death than anyone had thought. Maybe in her child's mind she was confusing the teenagers who were causing trouble on the estate at nights with the two Support the Miners men spotted walking around at the time of the murder. It seemed almost unfair to ask her anything about it, dredging the whole thing up again. She worried about whether Amy was enjoying the trip, and hoped the other kids hadn't isolated her for not being one of them.

But at five-thirty, as the coach opened its doors, Mary beamed at Clare. "Your Amy was something of a godsend for us today."

"She was?" Clare gave Amy a look.

"She's so good with younger kiddies, isn't she? She just organises them and plays with them and distracts them when they're feeling travel sick. Quite the little mother, isn't she?"

Clare felt irrationally proud. "Hey, well done, Amy."

Amy jumped up and down on the spot. "It's been brilliant.

259

The splash park was am-*aaaa*zing. I ate so much at the picnic I thought my belly would burst."

"Good, so you're not hungry?"

"Yes, I'm hungry again now. That was ages ago."

Clare thanked Mary.

Mary shook her head, smiling at Amy. "I gather she's staying with you for a few days, is that right?"

"Er, maybe. Nothing's really been decided. We need to speak to your mum, don't we, Amy, and the phone doesn't seem to be working." Clare touched Mary's arm. "Has Finn been in touch yet?"

Mary gave an exasperated shake of her head. "He does this from time to time. I never get a straight answer about where he's been. If he turns up, I'll send him your way."

Clare drove Amy back to her flat. She found herself glancing furtively around as she turned her key in the door, hoping that as few people as possible had noticed that this long-time single woman had suddenly acquired a child.

She'd got food in, although she rarely cooked. But the last thing she wanted was for some police officer to spot her out for dinner with Amy. The little girl seemed to have had such a good day, so Clare didn't want to spoil it by insisting that she went back over what she'd said in her statement. And she knew that Amy was a little afraid of the police, thanks to Tina's unhelpful attitude. She just couldn't help feeling like someone who was harbouring a fugitive.

"I figured you'd had quite a long day, so I thought we might just watch some TV and play cards, if you like."

"Yeah. And what will we do tomorrow? It's Sunday. You won't have to go back to work yet, will you?"

Clare skimmed the listings page of the paper. "Not much on. *Born Free*, again. Even I've seen that a thousand times."

"You should get one of them VCRs, though. Then you can buy films to watch."

"Maybe I will."

"Mickey has one. He brought it over to ours once. But he

just has dirty films."

Clare curled her lip. "I hope he didn't let you watch them."

"Not really."

Clare decided not to probe what that meant.

By around nine, Amy's eyelids were beginning to droop and Clare suggested that she had an early night, for a change. Amy didn't object. Clare was busy closing all her curtains when she noticed a figure standing on the other side of the road. It was Finn.

He half-turned away, but she waved at him. He crossed the road towards her, almost reluctantly.

She opened the door and held it wide. "Where've you been? Your mum's worried. I've been worried. Are you okay?"

"Yes." Finn stepped inside and closed the door behind him, leaning back against it. "No. Never mind me. Are you feeling better?"

"Come in. Let's have a drink." Clare led him by the hand to the kitchen, where she leaned up to kiss him. "I've missed you, that's all."

"Clare." Finn took the glass out of her hand and put it back on the bench. "I have to talk to you."

He took both her hands. "I... I know we haven't known each other very long. But you mean a lot to me. I want you know that."

Clare squeezed his fingers. "Good. I feel the same. You don't have to say anything. We can just see how things go."

Finn screwed up his eyes as if he was in pain. "We can't. I've done something, something I'm not proud of. And when people get to know about it, I can't be here."

"We've all done things we're not proud of. I should know." Clare put Finn's arms around her back. "Whatever it is, we can just work through it. It'll be fine."

"Not this. I need to get away from here. But I wanted you to know why."

Clare felt her blood pulsing through her. She wanted to

261

stop the conversation before Finn said anything he couldn't take back. "Tell me later," she said and pushed her mouth against his.

A moment later, a loud gagging noise made them jump apart. Amy was standing in the kitchen doorway, pretending to put her fingers down her throat. "Bleaaagh. I hope you're not going to start *doing* stuff."

They both laughed.

"I'd better go," Finn said.

Clare made a pleading face. "When will you come back?"

"Take care," Finn said. "I'll call. Soon."

Shortly before midnight, Clare woke up from a deep sleep to the sound of running water. It took her a few moments to work out what it could be. She went into the kitchen to find Amy kneeling on a stool next to the sink, trying to shove a bedsheet under the tap. She jumped when Clare spoke.

"You okay? What's happened?"

In the bright light of the kitchen, Amy's face went a deep pink. "I spilled something on the bed."

"Oh, right. What was it, just water?"

"Erm... juice."

"Juice?" Clare didn't recall Amy having any juice. She guessed that Amy had wet the bed and was too embarrassed to say so.

"Okay, but you don't need to wash it under the tap. I've got a machine, look."

"I know. But I didn't know how to work it."

"I'll show you." Clare squeezed water out of the sheet and pushed it into the machine. She taught Amy how to add the powder and which setting to use. "And now I'll get you a clean sheet. Feeling better now?"

Amy nodded. "Sorry."

"There's nothing to be sorry for. Accidents happen. I know you didn't do it on purpose."

Amy perched on the stool. "My mam goes mad with me

262

when I do it at home. She says I have to take the sheets to the launderette myself, but I never have the money. So sometimes I just have to try to dry them out."

"I don't want you to worry about it here." Clare wondered if she should ask Amy directly, but decided against it. "Does it happen very often? You, um, spilling something on your bed?"

Amy looked shifty. "Can we stay up for a bit? I don't want to go back to bed yet."

"Go on then." Clare made Amy's bed again, then filled the kettle. "Is it too warm for hot chocolate?"

"Nahh."

Amy moved to the sofa and hugged her bony knees. "Shall I tell you a secret?"

"If you want to." Clare wasn't sure what to expect. "Is it a good secret?"

"Not really."

"If you want to," Clare said again.

"I think my mam and Mickey might've gone on holiday."

"You're kidding? What makes you think that?"

"I heard them talking about it. Mickey said he could get a good deal to go to Spain, but not if they had to drag a kid along with them."

"So all that stuff about you being a target?"

Amy sniffed. "That did happen. I think they were just going to go away and let me stay on my own, only when people started banging on the door and calling me a grass, they got worried." She darted a glance at Clare and then back down to her mug. "It was my idea to come here."

Clare resisted the urge to swear. "So why didn't your mum just tell me? At least then I would have known how to get hold of her. Now I haven't a hope of talking to her until she comes back. Tell me they've booked a week and not a whole fortnight?"

"I think it was a week. Sorry, Clare."

"It's not your fault. But Tina should've put me in the

263

picture." She looked over at Amy's hunched little figure. "I bet you'd have liked to go to Spain, though."

"Mmm." Amy pouted. "Not with that Mickey."

"You really don't like him, do you?"

"Nuh. He just… he does stuff I don't like."

Clare suddenly felt her skin crawl. "What do you mean?" She swallowed. "I know about the Walkman. That was awful. But is there anything else? He doesn't hurt you, does he?"

"Yeah, sometimes. Sort of."

Clare waited. She didn't want to press Amy for any more details. She wasn't sure if she could cope with what the girl might tell her.

"Your turn to tell me a secret," Amy said, suddenly, her face brightening.

"Oh." Clare ran a hand through her hair. It was a very warm night and she was finding it hard to cool down. "I'm not sure I have any interesting ones."

"You must have. Anyway, I know one of your secrets already."

"You do? You tell it to me then."

"You're having a baby."

Clare gasped, as if she'd been hit across the face. It took her a moment to recover. "No, I'm not."

"Yeah, you are. You've got baby clothes and nappies and stuff in your bedroom. I found them when I was tidying up for you. And there's a baby bed on top of your wardrobe, all wrapped up in a bin bag."

"I'm not sure how you managed to find that, Amy. You must've climbed up and had a good root around."

"I peeked inside the bag, that's all. Just to see what it was."

"You're very nosy."

"I know. But you said it's good for reporters to be nosy, right?"

"I suppose I did."

"So, are you having a baby? You look sort of skinny if you are. You should be getting a big belly."

264

Clare swallowed hard, fighting the lump that was hurting her throat. "I'm really not having a baby. That stuff is waiting to go to a charity shop."

"So where's it come from, then? It's new. Whose is it?"

Clare put the knuckle of her index finger in her mouth and bit on it. She was going to have to say out loud the thing she didn't want anyone to know.

"I was having a baby. But I had a miscarriage, a couple of months ago. Do you know what that means? It means I lost the baby, before it got big enough to be born properly."

"Oh." Amy took a sharp breath in. "Ah! Was it in my bedroom? Where the baby came out?"

"Well, it wasn't really a proper baby. It hadn't grown enough. But yes, it happened in my spare room, where you sleep. It happened on the day I was supposed to be having a job interview at work. The one that man Chris Barber got instead. Everything seemed to go wrong after that."

"Right. That's what the ghost is, then. I thought it might be Jamie following me all the way here, because I suppose a ghost can do that, can't it? But it's the ghost of your baby."

"I've told you, there's no such thing as ghosts. You're imagining all that."

"I am not."

"Amy, please." Clare reached for a tissue and wiped at her eyes. "I don't really like talking about it."

"Okay." Amy patted Clare's leg. "Don't cry. I don't think your baby's ghost is sad. Not like Jamie's."

"Amy, this stuff about ghosts… "

"Jamie's ghost is really angry with me."

Clare sighed. "That's daft, in all sorts of ways. But let's imagine there is a ghost. Why would it be cross with you?"

Amy stuck out her lower lip and thought for a minute. "I think I should go to bed now," she said.

Clare stared as Amy got up and took the hot chocolate mug into the kitchen, where the washing machine was whirring. She got up and followed her.

"Are you sure you're all right?"

"Yep." Amy didn't look Clare in the eye as she swerved past her and headed for the spare room. Clare listened as the door clicked shut. She sat on her own bed and thought. These days, it felt like Amy was always on the point of telling her something. Something big, at least big to Amy's ten-year-old mind. But then she kept backing out at the last second.

twelve

Sunday 5th August

It was shortly after four in the morning, when it was starting to get light, that Clare woke to a sound in her back yard. She sat up and inched back the edge of the curtain. Amy was quietly replacing the lid on Clare's dustbin and slipping back through the kitchen door, clicking it shut as silently as possible.

Clare lay still, waiting until she was fairly sure Amy had gone back into the little bedroom. Then she pulled on a T-shirt and went out to look in the bin, to see what Amy had dropped in there. She hoped it wasn't more bed sheets.

At first Clare couldn't see anything obvious among the piles of cartons and newspapers. She leaned over and poked around, her hand finding something wrapped up in a sort of bundle. She pulled it out and opened the layers of paper. It had been well wrapped, she thought. It reminded her of the child's game of pass-the-parcel: layer after layer of paper. And just when she was beginning to think that that's all there was, and there was nothing at the centre of the bundle, she peeled back the final layer to find something small and soft. It was a baby's blue and white checked sunhat.

Clare jumped and her skin felt as if electricity was jolting through it. She could feel her heart palpitating. She wrapped the hat quickly back in its final layer of newspaper and ran back inside. She put the little parcel on the kitchen bench and stared at it, her heart thumping so hard and her breath so short it was making her feel dizzy. Her thoughts raced, unable to form any sense. How had Amy come by this? Why was she carrying it around with her? Fingers shaking, she edged the paper back again just to be sure she had seen what she thought she'd seen. There could be no doubt about it. This had to be baby Jamie's missing sunhat.

She heard a tiny shuffling sound and turned quickly to see Amy standing in the doorway, watching her. She found herself going hot, as if she'd been caught in the act of doing something she shouldn't.

"Amy. Hi."

Amy said nothing. She just stared at the bundle on the kitchen bench. Then she looked back at Clare. Clare couldn't read her expression.

"Look, I heard you putting something in the bin so I got up to see what it was, that's all. I have to ask where you got this. Is it what I think it is?"

Amy nodded.

"How did you get hold of it?"

"I found it, that's all. Out beside the bins at home."

"When was that?"

Amy blew air out of her cheeks, thinking. "Just the other day."

Clare leaned forward and put her head in her hands for a minute. "You're saying you found baby Jamie's missing sunhat beside the bins, just a few days ago?"

Amy said nothing. She pressed her lips together and looked at Clare. She took a step backwards and the wariness in her eyes suggested she was expecting Clare to get angry.

"The thing is," Clare went on, "I can't see how that would be possible. The police went through that area very carefully just after Jamie died. They would have found it then, wouldn't they?"

Amy still didn't reply. She twirled a ratty strand of hair

round her fingers, her eyes still fixed on Clare.

"You must have found it quite a long time ago," Clare went on. "And you knew the police were looking for it. Why didn't you hand it in? It could be really important in helping them to catch Jamie's killer."

Amy's chin crumpled.

"Don't cry. I'm not angry, I promise. I'm just trying to understand."

"I wanted to give it to you." Small tears trickled slowly down Amy's face. "I thought if I gave it to you then you'd get a really good story on the front page. But then I got scared. So I thought I'd just put it in the bin and forget about it."

Clare didn't know what to say, for a moment or two.

"Okay, Amy. We are going to have to give this to the police and tell them, you know that, don't you?"

Amy's mouth dropped wide open. "You can't. They'll put me in prison."

"They won't."

"They will. It's called holding evidence or something. I've seen it on the telly. They always put people in jail for it."

"But you're a kid, Amy."

"They might put me in care though. I don't want that."

"You're really scared of that, aren't you?"

"Me mam says it's just like prison. She says people beat you up all the time and lock you up in your room and it's really scary and there's no one there to be nice to you."

"I'm sure it's not really like that. Anyway, they won't do that. They might tell you off a bit, that's all."

"Me mam said I hadn't got to speak to the police anymore, about anything, because it just causes trouble."

"I'll speak to them, then. Your mum's not here to decide. But you must promise me that you'll never do anything like this again. Tell me again exactly where you found it. And when."

Amy bit her lip. "I'm hungry."

"It's a bit early for breakfast."

"But I'm starving."

Clare sighed. "I'll make some toast. And then we have to think about this. It's important."

"We don't have to see the police today, though?"

"Yes, we do."

Amy's face twisted. She didn't eat her toast and her usual constant chatter dried up completely, no matter what Clare tried to talk about. At around five-thirty, she started yawning.

Clare looked at her and softened. She was being too hard, expecting Amy to respond like an adult. "You know what? It's still really early. Neither of us have had much sleep. Why don't we both go back to bed and try to get a couple of hours? And then we'll go and see my friend Chief Inspector Seaton and explain everything.

"I promise they won't put you in prison. And when we're done, we'll do something nice. We'll go out for a picnic. Or maybe see what's on at the cinema. And we'll forget all about it, okay?"

Amy nodded and got up. She turned to Clare. "When it's all sorted out, can I come and live here?"

Clare blinked and smiled. "No, Amy, you can't."

"Why not?"

Clare had to think about that. "Your mum will miss you. You belong to her, not to me."

"She won't miss me, not one bit. She wants Mickey, not me."

"I think she wants both of you."

"Do you not want me, then? Is it because of your new boyfriend?"

Clare hesitated. "I really like you. Amy. And it's nothing to do with Finn. But the law wouldn't let you just come and live with me. It could never happen. I'm sorry."

Amy gave a little sigh and went into her room, without another word. Clare closed her own bedroom door. She lay down on top of her bed, not expecting to be able to rest. But she drifted off, into a heavier sleep than usual, and when she slowly opened her eyes it was almost eight o'clock. She jumped up and opened the bedroom door. The place felt strangely quiet. Amy must still be asleep. Good, Clare thought. For such a little girl, she had unnaturally dark rings around her eyes. A long lie-in would do her good.

By the time Clare was dressed, Amy still hadn't stirred. Clare turned on the radio, in the hope that Amy would hear it and emerge from her room. But when time ticked on, Clare thought perhaps she ought to wake the girl up, if they were going to do anything with the rest of the day. She tapped lightly on the bedroom door. "Hey, Amy. Want any more breakfast? How about scrambled eggs? It's the one thing I know how to cook."

There was no answer. Clare tapped a little louder. Then she opened the door. The room was empty.

Clare's stomach lurched as if she was travelling down fast in a lift. Amy had taken her little carrier bag of clothes. She had left a scribbled note on the bed, written in her childish handwriting. It read: *Dear Clare, Im sorry Im so much trouble. Im gone away now and I will be okay. Amy.*

"Oh god," Clare said out loud. She grabbed her bag and ran out to the car. Then she drove slowly around some of the nearby streets, trying to spot Amy, before heading off to Sweetmeadows, hoping against hope that the child had done the obvious thing and gone back home.

But there was no answer at the flat. There wasn't even the sound of barking. After Clare had thumped and banged at the door for a while, a woman put her head out of the next door along. "There's no one there, pet. I saw them leave the other day with their bags."

"Yes, I know, but I'm supposed to be looking after the little girl and she's gone missing."

"Amy? She goes where she likes. I wouldn't fret about her."

"I really have to find her. Are you the neighbour who was feeding their dog?"

The woman shook her head and shrugged.

Clare wandered back to her car and drove home, in the faint hope that she would find Amy sitting on the doorstep. She wasn't there. Clare flicked through her contacts book until she found an out-of-hours number for Geoff Powburn.

"Geoff, it's Clare Jackson from the *Post*. Are you busy?"

"It's Sunday. I'm sitting in front of the telly. I can think of only two reasons why you would be calling. Either I've made some massive cock-up and there's a big scandal about our social services ready to break in the paper. Or you're asking me out, at last. Please say you're asking me out?"

"Remember I mentioned I was worried about a child? I think I need to speak to someone about it. Urgently."

Geoff sighed. "It's not my weekend on, strictly speaking, but seeing as it's you. Where are you?"

When Geoff arrived, Clare told him an edited-down version of Amy's story. "So she thinks she's in all sorts of trouble and she's run away from here. And the mum's nowhere to be found. Off with a boyfriend somewhere, no contact numbers, possibly away abroad."

"You shouldn't have got so involved, you know. You should have told someone like me, as soon as you had concerns."

"Yes, thank you, I know that. But can we start from where I'm at now? How can we find her? And then what will happen to her?"

Geoff rubbed his eyes and sighed. "I'll get a colleague to come with me. We'll check out her flat first of all and talk to the neighbours."

"I've already done that, I told you. She's not there."

"We have to start somewhere."

"If you find her... "

Geoff raised his eyebrows. "What?"

"Just... be kind."

"I'm always kind."

As Geoff drove away, Clare spotted Mary McKenna

walking down the street towards her, her face tight. She frowned at her. "Mary? Is everything okay?"

For a second, Mary just looked at Clare. Then her tense face seemed to crack and crumble, like a stone dissolving into sand. She let out a small sob. "Oh, god. He's not here, then."

"Who? Finn? Of course he isn't. Have you not seen him?" Clare stopped and put her arms around Mary. "Look, come in. Come in and sit down. Tell me what's going on."

Clare made Mary tea, but she didn't drink it. "We've had a letter."

"From Finn? What's going on with him?"

"He told us that he's working for... " Mary pursed her lips and put a hand over her mouth. She closed her eyes. For a moment, Clare thought she was going to be sick. Instead, she spat out the words. "He's been working undercover. Infiltrating the strike. Passing things onto the police."

Clare felt dizzy. "No. That can't be right. Finn was passionate about the strike."

Mary shook her head, her lips still pursed as if she was trying to stop herself from screaming. "It's been a lie. He says he did it because he didn't want to go to prison. But to be honest, I'd rather see him in jail than disgrace us like this."

She leaned over and grasped Clare's hand, hard. "I want you to know we had no idea. He lied to his family and he lied to the men he called his friends. We had absolutely no idea." She paused and looked at Clare, her eyes bright and wet. "Did you?"

Clare shook her head, dumbly. Shapes passed in front of her eyes, as if she'd been hit hard across the head again. "I think he wanted to tell me, but I wasn't ready for more bad news. I stopped him I still don't understand."

"I don't think I'll ever understand. His dad's disowned him. From now on, Finn's dead as far as we're concerned."

"So where is he now?"

"He didn't say. Only that he'll be changing his name and

we won't hear from him again. Off to betray some other poor beggars, no doubt." She stared into her cold tea. "I don't know how anyone can do that sort of thing. Especially not a son of mine."

Clare wiped her hand across her face, surprised at how wet it was. "I owe him money."

"What?" Mary looked at her as if she had started talking gibberish.

"He paid some bills for me." Clare groped around for a tissue. "I didn't know. But when I was in hospital, someone cleared all my red bills. It must've been him. He had my keys for a while."

Mary sniffed. "Now and again, he'd turn up with a bit of extra cash for us, or a cut of meat, that sort of thing. He told us not to ask how he'd got it, he just promised he hadn't pinched it." She curled her lip. "He was using his blood money. It makes me sick to think about it." She gripped Clare's hand even tighter. "Don't tell anyone. I know you're a journalist but please – just think what it would do to our family, if the word got out. The shame is bad enough, without everyone else knowing about it too. Just let them think he's gone off somewhere. Anything but the truth."

Clare gave a small nod, the best she could manage. "Did he... did he say anything in the letter about me?"

"He said tell Clare I'm very sorry."

thirteen

An hour passed after Clare watched the hunched figure of Mary make her way back down the street. Clare crouched on her sofa, her curtains drawn, clutching her arms around her queasy stomach. The whole day felt surreal, as if she was in a very lucid kind of nightmare. When the phone rang, she leaped at it. It was Joe.

"Hey, Clare? Haven't heard from you for a couple of days. A few of us are in the pub at the sea front if you want to join?"

Clare resisted the urge to scream. "I'm waiting for an important call. Sorry."

"No worries. I hope you're not working, though."

"It's not work."

"I'm glad to hear it. Hey, I'll tell you who I saw when I was parking the car up here. Your little pal. What's her name again? Amy?"

"Seriously? You saw her just now?"

"Yes. She was with that beast of a dog. I told her not to wander along the edge of the cliffs and she gave me the V-sign. What a little charmer. Clare? Are you still there?"

Clare dropped the phone and grabbed her car keys. She drove out to the sea front so blindly she could barely remember how she got there. There were cars in the car park and dozens of families with kids and people walking dogs. Clare rubbed her eyes, staring around. The whole scene seemed so wrong:

parents and sunshine and children laughing and playing. She found it jarring.

Clare couldn't say for certain, but there was a little figure in the distance that could possibly be Amy, walking erratically next to a big dog. Clare started to run, dodging anyone strolling in the opposite direction. As she got closer, she knew for sure it was Amy. Clare opened her mouth to call out, before instinct told her not to. The girl might panic and run away again. Clare slowed to a walk, but gained on the child, keeping a distance behind her until they were a little way away from most of the day-trippers, further along the cliff edges.

Something made Amy stop and turn. If she was surprised to see Clare, she didn't show it. She just stayed still, waiting for Clare to catch up.

"I'm so glad I've found you. You gave me such a fright. Are you okay?"

Amy didn't say anything. As Clare got closer, trying not to look over the edge of the cliffs, she could see that the girl's face was red and her eyes were swollen and veined with crying.

She held out her hands. "You mustn't be so upset. I've told you, I'll talk to the police with you. We'll explain that when you found the hat you were too frightened to hand it in. You're only a child, Amy. They're not going to be hard on you."

Amy sat down on the yellowing grass. Max flopped down beside her, his huge tongue lolling out of his mouth. Amy cuddled him closer to her. "He's hungry and thirsty," she said. "No one's been feeding him. Me mam lied. She just left him on his own."

"Let's go back to mine and get him some dog food, then."

"I gave him a pie already." Amy stared out to the sea. "I took some money out of your purse. Sorry." She turned out the pocket of her shorts and some coins fell out.

"Tina said a neighbour was looking after him," Clare said.

She could have slapped the woman.

"I know. I just wanted to see him, though. And when I found him, he was on his own. He was all whiney and sad." Amy hugged the dog a little tighter.

Clare hated heights. The cliff edge wasn't making her vertigo any better. How were these cliffs not fenced off? She tried hard not to look over the top, but her gaze kept travelling back over the edge. Her body felt covered in sweat.

"It doesn't matter about the money. But how about we go back now? You can bring Max, for the time being. We can take care of him."

Amy shook her head. "You don't mean that. You don't want him. Or me." She didn't turn to face Clare, but she could see that the little girl had started crying again.

"Hey." Gingerly, Clare sat down and edged a little closer to Amy. "What is it? What's getting you so upset?"

"I can't talk to the police."

"Look, I promise I won't let them give you a hard time."

"But they will. They'll ask me questions and questions until they find everything out. I know they will."

Clare put her hand over her watering eyes to shield them from the glare of the sun. "Don't be so daft, there's nothing to find out. You made a mistake, that's all, because you were scared."

Amy started to sob loudly, like a much younger child. Clare put a hand on her bony shoulder and gave it a little squeeze. "Hey, you mustn't get like this. Is there something else you haven't told me?"

Amy nodded, still sobbing.

"Come on then. Tell me. It can't be that bad."

"It is," Amy whimpered, between gulps. "It's really, really bad."

Clare's insides twisted. She felt sure that Amy was about to tell her something about Tina's boyfriend. There had to be a reason why the kid hated him so much and why Tina was just as anxious to keep them apart. Clare tried not to think about what he might have done to the child. "Is it about Mickey?" she prompted.

Amy shook her head and gave a long, sticky sniff. Clare handed her a tissue. Amy wiped her eyes but not her nose.

"If I tell you, you have to promise not to tell anyone else. 'Specially not the police. Will you?" Now Amy had her gaze fixed on Clare, looking directly into her eyes.

"All I want to do is make sure you're safe."

Amy leaned into Max's fur and said something that Clare couldn't quite make out. "I'm sorry, what did you say?"

Amy lifted her face. "I killed baby Jamie."

For a second or two, Clare couldn't quite grasp the words. Then she gave a little sigh. "Amy, you mustn't say things like that. I know you feel guilty because you didn't save him. But it wasn't your job, I've told you."

"No." Amy's face dissolved and more tears started. "All that stuff about the men. I made that up. It was me. I dropped him."

For a second, Amy's words seemed to ring and echo inside Clare's head. She felt her chest ache as it was hard to breathe. "This mustn't be another fib, Amy. Do you hear me?"

"It's not a fib. I wish I was fibbing right now. I was playing with Jamie and we were doing *This Little Piggy Went to Market*. He loved that game, it made him laugh. I sat him on the ledge and I was counting his toes. And he wriggled and I dropped him. He went over the edge before I could stop him." Amy was shivering hard, in spite of the heat. "I never meant it. I never meant to drop him. It was an accident, Clare. Honest it was."

The heat made Clare's head feel ready to explode. Sweat trickled down her back. She tried not to breathe too hard, terrified of fainting out here on the cliff edge. She had no idea what to say. Except she had a painful certainty inside that this time, Amy was telling the truth.

"Do you hate me now?" Amy was tapping Clare's arm.

Clare shook her head, slowly, trying to ignore the loud

buzzing inside her head and think straight. "Of course I don't. Don't ever think that."

"But I can't go to the police, see, because they'll find me out. And then they will put me in prison, won't they? I'm a murderer."

Clare tried to swallow. "You're not. You're not a murderer. You're someone who had a terrible accident and didn't know what to do."

"But I'll still go to prison, won't I? 'Cos I told lies to the police. They can put you in jail for that, I know they can."

"So you ran down and tried to hide Jamie, right?"

Amy nodded. "I went and hid with him, by the bins. I was hoping he might just wake up and be okay. I sang to him and nursed him and tried to make him better. Only he wouldn't wake up."

"So what did you do then?"

"I ran away. I felt bad leaving him because he was just a little baby. But I was afraid of getting in trouble, really big trouble. I thought they'd put handcuffs on me and all the other kids would laugh when they put me in the police car."

"So you just went home?"

Amy nodded. "I had some blood on my T-shirt and it was me mam's top really. I thought she'd give me a clip for wearing it and getting it mucked up. So I got changed. Then I came down here and put the top in the sea. So that no one would find it and the water might wash the blood out."

Clare rubbed her temples, trying to stop her head thumping. "You thought it through. How did you know to do all this?"

Amy shrugged. "Cop shows on the telly, I s'pose. Murderers always throw their clothes away. And when I was getting ready for bed, I remembered I'd taken Jamie's hat off when I was playing with him and put it in my shorts pocket. And then I was really scared 'cause everyone was going mad about the baby and I had his hat."

She drew her knees up towards her. Max flopped his big head onto his front paws. "I think that's why Jamie's ghost kept coming to bother me. Because I had his hat. But I didn't know what to do with it."

Clare stared at Amy, not sure what to say next. "I still say the ghost is in your head. Because you feel guilty. But you didn't mean it, remember. It was an accident. The police will…"

"You're not going to tell the police. You promised." Amy ruffled Max's matted fur. "Anyway, then there was the thing with Debs."

"Debs? What about her?"

"I went in to see her because I looked in the window and she looked all sad. Only she knew. She looked at me and she said, 'Hey, you were there, the day Jamie died, I remember now.' I tried to say she was wrong but she kept going on at me. She was crying. And she was saying I must know what'd happened to him."

Goosebumps crept up Clare's arms. "So what did you do?"

"I wanted her to just shut up. I pushed the cushion in her face. I killed her too."

"Amy…"

"I didn't really mean for her to die," Amy went on, her voice coming out in gulps, getting faster and faster. "I just wanted to shut her up. That was all. Just to stop her crying and saying that I must know what happened. She was a bit dopey, you know? Because of the pills, I suppose. She put a big handful of pills in her mouth while she was talking to me and she was spitting because she was shouting at me and it was all horrible. I just wanted to stop it, for a minute."

No one spoke for a moment. Clare edged slightly, almost imperceptibly, away from Amy. The sounds of the sea, the breeze and families chatting and laughing nearby seemed as if they were a long way away, along some tunnel, in some other world.

Then Clare said: "You didn't kill her."

Amy turned to look at her. "Yes, I did."

"I just spoke to the police about Debs the other day. She was already very weak and ill. She took too many tablets, Amy. That's why she died." Clare tried to keep her breathing steady and her voice calm.

Amy started to shake, quite hard. In spite of herself, Clare found she was putting her hand back on Amy's shoulder. "And you got the ambulance, remember?"

Amy was still shaking hard. Clare wished she could make it stop.

"Yes. But I waited a few minutes first. Maybe I could've saved her?"

Clare shook her head. "I don't think so."

Amy picked up a handful of dried cut grass and scattered it over the cliff edge. "What's going to happen to me, Clare?"

"I really, really don't know. But I'm sure they don't send kids your age to prison." Something niggled at the back of Clare's mind about ten being the age of criminal responsibility. But she was sure that wouldn't mean jail.

Amy gave a small smile. "I do feel a bit different. I think it's 'cos I've told you all about it."

"Maybe you feel a bit, I don't know, lighter. You shouldn't be carrying such awful stuff round in your head. That's the only reason you hear ghosts."

"Except for your ghost. The one of your baby that was lost. That should've been in your head, not mine."

"It is in my head, Amy. I promise it is. It's in my head all the time."

Amy reached out and slipped a sticky hand into Clare's. She wrapped her fingers around, very tightly. "I think there's a way to make the ghosts go away."

Clare tried to shuffle backwards a little, surprised at how strong Amy's grip was around her hand. "What do you mean?"

"I did a really bad thing. Maybe I did two really bad things. I think that if the same thing happens to me that happened to Jamie, everything will be okay."

Clare tried to uncurl her fingers, but Amy was not letting go. "That's why I came here. Look." She raised her and Clare's hands and pointed with one of her dirty fingers out over the drop. "You know what? I've always wanted to jump over there. Just to see what it feels like. I bet for a minute you feel like you're a seagull, flying in the wind."

"Amy. You mustn't think about ever doing that. It's too high. You would kill yourself."

"I know that, you stupid. That's what I mean. You would feel like you were flying and then you would be dead. And everything bad would be gone away."

Clare tried to pull herself and Amy backwards, but the pounding and banging inside her head was getting louder and black shapes kept dancing in front of her eyes. Amy stood up, tugging on Clare's arm. "Your ghost will be gone too. You won't be sad anymore. Come on... "

Clare tried to struggle to her feet, every part of her body still in pain and yet, at the same time, not feeling quite real. Again she tried to pull her hand away, confused at how weak and disoriented she still was. Without looking at the cliff edge, Amy just ran backwards, and tumbled over the edge. Clare's arm wrenched as she fell with her, to the sound of Max letting out a low howl and the sight of rock and grass rushing past her, before she passed out and couldn't see anything anymore.

fourteen

Monday 6th August

Joe sat outside the church as the two coffins – one adult-sized, one heartbreakingly small – were carried inside. They were covered in so many white flowers that Joe thought the damp blooms could well weigh more than the people whose names they spelled out. From inside, the soft sound of the hymn Lord of All Hopefulness streamed out onto the summer morning air. Joe had been brought up as a Catholic but he didn't find the music any comfort. He hadn't even wanted to come at all; he didn't like churches and he hated funerals even more. He was only doing this for Clare. He pulled out a cigarette from a newly-bought pack and lit up, turning his back and taking long, desperate drags as quickly as he could. Throwing it down half-finished on the grass, he went inside the church to sit at the back.

Later, in the hospital, he sat at Clare's bedside and tried to recount the details. "Loads of people, as you'd imagine. Most of the estate turned out. They had those awful flowers shaped into teddy bears and the words 'Mum' and 'Jamie'. The priest was going on about how he'd married Debs and christened baby Jamie. And there he was doing their funeral. I don't know what point he thought he was making. It just made me think how senseless everything is. And what a mess it's all been. One horrible accident, a whole string of pointless deaths, a whole estate that will take years to recover."

"I know what you mean."

Joe looked at Clare, with her arm and leg in plaster and cuts and bruises across her face. "But you're still here. Thank god. I don't know what I would have done if... "

"Shut up. I was lucky."

"Lucky? Landing on a ledge instead of falling all the way down the cliffs. And that mutt of a dog baying until someone spotted you and called the coastguard. The doctors said it was a miracle. And if I was a believer, I'd agree."

"Let's just stick with lucky, then." Clare shifted in the bed, groaning at the pain. "Any more news about Amy?"

"The hearing's tomorrow."

"Tomorrow? That's quick. Will she be well enough?"

"She might not have to be there."

"That doesn't seem fair, does it? Not when they're deciding what to do with her whole life."

"I wish you'd stop caring about her. She tried to kill you. She nearly succeeded."

Tuesday 7th August

"I can't believe I'm doing this. I can't believe the hospital staff agreed to it. And I really can't believe you want to be here." Joe nodded at the court official who held open the doors so that he could push Clare's wheelchair through. "No, hang on. Strike that last bit. Of course you want to be here. You're an idiot."

"I was asked to be here, remember? In case they needed to check anything in my statement."

"Yes, but you could've said no. I think you have a reasonable excuse."

In the small court room set up for a family hearing, two care home staff flanked Amy, who was pale but much cleaner than usual and with her arm in a sling. Tina was there too, a bewildered expression on her face as Geoff Powburn detailed the squalid state of the house and the way she regularly left

284

Amy alone. He read out a letter from Amy's school, which said that she often truanted and that when she was at school, she could be difficult and disruptive. A psychiatric report wasn't any more complimentary but said there would be a police investigation into the fact that the child had clearly suffered abuse. When the details of Jamie's death were read out, Amy covered her face. Tina cried, quietly.

"Amy is not yet ten years old," Geoff told the court. Clare frowned. She looked across at Tina and then at Amy, but neither of their faces suggested that he had his facts wrong. "She is below the age of criminal responsibility. So the best option for her, we feel, is to place her under the care of the local authority."

Amy wailed. Tina stood up, wobbling slightly. "Do I get any say here?"

The judge nodded. "Of course."

Tina steadied herself by holding onto the back of her chair. She looked around the room. Clare stared down at the floor, not wanting to meet Tina's eyes.

"I know I'm a bad mother. I never knew what to do with Amy half the time. But I... " Tina swallowed.

She must know, Clare thought, that she's out of her depth here. Why didn't she have a lawyer to speak for her?

"When she said Mickey hurt her, I didn't know whether it was one of her stories. But I never left them alone together again. That was good, right?" She stared around the court room. No one spoke.

Tina's voice trembled. "I was brought up in care. I hated every minute of it. I don't want that for Amy. All that stuff with the baby. I think she just got it all off the telly. She's not a really bad kid, not at heart. Can I... can I try again?"

There was a short silence. The hopeless inadequacy of Tina's words seemed to have the effect of embarrassing the panel, more than anything else. They left the court briefly to consider what to do, but came back after a few minutes to rule that Amy would, of course, be put into care. As she stood up, Tina gave her daughter a hard hug. She slid a bar of chocolate into the pocket of the girl's shorts and promised to come and see her soon. Clare looked down, hoping that no one could see her eyes filling up. The painkilling medication only helped with the physical wounds.

"*Wait.*"

Everyone stopped rustling their papers and scraping their chairs as Amy spoke up. The chairman of the bench looked at her and gave the court room a nod, to indicate that he would hear what she had to say.

Amy took a deep breath in, as if she was about to read out her script in a school play. "I don't have to go into care. Clare will look after me, as soon as she's better. Won't you, Clare?"

Everyone turned to look at Clare. She felt frozen in everyone's gaze, caught out by Amy once again. The thought flashed through her mind: this is what she'd imagined, although not in these circumstances. To rescue Amy. To give her a better chance. To appease her own aching body for the loss of a baby that she hadn't even known she wanted.

She closed her eyes. And acting against all her instincts, she shook her head: no.

It was Geoff Powburn who spoke up. "That's not a viable option, your Honour, even if Miss Jackson was in full health. Although Miss Jackson clearly befriended Amy with the best of intentions, she would not be able to properly care for a child with such complex emotional issues."

The chairman of the bench spoke kindly to Amy, explaining that she was not in a position to choose who to live with at the moment and that care was the best option for her. Clare sat staring at the dull wooden floor, while voices murmured around her like buzzing flies, until things went quiet. Amy, her fingers gripping the chocolate, looked over at Clare for a split second. Clare knew what the look meant. It said: *You let me down.*

As the two women from the council care home indicated to Amy that she needed to leave the court, and one of them placed a hand on her back, the girl started to scream. They each took an arm and pulled her, kicking, biting and struggling, out of the door. Clare heard her name being yelled repeatedly as they took Amy down the corridor. It seemed to take a long time until the sounds faded away. The people on the panel had already gone.

"Back to hospital you go," Joe said. "I knew you shouldn't have come. At least I know you won't try to write this up and get it in the paper." Joe started wheeling Clare towards the door, waiting patiently while she stopped to chat to Geoff Powburn and the regular lawyers and clerks. "If I can get you away from your fan club."

Tina was hovering, waiting to speak to the social workers.

"I'm sorry," Clare said. "For the way things turned out. I didn't want this to happen."

Tina nodded. She looked as if she didn't quite grasp what was happening.

"Can I just ask something? It's a little thing. The other week, Amy told me it was her tenth birthday, but everyone keeps saying she's still only nine."

Tina gave Clare an odd look. "She is still nine. Her birthday's not till November. November the fifth, easy to remember."

"Right." Clare smiled to herself as Joe turned the wheelchair around. "I walked right into that one, didn't I?" When it came to little lies, Amy was pretty expert. But she couldn't carry the big lies around as well as she wanted to. And that was something that she'd spotted in Clare. Something they had in common.

She asked Joe to take her for a coffee before they went back to hospital. "Somewhere that's not very nice. Somewhere that it wouldn't matter if you never went there again."

"O-*kay*. I'm assuming there's some method in your madness." He took her into a greasy spoon near to the court. "This place is so awful I'd recommend you stick to the coffee and don't eat. Now what's this about?"

"I didn't want to be anywhere that we like, because I have to tell you something awful and I didn't want it to spoil any of your favourite places."

"Oh, god, what have you done now?"

"Shut up and listen. But you're going to hate me."

Joe was quiet and waited.

"Remember your birthday, back in May?"

Joe's face gave just the slightest hint that it might mean something to him. "Yes. Or I should probably say, no, I don't remember a hell of a lot. It was one of the booziest nights we've ever had in our long and sorry history."

"That's right, it was. We were… a bit stupid."

Joe breathed in. "We were. I haven't forgotten that. You know I haven't. But I guessed you didn't want me to bring it up again."

Clare chewed the edge of her thumb. "What made you think that?"

Joe smiled. "When we woke up the next morning, you said something like, 'well, that was fun, but now we have to return to our own planets'. That kind of sent a message."

"Right. The thing is, Joe, and I know I should've told you this – I got pregnant."

Joe sat forward with a jump and swore.

"I didn't know what to do. I didn't know how to tell you. And while I was still working things out in my head, I lost the baby."

"You had a miscarriage? When was… oh. That was round about the time you were supposed to have the job interview, right? That explains a lot." Joe put his hand to his head and closed his eyes, trying to take it in. "Were you okay? No, dumb question, of course you weren't okay. You haven't been okay since. Jesus, Clare."

"I'm sorry. I know I should've told you." She leaned towards him. "Are you crying?"

"Nope." Joe wiped a hand brusquely across his eyes. "But yes, you bloody well should've told me."

288

"Sorry. Again. Don't tell anyone else, obviously."

"Who would I tell? There's only you." He sniffed. "I could've been there for you, that's all."

"I didn't know I needed that." She paused. "If I had told you I was pregnant, what would you have done?"

"Anything you wanted me to." He gave Clare half a smile. "I always do anything you want me to. I thought you'd have worked that out by now."

Sunday 3rd March, 1985

Outside, Joe's car horn beeped three times. Clare wiped her eyes quickly and went to the door.

"You okay?" Joe looked at her and reached out to put a hand on her shoulder.

"Yes." Clare sniffed. "No. I've been watching the news."

"I'm sure I've told you that's bad for your health." Joe followed Clare into her living room. On the TV screen was an image of a miner, weeping on the steps of Congress House, after the narrow vote for the men to return to work.

"All that effort. For nothing," Clare bit her lip. "It's heartbreaking." She swallowed. "I should go and see Mary. She worked so hard to see everyone through." And she's lost a son because of it. Nothing will be the same for her again, Clare thought.

"It is heartbreaking. But remember what the counsellor said? You need to try to be more detached. Good time to start." He glanced at the half-packed case lying still open on the floor. "Do you need more time to get ready? We should get going in the next hour or so, if we're going to get to London early evening."

Clare looked at her feet and said nothing.

Joe blinked. "You've changed your mind."

Clare sat down heavily on the sofa. "I'm sorry. I really am."

Joe flung himself down beside her. "For god's sake. We've talked this through a hundred times. You know what'll happen if you stay. You'll wake up one morning and realise you're just like Sharon Catt. Angry, thwarted, jealous of anyone new. Let's leave all that behind, Clare. We've got the loan of a flat for the next couple of months and we've got shifts on the nationals. Let's go and be little fish in a big pond. It'll be more fun, I promise."

Clare shook her head. "No. I can't go and work for the papers that told all those lies about the strike. I'm sorry."

"So go and write something better for them."

"I can't change the system. I want to be somewhere where I can make a difference. I'm not ready to leave."

Joe sighed hard and got up. "You're crazy, you know that?"

"Probably."

Clare held out her arms and Joe held her tight, for just a few seconds. "You know where I am if you change your mind."

Clare nodded, her eyes pressed tight shut to stop herself crying.

Joe stepped back to look at her. He gave a slight shake of his head and walked out without saying anything else.

Clare waited until she heard him closing the car door. He'll be back, she thought. I know he will. Then she pulled out of her bag a letter, written on rough grey-white paper. The envelope was addressed to Clare in untidy writing but the letter itself was written in a neat, near-perfect Teeline. Amy had clearly been practising hard.

Dear Clare, the letter said, in shorthand outlines. *I hope your leg is all better now. I am reading your columns in the paper to see how you are doing. I am sorry for hurting you. The doctors say I was sick in the head after the accident with Jamie and 'cos of some other stuff that happened at home. Mickey said I was a bad person and I believed him. They said it would be good to write to you and say sorry. I wrote to Jamie's dad too.*

It's really bad here. The other kids pick on me all the time.

I told them they should watch out because I can kill people. So now they have put me on my own and I can't go out.

I still want to be a journalist. Do you like my shorthand now? I wish you would come and see me.

From Amy x

Clare folded up the letter and placed it on the table. Then she picked up the phone and dialled the number of the care home. There was only one thing she could change about the last few months and she meant to do it. It didn't have to be the end.

acknowledgements

Huge thanks to everyone who helped with *This Little Piggy*. Former DCI John Halstead's information on police procedures in the mid-1980s was invaluable, as were my daughter Naomi's reminiscences about growing up during that decade.

Special thanks to Lauren, Lucy, Tom and all at Legend Press for their wise input and for being such a pleasure to work with.

As always, thanks and love to Mark, Naomi, Patrick and Mary for their faith, love and support, which means everything to me.

If you enjoyed *This Little Piggy*, here's an extract from Bea's debut novel, *In Too Deep*.

Chapter One

Two paramedics are lifting the body of a young woman out of a large, wooden tank of water and carrying her, quickly and with surprising smoothness, across the market square to their ambulance. I am watching them through the dusty window of the office, my hand across my mouth in case I vomit, my back to the wall and my head turned to the side. The window is so small I can't see what happens next. But what I do know is that Kim is dead. And I know this, too, that I helped to kill her. Kim, my lovely, only, best friend.

This memory is five years old. So is the photo of Kim in today's newspaper. I am staring fixedly at the page. I have, as they say, seen a ghost. The newspaper's computer has touched up Kim's face so she has unnaturally dark eyebrows and outlined lips. But, as Kim might have said, not bad for five years dead. When the photo was taken, she was just twenty-seven years old and beautiful. And I was Maura.

I say I was Maura, because I haven't answered to that name for a long time. After her death, I ran away and became another person. It worked. Or I thought it did. I convinced myself I'd become invisible. I should've known it wasn't really possible. I thought I'd done a pretty good disappearing act. It's surprisingly easy to do the thin-air thing, if you really want to. Five years ago I was Maura Wood. A bit plain, a bit non-descript. I'm still ordinary; my hair is mousy blonde, not mousy brown. I wear glasses in public, glasses I don't really need. And of course I use a different name. But you'd never spot me in a crowd.

So how has Kim found me and managed to haunt me, after all this? The newspaper says there are plans to revive Dowerby Fair. It was cancelled after Kim's death. A respectable five-year period has elapsed, or I guess that's how they're looking at it. After a little time, it no longer seems callous to celebrate an event where, once, someone tragically died.

It's easy to find Dowerby, and lots of tourists do, every summer. Dowerby, like every other little market town in England, has its castle, its haunted pub and its gift shops. It seemed to me that everyone I ever met had been there at some point in their lives, usually as a child. They would say: 'There used to be a tea shop on the corner - oh, but I'm talking about fifteen or twenty years ago.' And I would reply: 'It's still there.' 'And a clock tower, with a funny sounding chime?' 'Still there, still sounding tinny.' And they'd be delighted and launch into misty-eyed stories about their childhood holidays. When Kim died, the place was full of reporters and photographers from London, Manchester, even one from America. It was amazing how many of them found they'd been there before.

To get to Dowerby, you come off the trunk road they still call the new road, and it's very well signposted for such a little place. When you've driven in a straight line for miles, probably stuck behind a tractor or two, it's very tempting to turn off, following the big brown road sign with its storybook pictures of the castle, the bed and the teacup.

But I'm telling you, up close, Dowerby is a huge disappointment. The service in the tea rooms is always sullen and the cakes are always dry. The ghost in the haunted pub hasn't actually been seen since 1862. The castle is remarkably well-preserved, but that's because it's still lived in, so you have to pay £9.50 for a ticket only to come across a large TV squatting in the grand Regency lounge. Everyone laughs at that.

When I first went to live in Dowerby, I was always being taken for a tourist. And in a way, I was, because you don't qualify as local here until you're about fourth or fifth generation.

I wasn't very good at making small talk and getting to know people. It was my husband, Nick, who was the talker. Nick brought us to live there, because it was where he'd grown up, although his parents had since moved abroad. Some old friend of Nick's dad had got him a job at the local pharmaceuticals factory, and it seemed that within a few weeks of moving in, Nick was a member of the Rotary Club and on every social committee. He sort of forced people to make us welcome. If it had been left to me, Nick complained, we would never speak to anyone for years. I'm just like that. Closed. It's been a useful trait, recently.

Funny, looking back, that Nick and I ever got it together in the first place. We were so very different. But it made sense at the time and I was really happy, at first. Totally in love. We had a little girl, Rosie, who was just a year old when we first came to Dowerby. She was a naturally undemanding, good child and I spent my days decorating the cottagey house we'd bought, reading, walking, listening to the radio, feeling blissful. Nick made me laugh and we made love every week. Ordinary, you see.

I didn't really want anything else, not even friends of my own. I thought I didn't need any. It was quite enough for me when, eventually, people started to nod at me in the street. I didn't even mind not working, which seems strange to me now, even though I've only reached the dizzy heights of bar and waitressing jobs. It still means I don't have to ask anyone else for money. And there's only me to spend it on. Not exactly Businesswoman of the Year, but good enough for me. It's so hard to remember that, once, I lived off Nick's wages and it didn't feel old-fashioned or demeaning. It would now. The new me.

We'd lived there for about two years when Kim arrived. She was the new district reporter for the regional evening paper. Nick knew all about her before she came. He'd joined the Dowerby Fair committee, where there'd been mutterings that there was no local reporter to get them a bit of publicity. The post had been vacant for a few months after the last reporter retired. Nick took it upon himself to write to the editor of the *Evening News* and complain they weren't covering the area properly. It worked. The editor phoned Nick personally to say they were sending one of their brightest young reporters to cover the patch. And Nick promised to make her welcome.

Around ten-ish on a March Monday morning, Kim Carter came to Dowerby. I happened to see her arrive. I was sitting with Rosie in the café in the market square, right opposite the newspaper office. I had a window seat with a very good view. First, the newspaper's little car pulled up, with its logo emblazoned across the bonnet in yellow and black. The driver parked it, inconsiderately, at the end of a row of cars, making it difficult for delivery vans to get past to the shops. The car door opened and Kim swung her silky legs out of the driver's side door.

I watched as she fumbled with the keys to the dingy newspaper office, and disappeared up the stairs. Minutes later, she emerged and headed towards the café. She was quite stunning to look at, with dark long hair, a girlish face. All the café's customers and its dour owner, Jim, watched her quite openly. I was a bit embarrassed to be honest, about the way they were staring. I swear one old woman even had her mouth open. It's a northern habit, staring straight at people like that. Some people think it's open and direct. Personally, I've always found it rude. They don't do it in London, in fact they famously go to the extreme opposite and it's as if you're not there at all. I much prefer that.

Anyway, Kim didn't seem at all fazed by this. I guess when

you look like that, you get used to people's eyes popping. She just marched up to the counter and asked for some milk to take out. Jim served her without a word. Kim remarked that it was chilly outside. Jim said, "Yes. It's March, you know," and clattered her change down on the counter top. Kim raised her eyebrows and left. I glanced around the café at the Biblical quotations Jim had painted on the walls, to see if there was one about being bad-mannered to your customers, but there wasn't.

Kim must have felt the cold. She was dressed in quite a short skirt and jacket, sheer black tights and heels. Way too smart for Dowerby. The clothes looked like some I'd seen in last month's *Elle* (I had a weakness for glossy magazines). I'd also noticed she had small, clean hands and pointed, very white nails. I've often wondered if other women notice as much about each other as I do. I can't help it, taking in details. I enjoy it. But I didn't like to ask anyone if this was normal, just in case it wasn't.

I was watching Kim cross the market square when Sally, who works in Dowerby's little Co-op in the afternoons, joined me. Sally had also given Kim an undisguised stare, even turning her head as she passed by. She sat opposite me and leaned over to chuck Rosie under the chin. "So that's the new ace reporter," she said.

"Nick didn't tell me she was a supermodel." She grinned. "Bet he didn't tell you, either."

I shrugged. "Well. I don't think Nick will be having that much to do with her."

"Hah!" Sally gave me a bit of a leer. "She'll be beating the men off with a stick."

Sally made me wince, but Nick seemed to think she was a laugh. She managed to get a coffee brought to her at the table just by nodding at Jim from the other side of the café. "So," she said, leaning back and smiling at me. "Busy day?" It was only later I realised she was probably being sarcastic.

Kim didn't have a good first morning. A van driver and the

flower shop owner had sworn at her for the way she'd parked her car. She was thrown out of the café for doing what she said was a 'vox pop', which involved asking customers' opinions on some local story. I knew Kim had asked permission from a young assistant, who'd just shrugged, but when Jim came in from the kitchen he sent her out as if she was a naughty schoolgirl.

I told all this to Nick when he called home at lunchtime. He shook his head and laughed. "Do me a favour, Maura," he said. "There's a big envelope by the phone with a load of details about Dowerby Fair in it. Will you drop it off at the newspaper office for me? Give you a chance to apologise to Ace Reporter for the local yokels and their bad manners."

And so I did. I planned to drop it through the office letterbox, but the envelope was too big so I rang the doorbell. Nothing happened so I pushed open the door, hoisted Rosie onto my hip and climbed the staircase, with its shabby, brown carpet and its musty smell. I tapped on the door at the top of the stairs and Kim put her head round it. "Hi?" she said, with caution in her voice.

"Hi. I'm sorry to bother you. Your bell isn't working. I've got this to give you."

Kim gave me a small smile. "Is it explosive?"

I smiled back. "No, it's very dull. It's stuff about Dowerby Fair. Have you had a tough day?"

"Tough? I feel like I've stumbled onto the set of *The Wicker Man*." She held out her hand. "I'm Kim."

"Maura. Hi, again."

"Nice to see a friendly face. I've just made some tea, will you join me?" I hung back. Kim held her arms out. "Please?" So I sat down on a huge, black chair with a torn, fake leather cover. Rosie sat on the floor and Kim made a bit of a fuss of her, giving her a biscuit. "What did you say this was?"

"It's about Dowerby Fair."

"Right." Kim looked blank.

"Well, my husband, Nick, he's on the fair committee and

he wants to get some publicity for it. Umm, if you would, that is. I don't know how these things work. Getting stuff in the papers, I mean. This fair happens every summer and it's quite a big thing for Dowerby. People dress up in medieval costume and there are stalls in the market place. The big thing is a sort of re-enactment of history. It's like a court where they put women on the ducking stool or in the stocks, that sort of thing, like they would've done, a few centuries ago."

"You mean they don't do that all the time here anyway?" said Kim, wrinkling her nose.

I grinned. "Don't think they'd get away with it. But it's a bit of a crowd-pleaser, so Nick says it's a good thing to do. It always brings the TV cameras in. And he says the women queue up for it, they love it. Apparently."

She looked at me quizzically and it suddenly seemed hilarious. We both burst out laughing.

Later, I told Nick all about her. "She had a really grim day. No-one helping her, everyone treating her like she'd just landed. Awful. I felt ashamed."

He was bouncing Rosie on his knee. "She'll soon settle in."

"Well, Nick, I've asked her round for supper on Thursday. Is that okay?"

He stared at me. "Sure. Of course. Bloody hell, Maura, that's not like you."

"What isn't?"

"Being social. Letting someone in the house without me forcing you to."

I frowned, "God, Nick. I'm not that bad."

People came from all parts of the country to live in Dowerby, even though the joke is that everyone there is inter-bred. There is actually an RAF base, the factory where Nick worked, and of course the district council, all attracting lots of professional men with wives in tow - although rarely, for some reason, professional women with husbands in tow. I was never sure if this was because the employers in Dowerby didn't tend to take on women or whether career women just don't move around and expect their families to follow them, the way that men do. Or maybe most women just had more sense than to come here.

The first thing these newcomers remark on is the weather. It's so cold! It was March when Kim arrived to take up her new job, but in spite of the shocks of garish daffodils splashed along every patch of grass, there was little sign of spring in the temperature. The very sight of a daffodil still makes me shiver, because spring in the north of England is always so bitter. It's as if there is a different sun, one that blinds you with its light and makes your eyes smart, but offers no heat whatsoever. A sunny spring day in London warms you up.

Kim, I remember, didn't bow to the climate much. She wore jackets rather than jumpers and very short skirts. She said that people kept staring at her legs, women just as often as men. "I don't know what you expect," I said. "I think you like it, really."

"I tell you," she complained one day, "this woman looked at me this morning, like I was some sort of alien. She was wearing maroon tights – big thick ones – and green shoes. I mean, how can you go round looking like that? And if you do, how can you judge other people?"

But it wasn't all hostility. Kim was actually a good reporter. It was very hard to dislike her, even if you wanted to. She was very pleasant to talk to. She smiled a lot, and had a sweet, trustworthy sort of face. Her editor was pleased with her. People in Dowerby grudgingly said the town was getting some good coverage in the *Evening News...*

Come and visit us at
www.legendpress.co.uk

Follow us
@legend_press